～ THE MYSTERY OF ～
GOAT MOUNTAIN

THE MYSTERY OF
GOAT MOUNTAIN

MEL LONG

iUniverse®

THE MYSTERY OF GOAT MOUNTAIN

iUniverse books may be ordered through booksellers or by contacting:

iUniverse
1663 Liberty Drive
Bloomington, IN 47403
www.iuniverse.com
1-800-Authors (1-800-288-4677)

Because of the dynamic nature of the Internet, any web addresses or links contained in this book may have changed since publication and may no longer be valid. The views expressed in this work are solely those of the author and do not necessarily reflect the views of the publisher, and the publisher hereby disclaims any responsibility for them.

Any people depicted in stock imagery provided by Thinkstock are models, and such images are being used for illustrative purposes only. Certain stock imagery © Thinkstock.

ISBN: 978-1-4917-8471-6 (sc)
ISBN: 978-1-4917-8472-3 (e)

Library of Congress Control Number: 2016903027

Print information available on the last page.

iUniverse rev. date: 05/16/2016

CONTENTS

This book is dedicated to my wife Elaine and
our three sons, Matt, Mike and Martin and their families.

FOREWORD

A few years back Mel had mentioned to me that in his retirement he was writing a book about an area near where he lived and taught school. Mel had taken his sons camping on the Goat Mountain, which is high up on the west side of the Cascade Mountains above Colton, Oregon, many times. His description of Goat Mountain sounded idyllic and a place I would love to visit. Fast forward a couple of years and with the completion of the book, Mel asked me, a retired school teacher, if I would be willing to read through the book and "proof" it. This request was an honor for me as I had never been asked to proof read a book.

Welcome to Goat Mountain, which is a delightful memoir sprinkled with a little fiction to keep the reader's interest. The pace of life on the mountain is a lot slower and faced with the complexities and challenges of living in an isolated area. Although isolated, the character Eli is blessed with the companionship of his many animal friends and a mysterious two legged creature that form an unusual bond. Eli's story is interwoven with the love of family and dear friends.

Thank you Mel for the opportunity to be part of this project and get to know you better through the eyes of Eli. It was truly a privilege.

Liana Griffin
Magnolia, Texas

ONE

Eli And His Wife Move To Goat Mountain

Eli now lives alone on Goat Mountain. His cabin is located in the foothills on the west side of the Cascade Mountains of western Oregon, near the small town of Colton. He was born in the same cabin that he now occupied, almost eighty two years ago. He had moved away when he got married but he and his beloved wife, Francis Amelia, had returned to the mountain when his parents died and left the property to him. Other properties they owned near the coast had been left to Eli's other brothers and one sister. Unfortunately Eli's wife passed away five years after they moved to the old homestead. She had been in ill health for some time, while living in San Francisco, and they both thought getting away from the city and moving to the country would be good for her. They did have five wonderful years together on Goat Mountain before Francis died from a heart attack.

Eli was the oldest of four children. His two brothers and sister had moved to Arizona several years ago to escape the long, cold and wet winters of Western Oregon. They spent the summers at their properties on the Oregon Coast. Eli and Frances had three sons, who were all born in San Francisco, two daughter-in-laws and ten grandchildren. Eli and Frances, along with their three sons, visited his parents on Goat Mountain nearly every summer, while the boys were still living at home. His oldest son Matt and his wife Kim, lived in Bend, Oregon with their three children, Elly, Evan, and Siena at the time the author started writing this book. His middle son Michael Shane and his wife Ailene lived in The Woodlands, Texas with their four children, Kate, Jacob, Benjamin and Christene. His youngest son Martin lived in Katy, Texas with his three children, Marina, Brighton and Archer. All three sons came with their families nearly every summer to spend time with Eli on his beautiful Goat Mountain. The children loved spending time with their grandfather. There was so much to do at Grandpa's place and so much to explore. They all loved Grandpa Eli's animal friends and there were wild strawberries, raspberries and blackcaps to feast on. Best of all though was the Kool-Aid Grandpa made from the wonderful carbonated spring water which he collected from the spring high on the hillside above his cabin. They also loved the stories he would tell them about various sightings of Sasquatch, by people in the Western United States and Canada.

Eli loved his home on Goat Mountain. His closest neighbor was more than 15 miles away. He still owned the original 640 acres that his parents had homesteaded in 1896. Eli was a great conservator of the land and the beautiful Old Growth Douglas Fir timber that grew so profusely. Each year he hired his good friend, Bob Berge, and his crew to remove just enough trees so that he would have money to live his austere life style. His cabin was not connected to the outside world in any way. Eli burned wood for heat and cooked on a Home Comfort wood stove. He used several oil lamps for light. Water was piped into his cabin from a spring about 1500 feet above his cabin. His wood cook stove had a side reservoir for heating water and his bathroom consisted of an old claw foot bathtub, a toilet which had just recently been installed by his sons, and a small sink. Prior to his sons fixing him an indoor bathroom, Eli had always used an outhouse, which he still used when he was working outside in the summer time.

Life was never dull for Eli, as hikers would come for a visit in the summer and fall. He was always happy to see folks who had been coming to visit him for many years. He had made pets out of the fox, the deer, a young barren cow elk, and more recently a female black bear. He started befriending the bear when it was just a cub. It seems as though its mother had been killed by a poacher just shortly after the cub was born. Eli had not given anyone permission to hunt bear on his property since moving to Goat Mountain. Eli found the poor little creature as he was going up the hill to work on his carbonated spring box. Papa bear was nowhere in sight so Eli brought the little cub home. He named the bear Sampson. Eli spent many hours playing with the little cub. As the cub grew older Eli would romp and wrestle with her just as he had done with his sons when they were young.

The summer time was a very busy time for Eli. He kept busy getting wood for the long winter months, picking wild berries which had to be cooked and put in bottles for making jam later on. He grew what vegetables he could in the short growing season on Goat Mountain. Most of the vegetables he would need for food for the winter were purchased when he made his trip to Canby, Oregon in August to the County Fair. Eli had only missed two county fairs in his entire adult life, that was when he served in the Navy during the Korean War. He also made a trip to Colton at least once or maybe twice a year for additional supplies and to visit friends. It was necessary for Eli to have at least 500 pounds of birdseed for the winter as he fed so many Dark Eyed Juncos and other birds that did not migrate south for the winter. He could only make that trip when the dirt road was passable. Eli's dad had purchased a 1947 one ton Dodge flat bed truck new and Eli still used the old truck to go out to civilization. In fact the truck was Eli's only method of transportation, other than his one and only horse, Old Pet. Over the years he had made a trip or two to town on his horse but now that Old Pet was almost thirty years old he only used him for short rides or to pull his wagon or sled when he needed to haul fire wood or grass hay from the meadows. Every time Eli made a trip down out of the mountains he would always visit his best friend and old Navy buddy Mike Smith, and of course his best friend from high school, Bob Berge, and another Navy buddy Bob Jennings.

There were only five buildings on the entire property, the four room cabin, an adjoining small wood shed, a small chicken coup and two barns. One barn was used as a home for Old Pet and for a milk cow when Eli had one. The other barn was used to store Big Red, his old Dodge truck, other tools and equipment, a warm and secure place for his hounds, Big Daniel and Little Anne, his falcon Delightful, and his black bear Sampson. In one corner of the barn Eli had placed a huge hollow old growth log for Sampson to hibernate in, in the winter time.

Winter time was also a busy time for Eli. He had learned a long time ago that it was important for him to stay active year around. Exercise was an important part of his life as was eating healthy foods and getting proper rest. Because the days were so short in the winter, it was necessary to be well prepared. His daily schedule went something like this: Eli would get up around 6:00 am and build a fire in the fire place and the wood cook stove. He always fed the animals before he would eat breakfast. That was quite a chore in itself and took him the better part of an hour. He fed Old Pet and the milk cow and then the barn cats. Next he went to the other barn and fed his hounds, Sampson, Delightful, and the chickens. He fed the birds on his way back to the cabin.

Eli's breakfast usually consisted of Old Fashioned Quaker Oatmeal, with fresh milk, and a spoon full of raw honey that he collected from the honey bees in the summer time. Some days he would have poached eggs, a small serving of fried potatoes and hot biscuits at least once a week. After cleaning up the breakfast dishes and tidying up the kitchen area he would go to the woodshed and prepare the wood and kindling for the next day. He would then check the animals and gather the eggs if there were any. The chicken coup was the most secure of all the out buildings as it was a challenge to keep the skunks, the fox and weasels out. Eli was never one to kill a wild animal, except for food, but he would trap a fox or a skunk whenever he got the chance to do so, as they were predators he did not need around the cabin and chicken coup. By the time he did all of this it was time for lunch. After lunch he always tried to take a hike part way up the meadow above the cabin. There were many spots where he could look far down in the valley and see the communities near Colton.

Normally Eli did not eat a big supper. His evening meal usually consisted of a bowl of homemade soup, a glass of milk or carbonated Kool-Aid, a warmed over biscuit and some type of fruit. He ate a lot of wild berries in the summer time. He also ate a lot of watercress taken from the small stream as it left his pond.

Eli was an avid reader and his library consisted of such books as: "My Side of The Mountain", "The Far Side of The Mountain," "The Cay," "The Return to The Cay," "Where The Red Fern Grows," "The Adventures Of Tom Sawyer" and many others. He would read by the light provided by several oil lamps, until he would fall asleep. These were books he had collected during his entire life time.

Eli had read many stories about Big Foot and he believed every one of them. The stories were about a two legged hairy creature that supposedly lived in the Cascade Mountains of Washington and Oregon. He had concluded long ago if anyone had a good chance of actually having an encounter with this big creature it was him.

January of 1980 was a particularly cold month and the snow depth on Goat Mountain had reached well over five feet. When the snow got this deep Eli would break out his snow shoes and use them for his daily hike up the mountain meadow above the cabin. It was on one of these hikes through the forest alongside the meadow that Eli noticed large man like foot prints in the snow. The foot prints were at least five times the size of his foot prints, and that was very big as he wore a size 12 shoe. The tracks were much further apart than were his tracks. Eli moved cautiously between trees in hopes that he might get a glimpse of what- ever it was that had made these tracks. He could tell immediately that he was stalking a two legged creature that walked in an upright position. Although Eli never carried a gun, unless he was on a hunting trip, he wished this time that he had brought one along. On the other hand he had determined that if he ever did see Big Foot he would not pose a threat to him. He would much rather co-habitat with him on Goat Mountain. He might become the first human to actually befriend such a creature. He had also determined that the general public would never know about the encounter. If the public found out, his life on Goat Mountain would never be peaceful again. News reporters and curiosity seekers would hound him until he would have to leave his peaceful home and the mountain he loved so much.

As Eli approached the edge of the meadow he noticed the tracks were getting much closer together which meant the creature had slowed down. About half way up the mountain meadow there was an entrance to an old cave that Eli and his sons had explored many times in past years. The tracks seemed to be leading directly to the cave. Eli continued on towards the cave and upon reaching the cave entrance he stopped to listen and observe any movement. Eli did not have his lantern, which he always used to explore the cave, so he knew that he could not go into the cave today, and he was much too frightened to do so at this time anyway. He stayed out of sight of the entrance for at least an hour in hopes that the creature would come out. Finally, he heard a roar come from within the cave that was louder than fifty people could make screaming. This scared Eli and he could feel chills running up and down his back. He stayed quiet and out of sight and listened to the creature scream louder than he had ever heard a mountain lion scream. Next, he heard loud noises which sounded like someone was banging on the walls of the cave and then he saw a cloud of dust escape from the entrance to the cave. As much as he wanted to get a glimpse of the creature, he decided that it was time for him to make fast tracks back to his cabin. He hoped that the creature would not follow him. That was Eli's first and what he hoped would be his last encounter with Big Foot. He decided right then and there that he would not pursue the creature again, he would leave that up to others in other areas of the Cascades. He was satisfied that two legged hairy creatures did exist, but the roar from the cave convinced him that he did not want to have anything more to do with these creatures. In reality though he realized this probably was not going to be the case with the creature living so close to his cabin. He suspected that the big creature was already aware of him, his hounds and perhaps Sampson.

Darkness was approaching quickly as Eli made his way back to the cabin. Traveling on snow shoes takes a lot of energy and can be slow going at times. Eli was glad to be back inside the cabin. He lit the oil lamps and quickly built a fire in the fire place. After a small supper, it was time to settle into his favorite chair and spend some time reading a new book he had purchased on his last trip to the County Fair in Canby. This was a book by Jack London about his experiences while living in Alaska. Eli had only read for about an hour and he found himself falling asleep. He turned off all of the oil lamps and let the fire die down and crawled into his comfortable bed.

The next morning after Eli had completed his chores and finished breakfast he went out on the porch to bring wood into the house. As he did he heard the noise of an engine approaching from the west. This was something Eli did not want to hear. He hated snowmobiles, as they were so noisy, and they scared the wild game so that it was usually days before they would return to the area around the cabin. He loved people to visit but not riding snowmobiles. Whomever this was, they had ignored his 'NO TRESPASSING' signs.

As they approached the cabin Eli could see that they were wearing Oregon State Police Uniforms. The two officers identified themselves and Eli recognized both of their names. He knew both of their fathers. The officers told Eli that they were Game Officers, and they had been told that Eli had a bear caged up, and that it was against the law to keep wild animals captive without a permit. Eli stated that he had had

Sampson since she was a cub but that she was not caged up, and could leave any time. They asked to see the bear so Eli took them to the barn. Of course Sampson was hibernating. One of the officers shined his flashlight into the end of the log. All he could see was the rump of the bear. Eli showed the officers that a swinging door to the barn was always left unlocked and that his animals could come and go as they pleased. The officers were satisfied that the bear was not being forced to stay. They asked if Eli would mind if they went inside the cabin to fill out their report. Eli invited them inside and fed them a bowl of homemade soup and hot chocolate. As they were about to leave one officer spoke up and said, "Oh, by the way, we've had reports of a large animal that some people call Big Foot, being spotted in this area, so you might want to be careful when you are out and about." "We're not too concerned because we don't put much faith in such reports." Eli nodded his head but said nothing, just laughed a little and bade the officers good-by. Little did they know that Eli had just recently had a very close encounter with the Big Fellow.

The cold winter months finally passed and the weather was beginning to warm up. The snow was melting fast and water was beginning to run everywhere. The Dark Eyed Junkos were starting to leave and some of the birds that left in September and October were starting to return. Some of the early spring flowers were starting to poke their heads up out of the ground. In another month the meadows would be full of spring flowers and the Dogwood trees would be in full bloom. The wild Rhododendrons were starting to bloom in the lower elevation of Eli's Goat Mountain.

Spring was a busy time on Goat Mountain. There were fences to mend, trees that had fallen needed to be cut up for firewood, and there were repairs on the cabin that needed to be made before summer. The chickens that survived the winter finally started laying again, so Eli would have fresh eggs for breakfast and for cooking. Spring also meant that Eli would start getting some of his annual visitors again, and he was anxious to catch up on some of the local Colton news. Most of the news, he hoped, would be good news, but once in a while the news was not so good, such as when Eli would be told of the death of a long time friend. When Eli's best friend, Bob Jennings, did not show up by the end of April Eli asked the next visitor about his friend. The visitor just hung his head down, and in a very low voice told Eli that Bob had recently died from an illness the doctors believed was the result of injuries he had received during the war. Bob usually made the trip to Goat Mountain at least twice a year. He and Bob had gone clear through high school together and had joined the Navy at the same time and had served together in Korea during the Korean War. If Eli had only known of his passing he would have tried to get down off the mountain someway to attend his funeral and offer some comfort to his family.

Before the visitor left Eli went into his cabin and brought out something in a small box. He handed it to the visitor and asked him to give it to Bob's wife. It was a token of friendship, with Bob's name on it, and a picture of the two of them standing in front of a USO center in Tokyo while they were on R & R while serving in Korea. Eli was not one to tear up easily but when he handed the box to the visitor a small tear rolled down his cheek. He bade the visitor good-by and walked back to his cabin. He never went outside the house the rest of the day except to feed the animals and spend some time with them in the barn. This was truly a day of mourning for Eli. He did find comfort in being with his two hound dogs and the rest of the animals that he cared for each day.

As Eli said his prayers that night he thanked the Lord for his good friend Bob Jennings, and he knew that He would have a good home for him in heaven. He knew that Bob was a good man and that he had lived a good life. Bob was loved by all that knew him and had contributed much to the small community of Colton.

The days continued to get longer and a little warmer. The spring rains were not quite so cold and Eli was able to get a lot of repairs made. He loved the spring time as everything seemed to take on new life. Little fawns were always so playful and beautiful with their white spots. The Red Fox could be found scampering through the meadows trying to catch the little field mice. Birds of many species were busy making nest for the babies that would soon be hatched. The Red Tailed Hawk and an occasional Golden Eagle could be seen circling high above the meadows on Goat Mountain. Hiking was much easier now with the snow almost gone, except for a few spots that were still shaded for most of the day.

Eli continued to make trips to the barn several times a day, mainly to see if Sampson was beginning to stir. He always brought along his trusty flashlight so he could shine it into the end of Sampson's log. On one such trip, as he shined the light into the log he could not see Sampson. He panicked and ran to the open door to see if Sampson was anywhere in sight. He called to Sampson and fully expected her to come to his call, but no such luck. Just as he was about to go to the cabin to get his coat and hat and begin a thorough search for Sampson he heard a noise behind the barn. When Eli got to the back of the barn there was Sampson rolling and playing in a pool of water that had accumulated from the recent snow melt. Eli was so happy to see Sampson and to know that she was still 'his bear'. Eli was not surprised to see that Sampson did not want to go back into the barn. Her hibernation was over for the winter months. She was ready to start foraging for her own food and exploring the surrounding area.

As spring turned to summer the visitors increased in numbers. Eli found that a good part of his day was spent visiting and hosting old friends. He would try to spend a little time each day picking the little wild strawberries. He would also go to the stream behind the cabin and collect watercress to mix with dandelions greens. When he prepared the salad he would pour a little watered down vinegar on the mix. He was finally able to start catching fish from his pond as all of the ice was gone. Eli loved the taste of smoked Rainbow Trout. He did not have to spend very much time cutting wood as the days were getting warmer and he only needed a fire early in the morning and sometimes late in the evening. This allowed Eli more time for hiking and spending time with Sampson, his hounds and Delightful. He spent a lot of time teaching his hounds how to hunt raccoons. Coon hunting was a great sport for Eli and provided him with valuable hides and furs for making gloves, hats and vests. He loved to hear his hounds howl when they treed a coon. He only killed the coon if he needed the hide and fur. He also trained the hounds to leave a tree if he intended to let the coons live, which incidentally, was most of the time.

It was now well into June and Eli expected to see his good friend, Bob Berge, any day to discuss how many trees he would be taking to market this summer. After lunch Eli decided to take a nap in his rocking chair on the front porch. It was not long before he dozed off to sleep.

He woke up when he heard the noise of a vehicle coming through the woods. He was happy to see that it was his friend Bob Berge and his grandson Robert and his dog Lucky. He invited them to sit down and immediately went to the cellar to fetch a cold jug of carbonated water. Robert loved the cold carbonated water, especially when Eli added a little strawberry Kool-Aid.

While Eli and Bob were working out the details of the logging contract in the cabin, Robert and his dog Lucky decided to do a little exploring down towards the pond. All of a sudden Eli and Bob heard Lucky barking loudly. Eli knew it was not his hounds as they were locked up in their barn. As they rushed to the door Robert ran between both of them completely out of breath and very scared, in fact too scared to talk. Finally his grandfather got him to calm down enough to tell what happened to cause all of the excitement and barking. It seems as though he and Lucky had come face to face with a black bear. The bear was not at all aggressive, in fact it seemed to just want to play, but Robert and Lucky had no intention of joining in play with a bear. Everyone was greatly relieved when Eli told them that the bear was his pet and that he had raised her from a cub.

After conducting their business and having some lunch it was time for Bob, his grandson and Lucky to head back down the mountain to their home in Colton. The logging was to begin around the first of July, weather permitting. Eli was always glad to see the logging crew come, but he was even happier to see them go so that peace and quiet could return to his mountain.

Eli's Mountain Cabin

TWO

Eli's Family From Bend Comes For A Visit

With so much to do now that summer was in full swing, Eli found that he did not have much time to spend with Sampson, his hounds, Big Daniel and Little Anne, or his falcon Delightful. He could see the sadness in their countenance as he would feed them each morning and evening. He also realized that it was taking him a lot longer to get things done than in years gone by. He seemed to need more rest and afternoon naps. Eli felt good but he just did not have the same endurance he had in past years. He also found that he was sleeping later in the mornings. No longer did he get up by 6:00 am, in fact some mornings the sun shining in through his windows would wake him up.

Never the less, Eli was having a good summer and getting a lot done in a timely manner. All the wood he would need for the next winter was now in his woodshed. He was able to spend a lot time harvesting the wild strawberries, wild blackcaps and gooseberries for making jam. Many edible roots were stored in his cellar for food in the wintertime.

Eli noticed that Sampson was spending less and less time around the homestead. Sometimes she would be gone for two or three days. This concerned Eli. Eli would turn Big Daniel and Little Anne loose each day but he had trained them to stay in and around the front yard. He also always managed to allow Delightful to be free from her tether for at least an hour each day. He always turned Old Pet out in the east pasture.

Even though Eli was very busy he managed to get up to the carbonated spring at least once a week. It was on one of these afternoon trips that Eli again spotted the large man like tracks of the creature he was sure he had heard in the cave on a previous trip up the mountain. The tracks had been rained on so they were not too clear.

Again, the tracks led him directly to the cave but there were also tracks around the carbonated spring. Eli had Big Daniel and Little Anne with him and his trusted horse. This time he remembered to bring his 30.06 rifle with him, but only for the purpose of killing a rabbit or squirrel for his evening meal.

After filling his water canteen and allowing the animals to drink it was time to head back to his cabin. On the return trip he decided to take the long route home and go through the east meadow. At the far end of the meadow Eli spotted a rabbit. With one crack shot he secured fresh rabbit for his evening meal. He also saw a sight that warmed his heart, but at the same time made him a little sad. As he looked back up the mountain side he could see Sampson, but she was not alone. She had found a companion and no doubt it was a male. Eli whistled at Sampson as he had done hundreds of times before, but Sampson ignored him. Being the great lover of nature and having an understanding of the way things work in nature, Eli was quick to realize that this was the way things were meant to be. Eli was just grateful for the time that he was able to spend with Sampson when she was around the cabin.

The time had finally come for the logging crew to arrive on Goat Mountain. Eli kept the animals close to the cabin this week as he did not want them to be anywhere near the logging operation. The only pet he worried about was Sampson. He had only seen Sampson a couple of times in the last few weeks and that was at a distance. He was pretty sure the noise of the machines would cause her and her new companion to stay far away from the logging operation. Eli hoped that the week would go by fast and the logging operation would be done for another year. The weather was beautiful the entire week. Eli always posted a sign on the road leading through the gate at his property line, asking any visitors, other than family members, not to come during the week that the logging operation was going on.

Much to Eli's surprise he was awakened Tuesday morning with a loud knock on his front door. When he asked who it was? he got a pleasant surprise to hear a little girl's voice say "Grandpa its Elly, your granddaughter from Bend." The next voices he heard were those of Evan and Siena, saying "Grandpa where is Sampson"? How surprised he was to see his son, Matt and his entire family. Eli dressed quickly and had them all come into the cabin. The children had grown a lot since last fall. Elly was now in the fourth grade. She was the artist in the family, in fact she could not wait to tell Grandpa that she had won $100.00 in a recent art contest. Evan was in the second grade and he was playing Little League baseball and doing very well. Siena was in kindergarten, and all she could talk about was the neighbor's horses. She asked grandpa about Old Pet.

When Eli asked his son where their vehicle was, Matt told him they had had to leave it about one fourth mile down the road from the gate, as a large tree had evidently just fallen over the road and there was no way around it. Eli told his son they could go and cut the tree up so as to be able to get by, right after breakfast.

Eli prepared a great breakfast with Kim's help. The meal consisted of pancakes made from flour Eli had ground from some roots that he had collected down by the pond. He went to the root cellar and brought in a large bowl of fresh wild strawberries he had picked the day before. He made cream from canned milk that he purchased on his last trip to Colton. Eli made his own syrup, which he collected from the sugar maple trees his dad had planted years ago. His father had brought these trees as seedlings when he moved to Oregon from Vermont to claim the homestead. All of his grandchildren loved collecting the syrup when they came to Goat Mountain. Elly asked her Grandfather if they could go up the mountain later in the day and help collect some new sap from the maple trees? He said they could go after lunch if everyone felt up to it. Eli told the children they would have to stay in and around the cabin and barns, unless he or their parents were with them, as the logging operation was going on for the rest of this week. Eli's son was very much against trees being cut down, but he realized this was the only income his father had to live on. Matt had even offered, on more than one occasion, to send his dad all the money he would need for the year. Eli always refused the offer and would continue to do so when his other sons made similar offers.

With the breakfast dishes cleaned and put away and the cabin tidied up it was now time to go and retrieve the family vehicle and their belongings. The girls could hardly wait to get this over with so they could get into more comfortable clothes and get ready for the many adventures they were going to experience on Grandpa's Goat Mountain. Eli promised Elly and Siena that he would saddle up Old Pet so they could ride him to the meadow to collect maple sap. The girls loved Old Pet and he loved to have them ride on his back. Eli had made a small two wheeled cart that he could hook up to his horse. It came in handy for hauling fresh carbonated water from the spring and for hauling containers full of maple sap, which in turn would be made into maple syrup.

After unloading everything from their vehicle Eli and the children went down to the barn to see the hounds, and Delightful and Sampson. The animals loved to see the children. While they were gone Kim made a nice lunch for everyone. After lunch Eli got everything ready for collecting sap from the Maple Grove. He put the harness on Old Pet and hooked him up to the two wheeled cart and off they all went to the Maple Grove high up on the mountain side. The grove was not very far from the Carbonated Spring, so Eli put several water jugs in the cart in addition to the containers used for collecting the sap. Previously Eli had drilled holes in the trees and placed collecting containers on each tree. On this trip all that would be necessary would be to replace the collecting containers. Eli did have three more maple trees that were not part of the bigger grove that he had the children drill holes in and place containers to collect the sap. In addition to filling the water jugs with carbonated spring water and collecting the maple sap there was still time for picking a couple of small bowls full of wild strawberries.

After collecting the maple sap and picking the wild strawberries it was time to go to the spring. Eli hoped that the children would not notice the large footprints near the spring. In the meantime he was trying to figure out how he could come up with some story explaining the big tracks that looked very much like giant human tracks, if the children should ask about them.

Eli was in a total sweat by the time they reached the spring. He tried the best he could to divert their attention from spending any more time than necessary around the immediate vicinity of the spring. Everything was going pretty well until Siena stumbled by stepping right into one of the giant footprints, and fell to the ground. As Eli went to help her she looked right into the large track. That was it, now he was trapped. How was he ever going to explain what the tracks came from. Suddenly an explanation that might work came to his mind. Eli was not one to ever want to tell something that was not true, but in this case he just had to come up with something that was not the 'gospel truth' because he did not want to ruin the rest of the children's vacation. He tried the best he could to downplay the tracks by telling the children the tracks probably were his from a previous trip. He told the children that he had taken off his shoes to cool his feet in the runoff from the spring and that rain had made the tracks bigger.

It was finally time to head back down the mountain to the cabin. As they passed through the mountain meadow and neared the entrance to the cave Eli wondered if he should go ahead and tell the children about his recent encounter with the big hairy two legged creatures. After giving it some thought he decided that he would wait until the end of their visit. He knew that his family would want to visit the carbonated spring again before they left to go home to Bend. He was afraid telling them now about Big Foot might keep the children from wanting to go outside at all. He remembered that on their last visit the children and their Dad had discovered the remains of an old whiskey still that had evidently been used by earlier residents during the days of Prohibition. Eli loved to have the children spend time exploring with the animals at their heels.

Matt and Kim had a wonderful meal prepared when the group got back to the cabin. After cleaning up after supper Matt suggested they spend the evening down at the pond. The children thought that was an excellent idea so they hurried out the door and began collecting old dead limbs for the campfire. Kim brought marshmallows for roasting. It was a beautiful evening with a full moon. As they sat around the camp fire Eli ask the children about their school year and the plans they had for the rest of the summer. He expressed the joy he felt in learning of their successes in school. He again reminded the children of the importance of getting a good education.

After singing several camp fire songs Grandpa Eli could see that the children were getting pretty tired, so he suggested they put the fire out and return to the cabin.

After family prayer was said the children asked Grandpa if he would tell them an old Navy story to which he happily agreed to do so. He only got about half way through the story, when he noticed that all of the children had fallen asleep. By 10:00 pm the lamps were blown out and the day came to a close.

Eli awoke to the sound of power saws and quickly realized the noise was coming from Bob Berge's logging crews. He got dressed quickly and made a fire in the wood range in the kitchen. Matt and Kim got up but all three stayed as quiet as possible so that the children might continue to sleep for a few more minutes. Kim agreed to make breakfast while Matt and his father went to the barn to feed the animals. When they got back to the cabin the children were up and getting ready for breakfast.

The morning was spent in and around the cabin. Eli brought the hounds and Delightful out from the barn and turned Old Pet out into the east pasture. Elly asked if she could release Delightful from her tether. Everyone watched as she soared high in the sky. Suddenly Delightful spotted a small rabbit and made a dive for it. The rabbit got away and the children cheered. Grandpa reminded the children that the rabbit could have been their evening meal. They all laughed a little.

The afternoon was spent cutting fire wood from tree tops that the loggers had delivered from their logging operation. The children all helped with hauling the rounds into the woodshed so that grandpa would have nice dry wood for the winter time. After they finished with the wood Grandpa suggested they make a trip to the carbonated spring and cave in the early evening, as the day time temperature was pretty hot. Kim prepared an early evening meal so the group could be on their way by 6:00 pm. Grandpa suggested they leave the hounds and Delightful home since they were going to do some exploring in the cave.

Grandpa put the harness on Old Pet and then hooked her up to the two wheeled cart. Matt put a few more water jugs in the cart, and Evan and Elly put in three small bowls for collecting wild strawberries. They went down to the far end of the east meadow and then directly up to the carbonated spring. By the time they collected the water and filled the bowls with wild strawberries they only had a little over an hour of daylight to explore the cave and get back to the cabin. Eli planned it that way as he was not at all anxious to spend much time at the cave. When they got to the cave Eli remembered that he had conveniently failed to bring any oil lanterns along so he told the group that they would not be able to go very far into the cave. The group went just far enough to feel the ice cold water dripping on their heads. Suddenly everyone froze as they could hear some very unusual faint sounds coming from deep inside the cave. Eli quickly exclaimed that the sounds were probably coming from winds from earlier in the day, that were trapped in the cave and just swirling around and trying to find a way to the outside of the cave. This seemed to satisfy the children, but Eli could tell from the looks on their faces that Matt and Kim were not buying his explanation. Suddenly the sounds were becoming much louder and appeared to be coming towards the group.

With that Eli exclaimed that it was time to leave the cave and head back to the cabin. The grandchildren were starting to whimper, and they told their parents that they wanted out of the cave now! When they got to the cart they heard very loud banging noises coming from the cave. Eli did not comment, as they moved rather quickly down the mountain side towards the cabin. Everyone seemed glad to have this cave experience over with for the time being. By the time they reached the cabin it was almost dark. Siena had fallen asleep in the cart.

Elly, Evan and Siena always loved night time in Grandpa's cabin because they got to sleep in bunk beds in the loft. They loved to look out the window and see the beautiful night sky. Grandpa had taught them the names of several constellations and they always tried to name as many as they could see. It was also fun to look for shooting stars and satellites. The last time they were up to Grandpa's mountain property they had seen a shooting star come directly towards the cabin. It appeared to have actually hit the field just west of the cabin. When they all went out to look the next morning they found a wide burned spot in the grass and a very hard black rock about the size of a baseball. Grandpa told the children this was a meteorite. He gave it to the children and told them to take it to school in the fall when they returned to Bend. Needless to say the children were thrilled.

Road leading to Eli's mountain cabin

THREE

Grandpa Takes The Grandchildren Hunting

The next morning the children woke up very early. They reminded grandpa that he had promised to take them on a hunting trip with the hounds and Delightful out into the east meadow after breakfast.

Everyone got a pleasant surprise when they got to the barn to fetch the hounds and Delightful. As soon as they opened the barn door Sampson was there to greet them. Eli was so happy to see her as she had been gone for several days. The children were a little nervous as this was their first experience with the bear. Eli assured them that Sampson would not hurt them, so it was only a few minutes until they became relaxed around the bear. After spending several minutes with the bear and the hounds it was finally time to go hunting. Eli explained that it was necessary to keep the hounds penned up as they would probably ruin the hunt for the falcon. He had not yet trained them to hunt together. Eli was satisfied that Sampson would not have a negative effect on the hunt, in fact she would probably wander off and they might not see her again for several days.

Eli told the family that they would need to hunt at the far end of the east meadow so they would be far away from the logging operation. Kim decided that she would stay at the cabin today as there was some deep cleaning that she could see needed to be done. Besides she wanted to spend some time alone as she had brought along her water color painting materials and she really wanted to do a painting of the cabin and give it to Eli as a surprise for his upcoming birthday. After she and Matt fixed a nice lunch it was time for the group to leave for the day long hunting trip with the falcon. It only took a few minutes for Eli to make one final check to make sure they had everything they needed for the day. Each person had a small backpack for carrying snacks and strawberry Kool-Aid.

Delightful could hardly wait to be turned loose from her tether. As they approached the far end of the meadow it became very difficult to hold her back. She would lunge forward as hard as she could and then when she came to the end of the tether line she would be jerked to an abrupt stop. With great excitement Elly spotted a large rabbit scampering across the field. She yelled to Eli and he immediately released Delightful from her tether. She soared into the sky and quickly spotted the rabbit down below. She made one long beautiful dive and caught the rabbit with her talons, but it was too heavy for her to lift so she pounced on it until Eli came to claim the catch. Before the morning was over the hunters had claimed two more rabbits and one squirrel. These would make a great barbeque that evening. The children were still not too excited about eating squirrel and wild rabbit. Old Daniel and Little Anne were having the time of their life trying to keep up with the children.

Finally Eli announced that the hunt was over and that it was time for lunch. He asked the children where they would like to have lunch. All three answered in unison, "in the cave". Grandpa tried to talk them out of it but they would not hear of any place else. Upon seeing their determination Eli gave in and they headed for the cave as that was the only cool place to get out of the heat. Matt and his father carried the lunch and the children each carried the small bottles of carbonated strawberry kool-aid. The group went about 100 feet into the cave and located a comfortable place to set. Matt handed out the sandwiches, chocolate chip cookies and wild strawberries. After lunch everyone seemed to just want to relax and take a little nap in the cool of the cave, that is everyone except Evan. He wanted to go a little further into the cave. Again, he could not go very far because Grandpa had not brought a kerosene lantern or flashlight. Grandpa, Matt, and the girls had just gotten to sleep when they heard Evan screaming and running towards them as fast as he could. He was so frightened that he could hardly talk. After catching his breath and calming down a little bit Grandpa asked him what had happened. Evan told him that he had heard the same noise as before, but it was much louder and seemed to be coming towards him.

Eli came out with the same explanation as before, but he could see even the children were not buying his story. After getting the children calmed down and gathering up the leftover lunch stuff, Eli had no trouble of convincing the group that it was time to head back down the mountain to the cabin. The trip down the mountain was uneventful.

With several hours of daylight left the children asked if they could do some exploring nearby while the adults visited. After getting the hounds and Delightful from the barn they went to the pond and did they ever get a pleasant surprise. Sampson was eating some green apples that had fallen from the lone surviving apple tree in the vicinity of the cabin. The only other apple trees on the entire property were located near the carbonated spring high up on the mountain side. The children were a little reluctant to approach the bear but any fear they had soon vanished as Sampson came to them. She just wanted to play. She would chase them around the tree and then they would turn and chase her around the tree. The children soon realized that Grandpa probably had done this same thing with the bear. Finally the dinner bell rang and it was time to end the play and return to the cabin. Grandpa was very happy when the children told him about their time with Sampson. This was the first time the children had been alone with the bear.

After dinner and clean up it was time to prepare for bed. The children asked grandpa if he would tell them one last story about their Great Grandparents, John and Anna Bailey. While grandpa was telling the story Matt and Kim decided this would be a good time to spend a few minutes alone by taking a short walk down to the pond. Matt loved to be down by the pond at night, particularly when the sky was clear, with just the stars and moon giving light. The stars seemed so close, and there was no pollution from city lights and automobiles. As they approached the pond they saw a shadow of what looked to be a giant creature walking in an upright position. The shadow was being reflected in the water. After experiencing what they had with the giant tracks near the carbonated spring, and the sounds coming from the cave, they became very frightened and rushed back to the cabin as quickly as their legs would carry them. On the way back they agreed that it would not be wise to mention this experience to the children. Matt said that he would discuss the experience with his father after the children were sound asleep.

At this point in time Matt and Kim were starting to get concerned about Eli's safety on Goat Mountain. At the same time Matt knew that he could never convince his father that it might be best if he moved from Goat Mountain to the little town of Colton where he had many friends. He knew that his father loved this place and that he intended to spend the rest of his life on his beloved mountain. When Matt and Kim told Eli about the encounter he just shrugged his shoulders and told them that he had no fear, and that there was no reason why he and this creature, if he in fact existed, and Eli believed he did, could not cohabitate on this mountain. This gave Matt and Kim some peace of mind, and they concluded that there was no reason for worry.

The only thing that Matt always worried about was his father's health and him being alone for long periods of time. Matt could see that age was creeping up on his dad. He was moving a little slower each year. Matt and Kim wondered just how long he would be able to be alone so much of the time. What would happen if he needed medical attention or if he fell and broke a leg or arm? Not being connected to the outside world in any way, there would be no way of anyone knowing if he was in trouble or needed help. Matt intended to discuss this situation with his brothers in the near future. With what had happened at the pond and worrying about his dad's well being Matt did not have a very restful night's sleep.

6:00 am in the morning came very early and it was time to get up and start packing for the return trip to Bend. They needed to leave right after breakfast, as they had a church function that evening in Bend. This was to be a very hard time for the entire family. They loved the time spent with grandpa and they found it very difficult to leave him alone on Goat Mountain. They had experienced so much on this short visit, memories that would last a life time. And of course Matt and Kim had another reason for not wanting to leave Eli alone. They had some concerns that they had not had to deal with in past visits.

Good-bys were said and each member of the family gave Grandpa a big hug and told him how much they loved him. As they drove off grandpa could see the children turned around in their seat and waving good-by. Big tears rolled down his cheeks and he turned and walked slowly back towards his cabin. He turned and looked in the direction their car was heading before going into his cabin. As he did so Matt stopped the car and the children stepped outside the car for a moment and waved one last time before heading into the woods and out of sight.

Eli was so grateful they had come, but how it hurt to see them leave. Eli could only hope that the time would pass quickly as he knew that his other two sons and their families would be coming from Houston in August. Their visits were to be just one week apart. With that in mind he knew there was much to be done to prepare for their visits. He also knew that his friend, Bob Berge, would be coming by in a couple of days as their logging operation would be finished for the year.

There was no time to sit around and feel sorry for himself. At the present time he felt pretty exhausted and a little sad so he decided to spend the rest of the day with his hounds, Delightful and Sampson if she was in the barn.

FOUR

FAMILIES ARRIVE From Houston

As Eli relaxed in his favorite rocking chair it was not long before he fell asleep. Suddenly he was awakened by noises that appeared to be coming from behind the barn. He decided to go and investigate and what a pleasant surprise awaited him. There was Sampson but she was not alone. A male bear was with her. This was something Eli knew would happen sooner or later. Eli whistled and Sampson turned towards him and the male bear scrambled off into the nearby woods. Eli was a little surprised when Sampson turned and followed the male bear into the woods. He thought Sampson would at least come for a little back scratching but obviously she had other things on her agenda that were much more important.

Eli spent the rest of the day doing little odd jobs that needed to be done before his other sons and their families arrived. There were still a few repairs he wanted to complete on the cabin and the woodshed had developed a leak in the roof that needed to be repaired before next fall. Both barns needed a fresh coat of paint but that would have to wait until his sons and their families arrived from Houston. Painting would involve getting on a ladder and Eli was not about to do that without someone else there to help him. Eli had purchased the paint on his last trip to Colton.

Eli was not up to eating any lunch as he had prepared a huge breakfast or brunch for Matt and his family before they left. Late in the afternoon Eli decided to walk down to the pond and see if he could find any foot prints of the big two legged creature that Matt and Kim claimed they had seen a shadow of in the pond last night. Sure enough, when he walked to the far side of the pond there were many huge tracks in the soft dirt. Eli had an old camera in his cabin and he decided that he would get it and take some pictures of the tracks. He hoped the film would still be good as it was at least two or three years old. He would take the film to be developed to Canby when he went to the Clackamas County Fair in August. After taking the pictures Eli took the hounds and Delightful out in the west field for an hour or so. After that he returned to the cabin and prepared a small evening meal of homemade soup, left over cornbread and a large glass of carbonated strawberry Kool-Aid.

This was going to be a long evening as it did not get dark until about 9:30 pm. Eli decide this would be a good time to wash some clothes as it had been some time since he had done any laundry. He started the old ringer washing machine which was powered by a small Briggs & Stratton gasoline engine. It took him about an hour to complete the laundry and hang the clothes out to dry on the clothes line out behind his cabin. With that little task completed it was time to spend the rest of the evening reading from his Jack London book about an adventure in Alaska. Eli had realized a long time ago that he was too old to even think of moving to a remote area of Alaska, but it was always fun to dream of what life might be like if he were living in Nome, Alaska. He finally fell asleep reading his book.

Rain pounding on the roof awakened Eli early the next morning. When he went out on the front porch to bring in some kindling there was Sampson playing with an old ball in the front yard. This is just what Eli needed this morning. Eli decided to dress quickly and grab some leftovers from the kitchen and head down to the pond and try his luck at catching some fish for breakfast. The rain only lasted about fifteen minutes. Eli hoped that Sampson would spend the morning with him.

He kept the hounds in the barn because they always spoiled his fishing by jumping into the pond to play in the water. After catching six nice Rainbow Trout, three for him and three for Sampson, it was time to spend some time with his hounds and Delightful.

As Eli was eating breakfast he heard a knock on the door. His friend Bob Berge came to settle up with him on the logging and to say good-by. Eli invited Bob in for Breakfast to which he quickly agreed. He was really tired of campfire food by now as the logging operation had taken a little over a week this time. Bob wanted to know how Eli's visit with his son and family had gone. He also wanted to know when Mike and Martin were coming. As usual they had a great visit and Eli told Bob that he would be coming to Colton in August as he also planned to go to the Canby fair.

The next several weeks found Eli busy making small repairs on his cabin, the barns and the woodshed. There were many fences and gates that needed to be repaired from damage from the deep winter snows. Of course there were trips to the carbonated spring and the cave. Eli had not seen any sign of the big fellow he now called Big Foot. Eli made it a point to start his old flat bed Dodge truck each day and drive it around the barns. He spent several days cutting up the tops of trees that Bob and his crew had left for him, for wood to be used during the long winter months. Eli also spent a couple of days collecting raw honey from bee hives near the old orchard above the carbonated spring. He knew how much his grandchildren loved his homemade biscuits and honey.

Eli always took his hounds and Delightful on these trips to prepare fire wood and collect honey from active bee hives. Delightful would ride in the cab of the truck until Eli would stop and then off he would fly high in the sky. Eli loved to watch the falcon soar high in the sky and then swoop down into a meadow and catch a small rodent. While Delightful was doing his thing the hounds would be busy trying to scare up a rabbit or squirrel. Eli would go about his task of collecting the raw honey while most of the bees were away from the hive. When it was time to go all Eli had to do was give his familiar whistle. The hounds would come running and Delightful would return to the cab of the truck for the ride back to the cabin.

July rolled around and Eli knew that his sons, Mike and Martin would be coming. He felt that he was well prepared. He had put up a large tent next to his cabin as the children loved to sleep in the tent, as his small cabin would certainly not accommodate the grandchildren and the parents for sleeping. Eli had repaired the outdoor fireplace that had been used many time for visitors and family. He had recently made an unscheduled trip to Colton in the old Dodge to buy some supplies and produce. He had also purchased birthday presents for each grandchild and he planned to have a big birthday party for all of the children.

It was on July 2nd that Mike, Martin, and their families arrived in what appeared to be a VW Mini Bus. Eli was greatly surprised as he thought they would be coming about a week apart, however he was so happy they came together. Eli had just finished checking and feeding all the animals and was about to prepare his breakfast when he heard honking and yelling from their vehicle as they approached the cabin. Eli rushed to open the door and ran to meet the bus. His son Mike brought the vehicle to a quick stop and the children all piled out, that is all except Archer, as he was not quite walking yet. The children ran to greet Grandpa and after a quick hug from each child he embraced the rest of the family. They had flown from Houston together and rented the Mini Bus at the Portland Airport. They had had an early breakfast at the only cafe in Colton. Grandpa was so excited to see everyone that he forgot about being hungry. It was not long before the children wanted to know where this pet bear was that they had heard about in Grandpa's last letter to their families. Of course they were also anxious to see the hounds and this falcon he had also mentioned.

The children were reminded by their parents that some chores needed to be done before they could go and see the animals. Sleeping bags needed to be placed in the tent and suit cases needed to be stowed away. With these jobs accomplished it was now time to go to the barn to spend time with the animals. Eli reminded the children that Sampson was spending less and less time around the barn and the cabin and more and more time away in the woods. She seemed to only come around when she needed a good back scratch or when she wanted some of the honey Eli had stored in the root cellar for her. The hounds were always excited to see the children. Delightful was far more shy as this was her first encounter with the children. As it turned out Sampson was nowhere in sight. Eli told the children that if she didn't show up in a couple of days he would put some honey out for her. He knew that would bring Sampson around for sure.

Eli and the two families spent the rest of the morning with the hounds and Delightful. The children got to see the falcon put on and incredible air show. She caught two rabbits and one squirrel. Eli released all three back into the wilds of nature in the east meadow. He did remind the children that this would not always be the case. He told them there would be fried rabbit for at least one or two suppers while they were visiting.

After lunch the entire group spent the afternoon playing in the water at the pond. Coming from Texas the children and their parents had a hard time getting used to the ice cold water.

After supper the children asked if they could take Old Pet and the hounds out to the east meadow. Eli thought that would be an excellent idea. He went along with the children but the parents stayed in and around the cabin. By 9:30 everyone was very tired and the children were more than ready for bed.

The next morning Eli was awakened by noises familiar to him. As he looked out towards the old barn there was Sampson but she was not alone. A much larger male bear was with her. Eli walked out onto the porch and gave a loud whistle. The large bear scampered off into the woods but Sampson remained. Eli quickly woke the children up and they all followed Grandpa, in their pajamas, down to where Sampson was. Sampson was acting a little strange since she had a new found friend. She would allow Eli to come near but she was very hesitant about allowing any of the children to approach her. Eli was very careful not to push the issue. He figured it was best to take his time and allow Sampson time to get used to the children being around. He was sure, before long the bear would accept the children and perhaps even allow them to scratch her back with the old broom. Eli was always very careful when visitors were around the bear as he knew she had never been de-clawed. Eli knew in his heart the day would come when Sampson would leave and not return and he wanted her to be able to survive in the wild. Eli knew that even though he had raised Sampson since she was a newborn, she was still a wild animal.

After breakfast Eli and his sons and the children spent the entire morning with the hounds, Big Daniel and Little Anne, and Delightful. They left Sampson in the barn. His sons wanted to see where the logging operation had removed the trees for this year and the children loved exploring in the woods. Before long they all heard the dinner bell ringing and that meant it was time for lunch. Meal time was a real experience in itself. Most of the things which were prepared for meals came from the root cellar or from Grandpa's small garden. During the summer time there were usually wild berries served for desert. These were all things that his families from Houston hardly ever ate. Eli always had homemade bread made from flour he made in his small grist mill, which was located below the pond. He would buy raw whole wheat each fall when he went to Colton for supplies to get through the long winter on Goat Mountain.

After lunch and clean up it was time to go swimming in the pond again. In August the afternoons were very hot on Goat Mountain, and playing in the water was a great way to cool off. Sampson came out of the barn and just watched from a distance. Of course the hounds were in the water right along with the rest of the group. Delightful was allowed to be free to fly and soar in the sky overhead. Old Pet was always put our in the east pasture every morning. The children asked Grandpa if they could have a bonfire down by the pond in the evening, to which he readily agreed. Kate said they had brought hot dogs, buns and marshmallows. The parents thought this was a great idea as they would not have to build a fire in the wood stove to prepare supper.

After the children got tired of swimming they all went to the cabin and tent to dry off and get dressed for the evening. Grandpa had promised them that he would teach them some fun games that his sons used to play when they were small and still at home in Seattle.

The children had so much fun playing kick the can and run sheep run. Grandpa insisted that the adults participate in the games. There was a full moon and so there were some scary shadows dancing around in the woods as well as strange noises from the pair of great horned owls that lived in the woods nearby. By 9:00 pm the children were getting pretty tired and they did not want to venture far away from the adults and the bonfire. Grandpa said that he would go with them to the tent so they could get their pajamas on. Eli had placed his cot and sleeping bag in the tent earlier in the day. He also told them that he would tell them an old Navy story. Martin offered to help, mainly because he still loved to hear his dad's old stories even though he had come to realize they were mostly made up with events that probably never really happened.

Mike and Ailene decided they would take a walk around. As they approached the far side of the pond they were startled to hear what seemed to be a loud noise of something running away through the woods. They assumed that it was probably the big male bear that Eli had seen that morning. They quickly made their way back to the bonfire. After putting the fire out they headed on back to the cabin. By the time they got to the cabin the children were asleep and Eli was preparing for bed himself. Mike and Ailene told Eli what they had heard. He shrugged it off by saying it was probably a curious Elk. They often came down to the pastures at night time to feed.

Eli got up from his cot in the tent around 2:00 am to go to the outhouse. It was very bright outside from the full moon. As Eli was coming back from the outhouse he glanced down towards the pond. As he did, he saw a beautiful sight. There was Sampson and the large male bear playing and chasing one another. Eli realized then and there that Sampson had found a male companion and he expected there would be a new baby cub in the spring. He just hoped that Sampson would not forget him and that the cub would be born in the barn. After watching the bears for awhile Eli returned to the tent. It did not take him very long to fall asleep.

The grandchildren were awakened by the bright sunlight pouring in through the open flap of the tent. Grandpa would have liked to have slept a little longer but the children would not hear of it. They all complained of being hungry so the first thing that came out of their mouths was "Grandpa what's for breakfast?" When he told them there would be pancakes made from scratch with homemade maple syrup and carbonated strawberry Kool-Aid they got very excited. They all got dressed quickly and went into the cabin.

With breakfast and cleanup out of the way it was now time to begin the day's activities. Grandpa had been planning this day for some time. First, Eli and the children would go to the barn and see if Sampson would allow the children to come close. When they got to the barn they discovered that Sampson was already gone to the woods to be with her new companion. Grandpa had promised the children that he would take everyone to the carbonated spring so they could eat wild strawberries and collect some fresh ice cold carbonated spring water. The older children had visited the spring on their last visit but this was to be a first for the younger ones.

Ailene and Mike made a big lunch while Eli and Martin readied the old 47 Dodge flat bed truck and fetched the hounds and Delightful from the barn. Everyone loved the old truck. Grandpa would let the older children take turns riding on the outside. Two would straddle the head lights and two would stand on the running boards. The rest of the children would ride on the flat bed with their fathers. Ailene would ride inside with Christine. Grandpa would drive very slow as the road going up the mountain side was very rough in places. In fact it was so rough that Eli seldom took the old truck. Most of the time he would hook Old Pet up to the little two wheeled cart for the trip.

As they passed the cave Eli quickly glanced at the opening but there was nothing in sight. As the group approached the carbonated spring Eli wondered if there would be large tracks from the 'big fella', as was the case on the trip to the spring with his family from Bend. He sure hoped not as he hated to try and explain what the tracks might have come from. Grandpa was not one who liked telling little white lies to cover up telling the truth. He was pleased when he remembered that they had had a couple of very hard rains since his last trip to the spring, consequently there were no tracks in or near the spring.

After collecting several jugs of fresh cold carbonated water it was time to do some exploring, before eating lunch, Jacob released Delightful from her tether and Ben and Archer released the hounds. Grandpa suggested they look for edible mushrooms and wild strawberries. Grandpa took great pains to show the children which mushrooms were ok to eat. The only ones Grandpa ever collected where the Morels. They were shaped like a little sponge tree. There was always an abundance of these wild mushroom after a hard rain. The grandchildren loved collecting the mushrooms, it was kind of like a treasure hunt. The children were a little startled when suddenly Delightful dove to catch a rabbit only a few yards from where Brighton was standing. The children were happy that the rabbit had managed to escape from the falcon's talons.

It was time for lunch, and of course the wild strawberries and carbonated cherry flavored Kool-Aid were the high-light of the meal.

Marina asked if they could take some of the carbonated water back to Houston. Everyone got a little chuckle out of her request. After lunch Eli again release the hounds and Delightful. The goal for the falcon was to catch at least two rabbits which would be prepared for supper when they got back to the cabin. Delightful soared high in the sky and the children watched in complete silence and awe. Delightful made several circles high overhead and then all of a sudden she dove at full speed towards the ground. Everyone looked to where they thought she might land but she fooled them. When she was about twenty feet from the ground she swooped back high in the sky. Delightful made several more circles and then she spotted her prize. The only problem was that it was not a rabbit but a large blue grouse. It had been a long time since grandpa had eaten blue grouse. This would be a special treat for everyone. In Grandpa's opinion grouse meat was far superior to rabbit or chicken. The grandchildren had never eaten grouse meat and Katy and Jacob became quite vocal in their opposition to the idea of having grouse for supper. In fact all the children were not in favor of having Delightful catch any of the wild critters. Grandpa spent several minutes explaining to the children that it was necessary for him to use Delightful for this purpose. The only way he could survive here on Goat Mountain during the long winter months was to have plenty of protein in his diet and he enjoyed having a variety of meat to eat. Grandpa assured the children that he never caught more than what he needed to survive the long winter months. The children were satisfied with his explanation and nothing more was said about using Delightful for this purpose. The children grew to love the falcon and they really enjoyed watching her perform. Old Daniel and Little Anne contributed by catching a large rabbit.

Finally it was time to call in Delightful and the hounds and head down the mountain. Unfortunately the road down the mountain passed very near the mouth of the cave. The same cave where the children from Bend had had the scary experience with the creature just a month or so ago. Grandpa hoped that he could get by the cave without the children paying much attention to it. That was only wishful thinking on his part because as the old 47 Dodge truck neared the entrance the children all screamed in unison "grandpa a cave, may we stop and explore in the cave"? Again, he had not brought any lanterns or flashlights so he was sure they would not want to go very far into the cave. The children's fathers led the way. Ailene and the smaller children stayed in the truck. Martin and Mike had gone into the cave several time in years past. Grandpa looked around for the giant tracks prior to going into the cave but evidently the recent rains had washed them away here as well as by the spring. Eli stayed near the entrance while his sons went into the cave with the older children. They were only gone about fifteen minutes. They only went as far as there was a little light coming through from the entrance to the cave. Jacob, Kate and Marina could hardly stop talking about what they had seen in the cave. Grandpa was surprised with the knowledge the children seemed to have about caves, bats, stalactites and stalagmites. Marina told grandpa about visiting some large caves between Austin and San Antonio, Texas. In fact she told Grandpa that she had brought some pictures of their trip through the caves and that she would show them to him when they got back to the cabin.

Grandpa hurried everyone back to the truck as there were thunder clouds starting to form, and he wanted to be off the mountain before any rain started falling. By the time they got back to the cabin and after putting the jugs of carbonated spring water in the root cellar it was time to start preparing supper. When the children and Eli took the hounds and Delightful to the barn they got a pleasant surprise. Sampson was lying down in the barn. Grandpa asked everyone to stay back as he approached Sampson. He wanted to see what mood she was in before letting the children approach her. Eli quickly realized that Sampson was in a playful mood and so he let Kate and Jacob come near to where he was standing as he scratched Sampson's back. Sampson could sense that the children were not a threat and before long she was letting them scratch her back with the old broom. Sampson even got to the point where she would lie on the ground or floor on her side and let the children set with their backs against her. The children loved the softness of her fur, that is all but Brighton. Brighton exclaimed loudly "grandpa Sampson stinks." Eli assured her that this was just the smell of a wild animal and that bears don't bathe very often like humans do. With that explanation Brighton finally cuddled up next to Sampson and nothing more was mentioned about the smell. After spending some time with the bear it was time for Eli to go inside and prepare the rabbit and blue grouse so they could be cooked for supper.

The children took the hounds and Delightful down towards the pond. They were only gone for a few minutes and all of a sudden the adults in the cabin heard loud screaming and yelling. Eli rushed to the door to see what was going on. The children were making a beeline for the cabin and yelling at the top of their lungs "Grandpa another huge black bear is down by the pond". Grandpa immediately ushered the frightened children inside the cabin and explained to them that this was probably Sampson's new found companion. He told the children that they could probably expect to see a new born cub on their visit next year. With that the children calmed down but they did not want to go down to the pond without grandpa or their parents. Big Daniel and Little Anne did not get too excited as they had already made their peace with the big bear but only because they knew he was Sampson's new mate. It was finally time for supper. The children were told to wash up and get ready for a great meal in which they would get to eat meat they had never eaten before. Everything smelled so good and the children were very hungry. The blue grouse looked just like a chicken and the rabbit was served in pieces. After each one ate at least two homemade biscuits with fresh wild strawberry jam, their parents reminded them that there were lots of other good things on the table. The only part of the dinner that the children did not eat very much of was the fresh dandelion greens salad. Eli said that he understood their dislike and he realized that it took some getting used to wild dandelion greens. Unless they are very young and tender they can sometimes have a bitter taste. For desert Grandpa made a blackberry cobbler from berries they had picked up by the carbonated spring. The children all loved Grandpa's cobblers.

With supper over and the dishes cleaned and put away it was time for everyone to walk down to the pond and also view the beautiful night sky. Going outside at night on Goat Mountain was always an enjoyable experience. The stars and planets seemed so close. Grandpa pointed out several constellations and planets. Jupiter was just above the horizon. Venus would not appear until morning. There was only a sliver of a moon. As they approached the pond there seemed to be a flurry of activity with several smaller animals scampering away from the pond and disappearing into the forest. Grandpa certainly hoped that the 'big fella' was not one of the creatures. He did hear some louder noises and what appeared to be branches being broken. As was the family custom, everyone was asked to set quietly in a row near the water's edge and observe the sights and sounds near and in the water and in the nearby forest. This always proved to be a good experience for the children and the adults. Soon Grandpa said that it was time to return to the cabin and get ready for bed as he had a big day planned for tomorrow.

When the children were ready for bed they all reminded grandpa that he had promised to tell them another one of his old Navy stories. The story was about an experience Grandpa had while his ship was traveling in the area of the famous Bermuda Triangle. As usual Grandpa only got about half way through the story and then he started to doze off. The children had to shake him every few minutes so that he could finish the story. The children loved Grandpa's stories and especially the old Navy stories. Grandpa finally had to beg the children to let him finish the story at another time as he was just too sleepy to finish the story tonight. With reluctance the children finally consented, but only on the condition that Grandpa promise to finish the story tomorrow night. After Grandpa fell asleep the children also fell asleep and there was no noise coming from inside the cabin where the parents slept.

FIVE

Mr. Weasel Makes a Visit

The next morning, long before Grandpa awakened, the children were up and playing outside in the front of the cabin. In fact it was the noise of the children and Big Daniel and Little Anne running and barking that awakened grandpa. The parents didn't seem to be bothered by all the noise. They were still sleeping in the loft. Grandpa Eli slipped on his trousers and joined the children outside. He invited all of the children to help him with the morning chores of feeding and caring for the animals which included taking Old Pet out to the east pasture. There were also chickens to feed and eggs needed to be collected. As they approached the chicken house everyone sensed there was something wrong. Sure enough in the middle of the floor there were three dead chickens. Right away Grandpa knew what had happened. He saw signs of the evil weasel. He had spotted the little creature several times in the last few weeks but he had not been able to catch him in the trap he had set. Now he knew that he must get much more aggressive in his attempts to catch the little chicken thief or he would be out of the chicken business. That would be a disaster as he needed the eggs for food and for cooking certain dishes like egg custard pudding.

When his two sons and daughter-in-law got up, Grandpa called a grand family council. The topic was to see who could come up with the best idea for catching the little chicken killer. The children were encouraged to participate by coming up with ideas as well as the adults. Grandpa would appreciate all of their input. Brighton had a problem with this discussion as she loved the chickens but she still did not want to see the poor little weasel hurt or killed. Her comment was "Grandpa can't you just catch the little creature and move him far up on the mountain side by the carbonated spring?" To which Eli replied "Brighton if we did that the little weasel would be back here the next day." Everyone was asked to come to supper in the evening with their ideas.

With the chores done and the chicken coup cleaned up from the bloody mess left by the weasel, it was time to prepare breakfast. Grandpa asked the children what they would like for breakfast. Archer, the youngest of the grandchildren, piped up and said "Grandpa may I have a Sausage and Egg McMuffin"? Everyone chuckled including Grandpa. He had never eaten one and had only recently heard of such a thing when the children from Bend visited earlier in the summer. Ailene told Archer that she could come pretty close to fixing him something quite similar if Eli had any canned sausage. So Eli went to the root cellar and brought in a can of sausage that he had purchased on his last trip to Colton. Wow, did that make Archer happy. The rest of the children put in their request for eggs and pancakes made with wild huckleberries and real mountain maple syrup that grandpa had collected from the sugar maple trees.

With breakfast over and dishes washed and put away, it was time to start the big project of painting the barns. Eli was so thankful to have his two sons and their families to help with this huge undertaking. He would be satisfied if they even just got one barn done this summer. Eli was too old to climb the ladders. He and the children could do the lower sections of the barn.

There was only one tall ladder and Martin decided that he would be first up the ladder. The idea was to start at the very top of the south wall and work down. Grandpa gave each grandchild a paint brush and demonstrated how he wanted them to use it. Little Archer and Christine were so cute with their little paint brushes. Grandpa had given each grandchild and old shirt to put on so as not to get paint on their play clothes. The older children did very well with the area they were assigned. Mike's assignment was to keep everyone in paint and to supply Martin with pain so that he did not have to come down the ladder.

The morning went by fast and it was now time to break for lunch. Ailene prepared a very nice lunch and brought it out to the barn. The children had really worked up an appetite and were also very thirsty for the carbonated strawberry flavored kool-aid. When Martin came down the ladder they all stood back to evaluate their progress. To say the least they were all surprised and pleased. They had almost finished the entire south side of the barn in just a half day. With any luck they would finish this wall and part of the east wall by evening. Little did they know what was going to happen during the afternoon shift.

With lunch over with it was time to return to the task at hand. It was now Mike's turn to spend the afternoon on the ladder. Ailene's assignment was to hold the ladder for her husband. Grandpa's job was to supervise and oversee the entire operation as well as paint the areas that he could reach standing on the ground.

As Mike approached the top of the ladder he let out a scream that could be heard for miles. You guessed it, he had placed the ladder right next to a bee's nest. He came down the ladder so fast and started ripping off his clothes. It seems as though several bees had gotten inside his shirt and down into his pants. Luckily he only got stung a couple of times. Grandpa took a drinking cup and filled it half full of water and dirt. He mixed it up and put the fresh mud on each sting. It worked and Mike was greatly relieved of the pain from the sting.

Everyone else scattered to avoid the mad bees. Grandpa decide that it would be best to take the rest of the afternoon off and give the bees a chance to settle down. The plan was to wait until dark, go out with a flash light and trap the entire hive and remove it away from the barns and cabin.

After supper grandpa asked the children if they would like to go down to the pond for a swim and bonfire with marshmallows. It was a very warm and humid evening and everyone was so excited to get into the water. Grandpa was having such a wonderful time that he forgot about the one worry he had in spending such a long time at the pond in the late evening. As they were just finishing roasting marshmallows and getting ready to put the bonfire out, Grandpa looked to the other side of the pond. It was starting to get dark. As he looked back under trees he saw a sight that startled him. There standing in an upright position was the big hairy two legged creature. He was looking right at the group and especially, it appeared, that he was looking at little Christene. The hair stood straight up on the back of Grandpa's neck. Eli knew that he must not let the others know of his great concern. He knew that he must quickly and quietly get the crew back up to the cabin. He turned away from looking at the 'big fella' and very calmly stated that it was time to return to the cabin and prepare the children for bed. This was the first time that he had such a clear view of 'Big Foot'. He was greatly relieved that no one else saw what he saw. Grandpa told the children a quick bed time story and then tucked each one into his or her sleeping bag in the tent.

Afterwards Eli went back into the cabin and sat down at the table with his sons to have a small snack. He wondered if he should tell them about what he saw in the woods on the other side of the pond, but decided not to, at least for a few days. After retiring to his bed in the tent he stayed awake a very long time wondering if there would be another encounter with the big fella while his family from Houston were visiting, he certainly hoped not!

Morning seemed to come so quickly. Grandpa was anxious to get up and continue with the painting of the barn. The bees were gone and the group made great strides in the painting project. They finished the side they stopped on when the bees attacked the day before.

Grandpa had promised the children another trip to the carbonated spring. There was no carbonated water left in the root cellar to make kool-aid. Every one helped with loading the water bottles onto the bed of the truck in a box grandpa had prepared.

Grandpa had told the grandchildren that Delightful and the hounds could go long on this trip up the mountain. Little did he know what troubles this decision would cause later in the day. Before starting out he had Mike and Martin put on the side boards and also get some straw from the barn for everyone to sit on. It was decided that Mike would drive up to the spring and Martin would drive home. Ailene packed a big picnic lunch and they also took some food for the hounds and Delightful. The ride going up was uneventful, except that Kate and Marina put up quite a fuss because grandpa would not let them stop at the cave. Grandpa was not about to stop at the cave, especially after what he had seen down by the pond the night before. He was sure the 'big fella' was probably in the cave today. Grandpa wondered how long the hairy two legged creature was going stay around before going further up into the Cascades and perhaps even over to the east side of the mountain range. One thing for sure, he did not want another encounter with the creature while his families were visiting.

As they approached the spring Grandpa was terrified with the tracks he saw. The hounds went crazy as they picked up the scent of the man like creature. They raced off in the direction of the cave. Grandpa told everyone that he would explain later but now everyone needed to get back into the truck. Jacob asked his grandpa why he had brought his rifle along but grandpa acted like he did not hear the question. Off they headed towards the cave. The hounds were far ahead of the old truck. Grandpa was really concerned and needless to say, very frightened. He was afraid to think of what might happen if the dogs went into the cave. As they approached the entrance to the cave Eli began calling for Big Daniel and Little Anne. He asked Mike and Martin to go with him into the cave and instructed everyone else to remain at the truck. He took the small flashlight that he had recently placed in the glove compartment of the truck and his 30:06 rifle. They had only traveled a short distance when Old Daniel and Little Anne both came running as fast as they could towards Eli and his sons. They were both barking loudly, and in between barks they were whimpering. Upon examination Grandpa discovered that both dogs were bleeding from cuts on their backs and faces. They did not appear to be life threatening but Grandpa knew that he needed to get them home and take care of their wounds before infection started to set in. Mike and Martin carried the dogs back to the truck and the group headed down the mountain. So much for the afternoon Grandpa had planned at the carbonated spring and meadows nearby. Delightful was disappointed because she was never released from her tether. The children were disappointed because they were looking forward to exploring in the mountain meadows near the spring. Their grave concern for the hounds far exceeded their disappointment in not being able to spend the afternoon on the mountain.

Grandpa and his sons took care of doctoring the hounds wounds while Ailene placed the picnic lunch on the outside picnic table. Prayers were said, giving thanks for the food and for the safe trip back to the cabin and for the dogs surviving what must have been a terrible fight inside the cave. Fortunately they had been able to escape rather quickly when they realized they were far outmatched by the big creature. After all, the dogs were only doing what was natural and of course Grandpa was sure that Big Foot was defending himself and his territory. Eli just wished this whole thing would not have happened. The other thing that made this whole event so bad was that now grandpa knew he would have to explain the whole series of events that had led up to this happening. He could no longer keep all of this a secret from his families.

At the present time he had no idea of how best to go about explaining what he knew to his sons and their families. He decided to ignore the subject for the rest of the day so that he could have some time in the evening to think about what he might say when the time came. He was now more concerned with the well being of the hounds and the children were also deeply concerned so they did not ask any questions about who the dogs might have encountered in the cave. His sons though it might have been a mountain lion but they said nothing. After giving it some thought Eli decided that he would have a talk with his sons first and get their reactions to what he would tell them about previous encounters with the big two legged man like creature.

Most of the rest of the afternoon was spent dealing with the hounds and preparing the evening meal. Grandpa brought some cured elk meat from the cellar as well as some dried fruit that he had prepared last fall. He invited the grandchildren to go with him down to the stream by the pond to collect some fresh watercress. The entire family had learned to like watercress and most of the other greens that grew wild on Goat Mountain. The children loved all of the wild berries but their favorite berries were not ripe yet, the Thimble Berries. They did not ripen until late August.

All of the adults pitched in to prepare a delicious supper which consisted of watercress, freshly caught trout from the pond, potatoes and carrots from grandpa's garden, homemade biscuits, and of course carbonated spring water. Last, but certainly not least, fresh strawberries and blackberries as desert. Grandpa loved having meals that consisted of a variety of foods which came from the land.

After dinner grandpa faked being very tired and begged the children's forgiveness for wanting to go to bed early. The truth was he wanted time to himself to think about what he was going to tell his families in the morning about this creature he now knew was Big Foot. His sons and Ailene did not object and the children were still too upset to want to talk about what happened during the trip to the carbonated spring. They did ask if they could check on Big Daniel and Little Anne to make sure they were doing ok. Grandpa told them it would be ok but please make it a quick visit. Since the dogs were staying down in the barn Martin and Mike agreed to go with the children to check on the hounds. Grandpa waited up until they all got back and then he suggested they have a family prayer. The children loved to snuggle close to grandpa as he offered prayers during their visits. He always offered special thanks for his families and for having them visit him on his beloved Goat Mountain. This time he also offered a prayer for Big Daniel and Little Anne and asked that God might heal them quickly.

At the end of the prayer the children had tears running down their cheeks. They all gave Grandpa a special big hug and kissed him on his cheeks. Grandpa excused himself and went directly to his camp cot in the tent. He lay awake a long time thinking about what he was going to say to his families in the morning. He knew there would be difficult questions about what went on in the cave. He finally decided that he was going to just tell everything just as things and encounters had happened. He was not going to hide anything including the sighting of Big Foot down by the pond a couple of nights ago.

The Chicken Thief

SIX

Grandpa Tells It All

The children were up early and Eli's daughter-in-law was already milling around in the kitchen area. Michael and Martin were evidently out and about. It was another beautiful morning on Goat Mountain. Eli could hear the dogs outside playing with the children. He felt good about that, after all that had happened yesterday. He apologized to Ailene for sleeping in so late.

Breakfast consisted of scrambled eggs, homemade biscuits left over from dinner, wild strawberry jam and ice cold water from the spring. After breakfast the children went back outside to see Sampson. They had noticed her milling around down by the barn. This gave Eli just the opportunity he was hoping for. He was now alone with the adults and ready to talk about yesterday's events. He started by telling them about his very first experience with Big Foot. He described every detail to the best of his memory. He also made it very clear that he did not wish this information to go any further that his immediate family! His sons and daughter-in-law listened carefully. The truth is they could hardly believe what they were hearing, in fact there were only two reasons they believed what Eli was telling them; (1) this was coming from someone they loved and trusted to always tell the truth; (2) they had witnessed seeing the dogs badly injured from the fight in the cave yesterday. The children's parents decided that it would be best if they all sat down at lunch time and gave Grandpa an opportunity to tell it all, just as he had told everything to them. Grandpa felt a great deal of relief now that he knew he no longer needed to hide all of this stuff about Big Foot from the family. He was so thankful to have someone to talk to about all of this.

Chores needed to be done and Grandpa Eli wanted to examine the dogs carefully to make sure their wounds were beginning to heal properly. Grandpa applied more Ground Yarrow to their wounds. Yarrow was Grandpa's main natural medicine he used to heal open wounds. He had used it on himself and his immediate family for years. He was told about the healing powers of Yarrow many years ago when he first moved to Goat Mountain and became acquainted with an old trapper. The trapper had seen the Indians using this remedy many times in his travels. The trapper was ninety years old when Eli met him. He told Eli many stories about his early trapping days among the Molalla Indians. He also told Eli about many of his experiences living near Goat Mountain. He had actually witnessed some of the late Indian wars. He had made friends with the Molalla's, especially those that came to the Goat Mountain area on hunting trips. In fact it was the Indians that had told him about seeing a Big Strange Creature that walked on two legs, on Goat Mountain. When the trapper told Grandpa Eli about the Big Creature' Eli shrugged it off as being 'Hog Wash'. The strange part of this was that Eli never experienced an encounter with The Big Fella during the time his wife was alive.

After lunch Michael and Martin told the children to remain seated because Grandpa had something important to discuss with the entire family. Grandpa again related every experience he had had with The Big Harry Creature which legend calls 'Big Foot'. The children listened intently with wide eyes. Not a peep was heard from the children or parents. When Grandpa got to the part of the cave incident and the citing last night at the pond, the children moved closer to their parents and began to whimper slightly. Grandpa ended by telling the children they were not to discuss any of this with their friends or anyone else, ever! This was all to be kept from the public. Grandpa told the children that he felt that he had developed some trust between himself and 'The Big Fella'. He knew that if any of this got out his life on Goat Mountain would have to come to an end. He would have to leave his home and way of life that he loved so much. The children and adults promised Grandpa that this would be kept as a family secret. While this information would be documented and kept in private family journals, nothing would be publicized as long as Grandpa was alive. Eli was again greatly relieved that he had finally been able to share this information with trusted family members. He had wanted to be able to talk to someone about all of these experiences with Big Foot for some time now. He assured the children they need not fear Big Foot and as much as they wanted to trust everything Grandpa told them, they just could not go this far in their trust. During the rest of their visit they did not wander very far from the cabin without adult supervision. Even the adults were more careful to not stray far from the cabin unless Grandpa was along. Grandpa never changed his goings and comings at all. He guessed they would not have another experience with the big fella during the remainder of his son's visit. That would be fine with him.

The afternoon was spent down at the pond. The weather was hot and the children and adults decided it would be a good time to spend the afternoon swimming and relaxing after all that had happened yesterday. All of the children were good swimmers. Everyone's ears perked up when they heard what they determined to be the sound of an automobile coming towards the cabin. Grandpa got out of the water quickly and headed towards the cabin. Sure enough it was Bob Berge, his friend, who harvested a little bit of Eli's timber each summer. He told Grandpa that he would like to come next week and start removing the trees that Grandpa had said he wanted to market this year. Grandpa agreed that would be fine and invited Bob and his grandson to come by the cabin when they arrived and say hello to his two families that were visiting from Houston. Eli thought perhaps this would make his sons feel a little better about the logging operation. His sons and their families were not too happy about this whole thing with the beautiful trees being cut down and marketed but they realized this was Grandpa's property and his decision and that it was necessary. It was his only source of income. Grandpa did not want to be a burden on anyone, especially a financial burden. Besides the loggers were doing an excellent job of carefully selecting which trees should be cut down and they were cleaning up the tree tops and limbs and making nice piles for habitat for the small critters. With the business over with, Bob was on his way and Grandpa returned to the pond. What he found surprised him a little bit. The children and parents were all lying on blankets in the shade of a large beautiful mountain maple tree, asleep. He decided not to disturb them so he walked quietly to the barn to check on the dogs and to spend some time with Sampson.

Eli had recently noticed that Sampson was spending more time just lying around the barn. Sampson was glad to see Eli alone. After checking on the dogs Eli devoted his full attention to Sampson. Eli had been so busy this summer with all of the company that he had really not spent very much quality time with Sampson. He was glad that Sampson was not along on the recent trip up to Goat Mountain Meadow and the cave. He surmised that Sampson and Big Foot were aware of each other but that each had respect for one another's territory and he wanted to keep it that way. After spending some time scratching Sampson behind her ears he decided that it was time to go back to the pond and check on the family.

When he got back to the pond he found everyone awake and swimming in the pond. They appeared to be rested and having great fun. Michael and Martin were allowing the children to climb on their shoulders and jump into the water. Grandpa decided to join in on the fun. Grandpa did not own swimming trunks. He always swam in his long handled underwear. The children got a kick out of seeing Grandpa in these strange looking red underwear. After spending another hour in the water Grandpa suggested they all get dressed and make a quick trip in the old Dodge Truck up to the spring on Goat Mountain Meadow. They had depleted the supply of carbonated spring water and needed a fresh supply. The children were excited about going but asked Grandpa to please stay clear of the cave area. Grandpa assured them that he would take another route to reach the spring. The ride up the mountain was uneventful. They spotted a couple of black tailed deer and at least two red tailed hawks. Grandpa noticed that some of the early varieties of black berries appeared to be getting ripe. He suggested they stop and eat some and perhaps bring some back home for dinner. He also suggested that they plan to come back tomorrow and pick a good supply so that he could make blackberry jam and syrup. Everyone thought that would be a good idea.

After spending about an hour picking and eating delicious mountain blackberries the group continued on to the spring. Grandpa was not surprised to find several of Big Foot's tracks around the spring area. He assured the family that there was no need to panic. He told them that the big fella needed water just as they did. He assured them that he honestly felt that the big creature had no intention of hurting them. He hoped that over the next week he would be able to build some trust in his family's minds and hearts for 'The Big Fella'. He knew this would take time, especially after what had recently happened in the cave with the dogs. He also hoped that he could eventually develop some kind of a relationship between Daniel and Anne and the big hairy creature, so that they would at least tolerate each other. He knew that this would take a very long time after the events of yesterday, but time is something he had a lot of.

After collecting several jugs of delicious spring water, and each person getting a drink, Grandpa said that it was getting late and they needed to head back down the mountain. The children asked if they could ride on the fenders and the head lights. Grandpa consented but wanted them to make sure it was ok with their parents. The children loved to ride this way so they could feel the cool breeze against their faces. Grandpa always drove a little slower when the children were on the outside of the cab. They had only driven a little way when Jacob spotted a badger going towards his den. This was a rare citing as badgers are usually nocturnal and rarely seen in the day time. Grandpa stopped the truck and Kate took a picture of the creature with her little Kodak camera. The badger only gave the group a quick look and then he was safely in his den. The group continued on their way. They next spotted a couple of turkey vultures circling around and so grandpa decided to drive over to check the area out. As they rounded the corner they all discovered why the turkey vultures were circling. There up ahead were the remains of a young black tailed doe. The children started to get upset but Grandpa assured them that this was all part of nature. He expected that the doe had been killed by a coyote or a mountain lion. The animal was already starting to smell so grandpa decided not to stop but turned around and headed back down the mountain. What started out to be a quick trip up to the spring ended up being a rather event filled couple of hours. They got back just in time to start preparing dinner.

Ailene helped Grandpa Eli prepare supper, which consisted of boiled potatoes with brown gravy made from the drippings of fried elk meat, miner's lettuce collected fresh from the stream down by the pond, homemade biscuits with wild blackberry jam and of course delicious carbonated strawberry Kool-Aid made with the spring water.

The children had grown to love the food Grandpa prepared. It was so different from what they were used to.

With supper over early, and still a couple hours of daylight, Grandpa suggested they take a hike out to the meadow east of the cabin. The children had not visited this meadow on this trip to Goat Mountain. Grandpa suggested they bring at least one flashlight along in case it got a little dark before they got back to the cabin. The children asked if they could take Delightful along to which Grandpa quickly consented. It only took a few moments to put Delightful on his tether. As they approached the west end of the meadow they saw a sight that made the hike well worth the effort. At the edge of the trees they saw a beautiful mother doe and her twin fawns that were born in the spring. Near-by they saw the buck which undoubtedly was the father. Grandpa explained that this was very unusual to see an entire family. Grandpa motioned for everyone to quietly move behind the willows nearby and watch until the family scampered off into the woods. Finally it was time to move on if they expected to reach the east end of the meadows and still get back to the cabin before dark. They had only gone a short distance when grandpa signaled for everyone to stop. He pointed towards the east end of the meadow. In full view the group spotted a huge black bear eating wild blackberries. Grandpa suggested they wait for a few minutes to see if the bear would leave. Grandpa suggested this bear was probable a male and perhaps a part time companion to Sampson. He had been noticing new tracks around the barn and the pond. He had also noticed that Sampson was acting a little strange lately, not as interested in his paying attention to her as in the past. The children were a little frightened and stayed close to their parents and grandpa. After about 15 minutes the bear rambled off into the forest. Grandpa indicated that it was safe to move on to the end of the meadow. After eating wild blackberries which the bear had not eaten it was time to head back to the cabin. It was a good thing they had taken a flashlight along as it was getting a little dark well before they arrived back at the cabin.

After Grandpa finished telling the children a bed time story they were anxious to go to bed. They were all very tired. Family prayer was pronounced by Jacob and the children snuggled into their beds for one last night in the tent. Grandpa spent every night in the tent with the children. The adults went quietly outside and talked and looked at the stars. There was no moon and so the stars shone brightly and looked as though one could just reach out and touch them. Venice was really beautiful and the brightest object in the sky. Grandpa expressed his joy and appreciation to his sons and their families for coming to visit him. He told them how much he loved each one of them and their children. They also expressed their love for him. Michael assured his father that this visit was always a highlight of the year and one that the children talked about throughout the remainder of the year. Martin always had to give his dad a little lecture about taking care of himself, not working too hard and being especially careful during the cold winter months. Both Michael and Martin had noticed their dad slowing down a little and taking longer to get things done. Everyone agreed that the visit was one they would all remember for a very long time. Both Michael and Martin cautioned their father to be very careful in his efforts to cohabitate with the big creature he called Big Foot. Their worry was that their dad would become too lax in dealing with the big fella and fail to remember that he was a wild creature and as such could deal great harm and possibly even death. They would have preferred their father contact the Game Commission and have the big guy trapped and removed from the area. On the other hand they also respected their father's good judgment and right to live the way he wanted to on Goat Mountain. The part that really bothered both sons was the fact that their dad had no phone and only occasionally received mail when an old friend would visit and bring his mail from the Colton Post Office. They recognized that something could happen to their father and it might be months before they knew about it. Even the children were getting old enough to recognize the unique life style Grandpa loved so much. They also knew that Grandpa was not going to change. They had come to accept the fact that grandpa was no doubt going to live here on Goat Mountain for the rest of his life. They also loved Goat Mountain and looked forward to every visit. Both sons gave their father a hug and said "good night". Grandpa was exhausted and returned to his bed in the tent. Even though the camp cot bed was not as comfortable as his bed in the cabin it felt extra comfortable tonight. He fell asleep almost instantly.

The next morning everyone awakened to bright sunshine and clear skies. Michael and Martin were the first up and they were already outside stacking some of the wood, which they had helped their father bring down from the forest a few days ago, in the wood shed. It was necessary to have a good supply of wood in the wood shed prior to winter. Grandpa Eli always made sure that he had plenty of food stored in the cellar and good seasoned wood in the shed. He had discovered that there were certain plants that grew in the wild that he could eat in the winter time which were very important to his diet. He had learned to dry many types of fruit and meat. To be sure, he was fortunate to be able to enjoy a fairly balanced diet most of the year. Perhaps that is the reason that he also enjoyed pretty good health. He also stayed very active year-a-round. In the winter time when there was snow he would bring out the snow shoes and take a little walk around the barn yard and pond almost every day. There was also wood and kindling to cut and fires to be made each day. Also Grandpa paid a lot attention to his dogs, Big Daniel and Little Anne, and Sampson. Eli was grateful for the time his sons and their families had been able to spend with him on Goat Mountain. School would be starting soon and it was necessary for both families to return to their homes in Houston. Both Michael and Martin agreed they would start coming for a couple of weeks every summer instead of every other summer.

This really made Eli happy. After breakfast Marina reminded Grandpa Eli that he had promised that they would go pick some blackberries today so everyone got ready and they loaded into the old Dodge flatbed one ton and headed for one last trip up to the mountain meadow and the spring. Ailene packed a nice lunch. The blackberries were ripe and sweet and the children had blackberry juice all over their hands and faces. After filling several pails with large, sweet, ripe blackberries it was time to head back down to the cabin. Ailene said that she would make a blackberry cobbler for their farewell dinner. This was to be their last full day with Grandpa and their beloved Goat Mountain. Tomorrow they must return to Houston. After dinner they all went down to the pond for some quiet time together and to reminisce about all that had happened during their visit. Finally it was time to return to the cabin and prepare for bed. Evening family prayer was said and everyone retired to bed, that is everyone except Grandpa. He decided that he would walk down to the barn to check on Delightful, the hounds, and see if Sampson was around. Daniel and Anne were happy to see him and Sampson was kind of standoffish. Delightful wanted to be fed. Old Pet got a little excited when Eli gave her an old apple from his pocket. Eli loved his animals and he knew they would be his only company for some time now. With fall approaching the only visitors he might still see were workers from the logging company. They had arrived a few days ago. Eli was always happy for the loggers to come but he was even happier to see them go. Eli was very strict about what trees he allowed them to cut each year and Mr. Berge always did everything to please Eli. He always had his crew pile the limbs so that Eli could burn them in the winter time when it was safe to burn. Mr. Berge always made sure that the dead or diseased trees were felled so that Eli would be able to cut them up for firewood. He also brought fresh vegetables and other fruits that were so plentiful down in the valley to Eli. They had developed a special friendship over the years. In fact Bob and his crew would spend the evenings with Eli around a camp fire near the pond. They would swap stories and also catch Eli up on all that had happened in and around Colton the past year. Eli checked his watch and discovered that it was well past 10:00 pm and time he retired to bed.

After breakfast the next morning Grandpa Eli asked if he could spend a few minutes alone with each child to which the parents quickly agreed. He started with the oldest granddaughter Kate and worked on down through the rest of the grandchildren. This took about 30 minutes. It was finally time for departure. That meant it was time for hugs and good-byes and the shedding of a few tears. Grandpa had called Daniel and Anne, placed Delightful on her tether nearby, and brought Sampson up from the barn. He even asked Michael if he would bring Old Pet up to the cabin. What a sight it was to behold as his families loaded into the Volkswagen Van and headed down the dirt road. Grandpa watched until they were out of sight. Grandpa moped around the rest of the day. He spent time reflecting on the events of the last few weeks, especially those that involved the big creature. Grandpa decided that he needed to take a long deserved afternoon nap. With that he headed down to the pond to take his nap in his favorite spot, the hammock.

Road leading from cabin through the thick forest

SEVEN

Another Big Foot

Eli awoke early the next morning to bright sunshine. This was to be a very busy day. There was always some work to be done around the cabin and barn. It was also time to start storing food in the cellar for the winter ahead. It took a lot of time to dry and season the meat for jerky. There was wild blackberry jam to be made and wild edible roots to be secured and stored in the cellar. So Eli knew there was very little time to waste. He was also anxious to take a ride on Old Pet, his horse, up to the spring. He needed fresh water and wanted to check things out. He also planned to look for any fresh tracks of Big Foot. He really hoped the recent encounters had not driven Big Foot away to higher ground. He spent the morning cleaning up after his company left and doing odd jobs around the cabin.

After lunch he called Old Pet and he came running. He appreciated the fact that he did not even need to place Old Pet in a corral or fenced area. He loved his horse and always appreciated his quickness to come when Eli called. Eli called his dogs Anne and Daniel as he wanted them to accompany him to the mountain. He also placed Delightful on her tether and tied it to the bridal. Sampson was nowhere around so Eli could not take her along. Eli never needed a saddle so it only took a few minutes and they were on their way up to the mountain meadow and the spring. As they passed the entrance to the cave the late afternoon sun was shining directly into the opening to the cave so a shadow was cast on the opposite wall from the sun light. As Eli looked into the cave what he saw next caused the hair on the back of his neck to stand up. He not only saw one shadow of Big Foot but another shadow of a companion creature. Needless to say he became a little nervous. Delightful got all excited but Daniel and Anne stayed right by Old Pet as Eli commanded them to do. He was just happy that he had not made this discovery while his family was visiting Goat Mountain; on the other hand he quickly realized that it was probably natural for there to be more than one of these creatures on Goat Mountain.

Eli continued on to the spring, filled his water jugs, picked some wild blackberries nearby and then headed on down the mountain and his cabin. He avoided the cave completely. He wondered when his next encounter with these big creatures would occur.

It was late afternoon when Eli got back to the cabin. He fed the dogs, and turned Delightful loose for awhile. He always enjoyed watching Delightful soar high above the cabin and barn. Delightful was only in the air a little while when Eli saw her dive down and catch a small rodent in the meadow next to the cabin. Eli decided to get out the check list of things he needed to do prior to fall and winter. He knew the only way he would get things done was to get started today. The first thing on the list was getting enough wood stored in the wood shed to get through the entire winter. This was a big project as Eli had to do it alone. In past years he sometimes hired a young man who lived down in the valley near Colton, but he was no longer available as he had gotten married and moved out of the area.

After supper Eli went down to the barn to see if Sampson was around. Sampson had made herself a little scarce while Eli's family was around. To Eli's delight Sampson was inside the barn in her favorite spot. Eli expected Sampson to be a little standoffish but that was not to be. Sampson was very glad to see Eli. Eli had brought her some carrots from the garden. Sampson always loved the vegetables and apples that Eli provided. Eli observed that Sampson appeared to be getting a little bigger stomach. After scratching Sampson's head it was time to return to the cabin and prepare for bed. The days were already getting a little shorter. Eli decided that he would get in bed and read for a little while. His son had brought several books. He chose first to read 'The Call of the Wild'. After getting comfortable in bed he heard something tap on the window. The sight he saw made him freeze in fear. Looking straight at him was the big hairy fella that he had been seeing on several occasions this past summer. Never before had he come so close, and in past encounters the creature always seemed to not have any desire for close contact with humans.

Eli realized that he had not locked the door. He never locked the door as there was no reason to do so. Quickly he got up and locked the door even though he knew the Big Fella could get in if he wanted to. Eli began to ponder on what he should do. He decided that he would not show any fear. He decided to ignore the creature and just continue reading. In a few moments he looked at the window and observed that the creature was gone.

He breathed a sigh of relief. He would check things out in the morning and make sure all of the animals were ok. He read for about one half hour and then fell asleep. He had only been sleeping for a few minutes when he was awakened again by a tapping on the window. He looked again and saw the two legged creature looking directly at him. The creature made a funny noise, a grunting noise. When he made the noise he turned away from looking at Eli and looked directly at the lamp. It was like he was saying "you went to sleep with the lamp still lit, which is a no, no". Eli had knocked the lamp over before but fortunately he woke up and was able to upright the lamp and cleanup the spilled lamp oil. Eli quickly realized that a miracle had just taken place and he was thankful 'The Big Fella' had made this rare appearance that may have saved his life. Eli said a little prayer and soon fell asleep.

Early the next morning Eli was awakened with the sun shining in his window. He felt rested and was eager to begin the tasks at hand from the list of things which needed to be done. After a light breakfast of scrambled eggs and homemade fruit juice made with wild berries and the wonderful carbonated spring water, it was time to return to securing his winter wood supply. Eli was always very careful with the power saw. He never operated it when he was tired. After cutting up several downed trees the loggers had left last year, into stove length pieces, he harnessed Old Pet and hooked him up to the wagon. He hauled in one big load before lunch. It would probably take less effort to use the old Dodge truck but he knew that Old Pet needed to be worked. Old Pet needed to know that he was still needed on Goat Mountain. After stacking the wood neatly in the wood shed it was time for lunch. Eli had really worked up an appetite. He fixed a sandwich, a glass of milk, and fresh green salad made from Miner's Lettuce from the nearby stream that fed the pond. After lunch it was time for a short power nap. Eli loved his power naps.

Eli spent the rest of the day splitting and hauling the wood he had cut in the morning. The wood shed was beginning to get full. Eli always stacked a little wood on the porch and in a few other places close to the cabin. Eli finished the wood project and then went to the woods to examine the trees he and Bob Berge had marked for cutting.

Eli's friend Bob had arrived early Monday morning with his crew but did not come to the cabin as he did not want to interfere with Eli and his family. This was a week that Eli did not necessarily look forward to but he knew it was necessary. He liked Bob and it was nice to have his company as he was really missing his family. Bob usually stayed with Eli in the cabin when he came to remove the trees. The rest of the crew camped down by the pond.

Eli just hoped there would be no encounters with the big fella. He was sure the big fella would go to higher ground when he heard the noise of the power saws, trucks and falling trees. Bob always brought all the food needed for Eli and the crew for the week. He even brought a cook, who was also part of his logging crew, so Eli got a rest from cooking and cleaning for the week. The only problem being the type of food Bob brought. Eli was not used to so many sweets and such huge amounts of food. But never the less he was grateful for Bob being so kind and thoughtful and he really enjoyed his grandson Robert. Robert spent a lot of time with Eli as he was not allowed in the woods while the crew was working. Robert had been coming the last three years and Eli treated him like one of his grandkids. Robert loved Delightful and he also looked forward to seeing Sampson and spending time with the coon hounds. Eli had promised Robert that he would take him on a coon hunt this year and Robert reminded him of that promise.

EIGHT

The Ring Tail Hunt With Robert

Tuesday night rolled around and Eli announced it would be a perfect night for the coon hunt as there was a full moon. With dinner over with and not having to worry about cleaning up it only took a few minutes to get the hounds ready. It was also necessary to take a lantern. Eli, Bob and Robert made up the coon hunting team. It was all Eli could do to hold Daniel and Anne back. They loved to run and they loved to chase raccoons. The hunting crew followed the stream that led to the pond. They had only gone a short distance when Anne opened up. Her howl made Eli so proud. Daniel took off running after Anne. In just a few minutes Eli could tell the hounds were no longer running. Eli told Bob and Robert to follow close behind. They had only gone a short distance and they spotted Anne and Daniel at the base of a huge Western Red Cedar tree. Bob shined his flashlight up into the tree and spotted the coon on a limb near the top. Eli needed the coon's hide for making a new cap and some gloves. Eli allowed Bob to shoot the coon. He only killed coons if he needed their hides for making clothes. With the coon over his shoulder it was time to continue the hunt.

They walked for several minutes before the dogs treed another coon. Robert paid close attention to everything Eli taught him about coon hunting. He kept asking his father when he could get a coon hound. He wanted his own hound to go hunting with. Eli always stressed gun safety and the importance of being careful with the lantern. It was Robert's responsibility to carry the lantern.

By the time they headed back to the cabin they had three large coons, two males and one female. Eli was please to announce that he would have enough hides to make the hats, shoulder wraps and gloves he so badly needed for the long and cold winter months.

It was necessary to dry and cure the coon hide prior to making hats and shoulder wraps. Robert spent the next three days staying close to Eli as Eli had promised him a coon hat from one of the hides. With the hot August sun and low humidity the coon hides cured fast. By Friday morning Eli was able to begin making the hats. He decided that he would make Robert's hat first.

Robert watched closely and helped whenever needed but he tried hard not to get in Eli's way. By Friday evening the hat was almost finished and Eli told Robert that he would bring it to him on his next trip to Colton. Wow! Was he ever excited and happy. He had wanted a coon hat for such a long time.

Robert could hardly wait for school to start so he could show off his new hat to his friends. Of course they would all want to know where he got it, but he had promised Eli that he would not reveal the source of the hat. Eli did not want fifteen or twenty young lads coming to look for him and asking for hats. Eli's position was that the fewer people from the outside world that came to Goat Mountain, the better.

Robert and his grandfather were scheduled to leave Saturday morning. The last load of logs had gone out Thursday evening. Bob had spent all of Friday cleaning up and storing things properly in his truck for the return trip down the mountain. The cook had gone home Friday morning after breakfast. Eli invited Robert and his grandfather for dinner. He prepared a farewell feast of red potatoes from his garden, lettuce greens with green onions, freshly picked blackberries, homemade biscuits and blackberry jam, and of course carbonated Kool-Aid from the spring. Robert loved the drink, he only wished that he could take enough of a supply home to last until next year, but that was not practical. With dinner over and dishes cleaned Eli suggested they all take a walk down to the pond to catch a fish or two. The evening breeze was wonderful after a pretty warm day. Unfortunately it was too dry to have a camp fire. Everything was so quiet, the birds had gone to roost for the night, and there were a few bats flying around and the usual mosquitoes. Bob caught the first fish and Robert caught the second fish. Bob offered to clean the fish to which Eli quickly consented. It was necessary to go down by the little stream that left the pond to clean the fish so flies would not be attracted to the immediate area. While Robert and his grandfather were busy cleaning the fish Eli walked to the other side of the pond. He was watching the reflection of the moon in the pond and so he did not notice something moving in the woods behind him. Suddenly her heard a limb break and turned around quickly. He froze in his tracks, not thirty feet away stood the big fella watching him. He wondered how long he had been there. Thank goodness no one else had spotted him. He did not want to draw attention so he turned quickly and returned to the other side of the pond. With this quick movement the big fella scampered into the woods. Eli breathed a sigh of relief when he saw Bob and Robert still cleaning the fish. It was difficult for Eli to keep this encounter to himself but he knew he must.

Saturday morning at about 6:00 am Eli heard a knock at his door. It was Bob and his grandson there to say good-by. Eli was glad that the logging was done for the year but he was always a little sad to see Bob and Robert leave. He had especially enjoyed the Coon hunt with Robert. It brought to memory the many times he had taken his own sons coon hunting when they were still at home. He made up his mind that when his grandchildren came next summer he was going to take them coon hunting.

The rest of the summer days were filled with doing things to get ready for fall and winter. Roots had to be collected, blackberries needed to be picked and made into jam, meat had to be smoked and dried and stored properly for use throughout the winter months. Fortunately Eli knew all of the wild greens that were edible so those could be picked fresh throughout most of the winter, except if there was deep snow. Eli had the barn full of loose hay that he had cut in the meadows. It normally took about four tons for the horse and the milk cow. The woods were full of huckleberries, thimbleberries, wild blackberries of both varieties, wild plumbs and of course delicious apples on some of the old apple trees that were planted when Eli's parents first moved to Goat Mountain. This meant that Eli was going to be busy for some time making jam and canning berries to enjoy during the long winter months. Eli made homemade apple sauce and he had even built a cider press for making apple cider.

Eli decided that it was probably a good idea to make one final trip down to Colton before the winter season arrived. The days were still warm and the rainy season had not arrived yet. He spent some time tuning up Big Red for the trip. He decided that he would make the trip on Saturday which would be the first day of September. He started making a list of supplies he would need for the winter. He also wanted to visit some of his long time friends including Bob and Darlene Berge. Bob had told him that he would have his money ready for the timber removed. Eli decided that he would stay in Colton for a couple of days so that required some additional preparation. Bob and Darlene had invited him to stay overnight with them. Eli was looking forward to the visit. He decided that he would take several gallons of the carbonated spring water to give to friends so that required another trip up to the spring.

Eli got up early the next morning, which was Friday, and headed for the spring in Big Red. He took the hounds, and Delightful. He placed the animals inside the cab on the way up to the spring. He decided that he would not drive near the cave, he did not want to risk an encounter with the big fella. When he got to the spring he turned the hounds loose but kept Delightful on her tether. As it turned out releasing the hounds was a big mistake. They headed straight for the cave. Eli left the water jugs and headed down to the cave. The sight he saw when he got to the cave was sickening. Daniel was coming out of the cave at full speed with deep cuts on his side. Anne was running by his side but she was not hurt. Eli quickly loaded his rifle, but hoped that he would not have to use it. Daniel quickly came to the truck. Eli loaded the dogs into the truck and headed to his cabin, leaving the water jugs at the spring. At the cabin he cleaned Daniel's wounds and fixed him a box near the fire place. He left Anne with Daniel and headed back to the spring.

As he drove by the cave the sun was shining into the entrance. As he slowed down he saw the shadow of the big creature on the wall at the entrance to the cave. He decided to stop the truck and just watch for awhile. As he was setting quietly in the cab with eyes trained towards the cave entrance he saw the shadow moving towards the entrance. He froze but decided to stay calm and quiet. After all he had protection with his rifle at hand. What he saw next was amazing. The creature came out of the cave and just stared at the truck. Next he sat down on his haunches and appeared to just be relaxing. It was as though he had no intention of advancing towards Eli or the truck.

After about thirty minutes Eli decided that he had better continue to the spring and get the water. He remembered that he had left Delightful tethered at the spring. When he got to the spring Delightful was glad to see him. He turned her loose for awhile while he collected several jugs of water to take to friends in Colton. With the jugs full it was time to head back to the cabin and to check on the hounds. When he got back to the cabin he saw that Daniel was in quite a bit of pain. He was really concerned about the possibility of infection setting in so he decided that he would take the dogs with him to Colton. He would take Daniel to a Vet so that he could look at the wounds and give him some antibiotics to fight off infection. The vet knew both hounds as he had given them their shots some time ago. Eli went to bed early so that he could get an early start.

Mt. Hood, Oregon's tallest mountain

NINE

A Trip To The Vet

Eli arose early Saturday morning, prepared a quick breakfast, fed the animals, checked on Sampson and then loaded the hounds in Big Ben and started down the mountain. He had only gone a short distance when he realized that he had forgotten the gift he had made for Robert. He returned to the cabin and retrieved the coon skin hat he had made from one of the coons they had shot the night of the coon hunt.

The trip down the mountain to Colton was uneventful. Eli decided that he would first go the Vet's office and have the doctor take a look at Daniel. Dr. Mike Smith was glad to see Eli and the dogs. After examining Daniel he gave Eli some antibiotics and told him to give Daniel two pills a day for 10 days. This should take care of any infection. He told Eli the wounds appeared to be healing quite well. He complimented Eli for the way he had doctored Daniel's wounds and then asked Eli the question he knew he would ask. Dr. Smith wanted to know how Daniel had received these wounds. Eli knew this was one time he could not tell the truth and it bothered him. He had planned well in advance the story he would tell the Vet. The wounds were the result of a fight with a bobcat. Dr. Smith seemed satisfied with the story and nothing else was said about the incident. Eli paid the doctor and said good-by.

The next stop was the local Colton Market to buy the supplies on his list. This took some time. By the time he completed the shopping he had filled two shopping baskets. With the supplies placed in a covered box on the back of the truck Eli decided that he would next stop at the little café down the road and have a hamburger, a milk shake and a piece of homemade apple pie. This was really a rare treat as Eli only came to town a couple of times a year. As usual the hamburger was excellent and the milk shake was made from hard ice cream in an old fashioned stainless steel container. Mrs. Berge made all the pies for the restaurant and brought them in fresh every other day. Eli managed to save a small piece of the meat from his hamburger for his dogs. He wanted them to have a special treat also.

Before going to visit Bob and Darlene, Eli stopped at a few of his old friend's homes to say hello and to give them a jug of his carbonated spring water. These folks always looked forward to Eli's visits. They were happy to know he was well and still enjoying life on Goat Mountain. Many of them had visited Eli in days gone by but most were not able to make the trip any longer. The friends he gave carbonated spring water to were so happy to get it and they always had a gift ready to give Eli. Usually the gift was a nice pair of leather gloves, a new down blanket, a homemade wool jacket, or a hat that covered his ears. They always tried to talk Eli into staying overnight but he always managed to convince them that he needed to be on his way. And of course the real truth was that he had already promised Bob that he would stay the night with he and Darlene.

When Eli arrived at the Berge's home he was welcomed with open arms. Darlene was a beautiful woman and when she gave Eli a hug he always blushed a little bit. Eli asked Darlene to call her grandson, Robert, and ask him to come over. He was not at home but Darlene got on the phone and called her grandson's friend's house and told him that someone was here to see him. Robert returned home quickly and was happy to see Eli and the hounds. He was very concerned about Daniel's wounds and wanted to know the details of the attack. Again Eli knew that he could not take a chance in telling the truth. Even though he trusted Bob's family he knew that one little slip of the tongue could mean trouble for him and his way of life on Goat Mountain. So again the story told was that Daniel had been attacked by a large male bobcat that came snooping around the chicken coup. Robert wanted to know how Sampson and Delightful were. He also asked Eli if he had been coon hunting again?

Darlene prepared a wonderful supper which Eli really enjoyed. Later that evening Bob started a fire in the fire place and the men folk spent the rest of the evening talking about life on Goat Mountain. Robert had something he wanted to bring up to his father and Eli. He had been planning this for some time and he decided that he had to get an answer to what he had been thinking about. He was just not sure how to approach the subject. Finally he just decided to get it out. He moved over close to Eli and looked him right in the eye and said "Mr. Eli I was wondering if I could come and spend a few weeks with you next summer? You know I am nine years old now and I am not afraid of the dark and I promise that I won't get home sick. I could come in early June as soon as school is out and then I could go home with grandpa when he comes to do the logging." Eli was a little taken back with the request and he looked at Bob to see if he was going to say anything. Bob in turn seemed to be waiting to see if Eli was going to say anything. Eli knew that his sons and their families would be coming in July but he quickly decided that he would love to have Robert come and spend some one on one time in June. He looked at Bob, then back at Robert and then cleared his throat before giving his reply. He then looked right into Robert's eyes and said "Young man I would love to have you come and spend some time with me. There are so many things we could do on Goat Mountain during the month of June. Besides you could help me get things ready for my sons and their families as they will be visiting with me in July". Robert jumped for joy and ran over to Eli and gave him a big hug. Darlene came into the living room just as Robert sat back down. She had overheard the last part of the conversation. She wanted to let Eli know that she and Robert had been talking about this desire of his for some time and she was in complete agreement with her grandson spending some time on Goat Mountain.

Darlene invited the men folks to come into the kitchen and have a piece of her homemade Marion Berry pie with a scoop of ice cream. After visiting a while Eli decided to check on the hounds and then retire to bed. He had had a very long day and was very happy but tired.

Eli awoke Sunday morning about 7:00 am and he could smell bacon cooking. When he walked into the kitchen Robert was waiting for him. Eli had a package in his hand and walked directly to where Robert was standing and handed it to him. Robert got so excited and asked if he could open the package. Eli said "sure go ahead." Robert got the surprise of his life when he saw the beautiful coon hat that Eli had made for him. He got tears in his eyes and gave Eli a big hug and expressed thanks many times. Darlene called from the kitchen and informed the men that breakfast was ready. She had prepared homemade biscuits, scrambled eggs, crisp bacon and fresh squeezed orange juice.

After breakfast Darlene asked Eli if he would like to attend church with their family. Eli mentioned that he had not brought along church clothes, but if she didn't mind him going with the clothes he had, he would love to go.

The Berge's attended the LDS church in Molalla. Eli told them that his son and his family who lived in Bend were LDS. This seemed to really please Darlene. Going to church was a rare experience for Eli and he knew that his son would really be proud of him. Eli felt a little out of place not being dressed up, as were the other folks at church, but everyone made him feel welcome. He was really impressed with the sermons. It was well after 1:00 pm when he and the Berge's left to return to their home in Colton. Darlene prepared lunch while the men took care of the hounds.

After lunch Eli told the family that he needed to get on the road back to Goat Mountain. They were very sad to see him go. Eli expressed his thanks for their hospitality and gave each member of the family a hug. Bob helped Eli load the hounds into his truck. Eli told Robert to take good care of his coon hat. He made a quick stop at the Post Office and mailed letters to his three sons and their families in Bend and Houston. To his surprise there were letters from his sons and the grandchildren to him at the post office. As he read the letters tears of joy came to his eyes. There were so many expressions of love and appreciation for the wonderful times they had during their stay with grandpa on Goat Mountain. His sons had also sent pictures that were taken during their visits during the summer. Eli cherished these letters and pictures and he knew that he would read the letters several times during the winter. Reading the letters made Eli a little homesick for his families. He thought of the many experiences they had during the summer and especially the frightening experience that involved encounters with the big two legged man like creature.

On his way out of town Eli filled Big Red with gas from the only station in town and then headed for his home on Goat Mountain. The trip home took about two hours because of several short stops along the way to enjoy the beauty of the early fall colors. Eli knew that he probably would not see very many people throughout the rest of the fall and winter months, maybe just a few who strayed onto his property during hunting season. He thought of the long winter months that were ahead and the many days that he would be alone on his Goat Mountain. Eli didn't mind being alone, but for some reason, as he got older, he seemed to think more about the times he spent with family and friends such as Robert and his grandparents, Bob and Darlene. Eli was in his 71st year now as he had just had a birthday on August 23rd.

As Eli approached the cabin Delightful and Old Pet were both very happy to see him. Delightful could hardly set still. She wanted to go for a hunt. Old Pet came to the corral gate so Eli opened the gate so she could roam a little and eat some green grass. The milk cow, which he had recently acquired, was down in the south pasture behind the cabin. Even the chickens came out of the chicken coup into the area that was completely fenced in with chicken wire. Eli went down to the barn to see if Sampson was around but was not able to find her. He was not too worried as Sampson was often gone for two or three days at a time. Eli was quite sure she was spending time with her male friend. After feeding the hounds he prepared a small lunch and then took a quick power nap. When he woke up he heard a rubbing sound on the front cabin door. He looked out the kitchen window and observed Sampson rubbing her right hip on the door. Eli was now content as almost all of the animals were now accounted for. He spent several minutes scratching Sampson behind her ears. Again he noticed Sampson sides seemed to be pushing outward a little bit more. He suspected there might be a baby Sampson growing inside that black fur. Evening was quickly approaching so it was time to unload Big Red and get things stored away. This chore took the better part of an hour. After everything was put in its place Eli drove the truck down to the barn and put it away in its usual spot. He decided that he would take Old Pet up to the spring in the morning and bring back a couple jugs of fresh carbonated water. He had a little two wheeled cart that he used for such occasions. He would usually ride in the cart up to the spring and then walk alongside the cart on the way down.

Eli got up early the next morning, prepared a quick breakfast, put the dishes in the sink, fed all the animals and put the harness on Old Pet. He put Delightful on her tether and put leashes on the hounds and tied them to the cart. He did not want them running loose as he passed the cave. In fact he would have to be more careful in the future about taking the hounds with him to the spring. He took a small bucket along to collect some of the plants and roots he would put in the cellar to have for food later on. He loved the wild onions that grew so plentifully in certain areas on Goat Mountain. He also found several morel mushrooms that had appeared after the shower last night. There were beautiful sweet thimbleberries a plenty and a few remaining blackberries that had ripened late in the season. There were also lots of wild currents and the mountain huckleberries were just getting ripe. Eli could see that he was going to be making many trips up the mountain in the next few weeks and that he would be busy canning some of the berries and making jam. There were apples and pears to pick and store in the root cellar as fresh fruit was an important part of Eli's diet, particularly during the winter months. He always made sure that the fruit trees were pruned and sprayed for insects so they would continue to bare the fruit he loved to eat. He used to be able to keep some berries and sliced apples near the back of the cave as there was always ice there but he doubted he would be able to do that in the future in light of the new inhabitants of the cave. He would have to have greater trust in the big fellas than he had at the present time. He did not want to push his luck. As he passed the cave on the way to the spring he again saw the shadows of two creatures on the wall which was exposed to the sun light. Now all the two legged hairy creatures that he had seen before, were accounted for. He could put that issue out of his mind.

After filling his jugs with fresh carbonated spring water, and giving all the animals a drink, it was time to begin filling his bucket and the small bags with the berries, fruits and roots he needed to collect. With all of the stops the trip down the mountain took several hours. The harvest was exceptional and he felt blessed. Eli didn't bring a lunch as he knew he would be feasting on all the wild berries, apples and pears.

Last summer Eli had found a wild plum tree that he had never seen before. He decided to check it out on this trip. The tree was full of ripe plums but unfortunately there was one problem. Hanging from one of the bottom limbs was a huge honeybee hive. Eli knew how to solve that problem but it would involve another trip with his bee mask and gloves and heavy long sleeve shirt. He decided that would be his project for tomorrow. He would come in the middle of the day and hope most of the bees were away from the hive.

As they neared the cabin Eli decided to turn the dogs loose and release his falcon from her tether. In short order Delightful caught a rabbit which Eli would fix for dinner. The hounds were happy to be able to run freely. Once in a while they would look up to see where the falcon might be. This was a game they played all the time. Once in a while they would spot what the falcon had spotted and the race was on. Once in a blue moon they would beat Delightful to the small animal.

The gang got back to the cabin a little before dark. Life was good again on Goat Mountain. Eli skinned the rabbit and decided to put it in an enclosure down by the spring so as to keep it cool and let some of the natural animal heat out. He would prepare it for dinner tomorrow night. He had eaten so many berries and several apples and pears so he was not really hungry.

Eli spent the rest of the evening reading the letters from his three families and one of the books they had given him. He received letters from each of the grandchildren in which they all expressed their love and affection for him. Kate asked him if she could take the falcon out for a hunt all on her own next year. Elly asked grandpa if she could ride Old Pet all by herself next summer. Jacob, Ben and Evan asked if they could go coon hunting. Siena asked if she could ride the horse with Elly. Kristine asked if she could ride on the headlights up to the spring. Marina asked if she could be in charge of collecting the eggs each day and also riding Old Pet up to the spring. Brighton wanted to know if she could bring her new bike to Goat Mountain next summer. Archer asked if he could take the horse and two wheeled cart out to the far pasture and bring it back full of fire wood. Kim said that she would be bringing a butterfly book and several butterfly nets next summer and wanted grandpa to join in catching and identifying butterflies. Ailene wanted to know if she could bring her mother Elaine along next summer. Her father had passed away a couple of years ago and she thought it would do her mother good to get away from her normal routine for a while. Her mother was 65 and in very good health so Ailene thought she would enjoy the outdoor life on Goat Mountain. Ailene had shown her pictures of Eli and of their family trips to Goat Mountain. Of course Eli would be delighted to have her come with the family and spend time on his mountain. Silently he wondered how she would take to his style of living and also all the animals that were a part of his everyday life. What would she think of this whole situation with two legged hairy man like creature and especially with there now being more than one of these big fellas? Matt asked when Mike and Martin were coming next summer and suggested that all three families come at the same time so that they could have a family reunion of sorts. Mike and Martin both suggested the entire family plan to spend a couple of days at the beach. They knew that it had probably been years since their father had been to the Oregon coast. It had been years since all three families had been together and several of the children had been born since the last gathering. Eli thought it was a wonderful idea and decided that he would write letters to all three sons and send them to the Post Office at Colton with the first hunter that showed up.

This had been a very long day and Eli was pleased with what he had accomplished and especially with the letters from his family. He quickly fell asleep listening to the sounds of the night coming in through the opened window.

TEN

Mountain Lions Raise Havoc

Eli got up early as he had so many things to get done. The days were getting much shorter. It was too dark to get much done outside after 5:00 pm. With breakfast out of the way and the animals all fed it was time to gather up his honey collecting clothing and head for the plum tree. He decided to drive Big Red up to the plum tree just in case he needed to make a quick escape. He did not take any of the animals with him. When he got near the hive he put on all of his bee equipment. It was difficult to drive with all of these bee trapping clothes and equipment on but he finally got to within about thirty feet of the tree. He parked Big Red and left the motor running with the emergency brake set tightly. Much to his delight he discovered that most of the bees were out of the hive. Eli removed the bottom part of the beehive to expose the honeycomb. He only took about half of the honey as he knew it was important to leave plenty for the bees. With the job complete Eli headed back down the mountain. Eli picked a bucket full of plumbs to store in his cellar. He would check on the hive in a couple of weeks to see if the bees had made repairs and perhaps collected more honey. He knew that he did not have nearly enough collected to get him through the long winter months. He had purchased several bottles of Jiffy peanut butter when he was in Colton, and there were very few things Eli loved more than a slice of his homemade bread with peanut butter and honey spread thickly on top. In fact Eli had often made the statement that if he were allowed only one food to eat for the rest of his life it would be peanut butter.

Eli got back to the cabin well before lunch time. He decided to have warm bread with honey spread on top and a glass of milk for lunch.

After lunch he decided he would spend the rest of the day with the animals. He put Delightful on her leash, and with the hounds, headed for the same meadow that he had visited with the family just prior to their departure. There were lots of wild thimble berries, some black berries and at least one apple tree on the west end of the meadow. The leaves were starting to fall from the alder and mountain maple trees and the air was getting a little cooler each day. The vine maple leaves were a bright red. Eli went by a small grove of those trees where his sons had spent many hours when they were little guys, on his trips to visit his parents. Matthew, Michael and Martin would climb to the top of the vine maple and swing from tree to tree.

The one who could go clear across the grove without touching the ground was the winner. Eli decided that he would bring Jacob, Ben, Evan and Archer to the grove next summer when they came and let them try doing what their fathers had done when they were young boys. He knew Archer was a little young but he also knew that he was very strong and would not let the older boys out do him.

After spending a couple of hours picking berries and picking up some of the apples that had fallen to the ground it was time to head back to the cabin. The hounds had been able to run and he had released Delightful for his daily hunt. It only took the falcon a couple of attempts to catch a rabbit. Eli skinned it and placed it in a wire basket down by the pond as soon as they got back to the cabin. They were all pretty tired and hungry by the time they got back home. Eli fed the animals, collected the eggs and checked on Sampson. She was spending more time just lying around these days. Eli scratched behind her ears and along her belly. Sampson loved the attention. After unloading Big Red and storing the berries, fruit and plant roots in the cellar, Eli walked down to the pond to retrieve the rabbit but when he got to the container where he had placed it the lid was open and the meat was gone. Sure enough there were tracks all around but they were not the tracks of the big creatures. They were mountain lion tracks. The cougar must have been nearby when Eli placed the meat in the basket. Now there was another wild animal to contend with. This could mean more trouble for Big Daniel and Little Anne. Eli knew there were mountain lions in the area but he had not spotted one for many years. He had come across bones from deer and elk that he suspected were killed by the big cats.

Eli returned to the cabin empty handed, quickly prepared a small dinner and then decided that he would spend the rest of the evening composing letters to all of his sons and the grandchildren. He would have them ready to send to the post office at Colton with the first hunter that showed up. The first deer season opened on Saturday so that did not leave any time to waste in getting all letters that he had previously received answered.

The next two days were spent writing letters, canning blackberry, thimbleberry and huckleberry jam. Eli canned several pint bottles of apple sauce. He also took the honey from the beehives and put it in small jars. He made plum jam and also canned some of the plums whole.

Saturday morning brought the usual hunters to the area. They always asked Eli for permission to hunt on his land. Eli always consented but with very strict regulations. They were not to kill does nor bucks with more than four points. He also asked one of the hunters to stop by when they were ready to leave and take his letters to the post office. He knew that his sons and the grandchildren would be anxious to hear from him. He also knew that he might get lucky and have responses from them by the time the elk hunters arrived just prior to Thanksgiving. Eli knew that all three families planned to come at the same time this coming summer as they planned to have a family reunion of sorts. This would take some planning and scheduling of vacations by his sons. Michael and Martin worked in the oil industry as they both had their master's degree in Geology. Matthew was a landscape architect for a large engineering firm in the Bend area. Kim and Ailene were stay at home moms. They were both very active in the schools their children attended. Most of the children were involved in summer activities sponsored by the Parks and Recreation District in their respective towns so scheduling was no doubt going to be a real challenge for all involved.

Saturday, the last day of hunting season, rolled around quickly and in the early afternoon one of the hunters came to the cabin and announced that he would be happy to take the letters to the post office. Eli had them all in a bundle with a rubber band securing them together. He thanked the hunter and asked him how the hunt had gone. The hunter shrugged his shoulders and said "another year without venison." Outwardly Eli showed sorrow but inwardly he was pleased that the animals were once again the winners. The hunter did say that he had spotted a full grown mountain lion, but that he did not have a cougar permit to kill it. Again Eli was relieved. Eli's position on the wild animals that lived on Goat Mountain was that they were here long before his parents came to the mountain. He had always tried to kill only what he needed for meat. He knew that all of the animals were part of a very important food chain and he had an obligation to not disrupt that chain by killing just to be killing. He even had his falcon trained to just catch the small rodents but to let him decide if the animal was needed for meat. He had trained the hounds not to stalk the deer and elk.

ELEVEN

A Face to Face Encounter With A Mountain Lion

By the late fall the weather turned cold and Eli decided to spend the rest of the day enjoying the warmth of his cabin. Earlier in the day he had brought a good supply of wood from the wood shed to the back porch. He had several good books to read and he still needed to finish reading Call Of The Wild. Prior to fixing his supper Eli made sure all of the animals were fed and in their proper places to spend the night.

When Eli got up Sunday morning there was a slight dusting of snow on the ground but the sun was shining brightly. Eli loved days like this. On his rounds to feed all the animals he could see animal tracks from all of the little creatures that lived near his cabin. He prided himself in being able to identify every single animal track. Since it was cold but sunny he decided that he had better make a trip up the mountain to the spring with the carbonated water as he didn't know just how many times he would get up there before deep snow came. He used to be able to snow shoe up there a few times during the winter but he had promised his sons that he would not do that anymore in the winter time.

With breakfast over with he decided to put the harness on Old Pet and hook him up to the small two wheeled cart as he would need to bring back several gallons of the spring water. He took Delightful but decided to leave his hounds at the cabin. Old Pet enjoyed going to the spring and pulling the small cart. Eli bundled up with warm clothes, his Russian style hat and warm gloves he had made from a coon hide. He decided to make a pass in front of the cave but saw no sign of the big fellas. He guessed they were probably sleeping further back in the cave.

As Eli approached the carbonated spring he was a little unprepared for what he saw, as he had forgotten to bring his rifle along. The mountain lion was drinking from the small water tank. Delightful got all excited and tried to pull free of her tether. Eli paused for a moment and then made a loud whistle. The mountain lion looked towards him and bolted quickly away. It appeared that he was more scared of Eli than was Eli of him. Eli collected several gallons of the delicious carbonated spring water and then headed down the mountain. By the time he got back to the cabin it was time for lunch.

After lunch Eli went out to check on Sampson. Sampson was glad to see him and as usual welcomed Eli's attention. Next Eli went to the chicken coup to check on the chickens and gather eggs. When he got inside the coup he found several dead hens. It appeared that a weasel had gotten into the coup again and killed them. Eli was very sad and this was a big loss. It meant he would have very few eggs to eat the rest of the winter. The remaining hens would not have little chicks until spring. Eli spent the next hour or so locating the spot that the weasel had come through. He put boards over the hole. Eli spent the rest of the afternoon with his hounds. They both loved to run. Eli took his double barrel shot gun with him. About an hour before dark Anne chased a big blue grouse from the underbrush. Eli took aim and downed the grouse with one shot. He would prepare it for supper. It had been some time since he had gotten a blue grouse. This would make a wonderful supper. He praised the hounds and gave them a treat from his pocket.

The next week was spent putting more wood on the back and front porch and collecting more edible roots and other edible plants. He had a wonderful root cellar and was happy that he could store food for long periods of time. He also spent some time grinding some of the roots into flour for making bread.

Each morning was greeted with a little sprinkling of snow but it was usually gone by noon. By now most of the leaves from the trees had fallen to the ground. Eli spent a lot of time collecting some of the biggest leaves and putting them in bags and storing them in the barn. They made excellent bedding for the animals in the winter time.

The rest of October was spent doing little odds and ends around the cabin, barn and chicken coup. He made sure all of his chicken feed was stored in a place where it would be dry and secure from predators.

He had purchased several sacks of bird feed for the birds that came in the winter time like the Dark Eyed Juncos and a few others. There were always Red Tailed Hawks and a few Bald and Golden Eagles but they were usually able to secure their own food.

Several weeks had gone by since Eli had had any encounter with the big two legged man like creatures. He supposed they were holding up far back in the cave. He had no intention of going into the cave to find out. He was more concerned with the mountain lion now. He was not sure what would happen if the mountain lion came around the barn where Sampson would soon be hibernating. It was now very obvious that Sampson was pregnant so it was even more important that Eli provide a safe environment for her. Eli spent some time building a fenced in area around the log he had brought into the barn a few years ago. Sampson always spent the cold winter months in the log. She would usually come out of hibernation around the middle of March, depending on the weather.

West pasture

TWELVE

The Elk Hunters Arrive

Elk season would start the first Saturday of November, which was only one week away. Eli hoped that he would have mail from his three sons and their families. He knew the elk hunters would bring his mail as they always had in the past. He decided that he would stay very close to the cabin on Saturday so as not to miss the hunters if they came.

Eli was not disappointed, early Saturday morning he heard a knock at the front door. Three hunters had arrived and asked permission to hunt. They also brought a small bag with letters from all three sons and their families. They also brought some fresh vegetable, bananas, and two small roasts. His friend Bob Berge also sent several loaves of homemade bread and a berry pie. Eli thanked the hunters for their kindness and thoughtfulness and told them they were welcomed to hunt on the ranch. He asked them to stop by before they left so he could give them outgoing mail. Eli invited the men to stay for lunch and they gladly accepted the invitation. He also gave them a gallon of his carbonated spring water. Eli assured the hunters that he would keep the hounds tied up while they were hunting.

After the hunters were gone Eli quickly opened each letter and spent most of the afternoon reading the many letters. He was happy to know that his sons and their wives and children were all well. They were all looking forward to Thanksgiving and Christmas and the children were looking forward to short vacations from school. Mike and Martin were going to be together with their families for both Thanksgiving and Christmas. Matt did not mention what he and his family would be doing but Eli was sure they would be with friends.

As usual this was a relaxing and quiet week for Eli. He kept the hounds in the barn through the hunting season. He had all the wood on the porch that it would hold. The remaining chickens were sill laying several eggs a day and so those needed to be collected. There was no sign of the weasel lately and he was thankful for that.

Eli decided that he would spend most of the time making gloves and hats for each of his grandchildren. He planned to give each one a coon skin hat and a pair of gloves when they came next summer. All three sons suggested they come in early June right after school was out for the summer. This was going to be an exciting time. Eli had been hoping something like this would happen for a long time. They all planned to stay two or three weeks.

The following morning he started to work on the project. He could make one hat and a pair of gloves in about a week. There were several other daily chores that still needed to be done so he could only work on the project for about four hours each day. He decided that he would make the ones for Matt and Kim's family first. He also had to spend several hours answering family letters as he wanted to have them ready to send back to Colton with the hunters at the end of their hunt. He knew all of his sons, daughter-in-laws and grandchildren would be anxious to hear from him and to know that he was ok. He told his sons that he also thought June would be a good month to have the family reunion. He told the grandchildren they could expect to find a baby cub when they came. He did not mention anything about the mountain lion that he had spotted near the carbonated spring. The only thing he told them about was the time one of the big creatures had tapped on his window one night when Eli had fallen asleep with the lamp burning. That tap on the window could have saved his life because the lamp was about to fall off the night stand by his bed. He also told them that he had seen shadows of two big creatures when he went by the cave after they left. Again he reminded the grandchildren not to worry about the big hairy creatures as he felt that he had developed somewhat of a workable relationship with them.

When the hunters came by the cabin Sunday morning he again asked them about the hunt. Apparently the elk hunters had been quite successful. They had bagged two nice bulls. They gave Eli some back strap to make jerky with. They also gave him a small roast and a couple of steaks. Eli thanked them and gave them his outgoing mail. They assured him that they would leave the mail at the Colton Post Office the first thing Monday morning. It was now time to get back to the glove and hat making project. Eli had collected some wild red berries and some Oregon grape berries and had made some red and blue dye. He was able to dye the coon tails and attach them to the hats. The gloves were nice and fury. He knew the children would love them. His only concern was that the children in Houston would not be able to wear them very often as the weather there was usually pretty warm and humid.

By the end of November he had the hats and gloves made for about half of the grandchildren. He was very pleased with the way they turned out. He hoped the children would like them as much as he did.

The weather turned very cold in December and the snow started piling up. The animals were all doing fine. Eli had moved the chickens to a small secure coup inside the barn where it was much warmer. He placed them by an outside window for light. He was still getting an egg or two a day for which he was thankful. Eli never got very far from the cabin and barn. He had plenty of food and several gallons of carbonated water from the spring and lots of wood on the front and back porch. The milk cow and Old Pet were doing just fine. They had lots of good meadow hay to eat. Eli milked the cow morning and night. He couldn't drink all of the milk but he fed the excess to the animals. The raccoons that came up to the porch loved the fresh milk. On the twenty third of December Eli measured the snow in his front yard. It was 35 inches deep. This was about normal for Goat Mountain for this time of the year. The elevation at his cabin was about 3800 feet; however being on the west side of the Cascades meant he usually got a lot of snow in the winter time. Eli had put his snow shoes on a couple of times and that was only to go down to the spring by the barn to get some fresh water. On one of these trips he saw fresh tracks in the snow of the mountain lion. He knew he was snooping around for food. In the future he would take his rifle whenever he left the cabin until this mountain lion had moved on to another territory. On another trip to the barn to feed Old Pet and the milk cow Eli found the leg of a deer that had been drug in by the mountain lion. Eli made sure the barn was completely closed in so other large animals could not get inside. When he took the hounds out for their daily exercise he always made sure he was close by. He never let them wonder off even though they wanted to on many occasions. Eli knew these hounds were no match for the mountain lion. With the snow getting deeper it wasn't long before the elk and deer left the mountain for the valley below and with them gone there were no more signs of the mountain lion. Eli could relax a little when he let the hounds out during the day time.

Eli awoke to bright sunshine on Christmas Eve Day. The temperature was just a few degrees below freezing. There was no wind and as Eli looked out the window he could see the beautiful sparkling snow. He always had a small Christmas tree and this year was to be no exception. He also put Christmas decoration on the fire place mantel and hung ten little stocking from the mantel even though he knew his grandchildren were far away. He got out his old hymn book with Christmas Carols and placed it by his big reading chair. On Christmas Eve he would sing some carols and imagine that his three sons and their families were singing with him.

THIRTEEN

Christmas Brings Surprise Visitors

On Christmas morning Eli woke up to bright sunshine streaming in his front window. He dressed quickly and built a fire in the wood cook stove and the fire place. As usual Eli fed the animals first and then made his own breakfast of pancakes, jerky and a boiled egg and of course delicious juice made with the carbonated spring water. After breakfast Eli washed the dishes in the small dish pan and put things away in the cupboard. All of a sudden he heard what he thought to be an engine. He looked outside and saw nothing. He guessed it was noise made from perhaps a small plane overhead. He sat down and started reading again from Call Of The Wild. Suddenly he heard the noise again but this time it seemed to be getting closer. He looked out the window again and still saw nothing. He sat back down and started reading again and fell sound asleep. Pretty soon he awoke to a loud knock on his front door. This startled him awake and he went to open the door. When he opened the door there stood his son Matt and his entire family. Eli was speechless. He started shedding tears, which was very unusual for Eli but they were tears of joy. He could not believe his eyes. Was this a dream? How could this be?

Eli ushered every one inside and immediately asked if anyone was hungry. Of course they were all hungry as they had made a long trip from Colton in a Skidoo snowmobile and sled. The trip had taken about three hours as they were not always able to stay on the road because of fallen trees and snow drifts. The children were so happy to be with Grandpa and especially at Christmas time. Elly, Evan, and Siena had never spent a Christmas with Grandpa. While the adults brought in stuff from the sled the children admired the Christmas tree with the simple homemade decorations and the stockings hung from the fire place mantel. Matt and Kim had brought presents for all and this was truly going to be a Christmas that none would soon forget. They even brought treats for the hounds, for Delightful and Sampson. They had forgotten that Sampson would be hibernating by now. The rest of the morning was spent visiting and getting things organized for the next day. Kim had brought a big Christmas ham, some yams, a baked minced meat pie, some fresh vegetables and another supply of raspberry Kool-Aid. Yes, this was going to be a great Christmas and Eli was happy that he would not have to spend it alone. He still could not believe this was really happening.

After lunch the children wanted to go to the barn to see the animals. Grandpa said they could take a flashlight and peek inside the hollowed out log to see if Sampson was asleep. After spending some time with the hounds and Delightful the children asked if they could gather the eggs. Grandpa told them to go ahead. When they looked inside the coup they noticed that there were fewer chickens. They asked Grandpa what had happened. He then told them about the weasel getting into the coup when it was outside the barn, and killing several chickens. They were saddened but understood those things happen once in a while. They were happy to see Old Pet and the milk cow. Evan asked Grandpa if he would teach him how to milk a cow. Grandpa was happy to honor his request, in fact he told him he could help do the milking tonight.

Eli asked if they had received his last letters to everyone. Matt said they had. Eli told his son how excited he was about the possibility of having the family reunion in June and having all of his families at Goat Mountain at the same time. Kim said she was reluctant to ask but wondered if Eli had had any more encounters with the big creatures? Eli told them about the time he went up to the spring shortly after Martin and Mike left and that he saw the shadows of two big creatures near the entrance of the cave. He also told them that he thought the two legged creatures were probably holding up way back in the cave for the winter. He was pretty sure they would only come out for short periods of time to get fresh water at the spring and he would not be going up to the spring until the snow left.

The children were anxious to get out in the snow and do some sledding. Grandpa had several old sleds that his sons had used when they were still at home. The hill going down to the pond was an excellent place to go sledding. Grandpa said that he would fix hot chocolate for everyone. With that they all went outside and played in the snow. On Elly's second run down the hill the runner on her sled hooked what looked to be the leg of small deer. She showed the leg to Grandpa and so he had to tell everyone about the mountain lion that had made a visit to the area. Eli had thought the cat was gone because he had not seen any sign of him lately but this appeared to be a very fresh kill. This frightened the children and they wanted to go back inside as it was starting to get dark.

Matt and Kim fixed a wonderful dinner while Grandpa spent time near the fireplace telling the children stories that he used to tell their father when he was a small boy. The children loved these old stories. Grandpa also told the children some old Navy stories about experiences he supposedly had when he was in the Navy.

Kim had placed all of the Christmas presents under and around the tree and after cleaning up from supper they all sat in front of the fireplace and sang some Christmas Carols. Life was good once again on Eli's mountain.

After kneeling for Family Prayer the children were anxious to go to bed so that morning would come soon and it would be time to open presents. There were sleeping bags wall to wall on the living room floor. Grandpa looked outside and told the children it was snowing hard. He kissed each child goodnight. The adults talked quietly for a while and then everyone retired for the night.

Christmas morning brought beautiful sunshine to Goat Mountain. The sky was clear with not a cloud in sight. Grandpa had kept a fire in the fireplace all night and so it was warm in the cabin when the children got up just a few minutes after 7:00 am. They all gathered around the tree and fireplace and each person got to open a present. After everyone had opened their presents Grandpa went to his bed room and brought out three brown paper bags, one for each grandchild. The children were very surprised when they looked in their bags and saw the coon skin hats and gloves. They ran to Grandpa and gave him big hugs. They wore their gifts almost every minute for the rest of the time they were at Grandpa's place.

Matt fixed poached eggs and fried toast for breakfast and hot chocolate. The children spent most of the morning playing with their

Christmas presents. After lunch they all went down to the barn to feed and check on the animals. The hounds were glad to see everyone as was Delightful. Siena asked if they could take the falcon outside and let her make a few flights. Grandpa said that would be a good idea. He also took Daniel and Anne out in the snow. The dogs were so happy to be out of the barn as they had been kept inside for some time with the mountain lion being in the area.

It was beautiful to see Delightful make her flights high in the sky. On the last flight she spotted a small white rabbit scampering on top of the snow just east of the cabin. She swooped down and gently picked the rabbit up and brought it to Eli, then turned it loose in his arms. The rabbit was unhurt and so Eli and the children took it into the barn where it was much warmer. Eli placed it in a small cage and gave it some chicken feed and water. The little rabbit was so scared; however after a short time the rabbit settled down and rolled up in a little ball and went to sleep.

The children had experienced a very touching and tender moment in time on Goat Mountain. Their love for the falcon had increased greatly. This would be something they would want to share with their school friends when they got back to Bend.

Matt and Kim were busy all morning preparing Christmas Dinner while Eli was outside with the children and the animals. Matt rang the dinner bell and all came inside. The cabin was warm and cozy with a nice fire in the fire place. The wood cook stove also gave off a lot of heat. Elly, the oldest of the three grandchildren, was asked to give thanks for the food. She offered a beautiful prayer. The dinner was delicious. The ham was prepared to perfection, there were candied yams, mashed potatoes and gravy, fresh vegetables and of course the minced meat pit. The drink was of course the ice cold carbonated strawberry Kool-Aid made from water from the spring. This was truly the most wonderful Christmas Dinner Eli had had in many years and it was so special because he had one of his families with him to help celebrate this Christmas Season. By 3:00 pm clouds began rolling in over Goat Mountain and within a few short minutes it started to snow very hard. The children were excited to look out the window and see large flakes falling to the ground. The family sang some more Christmas songs and then the children told Grandpa they had prepared a little

Christmas skit for him. Elly got a small doll that Grandpa kept for the girls when they came to visit. She played Mary, Evan was Joseph and Siena was an Angel watching nearby. The doll was the baby Jesus. The children sang Silent Night Holy Night. Tears flowed from Eli's eyes. He only wished that the Children's Grandmother was still alive and could be here. She loved her family but had passed away before any of these grandchildren were born.

As it was just getting dark the family was startled by a tap on the window. Eli, who was standing close to the window, looked out and became silent. No it could not be, sure enough he saw both of the big two legged hairy creatures standing in front of the window. Matt and Kim and the children froze in place. They did not speak or move. Grandpa moved close to them and put his arms around the children and told them not to be frightened that everything would be ok. The children had great faith in everything their Grandpa told them and this was to be no exception. In a moment the big creatures were gone. Grandpa told the children he was sure the big creatures had heard and perhaps seen the unusual activity around the cabin. Normally everything was extremely quiet on Goat Mountain this time of the year. He felt they had come down to check on Eli to make sure he was ok. The children asked Grandpa to check and make sure the doors were locked. It was some time before the children left Grandpa's side. As Dad and Mom began to relax so did the children. Before long they were all setting on the rug in front of the fireplace and grandpa was telling them a Christmas story. The snow continued to fall as the temperature continued to drop. Sienna was the first to fall asleep in Grandpa's lap. Matt offered the nightly prayer and everyone went to bed.

Eli was the first one up the next morning. He filled the fireplace with wood and built a fire in the kitchen stove. He then went outside quietly to feed and check on the animals. He also wanted to see if he could see any tracks of the big creatures who had made their appearance in the window last night. All tracks were covered by several inches of new snow, however, he could still see signs of their trail as the snow under their feet was packed down and the new snow was a little below the level of the surrounding area. Their trail led straight up Goat Mountain Meadow towards the cave. All of the animals were fine and warm in their cozy places in the barn. When Eli got back to the cabin everyone was up and moving around. The first thing the children asked Eli was "Grandpa, are all the animals safe and did you see any tracks of the scary creatures"? Eli assured them that the animals were fine and warm and the snow had pretty well covered the two legged hairy creature's tracks. He did tell them he could see signs of their trail and that they had gone up towards the cave on Goat Mountain. He assured the children that he doubted they would make another appearance while they were here for the holidays.

Matt made breakfast of homemade biscuits, flat eggs and hash browns made with the left over mashed potatoes. Kim served ice cold fresh cow milk and hot chocolate. The falling snow finally stopped and the children asked if Grandpa would take them outside to do some sledding. Kim and Matt said they would clean up and join everyone shortly. Grandpa went to the barn and got the sleds. It took some time to pack down a sled run but when it was completed the fun began. Elly and Evan were little speed demons and Sienna was right behind them. The hill led from the cabin to the barn. After about one hour of sledding Kim and Matt brought a large pot of hot chocolate to the barn and they all had a delicious hot drink. The children asked grandpa if they could play for a while in the large stack of straw grandpa had stored in the corner of the barn for bedding down the animals. Grandpa said they could. While the children played grandpa, Matt, and Kim went to the small barn that housed Old Pet and the milk cow. As they entered the barn Grandpa spotted the trap he had sat for catching the weasel that had killed the chickens. Sure enough Mr. Weasel was in the trap. The adults decided they would not say anything to the children about the catch. Grandpa knew they would be sorry for the poor weasel. Grandpa was not sad because he could not spare the lives of any more chickens. He especially needed the protein from the eggs in his diet.

When Eli, Matt and Kim returned to the barn the children were playing with the hounds and Delightful. They asked Grandpa if they could take the dogs and the falcon outside for some exercise and fresh air. Grandpa thought that was an excellent idea so out the barn door they all went. The snow was so deep the hounds had a hard time getting around. It was hilarious to watch them trying to run in the deep snow. Elly had Delightful on a tether and asked if she could turn her loose. Grandpa gave her the go ahead. The falcon flew around in circles high above the cabin and barn and after a short while returned to Elly's shoulder and the tether.

It was soon time to put the animals back in the warm barn and continue with the sledding. Evan asked his Dad to build a small jump in the sled run. Kim brought her Argus C-3 35 mm camera outside and took several pictures. After about another hour of sledding the children were ready to go inside the cabin as it was lunch time and they had really worked up an appetite. Kim made ham sandwiches and had baked a chocolate cake while they were outside sledding. Hot chocolate was served with lunch and of course Matt had to have ice cold fresh cow milk with his chocolate cake as did Eli. Kim's love for chocolate cake was a well know fact among all of the family and extended family. She loved anything made of chocolate. The only desert she liked almost as much was Grandpa's homemade wild black berry cobbler. In fact she hoped he had canned some berries and would make a cobbler before they left. After lunch they cleared off the kitchen table. Elly asked Grandpa if he had a game of Monopoly and if so, could they play the game. Grandpa told them that he still had the game that he had bought for their father when he was still at home and that he would love to play with the children and their parents. Matt put up some resistance to including Grandpa in the game as he had some bad memories of games played with Dad when he was younger. You see Grandpa had a reputation of spending most of his time in grade school playing monopoly. He was the Monopoly King of the eighth grade and was given a certificate for his achievements with the game along, with his Eighth Grade Diploma. It was finally decided that Grandpa would be the banker. After two hours and only Elly, Evan, and their father still left in the game the group decided to call it quits. Each person totaled up their assets and the banker determined that Elly was the winner.

It was still snowing outside and the children asked if they could go with Grandpa to do chores before it got dark. Matt and Kim said they would fix dinner. Siena carried the lantern and they all headed for the cow barn first. Grandpa told Evan this would be a good time for him to practice milking the cow. Evan got all excited. He sat down on the little milking stool with grandpa at his side kneeling down. The old Jersey cow knew that things were not quite the same. It was taking a very long time to get this unpleasant task completed and bossy cow was getting a little anxious. She finally had enough and made one swift pass with her tail across Evan's forehead. Evan let out a sharp painful sound. Grandpa grabbed the milk bucket just in time. Evan fell backwards and landed in a huge fresh cow pie. Grandpa asked him if he wanted to return to the cabin and change clothes. Evan said "no, let's finish the chores so we won't have to come back out till morning," to which Grandpa agreed. The smell on Evan's clothes was so bad no one wanted to get close to him, not Delightful or the hounds or his sisters. When they got back to the cabin Kim had Evan stand on the rug just inside the door while she brought him clean clothes. She then put the smelly clothes in a bag and put them on the porch. In addition to changing clothes it was necessary for Evan to take a bath in the old round tub. He loved that part of the mishap. Grandpa had made a small round portable wall made of colored sheets, to place around the tub for privacy.

Matt and Kim had prepared a wonderful dinner from leftovers from the Christmas Dinner. Kim made a fresh pumpkin pie for desert. After dinner everyone helped clean up and then they all sat in front of the fire place and listened to Grandpa tell stories about things that had happened to him when he was growing up. Before long Siena and Evan fell asleep and the rest of the family decided to retire to bed. Grandpa filled the fire place with good dry wood before he went to bed.

It was Saturday morning and as usual Evan was the first one up. Grandpa got up and put his robe on and filled the fire place with wood. He and Evan moved around quietly so as not to wake the others. They looked out the window and observed that it was still snowing hard and the snow was really piling up. Grandpa started a fire in the cook stove, put on a kettle of snow to melt and then got out the hot chocolate mix. In a few minutes he and Evan were drinking hot chocolate. Before long everyone else was up and Matt said he would fix breakfast. Grandpa said he would make homemade biscuits. The girls asked if they could have hot chocolate while they were waiting for breakfast. Matt prepared pancakes and Grandpa brought out jerky that he had made from the Venison the hunters had left. The biscuits were wonderful with Grandpa's homemade blackberry jam.

The snow finally let up about 11:00 am and so grandpa, Matt, and the children headed for the barn to feed and check on the animals. Kim said she would join the group in a few minutes. The hounds and

Delightful were excited to see everyone. Siena asked if she could look in the log where Sampson was sleeping for the winter. Eli told her to go ahead. Everyone got busy feeding the hounds and paying attention to Delightful and forgot about Siena. Pretty soon Matt looked around and did not see Siena anyplace. He checked the barn door and it was closed. He looked in the straw stack but she was not there. Pretty soon Eli came over and said "I'll bet I know where she is". Sure enough Siena, being so small, had crawled up in the log and was lying against Sampson, all warm and cuddled up to her rump. Oh, what a sight! Too bad Kim could not capture it on camera. She did get a picture of Siena as she was backing out of log into the barn. Everyone had a good laugh but Siena did not see the humor in the event. It was now time to go check on Old Pet and Bossy Cow.

Before long it was time to go inside and have lunch. The children asked if they could go back outside and play in the snow after lunch. Grandpa was of course please to say "sure". In fact Grandpa asked the children if they would like to try snowshoeing? They all said they would love to. Grandpa had made several pairs of snow shoes from willows and coon hides. He had snow shoes of many different sizes.

After lunch everyone put on snow shoes and followed Matt and Grandpa's lead. They decided that they would go east of the cabin just a short distance and then circle around the cow barn and then walk down and around the pond and then back to the cabin. Grandpa kept Siena right next to him. Elly and Evan of course found it difficult to stay in grandpa's tracks. Kim took the camera along and took several pictures of the children. The children did very well on the shoes. They marveled at how it was possible for them to walk in very deep snow. The trip took a better part of two hours. By the time they got back to the cabin everyone was very tired, in fact Grandpa had to carry little Siena the last fifty or so yards. The cabin was warm and cozy as usual.

After everyone got warm Grandpa told them he would like to make a special treat for them. The children got excited. Eli took a large kettle and went outside. He came back in with the kettle full of snow. He got milk from last night's milking, with rich cream on top. He added some honey he had collected from the bee hive and Vanilla Extract. He put all these things together and asked the children if they would like to stir the mix. Before long they had wonderful ice cream, and lots of it. Kim made hot chocolate. This was a first for the children. They had never heard of making ice cream from snow. Their father had as Eli had made it for them many times when they were still at home. What a treat! This was something else they would have to share with their friends back in Bend.

Grandpa Eli asked the children if they would like to help him with the evening chores, to which they all said yes, so off to the barn they went. Grandpa asked Evan if he wanted to help with the milking. Evan said "Grandpa I think I'll pass this time". The girls gathered the eggs, fed Old Pet some hay, gave the hounds their nightly ration, and fed the falcon while Evan and grandpa milked the cow. With the chores done they all headed back towards the cabin. All of a sudden Grandpa spotted some huge fresh tracks in the snow which were not there when they went down to the barn. Grandpa took the lantern from Elly to take a closer look. His first assessment was correct. These were tracks from the Mountain Lion. Grandpa did not want to frighten the children any more than they already were. He did bring all the children close to him and they walked back to the barn to make sure the door was well secured and then they went to the cow barn to make sure it was secure. They then proceeded quickly towards the cabin. Grandpa looked towards the east side of the house and spotted two eyes glowing in the dark from the light from the front window. With that the big cat let out a scream and ran off into the woods. By this time Grandpa and the children were inside the cabin. The children were crying and it took some time for them to settle down. Grandpa Eli was very concerned with this close sighting of the Cougar. They would have to be very careful the rest of the time the family was here. Grandpa would carry his rifle whenever they were outside. He hoped he would never have to use it as he felt the Mountain Lion certainly had a right to be on the mountain.

Matt and Kim prepared a wonderful supper and then they all gathered around the fire place to play some family games. The children asked Grandpa if he thought the Cougar had left the area. He assured them they were all very safe and the animals were safe. It was difficult for the children to concentrate on the games after what they had experienced while doing the chores. Grandpa filled the fire place with wood and closed the damper so that the fire would burn slowly. Prayers were said and everyone retired to bed for the night. Grandpa got up to check the fire about 2:30 am and noticed that all of the children had crawled in bed with their parents. He was not surprised.

The sun was shining brightly when Eli got up the next morning. Evan was the only one up and he was setting in front of the fire place. Grandpa started a fire in the cook stove and before long the rest of the family got up. Eli asked his son Matt if he would go with him to feed the animals and milk Bossy Cow. Eli took his rifle and the milk bucket. They fed the hounds and the falcon first and then went to the cow barn. On the way to the barn they saw where the Mountain Lion had been crouched down the night before. Eli suggested to Matt that they follow the tracks after breakfast to see if the big cat had finally left the area.

After breakfast the two men left with snow shoes. The trail led straight way up Goat Mountain towards the cave. Grandpa did not have a good feeling about what he might find. Both he and Matt had their rifles. They followed the cougar's tracks for about forth five minutes and then saw additional tracks in the snow. What they saw next caused the hair on the back of their necks to stand straight up. They saw the tracks of the two big two legged creatures and it appeared they were dragging the cat through the snow. They also saw blood stains in the snow. They followed the tracks for a short distance and then Eli suggested they return to the cabin. Matt was pretty scared but Eli was not scared at all. He knew exactly what had happened. He told Matt there was no need to be concerned about the Mountain Lion any more. He knew the big fellows were protecting him as well as the other family members. Eli said a silent prayer as they continued towards the cabin.

When they got inside Eli asked everyone to gather around so he and their father could tell them what they had discovered. Kim and the children listened without making a sound while grandpa did the talking. Afterwards the children asked a few questions to which grandpa answered the best way he knew how. They wanted to know if grandpa thought the big creatures had dragged the cougar to the cave after they made the kill. Everyone seemed much more relaxed now that they did not have to worry about the big cat being in the area. Grandpa told the family that he firmly believed the big hairy creatures were watching out for him and protecting him from possible danger.

The afternoon was spent playing in the snow near the cabin. The hounds were happy to be out of the barn and Delightful was allowed to make several flights over the meadow east of the cabin. The children asked grandpa if he would take them on snow shoes out into the meadow. Matt and Kim said they would prepare supper. Grandpa had a wonderful time with the children and the afternoon went by all too quickly. Grandpa knew the family would be leaving in a couple of days so he wanted to make every minute count.

Matt rang the dinner bell and everyone ran for the cabin. Grandpa made sure that little Siena was in front of him. The meal was wonderful as was the desert. After supper they cleaned the table off and decided to play some family games. Matt told his dad that they would have to leave Saturday morning as he wanted to get back to Bend by Saturday afternoon so they would have Sunday to get ready for school and work on Monday. Eli said he understood and told his son how grateful he was that they had been able to spend the Christmas Holidays with him.

The sun was shining brightly Friday morning when Eli got up. The rest of the family was up and Matt was preparing breakfast. The children were anxious to get breakfast over with and get outside. Grandpa had promised them he would help them build an igloo today. The children helped grandpa with the chores. The fresh milk from Bossy Cow was brought to the house, strained, and put in the screened in cupboard on the back porch to cool.

It took most of the morning to form chunks of packed snow into blocks for the walls. The children wanted to build the igloo in the meadow on the east side of the cabin. After lunch everyone helped in constructing the igloo. The walls were about six feet high and the door was three feet wide and six feet high. Grandpa brought some 2 X 4's from the barn to use as rafters for the ceiling. He spread feed sacks on top of the 2 X 4's and then the children piled snow on top of the sacks. Viewing the igloo from the outside it looked like one big snow hut. Matt brought several wheel barrow loads of straw from the cow barn for everyone to sit on. Kim said she would serve supper in the igloo. The children were so excited and pleased with what they had accomplished on this last full day of their vacation with Grandpa Eli on his Goat Mountain.

After going inside the cabin grandpa asked everyone to gather around the fire place and tell what they liked best about their stay with him during this Christmas vacation. They all agreed that building the igloo and eating supper in it was the highlight of their stay. Grandpa did not dare ask them what part they liked the least. He knew what their answer would be. No one mentioned one word about the mountain lion or the big two legged man like creatures.

The children asked grandpa if he would tell them one last Old Navy Story, to which he agreed to do. Again Siena fell asleep in grandpa's lap. Prayers were said and everyone went to bed.

Matt and Kim got up early and started packing things away in preparation for their departure on the snow mobile and sled. Grandpa asked the children if they would like to help him do the morning chores one last time. They were anxious to say their goodbyes to all the animals. The children gathered the eggs while Eli milked Old Bossy Cow.

Grandpa prepared breakfast while the rest finished packing for the trip back to Bend. Grandpa dreaded for this day to arrive. This had been a wonderful two weeks but it seems like all good thing must eventually come to an end and this was no exception.

The sun was shining brightly and there was not a cloud in the sky as the time for departure had arrived. The luggage was placed in the back of the sled along with the children. Kim rode with Matt on the Ski Doo snowmobile. Grandpa gave everyone hugs and watched until his family was completely out of sight. The thought he kept in the forefront of his mind was, they will be back in June, and that is not all that far off. He would have wonderful memories of the past two weeks to dwell on. At the same time he knew there were several long months of winter ahead and several months before he would probably see another person. He was feeling lonely already. He decided he would go down to the barn and bring the hounds and the falcon outside for some sunshine and fresh air.

East pasture

FOURTEEN

March Comes In Like A Lion

The animals were glad for the opportunity to be outside for a while. Delightful took several flights over Goat Mountain meadow and the hounds just had fun running around in the snow. Pretty soon it was time for lunch. Eli took the hounds and the falcon inside the cabin where it was warm. He fed them first and then made himself a sandwich. After a short nap it was time to go back outside. Eli decided to put on the snow shoes and take a short hike out into the meadow east of the cabin. He took the hounds and Delightful with him. They had only gone a short distance when the hounds spotted a white rabbit running on top of the snow. The chase was on. The hounds quickly learned that the rabbit had a real advantage. It could run on top of the snow while the hounds could not. They were just heavy enough to break through the thin crust on top of the snow. Eli laughed and laughed while watching this chase go on. Pretty soon the hounds tired out and the rabbit vanished into the deep, dark woods surrounding the meadow. The rabbit won this round but there would be another day. The sun was beginning to set and it was time to head back to the warm cabin and barn. Eli was tired and the hounds were all wore out from chasing the rabbit. Eli whistled for his falcon and down to his shoulder she came. Even though Eli was very sad to see his family go he had made the best of the situation by spending the afternoon with his wonderful animal companions. They in turn seemed very happy to have Eli all to themselves.

When they got back to the cabin it was time for evening chores. Afterwards Eli fixed a light supper and then spent the rest of the evening writing in his journal and reading. Once again life was good on Eli's Mountain.

Eli spent most of January in and around his cabin. The snow continued to fall and the temperatures remained unusually cold. Eli checked the snow depth on the 20th of January. It measured 48 inches in the meadow just east of the cabin. Eli had plenty of good food and a good supply of dry wood on the porch and in the wood shed nearby. He fed the hounds, the falcon and the chickens morning and night. Old Pet and Bossy Cow had plenty of good hay and seemed to do fine in their cozy barn. When weather permitted Eli would take his falcon out and let her fly for an hour or two. The hounds loved to run and play in the deep snow. The elk and deer had moved out of the area to lower elevations near Colton. Eli kept watching for the big two legged hairy creatures to make an appearance but that did not occur. He supposed they were holding up in the cave. The snow was too deep for Eli to even think about going up to the spring. He still had several gallons of carbonated spring water in his root cellar. He had several good books to read and he also spent a little time each day writing in his journal. He also had a fairly rigid exercise program that he followed each day. He knew how important exercise was and he had promised his sons that he would eat healthy and exercise every day. He had a routine that kept him busy. He also made sure that he gave the hounds opportunities to exercise several times a week. By the end of January the days were getting noticeably longer so Eli could spend a little more time outside.

By the middle of February the snow fall had pretty much stopped but the days were still very cold so the snow level stayed pretty much the same. Eli measured the depth and recorded in his journal that it was down to 28 inches. For the rest of the month there were several days of overcast and rain. It was very difficult to get around in the soft, mushy snow so Eli did not spend a lot of time outside. He went out in the morning and did his chores and again in the evening. On the last day of February he thought he heard some noise in the huge log where Sampson was in hibernation. He brought his lantern over to the open end of the log and looked inside. Was he ever surprised at what he saw. A beautiful little black ball of fur was nursing from its mother. Eli was so excited but he knew they must be left alone. Sampson was still sleeping. Eli had been reading about how bears could give birth while hibernating. They are not even aware of the birth of their young until they end their extended sleep. The baby bear gets along fine and continues to nurse and grow while the mother is sleeping. By the time the mother wakes up the little one has grown quite a bit and is ready to get out into the big world outside. Eli could hardly wait for spring to come. He wondered how the little cub would take to him. He also knew that he would probably have to be very careful with how he approached Sampson. He knew that Sampson would be very protective of her young cub. He intended to give them their space and just observe their behavior. He would let them come to him. The last half of February was very wet. There were several more days in which it snowed part of the day and several days of rain. Eli stayed in the cabin most of the time. He of course did continue to do the morning and evening chores. Occasionally he looked into the huge log to check on the cub and it's Mother. Both seemed to be doing fine. The cub slept and nursed most of the time. Sampson was still sleeping and not aware of the cub at all.

March came in like a lion and so Eli hoped it would go out like a lamb. The days were getting a little longer each day. There were only a couple days of snow showers. Fortunately there were several days of sunshine. The snow started to melt and by the end of the month most of the snow was gone. Eli was able to spend more time outside. He spent a lot of time with the hounds and his falcon in the meadows. He was able to ride Old Pet up to the spring and get a couple of gallons of fresh carbonated spring water. He went by the cave but there was no sign of the big creatures. Daniel and Anne were so happy to be able to run freely and Delightful was permitted to remain free of her tether for the entire trip. Eli took a small lunch with him and food for the hounds and the falcon. They got back to the cabin around 4:00 pm. Eli did the evening chores and then went inside for the remainder of the evening. He built a fire in the fire place and spent the evening reading and writing in his journal.

Just as he was about to blow out the lamp and go to bed he noticed a shadow go past the window and then another shadow. He quickly went to the window to look outside. There was a full moon and so he was able to see pretty well. As he looked towards Goat Mountain Meadow and the cave he saw the two big fellows going up the hill. He was sure they had come down to check on him and make sure he was ok. He suspected they had seen him go past the cave up to the spring. Eli was happy to know they were both doing ok and that they had survived the long winter. Eli said his nightly prayer, blew out the lamp and went to bed. Life was good on Eli's Mountain.

The last several days of March were marked with sunshine and daytime temperatures in the high 60s. Eli was glad for the warmer days and the sunshine. It had been a long winter but the visit at Christmas time by his family from Bend made it the best winter in many, many years.

On the first day of April Eli went to the barn as usual to feed the hounds, the falcon and the chickens As he opened the barn door he got a pleasant surprise. Sampson was playing with her cub. Eli decided to give them their space. He fed the hounds and Delightful as usual and then decided to take them outside for a while and leave Sampson alone with her cub. Eli could see that Sampson was giving her full attention to the cub and that's the way it should be. Eli decided that he would move the hounds and Delightful into the cow barn for a few weeks so Sampson and her cub could have some private space. Eli made sure that Sampson had plenty of food. Sampson was always glad to see Eli when he came to the barn. He brought fresh water every day to the barn. The cub grew quickly.

Around the middle of the month Eli decided it was time to open the barn door and allow Sampson to go outside with her cub. He decided he would keep the hounds inside for the first day or two. Finally on the third day he allowed all the animals to be out at the same time. Sampson spent all of her time with the cub. Daniel and Anne were happy to be able to run freely in the meadow east of the cabin. Eli released his falcon from her tether and watched her as she flew high in the sky above Goat Mountain Meadow. Eli watched Sampson as she took her cub down to the stream which fed the pond. They both drank from the stream. Afterwards Sampson brought her cub to where Eli was setting on a stump. She approached Eli slowly and then nudged her cub to come close to her. She came right alongside Eli and he reached over and scratched her on her rump. Tears came flowing, if ever so slightly, and fell to the ground. This was a day Eli would never forget. He could hardly wait for June to come and the visit by his three sons and their families. He knew the children would be thrilled to see the cub.

It rained almost every day the first half of April so Eli did not spend a lot of time outside. He always did the morning and evening chores and he made sure the hounds and his falcon got to go outside the barn every day. He also started leaving the barn door open several hours of each day so Sampson and her cub could go outside when they wanted to. He knew that it was necessary for Sampson to scrounge for food. There were hundreds of old rotten logs and stumps that were full of insects in the forest. It was important that Sampson teach her cub how to scrounge for food.

Mountain Lion on Goat Mountain

FIFTEEN

Spring Comes To Eli's Mountain

The last half of April saw several days of sunshine on Goat Mountain. Some of the trees started budding out and there were little signs of green grass in some spots. The days were getting a little warmer and Eli was able to spend much more time outside. He made several trips up to the spring to get fresh carbonated water. He never saw any sign of the big two legged man like creatures on any of these trips. He wondered if they had left the area for a while. Many of the birds were returning from their winter retreats to the south. Spring time was always a wonderful time on Goat Mountain. Eli had enjoyed good health all winter. He maintained a healthy diet as best he could and he exercised every day. All of this paid off. The hounds and his falcon were also very healthy and Bossy Cow and Old Pet had plenty of good quality hay and even some grain that Eli had brought back from the Colton Feed Store on his trip last fall. Eli would not need to feed very much hay now as Bossy Cow and Old Pet were able to get some new green grass in the meadow just east of the cabin. This was the only meadow on the entire ranch that was fenced.

On the last day of April Eli decided to make a trip up to the spring to get fresh water. The sun was shining brightly and there was a warm spring breeze. As Eli passed the cave he was thrilled to see shadows of both creatures on the east wall of the cave. He was happy they had returned. He kept both hounds on a leash and Delightful on a tether as he passed the cave. He hoped there would come a time when the hounds and the big creatures would accept each other. He was also very concerned about the safety of the young cub and he hoped Sampson would not take the cub that far away from the barn for several months. He hoped the big creatures would come down and observe the relationship that he enjoyed with all of the animals, without the animals knowing they were nearby.

Eli was very busy all of the month of May as there was so much to do in preparation for his three families coming in June for the reunion. He wanted to put up his big walled tent on the east end of the cabin. He would need to go into the woods and spend a few days cutting and splitting wood as he had pretty much used up his supply of wood, both on the porch and in the wood shed. There was a lot of clean up from the winter storms and deep snow. Several small trees had blown down near the cabin and there were limbs from other trees all over the place. He also needed to make some minor repairs on both barns. There were also a couple of boards that needed to be re-placed on the cabin. Fortunately there were only a few rainy days in May so Eli was able to spend a lot of time working outside. The hounds and his falcon spent most of every day outside. Sampson and her cub spent a lot of time outside. The cub grew quickly and gradually warmed up to Eli. The cub loved to have her back scratched as much as Sampson did. Fortunately Sampson stayed in the general area of the cabin and the barns and the woods nearby. Eli did make several trips up to the spring but Sampson did not follow. He saw the shadows of the big fellows more than once and he also saw their foot prints around the spring so he knew they were out and about. He surmised they had made more than one trip down towards the cabin and had probably observed Sampson and the cub. He was thrilled that there were no encounters. He was already getting a little anxious over what might happen when all three families were here at Goat Mountain if the big hairy creatures were spotted.

By the end of May Eli had everything pretty much ready for the arrival of his families. During the first two weeks in June he made several trips out in the meadow east of the cabin and picked wild strawberries and made fresh strawberry jam. He also collected edible mushrooms and placed them in his root cellar. He picked and cleaned fresh water crest from the stream leading into the pond. He placed it in the coldest part of the root cellar. He collected other edible plants and roots and stored them in the cellar. By the end of each day he was exhausted but very happy.

The morning of June fifteenth found Eli up very early. This was the day Michael and Martin were to arrive with their families. Matt and his family were to arrive on the sixteenth. Eli took care of morning chores including milking Old Bossy Cow and placing the milk in the root cellar. In the last week he had made several blocks of butter from the rich cream he collected from each milking. After breakfast he did the dishes and tidied up the cabin.

Old Pet

SIXTEEN

The Reunion

Eli had just sat down to review the notes he had made of things he would suggest they consider for the reunion, when he heard vehicles coming through the forest. He could hardly contain himself. It had been almost a year since he had seen his families from Houston. He quickly got up and went outside to greet his sons and their families. They came in two rented vehicles. Ailene, and her mother Elaine, got out of the car first. Ailene introduced her mother to Eli. He told her he was pleased she was able to join the families for this visit and the reunion. After hugs and expressions of joy and love the children asked if they could go down to the barn and see the hounds, Delightful and Sampson. Eli told everyone he had a surprise for them in the barn so they all headed for the barn. He went in first and suggested the children follow. When the children saw Sampson with her cub they were thrilled. Grandpa cautioned them to stay back and see if Sampson would come to him. Sampson moved away to the far corner of the barn with her cub. Eli told the children that it would be better if they gave Sampson her space. He assured the children that she would warm up to them in time. She was just being protective of her cub.

The children greeted the hounds with affection and asked if they could take them and the falcon outside. Grandpa suggested they unpack the vehicles first and get everything put away so the next hour or so was spent doing just that. The children asked if they could put their belongings in the tent to which Grandpa agreed. It was decided that Martin would stay in the tent with the children and Mike, Ailene and her mom would stay with Grandpa in the cabin. It was nearly time for lunch time so Ailene said she would fix sandwiches if Grandpa wanted to take the children outside until lunch was ready. The first question they asked grandpa when they got outside was if the big scary creatures were still at the ranch. Grandpa tried to brush their enquiry off but the children were persistent. He finally said he would tell them about the times he had seen the big creatures or their shadows since last summer, when they sat down for lunch.

Mike rang the dinner bell so it was time to go inside for lunch. Ailene had made toast by placing bread directly on top of the wood cook stove. There was homemade butter and fresh wild strawberry jam to put on the toast. The children were anxious to have carbonated Kool-Aid to drink with their sandwiches. Ailene had brought some brownie mix so she made hot brownies for desert. After lunch the children reminded Grandpa that he had something to tell everyone.

Eli told them about the encounter the hounds had had with the big creatures in the cave and the injuries Big Daniel had received. Grandpa told the children he believed the hounds had initiated the fight; after all they had gotten into the Big Fellows space. The big creatures were only protecting their habitat. He shared the incident about the mountain lion and the fear he had of him being in the area. He told them how the big creatures had taken care of the mountain lion. He also mentioned the times he had recently seen the big hairy two legged creatures shadows on the walls of the cave. The children became very frightened just hearing about these events. They asked Grandpa if he had seen any more cougars. He answered that he had not. The children wanted to hear more details but Eli said he would rather talk about the visit at Christmas time of their Uncle Matt and Aunt Kim and their children. He did say that the mountain lion incident happened while Uncle Matt and his family were visiting. He told them about seeing the eyes of the big cat when he and the children were returning from the barn at night. He shared with the grandchildren how the cougar started screaming and then ran off towards Goat Mountain Meadow. He related how he and Matt followed the lion's tracks the next morning and discovered where the big man like creatures had ganged up on the lion and killed it and then dragged it to the cave. By this time the children were so frightened they did not want to go outside for several hours.

It was finally time to do evening chores and the children were ready to go with Grandpa to help. They fed the hounds, the falcon and the chickens first and then went to the cow barn to feed Old Pet and milk Bossy Cow. Jacob asked if he could try milking the cow to which Grandpa agreed. Jacob did an excellent job of milking for his first attempt. Katy asked if she could do the milking in the morning and Grandpa said sure. Next Marina asked if she could milk Old Bossy Cow tomorrow evening. Again Grandpa said sure. Eli was thrilled that the children were so interested in learning new things and helping with the chores. He let Benjamin, Brighten, Christine, and Archer feed the hounds and take the falcon outside on her tether.

Martin brought some hamburger that he had purchased at the Colton Market and he suggested they barbeque hamburgers on Grandpa's homemade outdoor barbeque grill. Elaine and Ailene made a wonderful green salad and Elaine made a delicious apple pie with apples Eli had canned last fall. Mike and Martin made a bonfire in the meadow east of the cabin. This time Grandpa told everyone he wanted to hear all about what they all had been doing since their last visit. He asked each one to tell his own story. Eli listened carefully as each child and each adult talked. Mike was the last one to talk and by that time Archer and Christine had fallen asleep.

Finally everyone went inside and prepared for bed. After family prayer Martin and the children went to the tent and the rest went to bed in the cabin. This had truly been a wonderful day. Everyone was anxious for tomorrow to come as the family from Bend would arrive.

The next morning everyone got up early. The children helped Grandpa with chores while Martin and Mike made breakfast. While they were making breakfast Ailene and Elaine made a WELCOME sign for Matt and Kim and their children. After breakfast everyone quickly made their beds. Kate and Marina agreed to do the dishes. The temperature was 75 degrees F. so Grandpa did not build a fire in the fireplace. Jacob, Benjamin and Archer asked if they could take the falcon out on her tether to which Grandpa agreed. Brighten and Christine asked if they could go down to the barn and see Sampson and her cub. Grandpa said they could but only if he were with them. He still did not know how Sampson was going to act around the children or their parents. So off to the barn they went to check on Sampson. Grandpa told the children to wait outside for a minute or two. When he went inside Sampson and the cub were happy to see him. Both wanted Eli to scratch their side. The cub wanted to play. Just as Eli was about to put his hand on her side she would move away. Eli would start to walk away and the cub would run towards him and rub her side against his pant leg. Finally Eli decided that he would have the children come in. When they got inside Eli told them to set down along the wall. He asked Brighton to come to him. The two of them walked slowly towards Sampson. As they did so Sampson moved along side of Brighton at which time she reached out and rested her hand on his side. Grandpa told her to go ahead and scratch the bear's side. He then had her move back to the wall and he told Christine to come to him. She also got to scratch Sampson's side. All this time the little cub stayed a good distance away. Just as Grandpa Eli was about to approach the cub he heard Mike calling. The message was that a vehicle was heard coming through the woods towards the cabin. With that they all left the barn running. The plan was that everyone would be outside to welcome the family from Bend.

Eli was happy to see Matt, Kim and the children once again. There were many hugs and expressions of love. It had been some time since Mike and Martin had seen their older brother. And it was the first time that Matt's children had seen Brighton and Archer. Needless to say it was a very happy reunion. They were all excited and happy to be back at Goat Mountain. They were all looking forward to spending two weeks together with Grandpa Eli and all the animals. They were all happy that Ailene's mother, Elaine was able to join the family.

Ailene and Mike made a wonderful lunch for everyone to enjoy. They had set up some makeshift picnic tables so they were able to eat outside. This is where they planned to eat most of the meals as there were almost too many to sit down and eat inside the small cabin. Everyone loved the carbonated Kool-Aid and the fresh watercress from the stream flowing into the pond. They had venison meat sandwiches for the adults and peanut butter and fresh wild strawberry jam sandwiches for those that wanted them. Everyone helped to clean up after lunch.

The children all wanted Grandpa to take them down to the barn to see the newborn cub. Of course they also wanted to see the hounds and the falcon. Grandpa cautioned the children to not expect the cub to come near them at first. This was going to take some time to get the cub and Sampson to warm up to many people. As they all came inside the barn Sampson came over to Eli right away and wanted to be scratched but the cub stayed a good distance away. The children stayed close to the side of the barn and eventually the cub came over to Eli. Eli had the children come one at a time to him and as they did so the cub allowed them to scratch her side. This thrilled the children. They were already falling in love with the little bear. After spending some time inside the barn Eli left the barn door open so Sampson and the cub could go outside and scrounge for food in the woods nearby. Grandpa and the children took the hounds and falcon outside. They went to the meadow east of the cabin. Grandpa allowed each child to take Delightful on the tether and turn her loose so she could soar freely in the deep blue sky above. This was a beautiful sight. The hounds ran and played with the children for several minutes. Everyone got pretty hot and sweaty and asked grandpa it they could go for a swim, to which he quickly agreed. The parents joined in and pretty soon everyone was in the water having a good time and cooling off. The rest of the afternoon was spent in and around the pond.

It was finally time to get out of the water and go to the cabin and prepare for supper. Matt, Mike and Martin volunteered to prepare the evening meal. Matt brought fresh Halibut from his favorite fish market in Bend. Eli had not had sea food in a long time. Martin fixed a fresh green salad using watercress, miner's lettuce and green onions from his father's small garden. Mike made a desert using fresh wild strawberries and whipping cream made with fresh cream from the morning milk from Old Bossy Cow. There was a choice of fresh cool milk and carbonated Kool-Aid to drink. After supper Grandpa Eli suggested they take a short hike out in the meadow east of the cabin. Kate asked if they could take the hounds and the falcon, to which grandpa agreed. Evan asked if he could take the falcon on its tether. Eli said yes, but he needed to wear a glove on his right hand. Benjamin and Marina asked if they could ride Old Pet. Grandpa said he would hook Old Pet up to the small buggy and all of the children could ride. The children were so excited. It was a warm evening and there was a little breeze to make it very comfortable. The families from Houston were so happy to be enjoying a lot cooler weather with almost no humidity. It was so hot and humid when they left home. The sun was getting low in the sky but there was still plenty of daylight. All of the animals seemed to be very happy to have so much attention. They had not gone very far when Christine looked back and saw Sampson and the cub coming towards them at a dead run. She yelled to Grandpa and told him to look back towards the cabin. Evidently he had not closed the barn door very well. At any rate he was pleased to have the bears join the family outing. Sampson came right up to Eli but the cub stayed back a little way. Eli asked Christine if she wanted to ride on Sampson's back. She was a little hesitant but finally agreed to do so. Eli told each of the children they could have a turn if they so desired. Everyone said they wanted to with the exception of Elly. She said she would rather ride Old Pet. As they came close to the other end of the meadow all of the animals started acting funny and seemed to want to turn around and head back towards the cabin. The hounds tried to break away from Martin and Matt and Delightful started really making a fuss. Eli suspected he knew what was bothering them but he had no intention of saying anything except to tell everyone it was probably a good idea to head back to the cabin. The sun had gone down and it was starting to get a little cool and no one brought jackets or sweaters.

When they got back to the cabin Eli, Matt, Mike and Martin took all the animals to the barn. Mike asked Grandpa if there was a chance the animals were spooked by the big creatures possibly being nearby. Their father said yes, he suspected that was what had happened. All three sons wanted to know if Eli had had any more encounters with the big creatures since they were last here at Goat Mountain. Eli told them there had been. He told them again about the incident with the hounds in the cave. He rehearsed again the mountain lion incident that had occurred at Christmas time while Matt and his family were visiting. He again mentioned what had happened to the mountain lion. Matt chimed in and told them all of the details and how the big two legged creatures were involved. Eli also told them about the big creatures coming down one night in the spring time to check on him. All of this caused his sons to have heightened concern for their father and his safety; however they were coming to believe that the man like creatures were more concerned about protecting Eli than harming him.

When Eli and his sons got back to the cabin some of the children were playing a game of Aggravation and others were playing Chinese checkers. Elaine, Ailene and Kim were catching up on things that had been happening in their lives with their families since they had last been together.

It was soon time to prepare for bed and the children asked Grandpa if he would tell them a bed time story. They wanted him to tell them an Old Navy Story. Eli gathered them around his big soft chair and told them a wild story about the time they had sailed through the Bermuda Triangle. Before he got through the story Christine fell asleep on his lap. The older children slept with Martin in the tent and the younger children stayed inside the cabin. The cabin floor was pretty much wall to wall with bodies. Everyone was asleep by 10:00 pm.

The seventeenth of June was a special day. Everyone woke up early. The sun was shining and the sky was clear of any clouds. This was the day everyone had been waiting for. This was the special day of the long awaited family reunion for Eli and his family on Goat Mountain. The parents prepared breakfast while Grandpa Eli and the children went out and fed and tended to the animals. Sampson and the cub were happy to see Eli and the children. The hounds just wanted to get outside and be able to run freely. Delightful was anxious to get outside and find a good meal. The falcon loved to soar high in the sky and then pounce on a small rodent. In a few minutes all of the animals were outside. Grandpa even brought Old Pet and Bossy Cow out into their fenced pasture.

Mike rang the dinner bell so grandpa and the children returned to the cabin as they were all very hungry by now. The parents fixed a hearty breakfast. After breakfast everyone helped to clean up. It was then time to go outside and begin the activities for the day. As they started outside they heard what sounded like an automobile coming through the woods. Eli had no idea who it might be. Bob Berge was not expected until the end of next week, with his logging crew. Of course Matt, Mike and Martin knew exactly who it was but they kept silent. In fact even the children knew who was coming but they said nothing. Eli waited with anticipation. As the new pickup got closer Eli could not believe his eyes. It was his brother Al and sister Rita. Eli had not seen them in 7 years. They all had tears in their eyes as they embraced. With that Martin told his father that he, Matt and Mike had told Uncle Al and Aunt Rita about the reunion and encouraged them to come if at all possible. What a memorable day and week this would be. Eli introduced his brother and sister to Elaine. The next hour was spent just visiting and catching up on what everyone had been doing for the last several years. Eli was so happy to see his brother and sister. He was so happy to see they were both well and enjoying their retirement in Arizona. They in turn were very happy to be back at Goat Mountain and to see their nephews and their families. The children told their Great Uncle and Great Aunt about all the animals. They were anxious for them to see Sampson and her cub so the next hour or so was spent with the animals. Sampson and the cub stayed a little distance away. This was far too many people for them to feel comfortable around at this time. The hounds loved people and they loved all the attention. Delightful could care less. She just wanted to be released so she could soar in the bright blue sky.

Kim, Ailene and her mother Elaine said they would go in and fix lunch. The men had set up makeshift picnic tables outside so lunch would be served outside. After lunch it was decided they would all take a trip up to the spring and collect some fresh carbonated spring water. Eli thought about taking another route so as not to come even close to the cave but then decided against it. No one said anything to Uncle Al or Aunt Rita about the big two legged creatures. Eli thought that perhaps with so many people around the creatures might leave the area for a while, but he was wrong. As they passed the cave everyone except Al and Rita saw the shadows of the big creatures on the cave wall. Al and Rita were looking elsewhere and no one said a word about the cave or who was living in it. They arrived at the spring, collected several gallons of fresh water and then headed back down. They stopped to pick and eat wild strawberries and to also take a small pail full back to the cabin. The meadows were covered with beautiful wild flowers and there were so many birds that had returned to spend the summer. The mountain blue birds, scrub jays, stellar jays and meadow larks were there in abundance. This was truly a beautiful time of the year and the weather could not have been better.

When they got back to the cabin Matt announced that it was time to start some of the activities for the children and their parents. The first event was to be an old fashioned gunny sack race in the meadow east of the cabin. There were 10 grandchildren and five able bodied parents so each parent would have to run twice. Teams were organized and it was decided that Grandpa would be the judge at the finish line.

Elaine volunteered to be the judge at the starting line. The younger children were able to move up about twenty feet ahead of the starting line. Uncle Al volunteered to blow the whistle to start every race. Each team consisted of a child and a parent. Each member of the team had to place one leg in the sack. The distance of the race was fifty yards. The teams all lined up at their assigned starting position. Uncle Al blew the whistle and off the teams went. Martin and Marina had the lead for a while and then Martin stepped in a gopher hole and down he went. Mike and Kate were doing real well until Kate tripped and went flying to the ground. Matt and Elly made it almost to the finish line and then Matt slipped on some wet grass and went crashing to the ground. Ailene and Jacob both tripped and fell. By this time Martin and Marina were up and running again but Kim and Evan had been wise and decided to not run quite so fast and as a consequence they won the first heat.

The adults begged for a little break to catch their breath before the next race. The teams for this heat were Kim and Siena, Martin and Brighton, Mike and Ben, Ailene and Christene and Matt and Archer. Again there were many spills and a lot of laughing. Matt and Archer won this race hands down.

Everyone was pretty hot and sweaty after the race and so it was decided they would all go for a swim in the pond. The hounds were turned loose and Delightful was allowed to fly freely for the rest of the afternoon. Sampson and her cub were also allowed to leave the confines of the barn. They meandered off into the meadow on the east side of the cabin. Everyone had a great time playing in the water. After an hour or so it was time to get out and start doing the evening chores and preparing the evening feast. This was to be the main reunion meal. Many delicious dishes were prepared. Elaine volunteered to prepare Eli's favorite old fashioned dish, bread pudding. The meal was served outside. The children were all able to set at their own picnic table. Matt offered the blessing on the food. The carbonated Kool-Aid was of course the favorite drink. The desert was a fresh wild strawberry/rhubarb pie and of course the bread pudding. Everyone ate so much they were not able to do any physical activities for some time after the meal.

The children asked Grandpa if they could have a bonfire after it got dark to which he happily agreed. They wanted to know if Grandpa would teach them some of the games he used to play when he was a child. He said he would teach them how to play Kick the Can and Run Sheep Run. All the children and some of the adults gathered fallen limbs and brush for the fire. Before long they had a huge pile of wood for the fire. They used blocks of firewood for seats. The children and some of the adults had so much fun playing the games. The rest of the adults sat around the fire and had a great time visiting and laughing.

The days were very long now and it did not get dark till almost 9:30 pm. Kim and Ailene suggested it was time to get the children ready for bed. Archer and Christine were already asleep on a blanket on the ground by the fire. Those who were going to sleep in the tent went to the tent and the rest went to the cabin. Nightly prayers were said and before long everyone was asleep. This had truly been a wonderful day on Goat Mountain.

The children slept in Saturday morning but Eli and his sons were up early. Matt, Mike and Martin went outside with their father to do chores. Sampson and her cub were anxious to get outside. The hounds were restless and even Delightful was happy to be able to get outside. Matt volunteered to milk the cow and Mike and Martin agreed to take Old Pet out to the pasture for the day. When they got back to the cabin all the women folk were up and starting to prepare breakfast. Grandpa Eli went to the tent and woke the children up.

It was a beautiful day and there were no clouds in the sky. The sun was coming up over the Cascade Range to the east. The temperature was already 65 degrees f by 8:00 am. After breakfast the children asked their parents and Grandpa if they would take them high up on Goat Mountain to pick wild strawberries. The women folk said they would stay at the cabin and prepare for the activities of the afternoon. Grandpa decided it would be better if they did not take Sampson and her cub; however they did take the hounds and the falcon. They did not take the route that led by the cave. That part of Goat Mountain was pretty well picked over. Instead they went through the meadow to the east and then at the end of the meadow they turned left and followed a deer trail high up on the mountain. As they got into open areas there were huge patches of wild strawberries. Before long they each had a pail full of strawberries. Grandpa decided they would circle around and stop at the spring for a drink of water and then proceed on down by the cave and back to the cabin. Some of the older children had some reservations about going by the cave but Grandpa assured them everything would be ok. Grandpa led the way. The children were right behind him and then Matt, Mike and Martin brought up the rear. Siena and Christine wanted to stop along the way and pick some beautiful flowers to take to their moms.

As they neared the cave the big creatures were in clear view at the entrance of the cave. The children were frightened and stayed very close to Grandpa. Grandpa told everyone to just look straight ahead and continue on and to not act frightened. In his heart grandpa knew they were completely safe but he knew he could not convince the others of that fact and he did not even try to. He just wanted to get back to the cabin as quickly as possible. This was the first time his sons and grandchildren had had such a clear view of the big creatures. Grandpa Eli did look back a couple of times to see if the big creatures were following. Matt and Mike each had one of the hounds on a rope and Martin had the falcon on her tether. They made it back to the cabin just as the mothers had lunch ready. Everyone was hungry but the children could not wait to tell those that stayed at the cabin about seeing the big hairy creatures in the entrance to the cave. This is the first Al and Rita had heard about the big fellows. Everyone except Eli seemed quite frightened. Eli again assured everyone that he was quite sure they had nothing to worry about. Elaine, Al and Rita could hardly believe what they were hearing. They had all of course heard many stories about people who claimed to have seen a Big Foot but they never believed any of them and they were not sure they wanted to believe what they were now hearing, however, with so many of their own family members telling of the sighting and then hearing of previous incidents it was impossible to doubt what they were being told.

After lunch they all wanted to go down to the pond and go for a swim. It was a very hot day and thunder clouds were starting to form to the west. The water was perfect and everyone enjoyed cooling off. At the first sound of thunder in the distance Grandpa told everyone it was time to get out of the water to which they all readily agreed. Eli and his sons made sure all of the animals were secure back in the barn and then went to join the others in the cabin. Needless to say it was very crowded in the small cabin when everyone had to be inside, but they made due. It was only a short time until the clouds released huge amounts of rain.

It rained hard for about an hour. Water was running everywhere. Eli was very happy to see the rain as things were really starting to dry out. The trees and plants needed the moisture. This would also really give his small garden a good soaking. They spent most of the afternoon playing some board games and putting puzzles together. By 4:00 pm the rain showers were over and the sun came out. After letting things dry out for about an hour Grandpa Eli said it would be ok to go outside. The air smelled so fresh and everything looked refreshed and beautiful. The children asked if they could have another camp fire tonight to which Grandpa quickly agreed. Kim and Ailene suggested they have hot dogs, smore's and carbonated Kool-Aid for supper.

The rest of the afternoon and evening were spent playing games and gathering wood for the bonfire. Rita suggested they stay fairly close to the cabin in case any strange visitors should appear on the scene. Elaine, Kim and Ailene seconded the motion.

Martin started the fire around 7:00 pm. The ladies brought out the food. Matt and Mike had gone down by the pond and cut some willows for sticks for cooking the hot dogs on. Everyone ate hot dogs and smore's until they could eat no more. By the time they finished and cleaned up it was getting dark. Grandpa asked the children if they wanted to play some of the games they had played at the last campfire. The children all said no, because they were still frightened with what they had seen that morning at the cave. They all decided to go inside as Elaine said she had prepared a special desert. She made a fresh wild strawberry rhubarb pie. The strawberries came from a small field south of the cabin and the rhubarb came from Eli's garden.

After everyone was served a piece of pie, Brighton asked Grandpa if he had any ice cream to go with the pie. Everyone got a chuckle out of her request. Her father, Martin, reminded her that grandpa had no electricity and therefore had no way of keeping ice cream. He did promise her that they would go up to the cave some time and if the big hairy creatures were not there they would go to the back of the cave and collect some ice and bring it to the cabin and make some homemade ice cream from the fresh cream Grandpa collected from Bossy Cow's milk. This made all of the children happy. After finishing their desert it was bed time for the children. Family prayers were said and before long all of the children were asleep. The adults stayed up and visited for awhile.

Matt and Kim were the last to go to bed after checking on all of the children. It was Kim and Matt's turn to sleep in the tent.

Sunday morning was another beautiful June morning on Goat Mountain. This was to be a special day when everyone would stay around the cabin area. Eli's sons said they would make a brunch. They all liked to cook and each one prepared his favorite breakfast dish. The chickens were all laying and so there were plenty of eggs.

After brunch Eli suggested they play some family games outside. Jacob asked if they could have a family softball game. Grandpa said he thought that was a splendid suggestion. He asked Elaine and Rita to choose sides. Everyone got to play. It was decided that the men folk would bat with the hand they did not normally bat with. Siena asked if she could play third base on her team. When everyone had their positions a coin was flipped to see which team would bat first. Elaine won the toss. She chose to be in the field first so her team would get to bat last. There were five children on each team. In the bottom of the third inning Elaine was coaching third base and saw little Siena lying on the ground and picking apart a dandelion. This caused a moment of laughter. It was decided at the beginning to play only five innings. At the beginning of the bottom half of the fifth inning Elaine's team was behind by one run. With two out and runners on second and third base Grandpa Eli came to the plate. Rita was the pitcher for her team. Grandpa hit a foul ball on the first pitch. He took a strike on the second pitch. On the third pitch he connected perfectly with the ball and drove a line drive into right field. Archer came home safely from third and Benjamin came home from second base. Elaine's team won the game by a score of 5 to 4.

After the game the adults needed to rest for a little while but the children still had plenty of energy. Grandpa told them they could take the animals to the meadow on the south side of the cabin. He even let them take Sampson and her cub. The cub was getting used to the children and would allow them to scratch his back. In fact the children were getting very attached to both Sampson and the cub. Before long Grandpa Eli and his sons joined the children in the meadow. They all had a great time playing with Sampson and her cub and the hounds and the falcon. The children were developing a great affection for the cub and he seemed to love the attention.

The play ended when they heard the dinner bell ring. Everyone had really worked up an appetite and so it was no trouble at all getting the children to go to the cabin. The women folk had prepared a wonderful meal. Everyone helped with the clean up. All the dishes had to be washed by hand and dried with a dish towel. This was a new experience for some of the children. The only time they did dishes by hand was when they came to Grandpa's Goat Mountain cabin.

Afterwards they all helped to prepare wood for the evening camp fire. Mike brought his guitar and they all sang camp fire songs most of the evening. Everyone was a little too tired to do much running so they mostly sat around the camp fire and sang songs and told camp stories. Mike and Martin knew a lot of songs and camp stories as they had been camp counselors when they attended high school. Before long Archer and Christine fell asleep and so everyone decided it was time to end the day and get ready for bed. Matt offered the family prayer as they sat around the camp fire and then Eli and his sons put the fire out and they all retired for the night. This had truly been a wonderful and fun day on Eli's Goat Mountain.

The weather Monday morning caught everyone by surprise. It was cloudy and sprinkling rain drops. The temperature was only fifty degrees. Grandpa fixed a fire in the fire place and the wood cook stove, then asked the children if they wanted to help him with the morning chores. The children were not about to let a few rain drops keep them inside. They all followed Grandpa to the barn to take care of the hounds, the falcon, and Sampson and her cub. Grandpa let the children play with the cub several minutes. They were falling more in love with the cub every day and the cub seemed to love the children. Sampson seemed to be very pleased that her cub was so good with the children. Elly and Jacob spent time with the hounds and Kate spent time with Delightful. It was finally time to leave the barn and go to the cow barn to do the chores there. Elly asked Grandpa if she could stay with Evan, Siena, Marina, Brighton, Benjamin, Christine and Archer and play with the cub to which Grandpa quickly agreed. He took Kate and Jacob with him to the cow barn. When they finished milking and feeding Bossy Cow and Old Pet they returned to the barn where the rest of the children were playing. Grandpa told them the breakfast bell had rung and that it was time to return to the cabin for breakfast. They all gave the cub one last hug and headed for the cabin. By the time they got to the cabin they were all pretty well soaked and the rain was now coming down pretty hard. This was a good day to stay inside and play monopoly. Everyone agreed that Grandpa Eli could play. Elaine volunteered to be the banker. A time limit of two hours was set for the game. Those that didn't want to play monopoly played other games or just visited.

By lunch time the rain had stopped and the games were over with. Martin was declared the winner of the monopoly game. Everyone was on their own to fix a sandwich for lunch.

The children wanted to get outside as soon as possible. The sun was warm and the ground dried quickly. The children asked Grandpa if he would go with them up to the spring. Eli put up some resistance at first as he contemplated what the ramifications might be if they were to encounter the big creatures outside of the cave. Finally the children won out and grandpa consented. Matt, Mike and Martin quickly decided they would go along. Matt asked his father if it would be alright to take the 30/30 rifle along. Eli said it would not be necessary or a good idea. Elly asked if she could ride Old Pet to which grandpa agreed. Kate asked if she could take Delightful and Grandpa said "sure". Evan and Jacob asked if they could take the hounds, again Grandpa said "yes". Before long they were all on their way up the mountain. The children were all having a good time picking wild strawberries and learning about the many beautiful things in nature from their grandfather.

As they approached the area near the cave, Grandpa told Jacob and Evan to hold tightly to the hounds. In spite of this Evan lost control of Daniel and Anne jerked away from Jacob. Off they ran towards the cave. Everyone froze with fear of what might happen if in fact the Big Fellows were anywhere near the entrance to the cave. Eli cautioned everyone to stay calm and not advance any further until he gave the signal to go on. He left the group and headed towards the cave and the dogs. As he neared the cave entrance he saw something that he never would have dreamed of. The big man like creatures were just a few feet inside the entrance and Daniel and Anne were there with them. The dogs were not excited at all and the big hairy creatures were just enjoying their company. This puzzled Eli beyond words. He wondered how many times they had been together this spring and early summer.

Somehow they had developed a bond of unusual friendship that was almost impossible for Eli, his sons, and grandchildren to understand. Needless to say Eli was so happy. In fact this observation brought tears of joy to flow from his eyes. Everyone soon became relaxed and continued their journey towards the spring. This changed everyone's attitude towards the scary looking creatures of the wild. Eli cautioned everyone to not read too much into this incident. He had no intention of bringing the children or any other members of the family near the cave or the big fellows. After all, these creatures were not used to being around people. As far as Eli knew they had not ever been seen by other humans. People made claims of seeing 'man like' creatures but those claims had never been verified.

With the incident over, they proceeded up the mountain meadow to the spring. Everyone was thirsty by now and each took their turn at getting a drink of the cold carbonated water. Grandpa looked for fresh tracks around the spring but the hard rain had washed away all tracks. Several jugs were filled with water and placed in the small cart that Old Pet had pulled up the mountain. Christine and Archer asked if they could ride down the mountain in the cart to which grandpa agreed. Grandpa suggested they take another route back to the cabin so they could feast on more wild strawberries. Matt suggested they take some back to the cabin as Elaine had said she would make a strawberry/ rhubarb pie. Kate asked if she could release Delightful from her tether and Jacob and Evan asked if they could turn the hounds loose. Grandpa said yes to both request. The trip down the mountain was fun for everyone. Delightful caught a small rodent and the hounds enjoyed the attention they got from the children. Mike brought a small pail to put the fresh wild strawberries in that everyone helped pick. They arrived back at the cabin about 5:00 pm. The ladies had started dinner and Elaine had made a pie crust in anticipation of the arrival of the strawberries. Ailene had brought in several stalks of rhubarb.

Supper consisted of elk steak, mashed potatoes, fresh water crest, carbonated Kool-Aid, homemade biscuits, and elk gravy. The pie was saved for later in the evening. Everyone helped in preparing wood for the camp fire, which was to be down by the pond. The children had prepared several skits while the others had been helping with the supper preparation. Mike started the campfire just a little before dark. Elly asked Grandpa if she could bring the cub to the camp fire to which Grandpa agreed. Little did Grandpa know the cub was to be in at least two of the children's skits? Everyone got to participate and there were lots of laughs. The campfire ended around 9:30 pm and before long everyone was in bed. This had really been a wonderful day on Goat Mountain.

By Tuesday morning there was no sign of clouds and the temperature was already 68 degrees by 9:00 am. After breakfast Eli and the children headed outside to do the morning chores. On the way to the barn grandpa heard the sound of a vehicle coming through the woods. He was not expecting anyone so he was very surprised when the vehicle got close enough that he could identify his friend Bob Berge in the driver's seat. Eli waved for Bob to park the truck and join him and the children in the barn.

Grandpa introduced his friend Bob to all of the children. The rest of the adults came outside when they heard the truck approaching. Eli introduced Bob to those whom he had not met before. After the introductions everyone went about doing other things in preparation for the day ahead. Bob asked Eli if he could talk with him in private. They went a little ways from the barn and sat on a log. Bob asked Eli if the loggers could come early as the weather was supposed to turn very hot and dry and the woods might be closed to logging. Eli thought about Bob's request for a few minutes and then consented with some conditions. The logging was to be done on the far western part of the ranch. The timber crew were to be very careful and make sure there were no family members in the area where they were working, and they were to make sure there were none of Eli's pets in the area. Bob quickly agreed to these conditions and said the crew would be coming in the morning. After Bob left Eli found it very difficult to tell the family that the loggers would be coming early but he finally worked up the courage to break the news to his sons. They were not too happy but they understood why it was necessary.

The rest of the day was absolutely wonderful. Everyone participated in several outdoor games such as sack races, wheel barrow races, three legged races and a five inning soft ball game. Everyone was pretty tired by 4:00 pm and it was very hot on Goat Mountain. Perfect weather for swimming in the pond. Those who did not go swimming volunteered to fix the evening meal.

Kim rang the dinner bell about 5:15 pm and with that everyone quickly got out of the pond and headed to the cabin. After supper everyone helped with the cleanup. Matt and Martin had prepared a small camp fire and Mike said he would play some campfire songs on his Gibson guitar if they would all join in and sing with him.

SEVENTEEN

Tragedy Strikes On Goat Mountain

On June 22, Wednesday morning the logging crew arrived. Eli and his sons went over to make sure they were setting up camp in the proper place. The loggers were very polite as they had great respect for Eli. They brought Eli several new pairs of overalls and work gloves. They also brought mail that had been held at the Colton Post Office. Their kindness was very much appreciated by Matt, Mike and Martin. Eli and his sons got back to the cabin just in time for breakfast. The older children had done the morning chores, all except the milking. Matt agreed to do that after breakfast. Kim said she wanted to observe this event as she had never seen Matt milk a cow before.

After breakfast the faint sound of power saws working could be heard in the distance. There were many activities planned for the day in addition to a trip up the meadow to the spring. The last jug of carbonated water had been used for breakfast. Grandpa decided they would take another route to the spring and avoid the cave completely, even though he figured the big fellows would be long gone with the sound of power saws in the nearby woods. The trip to the spring was uneventful and several jugs of water were brought back to the cabin and placed in the root cellar to keep the water cool. The children asked if they could take Sampson and the cub out to the meadow to the east of the cabin to which Grandpa agreed. The children were getting very attached to the little cub and the cub loved the attention. Sampson also loved the children. They spent hours on end playing together. The children asked Grandpa if they could name the cub. The name they decided upon was Sambo. Eli liked the name as did the other adults.

The hounds always joined in the play. Delightful watched from a perch in the old oak tree in the center of the meadow. The morning passed quickly and the children were having so much fun they did not want to stop for lunch. As they were about to head towards the cabin they saw Kim and Ailene coming towards them with two picnic baskets. They brought sandwiches and drinks for everyone. They all sat down under the large oak tree and enjoyed a wonderful lunch. Pretty soon the rest of the adults came from the cabin. They all spent the rest of the afternoon playing with the animals in the meadow. By 4:30 pm they were all very tired and ready to go for an afternoon swim in the pond.

All afternoon they could hear the power saws working in the distant woods. Eli knew that his sons were not really in favor of the beautiful trees being removed so he tried to ignore the sounds coming from the west. After supper Eli suggested they all walk out in the meadow and watch the sunset. The children asked if they could take Sampson and the Cub. When they went to the barn to fetch them they noticed the barn door open and Sampson and Sambo were nowhere in sight. Jacob ran to tell Grandpa. Eli said not to worry; they were probably nearby and perhaps resting from all the activity of the day. With that they all headed out to the big oak tree. The sunset was spectacular as there were some clouds forming to the west. Before long it was time to head back to the cabin. Eli went directly to the barn to see if Sampson and Sambo had returned. They had not but Eli was not concerned. He left the barn door open and returned to the cabin to find most of the children asleep. Just as Eli got inside the cabin he saw a huge bolt of lightning in the sky to the east and then the thunder that followed was so loud that it awakened all that had gone to sleep. Those sleeping in the tent hurried into the cabin. They all watched the lightning and thunder storm for almost a half hour. About half way through the storm it started to rain very hard. The wind also started to blow very hard. The tent blew over and so everyone had to spend the night in a very crowded cabin. It took some time to arrange sleeping places on the floor for those who were sleeping in the tent. Those that did not go back to sleep watched the lightning through the windows and listened to the loud thunder that seemed to be so close. Fortunately it rained very hard during the entire storm and that prevented fires from starting. It was well past midnight when the last voices were heard. Before slipping into his bed Eli knelt down and thanked God that they were all safe.

The next morning Eli was awakened early by a loud knock on the door. He slipped quietly out of bed and opened the door to find his friend Bob standing there. Bob appeared to be in an almost state of shock and could hardly speak. He asked Eli to come outside and close the door. Bob walked a ways away from the cabin and then stopped near the door to the wood shed. Eli was puzzled by his somber and almost speechless mood. Finally Bob told Eli that one of his crew members had found Sambo dead at the base of a large tree not too far from their crew camp. It appeared that he had been killed by a bolt of lightning that had struck the tree. The grass was burned all around the base of the tree. Eli asked Bob how he could be sure it was Sambo. Could the dead cub possibly be a stray bear that happened to be in the wrong place at the right time? Bob assured Eli that it was Sambo because the logger that found him also saw Sampson walking away from the tree and into the nearby woods. Tears filled Eli's eyes and he thanked Bob for coming right away. Eli turned and walked away and Bob headed on back to his camp. Eli walked down to the barn to see if Sampson had returned. The door was open but there was no sign of Sampson. Eli went quietly into the cabin and woke Matt, Mike and Martin. He asked them to dress and come quietly outside. Fortunately none of the others awakened. When they got a good distance from the cabin Eli told them what had happened. They all decided to go immediately to where they would find Sambo. They met up with Bob and he showed them where the cub was lying. When they got to the tree the sight was almost unbearable. There stood Sampson at the side of her dead cub. She was nudging Sambo as if to say "come on little one, get up, let's go back to the barn where we belong, the storm is over." Of course Sambo was lifeless. Eli walked up to Sampson and started scratching her side. Sampson appeared to be pleased that Eli had come. He and the cub both had great affection for Eli and the cub had really started enjoying all of the children. Eli and his sons wondered how they would ever break this sad news to the children and the rest of the family.

Bob left Eli and his sons alone and returned to his camp. Eli and his sons stayed by Sampson and the dead cub for several minutes. No one spoke for a long time. Finally Matt spoke up and suggested that they return to the cabin and call all of the family together at which time he said that he would be willing to be the spokesman and break the sad news to the children. Eli and his other two sons agreed. Eli knew that he could not be the one to break the news. His eyes were red from the continual flow of tears. His hands were trembling and his whole body was shaking and he was so thankful that he had his three sons with him as they slowly returned to the cabin. Eli stopped his sons about half way to the cabin. He asked them if perhaps they should wait until everyone got back to their homes and then have each father break the news. His sons all said "No, Dad it is better that we be straightforward and honest with the children and tell them now." They discussed how it would be best to tell the children. Again Matthew said he would be willing to be the spokesman for the group. When they got inside the cabin everyone was up. Kim immediately asked Matt if there was something wrong. She then looked at Eli and noticed the tears in his eyes.

Matt asked everyone to sit down and then he told why Grandpa's friend Bob had knocked on the door. He continued to relay the entire tragic story of Sambo's death. The children started crying before Matt even finished the story. The parents and grandparents spent the next several minutes consoling the children. Several children spoke up and asked Grandpa if they could go and see Sambo. Eli said "No, that would not be a good idea." After everyone calmed down a little bit Kim and Ailene said they would fix some breakfast. The children all said they were not hungry now and they did not want breakfast at the present time. Perhaps a little later would be better. Eli asked his sons to go outside with him. When they got outside he suggested that they go over to where Sambo lay and dig a hole and burry the cub as soon as possible. His sons agreed. Eli did not want breakfast at that time either. They got shovels from the wood shed and walked over to the logger's camp. Bob said they would not be cutting down any trees today. He also offered to help dig the hole. Eli thanked Bob but said that would not be necessary. When Eli and his sons got to the place where Sambo lay they found Sampson still standing by her cub. She was still nudging Sambo to get up. The sight was more than Eli could handle. As he approached Sampson he again began to scratch her side. Sampson was happy to see Eli but refused to leave her cub. Tears again made it difficult for Eli to speak. He finally asked his sons if he could be excused from this most difficult task to which they immediately agreed. Eli left the area and spent some time alone in the nearby woods. Eli's sons spent about an hour digging a hole large enough to bury the cub in. With the task completed Matt, Mike and Martin returned to the cabin. They got there about the same time as their father. The mood in the cabin was very somber in deed. The children were still quite upset. They again asked if Grandpa would take them to the burial site. Grandpa said he would but not today.

After lunch Grandpa and the children went down to the barn to see if Sampson had returned. Sampson was not there. Eli assured the children that Sampson would return in the next couple of days. The children asked Grandpa if he would take them up to the spring in the afternoon to which he agreed. Kim, Ailene and Elaine prepared a nice lunch. Eli still was not very hungry but he knew he would need nourishment to make the hike up to the spring. The ladies decided to stay at the cabin and all the rest of the family went with Eli. Elly asked if they could take Old Pet to which Grandpa agreed. Matt put the harness on and Mike and Martin hooked Pet up to the small two wheeled cart. Eli took several jugs along to get fresh water from the spring. They took the road at the far end of the meadow so as to avoid going by the cave. The trip up the mountain was uneventful. They saw a herd of Roosevelt Elk way high up on the mountain above the spring. There were so many beautiful wild flowers and the huckleberries were just getting ripe. They picked several gallon cans full of the berries to take back to the cabin. Kim had volunteered to make some huckleberry jam if they bought enough back.

They got back to the cabin just before supper time. Eli and the children went down to the barn to see if Sampson was there. She was not. Eli decided now would be a good time to go to the site where Sambo was killed and see if Sampson was still there. He agreed to take the older children along. When they got to the tree and the burial site they found Sampson lying down under the tree. Eli took Kate, Jacob and Elly with him as he approached Sampson. Sampson was glad to see them and welcomed their scratching on his back side.

When they left to return to the cabin Sampson followed. They were all very happy about this turn of events. When they got to the barn the hounds and Delightful were very happy to see Sampson. The children asked if they could spend some time with Sampson in the barn to which Grandpa was about to say yes, when the dinner bell rang. Everyone was pretty hungry by now, even Eli. The supper was superb as usual. Elaine made a fresh huckleberry pie with some of the berries that had been picked on the trip to the spring. Mike said he would like everyone to join in an evening campfire at which time he wanted to talk with the children about forces in nature which sometimes do harm and take lives, even lives of animals. These forces cannot be controlled by humans.

Everyone helped gather wood for the campfire. Martin brought his guitar to the campfire and they all sang some campfire songs and then Mike gave the most wonderful explanation of things which occur in nature, such as lightning and thunder, hurricanes, tornados, etc. It was an excellent opportunity to teach a lesson about lightning and where and how it strikes. He taught the children an important concept about lightning and the importance of never standing under a tree in a lightning and thunder storm even though it is a natural thing to want to do to escape the rain.

Everyone was up bright and early the next morning. It was Saturday and the logging crew was supposed to be leaving today. Several loads of logs had been cut and taken to the mill in Colton. Eli was always glad to see Bob and his Crew come, but he was equally happy to see them leave.

Bob came to the door shortly after breakfast to say good-by and to again offer his condolence over the loss of their precious little cub bear. Eli told him that he would see him and pick up the check for the timber when he made his next trip to Colton in the fall.

After Bob left, Eli and his sons went to examine the forest where the trees had been taken. They were all very pleased with how neat the crew had left the entire area. All the limbs were neatly stacked and the tree tops were cut into stove length pieces and put in neat wood ricks. Eli really appreciated this and his sons agreed to help haul all of the wood to the woodshed. This would certainly lighten Eli's load of work to be done in the fall to get ready for winter. Eli and his sons got back to the cabin just in time to see the children all playing with Sampson in the field just east of the cabin. They also had the falcon out and placed on her tether. The hounds were having a great time chasing after the children. Life was once again good on Eli's Goat Mountain.

Everyone decided to sleep in a little on Sunday morning except Matt's son, Evan. When Matt got up he noticed that Evan was not in his sleeping bag. Not wanting to awaken the rest he quietly put on his shirt and pants and headed outside to see what Evan was up to. Matt saw the barn door slightly open. He walked quietly down to the barn and there Evan was playing with Sampson. The hounds were also nearby and Delightful was flying around inside the barn. Evan was happy to see his dad and asked if they could take the animals outside for some exercise? Matt said "sure, I'll lead the way." They placed the falcon on her tether and they all went to the field east of the cabin. They went far enough away from the cabin so as to not wake anyone with the noise they might make. Evan loved all of Grandpa's pets and he knew the time at Goat Mountain was drawing short so he wanted to take advantage of every opportunity to spend time with the animals.

They had only been in the meadow for a short while when the hounds started howling and made a beeline for the forest. Evan started after them but his father called him back. Matt sensed danger in the forest. He quickly went to the cabin and awakened Eli. He tried not to disturb the rest of the family but that was nearly impossible. Mike and Martin both woke up and asked what was going on. Matt told them that the hounds had made a beeline for the forest, yelping all the way. When they all got outside they headed straight for the forest. They had not gone very far when they saw the most touching site. The hounds were actually playing with a small creature that looked like the Big Foot. As soon as the small creature saw the people he ran as fast as he could into the woods. Eli called the hounds to him and they headed back to the cabin. Eli started putting two and two together and soon realized what had taken place over the last several months. The other creature he had seen with Big Foot was evidently a female and now there were three. When they got back to the cabin there were a lot of questions being asked and Eli was fortunate to be able to explain to all what had taken place. The children were so excited and asked Eli if he would take them into the woods to see the little Big Foot. Eli quickly said "No" with no explanation. Needless to the say the children were very disappointed. Eli had another concern in the back of his mind. He wondered how many more there might be in the future. He also wondered if there were other big creatures like these in other mountainous regions of the Pacific Northwest?

It was finally time for lunch and the ladies had prepared a picnic type lunch to eat outside. The children had gotten so excited with the events of the morning that they had not even gone inside the cabin to eat breakfast so they were really hungry.

After lunch the children asked grandpa if he would take them up to the spring high on Goat Mountain. They also asked if they could take the hounds, Sampson, and the falcon? Eli thought that was a good idea. This time Matt, Mike and Martin said they would not go but instead would start hauling in the wood that the loggers had prepared for their dad. When they went to the barn to collect the animals they discovered Sampson was nowhere in sight. The barn door had been left open. Grandpa Eli suggested they go without Sampson. Eli put the falcon on her tether and took the leashes for the hounds but did not put them on yet. The only time Eli thought they might need the leashes was when they passed near the cave. Eli did not fear the big creatures attacking the dogs any longer but he just did not want to have them go off into the cave.

Matt got the old flat bed running and they headed for the forest to collect the wood that had been prepared by the loggers. When they got near the spot where the little cub had been buried they saw Sampson setting down right next to the grave. The sight made tears come to the eyes of all three sons. They drove slowly by so as to not disturb Sampson. They loaded as much wood on Big Red as possible and then drove slowly back towards the cabin and the wood shed. When they got near the grave site they noticed that Sampson was gone. When they got back to the barn area they noticed the barn door still open but Sampson was not inside. They unloaded the wood and then went back for another load. When they returned the second time they saw Sampson way out in the meadow east of the cabin. Sampson was not a lone, she had a companion with her. They suspected it was the same bear that had fathered Sambo. Perhaps there would be another cub to replace Sambo next spring.

The trip up to the carbonated spring went very well. They passed the cave without an incident. In fact there was no sign of the big creatures at the cave or near the spring. Several of the children expressed concern in not seeing any foot prints near the spring. They no longer had the great fear of the two legged creatures they once had. In fact they now had more concern for their safety and keeping them away from the public. They knew if word got out that there were human like creatures in these foothills of the Cascades, Goat Mountain would no longer be a good place for their grandfather to live and it would end their visits to this beautiful and peaceful area. This would truly be a very sad turn of events in their lives. These grandchildren looked forward to their visits to Grandpa Eli and his Goat Mountain. The life style here was so vastly different from life in Bend and Houston.

After collecting several jugs of spring water it was time to head back down the mountain. Grandpa decided to take the long way back to the cabin. This route took them to the far eastern end of the meadow to the east of the cabin. As they started out across the meadow towards the cabin they saw Sampson. To their surprise she was not alone. There was another large male bear with her. Eli told them he thought it was the father to Sambo. When Sampson saw Eli and the children she started towards them. The big male bear did not follow but headed into the woods nearby. Eli and the children greeted Sampson by scratching the fur on her side. Sampson loved their attention. She followed them back to the cabin.

By the time they got to the cabin it was supper time and they were all very hungry. The children asked Grandpa Eli if they could have one last bonfire tonight to which he quickly agreed. After supper they all went down near the pond and gathered old limbs and other brush for the fire. Afterwards the children returned to the cabin and tent to put on their pajamas. Mike brought out his guitar so they could sing some campfire songs he had learned when he was a counselor at outdoor school when he attended Molalla High School many years ago. The night air was warm as it usually was this time of the year. The stars shone brightly in the night sky and everyone enjoyed looking at The Big Dipper and some of the planets. Jupiter was the brightest planet visible in the eastern sky. Grandpa Eli asked each of his grandchildren to tell what they liked best about their summer visit to Goat Mountain. They all expressed their love and appreciation to their grandfather and they all expressed their joy about the time they got to spend with each other and all the animals. Each one expressed the sorrow he or she felt over the tragic and untimely death of little Sambo.

They all heard a little noise in the woods on the other side of the pond. By this time it was getting pretty dark as there was no moon but they could just make out the two big creatures walking away and heading up towards the cave. The children were no longer frightened, instead they shed some tears and mumbled words of good-by to the two creatures. Grandpa asked if they all would like to join in a fireside evening prayer. He asked his oldest son, Matt to offer the prayer. After the children were escorted to bed and good nights were said the adults sat around the camp fire for a little while and talked about what a wonderful vacation this had been. They all agreed to return next summer if it were at all possible. This made Eli very happy.

Monday morning everyone got up early as there was much packing to do. All of Eli's families planned to head down the mountain by noon. The children were complaining about having to leave. They all would have loved to spend the rest of the summer with their Grandpa. Grandpa agreed to make breakfast so that everyone else could help with the packing. He made huckleberry pancakes with fresh huckleberries they had picked on the last trip to the spring.

The children asked if they could spend some time with all of the animals after breakfast to which Eli agreed. It seemed as though the animals sensed they would be leaving soon. Sampson wanted continual attention. He loved the children and he loved to have them scratch his sides. The hounds had taken a special liking to Evan, Jacob, and Benjamin. Delightful seemed to favor all of the girls. The milk cow and Old Pet liked the attention they got from everyone, children and adults. The entire group thought they probably had their last look at the big creatures last night. Most even doubted they would still be around by this time next year. Even though they were no longer afraid of the big creatures they had still not developed any special bond with them.

It was now time to prepare for departure. The vehicles were all packed and each family had their own special last moments with Grandpa. With good-bys completed everyone loaded into their respective vehicles and started the trek down the mountain. Grandpa continued to wave good-by until they were all out of sight. Eli moped around the rest of the afternoon. He was very sad to see everyone leave. He felt so alone.

He finally walked down to the barn and took all of the animals outside to spend the rest of the day. Eli walked with the animals far into the meadow east of the cabin. He kept his falcon on her tether until he reached the far end of the valley. He kept the hounds on their leashes as long as he could. He was glad he did so. As soon as they got to the end of the meadow Sampson bounded off into the woods. Eli looked in the direction Sampson was going and quickly saw the reason for the quick departure. Eli got a glimpse of the large male bear they had seen earlier. Eli was not concerned as he understood nature and what was happening with Sampson. After spending an hour or so with his pets, it was time to return to the cabin.

Eli didn't feel much like eating supper. He walked out to the barn to check on Old Pet and the Milk Cow. He made sure the door to the barn was left open so Sampson could return at a later time if she wanted to. El thought about the wonderful times he had had with his family over the past several weeks. These memories would stay with Eli over the winter months. The evening was beautiful and Eli decided to sit outside for a while. The full moon came up over the Cascade Mountains to the East. The night air was a little crisp for late June. After a long day it was finally time to turn in and hopefully get a good night's sleep.

Eli slept in until almost 7:00 am. The sun was shining in the east window and providing warmth to the cabin. Eli decided to start a small fire in the wood cook stove and heat some water. The aroma from the smoke from the fire was so refreshing. After washing his hands and face Eli decided to make a small bowl of hot cereal. His family had left so much food and Eli wondered if he would ever be able to eat all of it. After breakfast and clean up Eli went outside to check on the animals. When he got down to the barn he discovered that Sampson had not returned last night. He was not at all concerned as he knew what she was up to.

EIGHTEEN

Eli Is Alone Once Again

Eli spent the next several days cutting hay in the east meadow. He used Old Pet to pull the horse drawn mower and rake. The days were warm and dry and so it was easy to dry the hay. Eli left the hay in winrows for two or three days. When it was ready he hooked Old Pet up to the hay wagon and spent the next several weeks gathering the hay and bringing it to the barn. Finally the barn was full and there would be plenty of good quality meadow hay for Old Pet and the Milk Cow for the winter months when the snow was too deep to get outside. Life would continue to be good for Eli's animals on Goat Mountain throughout the fall and winter months.

Eli awoke early on the 1st day of August to unusual sounds just outside the front window. When he looked outside he saw Sampson and the big male bear romping and rough housing nearby. Eli decided he would not go outside and interfere yet. Instead he started a fire in the wood cook stove and made a light breakfast. After cleaning up he decided it was time to go out to the barn and feed the hounds and Delightful. When he went inside the barn he discovered that Sampson was there but he saw no sign of the big male bear. Next, he went to the horse and cow barn and took Old Pet and Milk Cow out to the pasture east of the cabin. This is the first time they had been allowed in the pasture for some time and they appeared to be very happy. Eli realized that it had been over a month since he had seen any sign of the big hairy creatures. It had also been a little over a month since his family left to return to their homes. Once again he realized how much he missed his family and how much they meant to him.

Eli spent most of August making small repairs on fences, the wood shed, the cow barn and the barn where most of his pets lived. The black berries were getting ripe and Eli spent several days picking berries and making jam. It was also time to collect the edible roots and put them in the cellar for winter. Eli also made several trips to the carbonated spring and collected several jugs of water to be stored for winter, in case the snow was too deep to get up to the spring. He never once saw the big fellows by the cave. He wondered if having all of his family there for so long might have driven them to higher ground.

Eli also spent time working on Big Red and getting it ready for his annual fall trip to Colton. He needed to purchase supplies that he was running low on or out of completely. He always enjoyed getting the old truck ready to go. He looked forward to this trip every year. He looked forward to visiting with his old friends and especially visiting with his good friend Bob and his family. He would also be paid for the timber that was removed so that he would have money for the next year. Eli wonder if Bob and Darlene would invite him to attend church with them this year, he hoped so.

The days were already getting shorter and the nights were getting cooler. High up on Goat Mountain some of the leaves were already starting to lose their bright green color. Eli loved this time of the year.

On the 29th day of August Eli rounded all of his smaller pets up and decided to take a test drive in Big Red up to the spring. The road was pretty steep but Eli had driven to the spring several times over the last 20 years. As he approached the Cave he saw shadows of both of the big fellows and the little Big Foot on the cave wall that the sun shone on. He was very pleased to know that they had not left the area for good. It had been nearly two months since he had seen any sign of them. He drove slowly by and kept the hounds and Delightful in the cab. Sampson did not make this trip as she was not in the barn when they left. Eli supposed that she was off courting with her male friend. When they got to the spring Eli saw many tracks the big guys had made. There were so many tracks Eli wondered if they were not made by more than two creatures; however he only saw three shadows when he drove past the cave. Eli had trained the hounds to stay away from the cave and so he felt comfortable in turning them loose while he collected several jugs of water. He also released his falcon from her tether and she quickly flew high in the sky. She was only gone a few minutes when Eli saw her dive for a rodent in the meadow above the spring. Delightful returned quickly to Eli with her catch. It was a large jack rabbit. The rabbit was still alive and Eli quickly turned it loose and it scampered off into the woods, very happy to be free again. Eli had trained his falcon to be careful with whatever she caught and his falcon was perfectly happy to have the catch go free. She just loved the sport of catching the animal.

The next flight did not turn out so well. Delightful dove down on another rodent but this was not a scared little rabbit but instead a mad and ferocious badger. The badger was heavy and Delightful immediately realized far too mean to deal with. The falcon let go quickly and the badger turned on her in an instant. Fortunately for Delightful she was able to get airborne before the badger could grab her with its teeth and claws. Eli saw the entire incident looking through his binoculars. He quickly whistled for his falcon and placed her back on her tether. He called for Big Daniel and Little Anne and they came running. Eli had all of the jugs filled with the delicious carbonated spring water and it was now time to head down the mountain. Eli had noticed a large elderberry tree on the way up and decided to stop and pick some more elderberries to make elderberry syrup. The berries were very ripe and easy to pick from the tree. Eli picked enough to fill the large sack. He loved elderberry jam and syrup. He also planned to take several pint jars of the jam to the Berge's and other friends on his trip to Colton.

When Eli got back to the cabin he decided to check the barn to see if Sampson was back. He had intentionally left the barn door open. When he approached the door he could hear quite a commotion inside. He approached the open door slowly and got a big surprise. The big male bear and Sampson were scuffling and just having fun. As Eli started to go inside both hounds bolted from the truck and raced toward the barn. Eli tried to stop them but to no avail. Daniel and Anne raced inside and immediately began to challenge the big male bear. Sampson didn't know how to react. She knew that Daniel and Anne were no match for the male bear, but she was also afraid to interfere. Eli called to the hounds continually but there was no stopping them. When the big bear moved towards Anne, Daniel moved in behind and nipped at the bears hind legs. The big bear quickly turned on Daniel and took a swipe at him. The force of his rapid moving paw knocked Daniel about 15 feet towards the door. With that Daniel realized that he was no match for the big bear and bolted for the door with Anne right behind him. Sampson quickly sensed the danger the hounds were in and she turned on the male bear and let him know that he was to leave the dogs alone. Eli quickly closed the door and decided it would be best to return to his cabin and keep the hounds inside until he could return to the barn and open the door so the big bear could leave.

It was well past lunch time so Eli decided to have something to eat and feed the hounds and his falcon from the leftovers. After cleaning up Eli decided it would be an excellent time to take a well deserved nap. The hounds and Delightful sensed the quiet in the cabin and soon all fell asleep. Eli awakened in about an hour and decided to go to the barn and carefully open the door. To his surprise the barn door was off its hinges and lying on the ground. Eli peeked inside and noticed that the big male bear was gone and Sampson was lying down and appeared to be sleeping. Eli called to Sampson and she rolled over and looked at Eli. Eli approached her slowly and started scratching her side. Sampson responded by rolling over onto her other side so Eli could scratch it also.

It was a beautiful fall evening and Eli decided to take the hounds, Delightful, the Milk Cow and Old Pet for a walk in the East Meadow. He freed his falcon from her tether but he kept the hounds on their leashes. Old Pet and the Milk Cow followed along as usual. When they got to the east end of the meadow they all got a surprise. As Eli looked far up on the hillside he saw the big male bear in the middle of a blackberry bush eating blackberries. The old fellow looked at the group and just kept eating. He had learned his lesson not to bother or attack any of Sampson's friends. After spending about an hour in the meadow it was now time to return to the cabin. Eli was very happy to be able to spend this beautiful fall evening with his animals. Eli felt very blessed to have a wonderful family and to have these beautiful animals in his life. Yes, life was good on Eli's Goat Mountain.

Eli was awakened about 2:00 am in the morning with terrible noises coming from the barn where the hounds, Sampson and Delightful stayed. The noise was not coming from the hounds or his falcon but from Sampson. The screams were defining to Eli's ears. He arose immediately, put on a heavy coat, grabbed his rifle and headed slowly towards the barn. There was a full moon so he did not need any additional light.

As Eli approached the barn, the door flung open and out came the big male bear with Sampson right behind him. The male bear was bleeding from several lacerations on his neck and sides. He headed towards the woods as fast as he could go, completely ignoring Eli. Sampson started to follow him but upon seeing Eli she stopped and returned to the barn. Eli continued into the barn and slowly approached Sampson. As Eli got near Sampson he saw several cuts on her right side. They were not bleeding very much and as Eli examined them he noticed that they were not very deep. He scratched Sampson on the side of his neck, checked the hounds over to see if they were ok, and then closed the barn door tightly and returned to the cabin. He surmised what had happened was that the male bear had started after the hounds and Sampson had intervened. When he returned to his cabin, sleep had left him, and it took more than an hour to get back to sleep.

Small creek leading away from pond

NINETEEN

The Coon Hunt

On the first day of September Eli awoke to the sound of an engine. He got up quickly, got dressed and went outside to see if anyone was approaching. He quickly realized that the noise from the engine was getting louder but he still could see nothing coming through the forest. In a few more minutes he finally saw a pickup coming out of the forest. He recognized the pickup as belonging to Robert's dad, Mike Smith. As the vehicle approached the cabin the door on the passenger side flew open and out jumped Robert. He ran to Eli and of course was greeted with a huge hug. It was then that Eli remembered that Robert's father had promised him that he could spend a week with Eli on Goat Mountain. He also remembered that the hunters who came late last fall, had brought him a message saying that Robert would not be able to come in the summer. He had a baseball camp to attend in June. Eli was thrilled to have him stay. Mike turned the pickup off and helped Robert bring his grocery bag with his clothes in it into the cabin. Eli fixed breakfast of fresh eggs that he had gathered yesterday, bacon left by his family, and cold carbonated kool-aid from the spring. Mr. Smith spent most of the morning visiting with Eli and then left a little before noon to return to his home in Colton.

Robert asked Eli if they could make a trip to the spring after lunch, to which he quickly agreed. Eli decided that he would harness Old Pet and hook her to the two wheeled cart. He put Delightful on her tether and put both hounds on leashes. He then gathered several clean jugs to bring back fresh carbonated water. He decided that he would not go by the cave so they took the long route to the spring. This took them to the far end of the meadow east of the cabin and then up the mountain to the spring. The thimbleberries were ripe and delicious to eat, so the trip took twice as long. As they moved up the mountain they came to Eli's favorite old apple tree. Eli was not surprised to see Sampson under the tree getting his fill of ripe red apples. Robert was frightened until Eli assured him that Sampson lived in the barn with the other animals and was a wonderful pet to his family. Eli took Robert with him and approached Sampson. Sampson was happy to see Eli as usual and quickly made friends with Robert. Eli invited Robert to scratch Sampson's side. After spending about fifteen or twenty minutes with Sampson it was time to move on towards the spring.

When they got to the carbonated spring Robert quickly got a drink of the ice cold water. He then asked Eli if he could release Delightful. He said "sure, he would love to show off, besides we need a rabbit or squirrel for our supper tonight." It was not long before they watched the falcon make a dive. In his talons was the meat for their supper. After spending a couple of hours at the spring it was time to head back down the mountain to the cabin. Again, Eli avoided going by the cave. He took the long route home by the far east end of the meadow which was directly east of the cabin.

The nights were getting chilly and Eli asked Robert if he would like to go on a coon hunt the next night?. Robert was thrilled and excited. They spent the day doing chores around the cabin and putting a little more wood in the shed in preparing for winter. Robert was a great help and he really enjoyed doing things with Eli.

It was finally time to fetch the hounds, put oil in the lantern and prepare supplies for their backpacks. There was a full moon, which made the conditions perfect for the coon hunt. This was to be the first hunt of the fall. It was difficult to control the hounds, they were ready and anxious to get going. They headed for the creek which came out of the pond down by the barn. They had only gone a short distance when big Daniel opened up with the most beautiful sound any coon hunter could hope to hear. Shortly thereafter Anne joined in. Eli and Robert picked up the pace and before long they reached the small cedar tree that held a small baby coon which the hounds had treed. Eli complimented the hounds, gave them a treat and then told them it was time to look for another coon. Again, one of the most difficult things Eli had to teach the hounds was to leave a coon in the tree and move on.

After the hounds treed two more coons Eli told Robert it was getting late and he was getting very tired and they needed to head back to the cabin.

When they got back to the cabin they had a snack which consisted of a peanut butter and jam sandwich and a glass of wonderful carbonated Kool-Aid. Robert thanked Eli for the wonderful day and especially the coon hunt. Eli just patted him on the head and said goodnight.

The next three days were spent taking short hikes with the animals, repairing a few weak spots in the pasture fence, and picking a few of the blackberries that ripened in the early fall.

Mr. Ringtail

TWENTY

Eli's Annual Fall Trip To Colton

On the sixth day of September Eli decided it was time to make his annual fall trip to Colton and the civilization below. He got up early and had breakfast and fed all of the animals. He turned the cow and Old Pet out into the pasture near the pond. There was plenty of grass there and of course fresh water to drink. Earlier he had made a fenced path way to the cow barn so the animals could get inside the barn if they so desired. He put the hounds in there make shift dog house on the back of the truck. He also had prepared a small cage for his falcon and placed it on the front seat of the truck. By noon he and Robert were ready to start down the long and sometimes rough road leading to Colton. It would take most of the afternoon to make the trip. His first stop was only a short distance from the cabin. He stopped and looked at the site where the little cub was buried. Again tears flowed from Eli's eyes as he reflected on those sad events.

Eli and Robert arrived at Bob and Darlene's home about 5:00 pm. They were happy to see Eli and their grandson. Bob's wife, Darlene, made a wonderful home cooked meal of roast beef, mashed potatoes and meat gravy and a homemade pumpkin pie. As soon as dinner was over Eli and Bob took Robert to his home. Robert's parents were very glad to see him. When they returned to Bob's place Darlene had the pumpkin pie ready to serve. Bob insisted Eli spend the night to which he gladly accepted the invitation. They spent the evening talking about everything that had happened on Eli's Goat Mountain since the logging crew left in June. Eli took his hounds from their safe place on the back of Big Red and placed them in Bob's small tool shed. Eli put Delightful in her cage in the same small shed. This had been a very long day and Eli was ready for a good night's rest.

Darlene fixed a wonderful breakfast of poached eggs, hash brown potatoes, homemade fried bread and fresh squeezed orange juice. After breakfast Bob and Eli sat around the table and went over the receipts from the sale of the timber. Afterwards Bob gave Eli a check for most of the money he owed Eli and he also gave him a considerable amount in cash as Eli needed cash to buy supplies. He signed the check and asked Bob to deposit the money in his banking account when he went to Molalla next week.

Eli thanked Bob and his wife for their wonderful hospitality. Bob helped Eli bring his hounds and Delightful to the truck. He told Eli that he would check on him when he came to Goat Mountain for the hunting season in late October.

Eli stopped at the Colton Post Office to pick up his mail. He was so excited to receive letters from all of his sons and daughter-in-laws and there were also letters from each group of grandchildren. He was pleased to learn that all were well and the grandchildren were doing well in school. Ailene mentioned in her letter that her mother, Elaine, had discovered that she had a first cousin living near Colton. This was a cousin she had not seen since her teenage years. She had lost contact with her when her parents divorced and her cousin stayed with her mom. Her father was Elaine's dad's brother but they were not close at all. Elaine had asked Ailene to ask Eli if he would mind looking her up. Eli was very happy to do this. He decided he would ask his friend, Tom Martin, if he knew a Jennifer Murray.

Eli's next stop was at the Colton General Store. Mr. Martin, who operated and owned the store, was very glad to see Eli. Eli asked if he planned on coming to Goat Mountain this fall for hunting season. Tom told him that he hoped to be able to. He told Eli that if things worked out he hoped to be able to bring his son Tom Jr. along. Purchasing those items on Eli's list took well over an hour. After he had made all of his purchases he asked Mr. Martin if he knew a Jennifer Murray. Tom said "of course I know her, she is my next door neighbor". He also told Eli that she had lost her husband in the Vietnam War. Tom Martin said that Jennifer had moved to the area about five years ago. He said that he would be happy to introduce Eli to her before he left to return to

Goat Mountain. Eli said he would like that and that he would come to his home before he left town. After loading everything onto the back of the truck, Eli decided to stop at the little Colton Café and have lunch. This was the only time during the year that Eli ate in a café. Eli even ordered a special treat for his hounds and his falcon.

After lunch he called on several old friends that he had known for years. He was pleased to learn that all of his old friends were well. Eli had purchased a writing tablet and some envelopes so he walked over to the small city park and wrote short letters to each family. He told Ailene that he had made arrangement to meet her mother's first cousin before he left to return to Goat Mountain. He returned to the Post Office and mailed the letters. It was evening time when he finished so he drove on over to Mr. Martin's home. Tom greeted Eli at the door and invited him in for dinner. He also invited Eli to spend the night, to which Eli agreed, as it was getting much too late to return to Goat Mountain, he would instead leave right after breakfast in the morning. Tom told Eli that he had stopped at Jennifer's home and told her that he would be bringing someone over tonight to meet her.

After dinner Eli and Tom walked next door to Jennifer's house. Jennifer was very pleased to meet Eli. They talked about the recent reconnection of Jennifer to her cousin Elaine. Jennifer was so sorry they had not made the connection prior to Elaine's visit the past summer to Goat Mountain. She wanted to know more about Elaine and her visit to the area. Jennifer also wanted to know more about Goat Mountain. She had heard the locals mention Goat Mountain but she had never ventured very far in that direction.

Eli offered his sympathy to Jennifer over the death of her husband in the war. Tom mentioned that he planned to visit Eli next spring and that he would be happy to take Jennifer along. She said she would like that very much. With that, good nights were said and Eli and Tom returned next door. It was getting late and Eli wanted to get a good night's rest so he could get up early and make final preparation for his trip home. He still had a few things to pick up at the feed and hardware store.

Mrs. Martin fixed a wonderful breakfast as usual. Eli loaded his dogs onto the back of the old truck and placed Delightful in her small cage inside the cab. He thanked the Martins and headed for the hardware and feed store. He picked up several 100 lb bags of grain for Old Pet and his cow. He also picked up several bags of cracked corn for his falcon and a good supply of dog food for the hounds. Big Red was pretty well loaded. Eli's last stop was the gas station. He asked the attendant to fill the tank and he also had him fill four 5 gallon cans with gasoline. It was almost 10:00 am by the time he got out of Colton. The sun was shining and the air felt warm as Eli started the climb towards his peaceful home high in the Cascades of Western Oregon. He had had a wonderful visit with his friends but he was anxious to get home. He hoped he would find everything in order. He had no idea of the tragic happening he would discover when he got home.

TWENTY ONE

Tragedy Strikes Goat Mountain Again

Eli arrived at his cabin about 1:00 pm. The hounds and his falcon were very glad to be home. Eli turned the hounds loose and released Delightful from her tether. The hounds ran around the cabin and then headed for the barn. Delightful flew high in the sky out over the East Meadow. Eli saw Old Pet in the pasture near the pond and he wondered where the cow was. He went to the barn to see if the cow was in her stall. When he opened the door he saw his cow sprawled over the floor. She was ripped into several large pieces of meat. There was blood all over the place. Eli was terrified and shocked. He saw mountain lion hair all over the place. The smell was terrible. The sight was unbelievable. Eli was mad. He determined right there and then that he would track the lion down and kill him for what had happened while he was gone. This was a great loss to Eli. Milk and the products Eli got from the milk were a very important part of his diet. He spent the remainder of the afternoon cleaning up the mess in the barn. He decided that he would use some of the meat as a trap for the mountain lion. He hung the meat from a tree between the cabin and the barn.

Eli decided that he would stay up late and watch for the lion. He returned to the barn to check on Sampson. As usual Sampson was very happy to see Eli.

After supper, he unloaded the truck and parked it in the barn. This had been a very long day and he was very tired but he was so upset that he could not sleep. He locked the hounds in the barn and brought his falcon in. He placed his rifle near the door and positioned himself near the window. There was a full moon and so it was very easy to see the meat hanging from the tree. He could only stay awake until about 10:00 pm and then sleep finally overtook him.

At about 2:30 am Eli was awakened by a noise outside. He got up quickly and went to the window. Sure enough the Mountain Lion was pulling meat down but not eating it. Eli quickly retrieved his rifle, opened the window and fired a round. His aim was deadly. Eli opened his cabin door, and with his rifle in hand, he approached the lion. He kept his rifle at ready just in case the lion should make a move. Upon closer examination he was able to determine that the lion was in fact dead. Eli was not happy about this killing but he knew it had to be done. He knew that once the mountain lion had made this kill he would be back to make other kills. Eli had really hoped he and the Mountain Lion could both live on Goat Mountain in peace.

It took Eli a long time to get back to sleep. It was starting to get light outside when he finally dozed off. Eli did not feel like eating breakfast when he awakened. He decided to get dressed and check on the hounds, Delightful and Sampson. He knew he now had the task of burying the remains of the mountain lion. He put the harness on Old Pet and loaded the dead lion on a small cart and hauled it to the far end of the east meadow. He dug a pit and placed the remains in the pit and covered it with the fresh, soft dirt. By the time he returned to the cabin it was almost noon. He decided to force himself to eat lunch. He spent the afternoon resting and thinking about what he should do about the loss of his cow. He wondered if he shouldn't return to Colton and try to purchase another cow. He decided not to make a decision right away, but he knew he could not put it off for very long as the weather could turn bad and make the roads impassable for the old truck.

Eli was awakened the next morning by a knock on his cabin door. He was surprised to see Jim, a member of his friend Bob's logging crew, at the door. He greeted him warmly and invited him in. Jim gladly accepted but stated that he could not stay long as he and Bob's crew were removing some logs from a place only about 2 miles from Eli's place. He wanted to stop by a see if it would be ok if he left some things for their hunting camp. Eli told him that would be fine. Eli then told Jim about his milk cow being killed by a mountain lion while he was down to Colton. Jim expressed his deep sorrow and asked if there was anything he could do. Eli expressed his thanks but said that he would have to deal with the situation at a later date. With that Jim said he would see Eli soon and bid him good-by.

Eli spent the rest of the day bringing wood from the wood shed to the front porch. He always kept a two week supply of wood on the front porch in the winter time in case of deep snows or bad weather. He also decided that he would take Old Pet up to the carbonated spring and collect several jugs of fresh water. He decided to take the hounds and his falcon along. The sun was shining when they passed the cave and to Eli's delight he saw the shadows of the big fellows on the west wall of the cave entrance. He stopped Old Pet and kept the hounds on their leashes. Before long one of the big creatures came outside the cave entrance. He looked at Eli and Eli looked at him for several minutes. The hounds just whimpered a little and wanted to be turned loose. Eli sensed this but had no intention of granting their desires. After a few minutes Eli decided he needed to continue on to the carbonated spring, collect the water and get back to the cabin. The days were getting much shorter and he had several more things to get completed at the cabin. When Eli got to the spring he was surprised again to find the remains of a young doe about 50 yards away. Again he saw mountain lion tracks all about. He wondered if there had been any encounters between the big hairy creatures and the mountain lions in the area.

The trip back to the cabin was uneventful. Eli spent the rest of the afternoon storing the carbonated spring water in the root cellar, collecting more edible roots from nearby, and preparing his evening meal. He took care of his animals and then decided to read by the lamp light for a while before going to bed. He was still trying to decide what to do about the loss of his cow. Not only was Eli concerned about not having milk to drink but he used milk in preparing many of the foods that he loved.

Eli spent the rest of September continuing to get things ready for the long winter that lay ahead. The weather had turned very rainy and Eli decided that he would not attempt to get another milk cow this fall. Somehow he would make it through the winter without fresh milk. He did have a fairly good supply of powdered milk ant that would have to do.

Eli got up early and prepared breakfast after feeding the animals. He no sooner finished cleaning when he heard the sound of vehicles approaching. He surmised that it was probably Bob and his crew or Tom Martin, as Black Tailed Buck Deer season opened the next day. Eli got the surprise of his life. He saw his friend Bob pulling a trailer. Jim was with him. In the trailer was a cow. Eli could not believe what he was seeing. Bob greeted him and told him Jim had told him what happened to his cow and wondered if he would like a replacement. Eli could hardly hold the tears back. They unloaded the cow and placed her in the small pasture next to the cow barn. Old Pet came to the opened window to see what the commotion was. He seemed pleased. Eli could hardly contain his emotions. He was so happy and thankful for wonderful friends like Bob, his family and Jim. Eli offered to pay for the cow but Bob would not hear of it.

Bob and Jim told Eli they would check on him before returning to Colton after the hunt. Eli asked them to plan on having lunch to which they both agreed. Eli spent the rest of the day doing little chores and walking the cow to the various pastures. The cow seemed to adjust to her new environment quickly. Life was good once again on Eli's Goat Mountain.

In the early afternoon of October the seventh Tom Martin stopped by to give Eli a portion of the nice buck he had killed. Eli was surprised to see Robert with him. Tom said that his son was not able to make it so he brought Robert instead. Eli was please to see them and to know they were successful in their hunt. He thanked Tom and told him he would see him when he returned with Jennifer in the spring. Eli spent the rest of the day canning the meat to preserve it. He was pleased to be able to fill several quart jars. This would give him much of the protein he so badly needed, especially in the winter time.

The next morning Bob and Jim stopped by to give Eli some more meat and see how the cow was doing. They were pleased to see how contented the cow seemed to be. They spent the rest of the morning helping Eli with some chores that required a helping hand. Eli then fixed a wonderful lunch of carbonated Kool-Aid, boiled potatoes, fresh fried rabbit Delightful had caught just two days ago, and watercress taken from the nearby stream. Just as Bob and Jim were preparing to leave Bob happened to mention that they had seen some very unusual tracks near the small spring by their hunting camp. Eli suggested they were perhaps Sampson's tracks that had been messed up by the hard rain they had had a few weeks ago. The answer seemed to satisfy Bob and Eli changed the subject quickly. Shortly thereafter Bob and Jim said their good-bys. Eli thanked them again for their kindness and the wonderful gift of the milk cow. After they were out of sight and a good distance from Eli's property he decided to go to their camp site and examine the tracks. Sure enough they were tracks made by the big hairy two legged creatures that he shared his Goat Mountain with. Now he hoped more than every that Bob and Jim bought into his explanation of what made the tracks. He was thankful that they were pretty messed up and not easy at all for the average person to identify. Eli now worried more than ever that future hunters would continue to see these unusual tracks and ask questions. His greatest fear was that one of the hunters would spot one of these creatures. He knew if that happened his Goat Mountain would never be the same. It would be impossible to keep their presence on Goat Mountain a secret. He hoped and prayed that the big fellows would stay in the cave during the hunting seasons. This fear was on his mind most of the time now.

Eli had done one very smart thing many years ago with the hunters. He did not allow any hunting in any part of the meadow between the cabin and the carbonated spring. This also included the entire area around the cave. He also did not allow hunting in any of the area east of the cabin. This still left several hundred acres to the west of the cabin which was heavily treed. Eli hoped the big creatures would stay near the cave when they started hearing gun shots. Since he had first encountered the two legged creatures he always went to the area near the cave just before any hunting season and fired off several rounds. In the past this seemed to keep the big fellows close to or in the cave for several weeks. He hoped this would continue to work for him and for their safety.

Eli woke up to discover a deep silence outside. He looked out the window and discovered three or four inches of fresh snow. The trees were covered with a beautiful white blanket. Everything was white and beautiful. Eli started the fire in the kitchen stove and fireplace and before long the cabin was toasty warm. Eli got dressed and went to feed all the animals. The hounds and his falcon wanted to go outside. Sampson was not as anxious to leave the warmth of her place in the barn. Eli took the hounds and Delightful over to the horse barn and fed Old Pet and the new cow. He left the barn door open so Old Pet and the cow could go out into the east pasture and get some exercise. He then returned to the cabin and fed the hounds and Delightful on the porch. He prepared a quick breakfast of hot oat meal and ice cold milk. Eli loved oat meal as did the rest of his family.

After breakfast Eli took the hounds and his falcon far out into the east meadow in search of some more edible roots that he could only find in the forest near the far end of the meadow. In spite of the fresh snow he was able to dig up a small pail of wonderful roots that he would keep in his root cellar. Before heading back to the cabin Eli decided to release Delightful from her tether and also to turn the hounds loose so they could run for awhile. The animals loved this freedom. After about an hour they were all ready to return to the cabin.

Eli spent part of the afternoon writing letters to his family so that he could give them to the Elk hunters when they came at the end of the month. Eli hoped they would also be bringing mail.

TWENTY TWO

Winter Arrives On Eli's Mountain

It snowed almost every day for the rest of October. With the deep snow it became more difficult for Eli to spend much time outside. He did keep a path open to both barns. He had plenty of good food and carbonated water from the spring. He also had meat and wonderful fresh milk. He had a wood shed full of good dry wood and both the front and back porch were almost full of wood. Eli felt so blessed to be so well prepared for winter months. He kept fairly busy just doing little things around the cabin and the barns. He took the hounds and his falcon out every day so they could get plenty of exercise. Sampson was now hibernating in her log in the barn. Old Pet now had his winter coat and the milk cow seemed to be loving life on Goat Mountain. Life was truly good on Goat Mountain.

On the last morning of October Eli was awakened by a loud knock on his cabin door. He got out of bed quickly and put his robe on and opened the door. He was so happy to see Bob and Jim. He invited them in and insisted they stay for breakfast. The first thing they gave him was letters from all of his sons and their families. This amounted to more than a dozen letters. Eli was so happy and could hardly wait to read each of the letters but that would have to wait until Bob and Jim left. He prepared a wonderful breakfast of pancakes with maple syrup he had collected from the sugar maples he had planted many years ago. Sugar maples were not native to this part of the country but Eli's father had planted more than a dozen of these trees that he had shipped from Vermont when he first moved to Goat Mountain. Bob and Jim thanked Eli for breakfast and told him they would stop by at the end of their hunt and pick up the mail he wanted them to take to the Post Office in

Colton. This was one time when Eli could hardly wait for his company to leave. After feeding the hounds, Delightful and the chickens Eli fed the milk cow and Old Pet and then returned quickly to his cabin. He spent the rest of the morning reading and re-reading the wonderful letters. The grandchildren all expressed their love for Grandpa and told him how much they enjoyed their stay at Goat Mountain the previous summer. They all were looking forward to coming again the next summer. They also sent pictures and Eli placed the pictures on his fire place mantle.

Ailene thanked Eli for visiting her mom's cousin, Jennifer, on his trip to Colton. She said they were all looking forward to visiting Jennifer on their next trip to Oregon. Eli was happy that he had made that visit. He was even looking forward to Jennifer's promised visit in the spring time to Goat Mountain.

Eli spent the next week writing letters, doing little chores around the cabin, some late fall cleaning, and piling some tree limbs that had fallen from trees around the cabin in the last storm. There was always work to be done and he loved doing the work because he loved his home on Goat Mountain.

November the ninth was the last day of Elk season. Eli got up early and started a fire right away. He knew the hunters would be coming sometime today but he was not sure what time they would arrive. He went outside and fed all of the animals and made sure they were all ok. He had heard some noises outside during the night but it sounded like they were off in the distance and not near the cabin so he did not get up. After the chores were done he returned to the cabin and had a light breakfast. He then decided to prepare a large beef stew and have it ready when the hunters showed up.

About 1:00 pm Bob and Jim showed up. They were excited to show Eli the two Elk they had killed. Eli was pleased with their success. He was also very pleased that they did not make mention of any sighting of unusual tracks. Evidently the big creatures had stayed in or near the cave and he was grateful for that. Bob and Jim enjoyed the wonderful beef stew and thanked Eli by giving him some elk meat. Eli loved elk meat but he had not killed an elk or deer in a several years. He had no need to as the hunters always gave him plenty of their kills. After lunch Eli gave Bob all the letters he had written and asked if he would mail them when he got to Colton. The men said their good-bys and left for their return trip to their homes in Colton. Eli was a little sad to see them go as he knew it would now be several months before he could expect to see another human. Even though he was well prepared for the winter he seemed to be bothered by the loneliness a little more in the last couple of years.

Eli woke up the next morning to bright sunshine coming in through the kitchen window. He got dressed quickly and started a fire in the fireplace and kitchen stove. He then went outside to feed all the animals. As usual the hounds and his falcon were anxious to see him. Sampson was sound asleep in her log. Eli decided that he would return after breakfast and take the hounds and Delightful out into the meadow east of the cabin. He then went to the cow barn and fed Old Pet and the new milk cow.

Eli looked down in the valley and noticed very heavy white clouds moving up the mountain side. This usually meant snow. He quickly brought extra wood inside and then went to the root cellar to get some tubers and other things to put into the stew he planned to make for supper. He loved homemade stew, especially when it had elk meat in it. By mid morning the temperature dropped 10 degrees and the snow started to fall. By mid afternoon there was about 3 inches of new snow on the ground. Eli decided to take the hounds and Delightful out so they could play in the second snow of the winter. The hounds went wild and his falcon was so happy to be allowed to fly freely. Eli even let Old Pet and the milk cow out for awhile. It finally stopped snowing about 4:00 pm. After putting the animals back in their cozy places Eli decided to take a walk down to the pond. On his trip around to the far side of the pond he was startled but pleased to see tracks the big creatures had made very recently. He wondered if they were not watching him this very moment. It was getting too dark to see very far into the woods on the north side of the pond. Eli moved slowly around the pond and then went back to his warm cabin.

The aroma inside the cabin was wonderful. The stew was nearly done. Eli had enough time to make some corn bread and bring in some ice cold carbonated spring water from the cellar. After supper he tidied up the kitchen, washed the dishes, and then sat down in his comfortable chair to read from 'Call Of The Wild', the book his sons had given him.

Eli had not been reading very long when he was interrupted by a tap on the window. He glanced quickly at the window and could hardly believe his eyes. There stood one of the big fellows. Eli got up and went towards the window. The big hairy creature quickly disappeared. Eli sat back down. Again the tapping started. Again Eli looked towards the window. This time he knew something must be wrong outside and so he put on his boots, coat and hat. He lit a lantern and approached the door very carefully. As he did so he heard this scream out by the cow barn. Eli grabbed his rifle and headed towards the barn. As he did so he saw a huge mountain lion trying to break into the barn. Eli had decided by this time he would not attempt to kill the mountain lions, he just wanted to scare him off. He wanted the cougars to know they were not welcomed around his animals or close to the cabin. He was able to fire one round in the general direction of the big cat and that was more than enough to send the animal scurrying off into the deep woods. Eli walked out to the barn, went inside, and spent some time trying to settle Old Pet and the milk cow down. With that done he returned to the warmth of his cabin and continued reading. The adrenalin in his body made it very difficult for Eli to get to sleep and so he read longer than usual. Eli was just very thankful that the mountain lion had not attacked Big Foot. Big Foot must have been too close to the cabin when the mountain lion came on the scene. Eli now knew for sure that there were probably several mountain lions in the area.

The following morning Eli did not awaken until well after 8:00 am. When he looked out the window he was surprised to see what looked to be well over a foot of new snow. He dressed quickly, put on his boots and went out to feed the animals. He was pleased to find them all safe and sound and excited to get out in the fresh snow. Eli returned to the cabin, prepared a quick breakfast, cleaned up and then went out to spend some time with the animals. He made the mistake of turning the hounds loose and they immediately discovered the scent of the mountain lion. In an instant they were off and yelping as they followed the tracks of the big cat. Eli panicked but he knew it would not be wise to go after the hounds unless he was properly equipped. He returned to the cabin, put on his snow shoes, got his rifle, made a sack lunch and headed out to find the dogs. The sky was clear and the sun was shining even though it was quite cold. Eli had only walked for about an hour when he saw the hounds standing and howling under a large old growth fir tree. He was happy to see them but frightened with what he saw high up in the tree. The mountain lion was straddling two large limbs. Evidently he had decided it would be easier to escape to the safety of the tree than to confront the dogs. Eli was grateful for that.

Eli could feel his hair stand up on the back of his neck. His muscles tightened as he contemplated his next move. The big cat moved ever so slightly. Eli never took his eyes of the treed animal. He bent down and took hold of the collars of both hounds and walked slowly backwards after deciding that he was not going to kill the big cat. He had really made that decision some time ago and he was going to stick with it unless his life or the lives of his animals were threatened. Eli had to admit to his self that the day could come when he would be forced to shoot another one of these beautiful wild animals but he hoped that would not happen today. He continued to walk slowly away from the base of the tree. The hounds were putting up a little resistance, but Eli was persistent in his backwards movement. In a few minutes they lost sight of the tree and the big cat. About the time Eli started to loosen up he heard the sound of limbs breaking. He figured the cougar had started down the tree, breaking limbs in his path. He turned quickly towards the tree, tightened his grip on the hound's collars, readied his powerful rifle and froze. He waited a few minutes but finally came to the conclusion that cat was evidently not following them. Eli was greatly relieved but stayed on high alert until he was far from the tree.

Eli was glad to be back to his cabin safely, and to know that all of his animals were safe. He hoped these encounters with the mountain lions would become few and far between, in fact he would be very happy not to see one again on his Goat Mountain but he knew that probably would not be the case.

Eli looked at his big John Deer calendar as soon as he woke up. He was pleased to discover that it was November twenty sixth, Thanksgiving Day. As usual, the first thing he did was feed the animals and milk the cow. After breakfast Eli took all the animals outside for a little while, but he kept them near the cabin. Afterwards Eli gave each animal a special treat that he had purchased in Colton. He then went inside and prepared himself a wonderful Thanksgiving dinner, which was difficult to do for just one person. He had roast chicken, mashed potatoes and chicken gravy and he had managed to store some yams in the root cellar for this special dinner. The only thing missing was his beloved family members, sons, daughter-in-laws, and grandchildren. Oh how he missed them!

Eli spent the next week making sure he had plenty of wood on the porch and he also went to the nearby woods and collected some of the edible roots and tubers that he found under some of the big old growth trees where there was very little snow and put them in his root cellar. It snowed almost every day but the temperatures were not cold enough and so the snow that came in the early morning hours melted in the afternoon.

Eli woke up to bright sunshine on the first day of December. He decided he would take Old Pet, the hounds, and Delightful and make one last trip up Goat Mountain to the spring. The snow was only about 6 inches deep as a result of a recent rain, so he knew Old Pet could pull the small sled. Eli packed a good lunch and took food along for the animals. All of the animals loved frolicking in the snow. Eli walked alongside the sled on the way up. He took several gallon bottles to collect water in. He loved the wonderful carbonated water provided by the spring. He also realized that it might be some time before he would be able to get to the spring again. He also wondered if he would see any sign of the big hairy creatures when they passed by the entrance to the cave. As it turned out there was no sign of the hairy man like animals that he now considered as his friends. This concerned Eli just a little bit. He hoped they had not had another encounter with the mountain lions. Eli collected the water and then the party returned to the cabin. He spent the rest of the day in and around the cabin.

The next morning Eli was sleeping soundly and a little later than usual. He was awakened by the sound of several loud knocks on his cabin door. He got up quickly and didn't even put on his pants. Instead he came to the door in his red long underwear. He was greeted by a man who identified himself as a Government Trapper. He told Eli that there had been complaints by several hunters of too many mountain lions in the area and he was given the job of thinning them out. He asked Eli if he had seen any on Goat Mountain? Eli said that he had in the past but not recently. The last thing Eli wanted was to have some Government Official tromping around the woods on his Goat Mountain. He could only imagine what would happen if the trapper happened to see his big hairy two legged man like friends or even unusual man like tracks. That would be the end of his wonderful and peaceful life on the mountain. Far back in the back of his mind he knew that perhaps he only had a few years left of his wonderful life style in this place that he had called home for more than fifty years, but he wanted to make it last as long as possible.

He invited the Government man in and asked if he would like to have breakfast before he headed back down the mountain. He started a fire in the old cook stove, got dressed quickly and prepared a small breakfast. He was also glad that he had kept the barn door closed last night because he was sure the Government man would have had some questions about Sampson. Eli just wanted to give him a good breakfast and then send him on his way. The trapper instructed Eli to shoot to kill any mountain lion that he might see on his property or in the general area. After breakfast the Government man left on foot. He had told Eli that he parked his snow mobile at the gate. Eli breathed a sigh of relief when the trapper got out of sight. He remained outside for some time until he could not hear the sound of the Government man's snowmobile.

Eli spent the rest of the day doing little chores around the cabin and spending time with his animals. The weather had been so mild that Sampson was able to get outside quite a bit and did not seem to want to crawl into his log and begin his hibernation for the winter. Eli did notice that she was lying around more and appeared to be getting a little bigger around the belly. He was pretty sure there would be a baby cub born in the springtime, at least he sure hoped so.

The next two weeks brought colder temperatures and heavy snow to Goat Mountain. Eli never ventured very far from the immediate area around the cabin. He spent a lot of time with the animals in the barn and also made sure that the milk cow and Old Pet had plenty of feed and fresh water. He could not let them outside as the snow was getting pretty deep. He wondered how the big fellows were doing in the cave. He had not heard or seen any sign of the mountain lion for some time for which he was very thankful.

The days were so short now that Eli was sleeping in until around 8:00 am. It had finally stopped snowing so Eli decided that he would take the hounds and Delightful outside for a little while. He knew the hounds loved to try to run in the deep snow. Delightful had an advantage as the depth of snow had no effect on her being able to soar in the sky. Eli noticed when he went to the barn that Sampson had decided it was time for her to crawl in her log and take a very long nap, like maybe until early spring. Before returning to the cabin Eli went to the cow barn and milked the cow and fed Old Pet. He could tell the cow barn animals were really getting tired of being made to stay in the barn. They were getting 'barn fever' while Eli was getting 'cabin fever'.

After lunch the snow clouds started moving up the mountain and the temperature dropped fifteen degrees in about thirty minutes. The next time Eli looked out the window is was beginning to snow again. He had measured the snow depth just before coming into the cabin and it was almost 60 inches. None of this bothered Eli as he had plenty of wood in the wood shed and on the covered porch. He had plenty of food in the cupboard and root cellar and he still had several jugs of carbonated spring water plus good water from melting the snow.

Eli wondered how his three sons and their families were doing. He imagined they were all busy getting ready for Christmas. They all had young children and so Christmas was a very big thing in their families. He knew that each family was active in their church and lived the true spirit of Christmas in their homes and in their lives. He was a little sad that he could not be with them during this special time of the year. Today he felt a little lonely. He decided to make a trip down to the barn and feed the hounds, Delightful and the chickens. He was pleased that the chickens were still laying a few eggs every other day. He opened the top half of the back door to the barn and looked towards the pond. What he saw caused him to freeze in his tracks, not with fright but with amazement. Both of the big hairy two legged man like creatures had broken a hole in the ice and were drinking water out of the pond. He watched them for about fifteen minutes until they headed through the woods up towards the mountain meadow and their home in the cave. Eli closed the barn door and returned to the warmth of his mountain cabin. He spent the rest of the afternoon reading.

The next day was a very relaxing day for Eli. After checking on and feeding all the animals Eli spent the rest of the day writing letters to each of his grandchildren. Even though he knew he would not be able to send the letters until spring time he still wanted the children to know that he was thinking of them at this special season of the year. Eli loved his grandchildren and wondered if he would ever live close to any of them in the future.

Eli was almost ready to retire to his nice comfortable chair and spend the rest of the evening reading when he heard the most horrible scream he had ever heard in his life. He also heard very loud sounds that he knew were coming from the big fellows. He grabbed his hat and coat and his lantern and 12 gauge shotgun. As soon as he got out the door he witnessed the most horrible sight he had ever seen in his life time on Goat Mountain. There was truly a battle royal going on. The two hairy man like creatures that he had grown to have so much respect for were in the fight of their lives. The mountain lion was screaming and clawing at both creatures. Blood was flowing from all three but mostly from the mountain lion. There was a lot of commotion inside the cow barn. The hounds were howling as loud as their lungs would allow. Eli just hoped they remained in the barn. He had locked the door and he hoped it would stay locked. The battle went on and on. The screaming never stopped and the sounds from the big creatures got deeper and louder. Eli tried to get in a position so that he could take a shot at the big cat but was never able to get a clear shot. He was afraid he would hit one of the big creatures. The battle continued for almost an hour and finally the big cat started to weaken, probably from the loss of blood. The big man like creatures would not let the lion get away. Finally the big cat was so weak that he tumbled to the ground as though he were dead. With that the big creatures stopped the attack and retreated into the nearby woods.

The cat lay still as Eli approached very slowly, shotgun in the 'ready to fire' position. Eli could see that the cat was very near death. Even though it was hard to do he pointed the barrel of his shotgun at the big cats head and with the pull of the trigger it was all over. Eli remembered thoughts he had had earlier when he wondered if the time would ever come when he would have to kill another mountain lion on his mountain. He knew that moment had just passed. He was not proud of the act but he knew it was necessary. He was just very thankful that the big man like creatures were victorious and he hoped their wounds would heal. There was just no way he could even check on them as the snow was too deep for him to venture up to the cave, even with snow shoes.

Eli had so much adrenalin flowing through his body, when he returned to the cabin sleep was not an option. He put some wood in the fireplace, prepared a little snack of dried fruit and a glass of carbonated strawberry flavored Kool-Aid and sat down in his favorite chair. He tried to read but just could not concentrate on what he was reading. He found himself reading the same paragraph over and over. Finally after more than an hour he started to settle down and the adrenalin level receded in his body. He finally started to feel a little bit sleepy. He knelt beside his bed an offered his usual nightly prayer. This night he had so much to be thankful for.

Eli awoke early to the sound of rain on his tin roof. He shined his flashlight through the window to his outdoor thermometer which read 42 degrees F. He lit an oil lamp and then started a fire in his wood cook stove. He then started a fire in the fire place. In no time the cabin was nice and warm. By the time he got the fires going the rain stopped and he heard the wind starting to blow pretty hard. He decided to check on the animals, see if the chickens had laid any eggs, milk the cow and feed the barn animals. All of the animals seemed to just want to stay inside their warm and cozy homes and Eli thought that would be a good idea. After feeding the animals Eli prepared his breakfast and then decided this would be a good day to catch up on his reading. He had many wonderful books to read, one of which was his family Bible that had been handed down from his dear mother. This was a Bible that had a copyright date of April 6, 1830. He wished that he was a scholar of the Bible as was his Mother.

The rain finally stopped at about 1:30 in the afternoon. Eli knew it would be difficult to get around in the slush so he did not even attempt to do his evening chores until around 4:00 pm. The animals were all glad to see him, especially Delightful. Eli hoped tomorrow would be a better day as he was anxious to take the hounds and Delightful outside for a little R & R. After his chores were done he returned to the cabin and prepared a light supper. He had kept a fire going in the fireplace all day so it was nice and warm in his cabin. After cleaning up from supper he again retired to his favorite chair and continued reading from some of the Reminisce magazines that his sons had left with him. He had just about read himself to sleep when he heard a familiar tap on the window. It startled him as it was a little louder than usual. He looked up just in time to see both of the big hairy two legged creatures look through the window and then quickly disappear into the night. Eli knew they had come to let him know that they were both ok. He was happy and relieved. The sight of the big fellows brought back fresh memories of what had just taken place the night before.

TWENTY THREE

Christmas Brings Two Surprise Visitors

December 24 (Wednesday Christmas Eve Day)

The snow was piling up once again. It had been snowing every day for the last 3 days. When Eli went out to feed the animals he measured the snow depth and it was about 68 inches. It was stunningly beautiful with the huge fir and hemlock trees weighted down with snow. Eli noticed fresh tiny tracks on top of the fresh snow. Some were rabbit tracks and then there were other small animal tracks. Eli froze when he got near the cow barn and saw new mountain lion tracks under one of the big fir trees. He returned immediately to the cabin and retrieved his 12 gauge shotgun and then headed for the cow barn. He was so happy to find the milk cow and Old Pet safe and just munching on some of the hay he had given them the night before. In fact there was no sign of the cougar tracks any closer to the barn. Eli had secured the barn door exceptionally well and he had also put iron bars over the windows as one of his projects last fall.

Eli had hung a large stocking from the mantel of the fire place and he had brought in a small, bushy fir tree that he had placed in the wood shed early in December. He had placed a few simple decorations, which the children had made during their last visit, on the tree several days ago. He also got out his battery operated phonograph and put on an old record of Christmas music that he always played every Christmas Eve and Christmas Day. He always remembered to buy new batteries for the phonograph each fall when he went to Colton. Eli finally fell asleep setting in his favorite chair listening to beautiful Christmas music. Way in the back of his mind he wondered how many more Christmases he would be able to remain on his beautiful Goat Mountain and the home he loved. He was now nearing 80 years old.

Eli had much to be thankful for this Christmas Day. The sun was shining through the window on the east side of the cabin when Eli finally awakened a little after 8:30 am. Before fixing his breakfast he went out and fed the hounds, his falcon and the chickens and then went to the cow barn and milked the cow and fed Old Pet. He then returned to the warmth of his cabin and prepared a light breakfast. Even though he was alone he planned to prepare a nice Christmas dinner. His thoughts turned to his sons and their families. He hoped they were all well and enjoying the day with their families. He decided that he would skip lunch and have an early dinner. He had saved a couple of young chickens, one he had for Thanksgiving and he would now have the other one for Christmas dinner.

Just as he was putting the stuffed chicken in the oven he heard the sound of an engine. He was startled and could not imagine who would be brave enough to attempt to come to see him through deep snow. He knew that only a snowmobile or snow cat would be able get through the road to his cabin. He waited with anticipation as the noise of the engine became louder and the vehicle appeared to be getting closer. Eli opened the door and stepped outside to greet the guest, whoever it was. As soon as the snow cat came into view Eli could see that it was his dear friend, Bob Berge. Eli became so emotional that he had a few tears streaming down his cheeks when Bob finally arrived.

Bob had his grandson Robert with him. Eli was very glad to see them and brought them inside quickly and offered them hot chocolate. He also asked them to please stay for Christmas dinner to which they accepted. They asked Eli if they could stay the night so that they could travel back to Colton in the daylight. Eli was so happy to have his good friends with him and very surprised to say the least. Until they arrived Eli was feeling quite lonely and really missing his family. Bob brought Eli up to date on news around Colton and the surrounding communities. He also told Eli about another one of the old timers around Colton passing away. Eli knew Charley Wilkins very well as he used to come to Eli's Goat Mountain every fall to hunt. Bob and Robert helped Eli with the final preparation for the Christmas dinner. The meal was wonderful. In addition to good food both Bob and Robert drank all of the ice cold carbonated strawberry flavored Kool-Aid they could hold. Eli still had several gallons of the spring water stored in his root cellar.

After dinner Robert challenged Eli to a game of checkers even though he knew who the winner would be. Bob said he would play the winner. As it turned out neither Robert or Bob were very much of a challenge for Eli. The three of them went to the barn and fed the hounds, chickens and Delightful and then did the chores in the cow barn. Eli told Bob and Robert about the encounter with the mountain lion but he made no mention of the big fellows and the horrible fight that had taken place prior to him shooting the big cat.

After they returned to the cabin Bob and Robert told Eli they had brought some little gifts for Eli and something ever more special, letters from his three sons and their families. Eli became very emotional as he opened and read each letter. All were doing well but they were really missing grandpa. Each son said that they were already making plans to be together on Goat Mountain in June. Each of his ten grandchildren said they could hardly wait to be with grandpa and all of the animals next summer. They all sent pictures including many they had taken last summer at Grandpa's ranch on Goat Mountain. They all asked about the hounds, Delightful, Sampson, the milk cow and Old Pet.

After reading all of the letters they all sat close to the fire place and visited the rest of the evening. What a wonderful Christmas this had turned out to be after all. When Eli awoke in the morning he was sure he would be spending this Christmas alone, which certainly turned out differently. He was so happy and so grateful and he expressed his gratitude to Bob and Robert many times. It was finally time to organize places for his guest to sleep. Eli had some wonderful camp cots with nice thick foam pads and plenty of blankets and quilts. Eli invited Bob and Robert to join him in evening prayer to which they gladly agreed. Eli asked Bob to offer the prayer. As Bob was about to climb onto one of the camp cots Eli protested by saying "Oh no you don't Bob, I am sleeping on the cot and you are sleeping in my bed." A friendly argument followed but Bob finally realized he could not win.

Eli got up once in the night and put wood in the fire place and then closed the damper and so it stayed warm in the cabin all night. Everyone got a good night's sleep. Eli got up early and started a fire in the wood cook stove. He choose to let Bob and Robert sleep a little longer while he went to the barn and fed and cared for the animals. He also milked the cow and fed Old Pet. When he got back to the cabin Bob and Robert were up and dressed and getting their belonging packed and ready for the return trip to their home in Colton. Eli fixed a quick breakfast and then asked Bob if he could wait long enough for him to write a quick note to each of his sons and his grandchildren, to which Bob said "sure." Bob asked Eli if it would be alright if he and Robert went out to the barn to see the hounds and falcon, to which Eli agreed. Eli put his short notes in three envelopes and addressed each envelope to a son. Bob assured him that he would see that they got in the mail as soon as he got back to Colton.

It was a few minutes before noon when Bob and Robert said their good-bys. Eli thanked them for the surprise visit and told them to be careful on their return trip home. Eli spent the rest of the day doing little things around the cabin and re-reading the letters from the children and his sons and daughter-in-laws. He also placed the pictures on the fireplace mantel so that he could look at them often. The last two days had been wonderful and yes, life was good on Eli's Goat Mountain.

TWENTY FOUR

Goat Mountain Becomes A Winter Wonderland

When Eli woke up on the morning of New Year's Eve day and looked out the window he could see it was snowing hard with big flakes. He quickly built a fire in the fire place and the wood cook stove. He then went down to the barn to tend to the animals and then over to the cow barn to milk the cow and feed Old Pet. He had to trudge through about eight inches of new snow. As Eli looked around he was overwhelmed with the natural beauty. Goat Mountain was truly a white winter wonderland. As he looked back towards the cabin he could see the beautiful gray smoke making its way far up into the sky through the snow flakes. Eli was filled with emotion as he thought of all the wonderful things that had happened this past year on Goat Mountain. He thought of the wonderful weeks that his sons and their families were with him during the summer time. He also thought of the very sad time when little Sambo, the cub, had been killed by lightning. He reflected for only a moment on the recent event with the big fellows and the mountain lion. He thought of the wonderful trip he had made to Colton and the opportunity to see so many of his dear friends that he only saw a couple of times a year. He remembered then that he had forgotten to ask Bob, on his recent visit, about his new found friend, Jennifer. He hoped she was well.

It finally stopped snowing about 1:00 pm so Eli got out his snow shovel and removed the fresh snow from the path to both barns. He then took the hounds and his falcon outside. The animals were very happy to be outside. He turned the hounds loose and released Delightful from her tether. What a beautiful sight it was to see her soar so high in the sky and then return when Eli would call her. Eli stayed outside for a couple of hours but when the sun went down the temperature dropped quickly and Eli knew it was time to put the animals back in the barn and return to the warmth of his cabin.

The sun was shining through the window when Eli woke up on New Year's day. Eli went through the normal morning routine of building fires, feeding the animals, and preparing his own breakfast. After cleaning up the breakfast dishes Eli decided he would write in his journal about some of the events of the past year. He had so much to be thankful for. He had also enjoyed good health this past year for which he was especially grateful. He had only been setting down for a few minutes when he heard the all too familiar tap on the window. This time it really startled Eli because it was a little louder than usual. When Eli looked up he saw one of the big man like creatures standing in front of the window. The normal pattern was that he would only get a quick glance at the big fellows and they would be gone. It was different this time. The big creature did not leave. Eli went to the door to see where the other Big Foot was and to his surprise there was only one who came to his cabin. When Eli opened the door the big fellow started to retreat towards the direction of the cave. Eli closed the door thinking the big Creature would leave and return to the cave. He imagined that the other creature just did not want to venture out into the deep snow. Eli closed the door and returned to his comfortable chair and again started to write. He had only sat down for a few minutes when again he heard the tap on the window. He looked at the window and saw the big fellow again. This time Eli knew there must be something wrong. Again he went to the door and looked in the direction the big fellow was going. This time Big Foot turned towards Eli and stopped. Eli went back inside the cabin, said a quick prayer, put on his warm coat and took his snow shoes down from the cabin wall. He also took his 30:06 rifle and some warm gloves. He wondered if he would even be able to walk with snow shoes. He made up his mind that he would be very careful and only go as far as he felt safe in going. As he started out he was amazed at how well he was able to walk as long as he stayed right in the tracks of the big hairy creature.

The big guy remained several hundred yards ahead of Eli but always kept within sight. Eli trudged slowly on gradually making his way up in the direction of the cave. Finally under a grove of huge hemlock trees the Big Hairy Creature stopped. Eli froze in his tracks. Neither moved for several moments and then Eli again began to approach slowly. As he approached the spot where Big Foot had stopped the creature moved out from under the trees and walked about 500 feet on towards the cave. The sight that greeted Eli broke his heart. Big Foot's companion lay dead in the snow. He was cut from head to toe with deep gashes. Eli began to weep, almost uncontrollably. He did not touch the creature, he just wept. He stood there for almost an hour. He immediately saw signs of several mountain lions and realized that it must have taken that many to finally bring the big guy down. What a fight it must have been. They were too far from the cabin for Eli to hear what went on, besides it happened during the night when he was sound asleep. The surviving big fellow slowly started making his way up towards the cave. Eli determined then that it was time for him to make his way back to the cabin. When he had gone about 300 feet he turned around and looked in the direction from which had just come. He was not surprised when he saw the lone big creature following along. He realized that his friend was making sure he made it back to the cabin safely. He went about another 500 feet and what he saw just up ahead caused him to again freeze in his tracks. Just ahead there were three mountain lions crossing his trail. This presented another moment that Eli hoped would never come. The animals did not back off and Eli knew the danger that could befall anyone if they got between a cougar and his kill. The decision was made for Eli, either he shoot the cats or be killed. He also did not want to draw his hairy friend into another battle.

Eli got close enough so that he knew the bullet from his rifle would bring death when it hit its target. He also knew that he might have to kill all three of the lions. His aim was accurate and deadly, with the pull of the trigger one of the lions fell to the earth. He had hit the animal right in the head. The other two animals backed off a little and then stood their ground, screaming loudly. The hair stood up on the back of Eli's neck. He took aim again and pulled the trigger. Another lion fell to the ground. Eli glanced back in the direction of the grove of trees and the big creature was only about 100 feet away. The third cougar was fighting mad and made a beeline towards Eli. Again Eli took aim when the cat was within 50 feet, pulled the trigger and the cat fell dead in his tracks. Eli could not move for several minutes. It was as though he was in a state of shock. After about fifteen minutes Eli looked in the direction where he last saw his friend and saw him moving slowly towards the grove of trees where his companion lay dead. Again Eli was overwhelmed with emotion and the tears started to again flow. Eli slowly made his way down the mountain to the safety of his warm cabin. What a day this had been. Eli collapsed in his big chair and spent several minutes thinking about what had just happened. Eli still had too much adrenalin to be able to calm down. He got up and put some wood in the fire place. When he looked out through the window he noticed that snow clouds had formed and in a few minutes it started snowing very hard.

Eli had not eaten anything all day. He was not hungry when he got back to the cabin. About 4:00 pm he finally started to relax a little bit and decided that he had better prepare supper even though he still did not have much of an appetite. He went to the cellar and got some vegetables and some canned meat that he had prepared in the summer time and put these in a small kettle and cooked the stew for about one hour. As the aroma spread throughout the cabin Eli quickly began to develop an appetite.

While the stew was cooking Eli went out to the barn down by the pond and spent a few minutes with the hounds and his falcon. He also fed the chickens and collected a few fresh eggs. He then went to the cow barn and milked the cow and fed Old Pet. All of the animals were very happy to see Eli. Eli had a feeling that the hounds and Delightful sensed that something bad had happened that day. Eli was so happy that he had made both barns extremely secure for the safety of his beloved animals. They were his only close companions during these long, cold winter months. He seldom saw the big hairy creatures during the winter as the snow usually got so deep it was not easy for them to get around much. He only surmised that they were coming down to check on him when the battle that brought death to one of the man like creatures occurred. He hoped that he would never experience another day like this in his life.

The next morning when Eli got up he looked out the window and noticed that it was snowing but the flakes were more like sleet. The temperature had really dropped over night. The temperature gauge registered eighteen degrees F. Eli built a fire in the fireplace and the wood burning cook stove. He looked at his battery operated clock and was quite surprised to see that it was almost 9:00 am. He then realized how exhausted he must have been to sleep this late in the morning. He decided that he would care for the animals first before fixing his own breakfast.

The snow continued to fall throughout the day and the size of the flakes increased so that by nightfall Eli measured 8 inches of new snow. He spent the day inside the cabin doing little chores that needed to be done and reading from a new novel his son Martin had given him when he was visiting last summer. The name of the book was "My Side Of The Mountain." It was an easy book to read which told about a twelve year old boy leaving his comfortable home in New York City and living in a tree house for a year on property that had at one time belonged to his grandfather. Eli read several chapters before sleep overtook him.

It continued to snow throughout the night and by morning there was another six inches added on to what fell yesterday. All the animals were getting restless and wanting to go outside the barn but the weather was just too bad. Eli wondered how the surviving big fellow was getting along in the cave. He hoped that his wounds had healed. He knew that the hairy creatures had learned how to get food, even in times of deep snow and nasty weather. He was hoping that there would be a break in the weather and that some of the snow would melt so that he could put on his snow shoes and make it up as far as the cave in the next few weeks. In the past there were usually a couple of weeks in January when the temperatures rose and some of the snow melted, but this was already shaping up to be a different winter.

On Thursday morning, January the fifth, Eli was awakened during the night to the sound of strong wind. There was a full moon as Eli opened the door to step outside for a moment to make sure everything was not being blown away, he was shocked to feel the warm air. The famous Chinook Winds had returned to Goat Mountain once again. This is what he had been hoping for. The snow was already melting fast. Eli hoped this would keep up for the next couple of days so that he might have a chance to get up to the cave and check on the remaining Big Foot. He had a snack and then went back to bed but he was not able to go back to sleep as the wind was making too much noise. After tossing and turning for about an hour Eli finally decided to get up and build a little fire and read.

After breakfast Eli went to the barn and tended to the hounds, the falcon and the chickens. The chickens had stopped laying eggs and were beginning to molt. Eli had to be very careful because parts of limbs from the big trees were being blown around. He finally made his way to the cow barn and milked the cow and fed Old Pet. He was glad to be back in the safety of his warm cabin. Several years ago he had removed all of the big trees that were close to his cabin so he never had to worry about trees or limbs coming down on his roof.

The wind finally died down about 3:30 in the afternoon. The snow was melting fast and there was water running everywhere, but Eli was very happy because he knew that there might be a chance he could make it up to the cave when things settled down and dried up or froze up again.

The Chinook wind and thawing continued for the next two days. Eli could only imagine the flooding that must be going on in areas of lower elevation such as Colton and Molalla. The snow level dropped by a couple of feet in just two days. Eli did not venture any further than the two barns. He was able to spend a considerable amount time with the hounds and Delightful in their barn. He also spent several days making repairs in both barns.

The warm wind from the east finally stopped during the night and the temperature started to drop very fast as a cold front moved through the area. Eli woke up to bright sunshine and temperatures just a little above freezing. This is just what Eli had been praying for. Eli determined that if this weather continued for another day he would attempt a trip on snow shoes up to the cave. He even planned to take the hounds and Delightful. His plan was to leave immediately after breakfast and thereby take advantage of the frozen snow.

The weather had been perfect and Eli decided this would be a perfect day to make his short journey to the cave. Eli had a light breakfast, fed all the animals and made final preparation for the hike. He always took a backpack that had emergency supplies and things he would need for survival if he got into a situation where he had to stay out overnight.

Eli moved slowly, but the hounds were anxious to get moving. It was difficult to hold them back. He was able to release the falcon and enjoyed watching her fly high in the sky. All he had to do was whistle and she would fly back and land on his arm. Eli made several stops along the way as it took a lot of energy to walk with snow shoes. Eli had only gone about half way when he ran out of energy. Fortunately Eli had brought a good supply of homemade Jerky, some dried fruit and water. He found a downed tree and stopped to have a snack. The sun actually felt warm on his back as he ate his lunch. After resting for a half hour Eli continued on towards the cave. He was able to walk on frozen snow all of the way so far.

As Eli approached the cave he became very apprehensive about what he might find. He hoped that he would not have to go very far into the cave to find the big two legged creature that he had come to have so much respect for. He was a little surprised that his friend was not at the entrance and this concerned him a great deal but he continued on for another fifty feet or so. The sight he saw then horrified him. He stopped dead in his tracks and could not move. He almost felt like he was going to collapse. He could not believe what he was seeing. He wanted to turn around and leave the cave and go to a spot and cry his heart out. All that remained of the man like creature that had been killed in the battle with the mountain lions was a pile of bones. There was total silence in the cave and surrounding area. The hounds knew something was very wrong. They came to Eli and stayed right by him. Tears started to flow down Eli's cheeks. Eli surmised that the big fellow had died from his wounds and the loss of blood. There was frozen blood all over the floor of the cave. Eli had to leave the cave and get out in the fresh air. He became so emotional that he did not know if he could make it back to his cabin. He felt like he was going into a state of shock. He knew there was only one thing he could do or he might become the next victim of the terrible battle that had happened a few weeks ago. When he got to the entrance to the cave he knelt down and said a prayer. He asked God to give him the strength to get through this terrible event that had happened on his Goat Mountain and to make it back to the safety of his warm cabin. As he ended his prayer it was as if something helped him get up, put on his snow shoes and back pack and head down the mountain. He whistled for Delightful and together they all continued down the mountain. They were home within an hour and back in the warmth of the cabin. Eli immediately dropped to his knees and said a simple prayer of thanks. Eli could not imagine the effort it had taken his big friend to drag the body of his companion from far down the mountain to the cave.

Goat Mountain received several feet of snow during the last couple of weeks of January and the first couple weeks of February. The weather had turned very cold about a week ago, and the snow level was back to what it was before the big melt. Eli spent most of time in the warmth of the cabin. He loved to read and he had several good books to choose from. He also had a couple of puzzles his daughter-in-laws had left for him to put together. He spent a considerable amount of time down in the barn by the pond with the hounds and his falcon. Eli loved his dogs and he was anxious for spring to come so he could spend more time outside with his animals. He had dried his milk cow up a couple of weeks ago as she was getting pretty big with calf. Old Pet seemed pretty restless and Eli decided that as soon as the snow level dropped to no more than a foot he would put the harness on her and hook her up to the sleigh. Old Pet loved to pull the sled. Eli would always take the sled into the woods and pull the thick bark off the Douglas Fir stumps and bring it to the porch to burn in the wood fire place. This allowed him to save the wood in the shed to burn at other times.

The last few weeks had been a very sad and lonely time on Goat Mountain for Eli. At least he still had his animals and Sampson for which he was very thankful. It snowed almost every day and Eli only saw the sun a couple of times during the rest of February. He hoped that March would come in like a lamb and go out like a lamb. That was not to be the case.

During the first week in March it snowed throughout most of the mornings and then the wind started blowing hard in the afternoons. This created huge drifts between the cabin and the cow barn. Eli spent a lot of the afternoons with the hounds and Delightful. He was not able to make it out to the cow barn every day. If the wind stopped during the night he would shovel a path to the barn in the morning. This was the first time that Eli found himself grumbling over the weather and the long cold winter on Goat Mountain. He actually had thoughts of how nice it might be in Houston where two of his sons lived as the winters were much warmer there.

On the ninth day of March Eli was awakened in the night by the sound of strong winds. He also noticed that the temperature inside the cabin was much warmer than it was when he went to bed. He slipped on his slippers and robe and stepped outside for a moment. The warmer than usual wind, felt good against the side of his face. This pleased Eli greatly.

Eli got up about 8:00 am and started a fire in the wood cook stove and a small fire in the fire place. He went out and fed the animals in the barn down by the pond and then got his snow shovel and opened up the path to the cow barn. The milk cow and Old Pet were glad to see Eli and get some fresh hay that Eli pitched down from the loft.

The snow was melting fast with the warm Chinook Wind. Eli measured the snow depth when he went to feed the animals just before dark. It had dropped nearly 6 inches today. If this warm easterly wind lasts through the rest of the week Eli knew there would not be much more than a foot of snow by Monday, the day he planned to hook Old Pet up to the sled.

The next morning Eli woke up to bright sunshine coming in through the front window and he could not hear the sound of any wind. He fed all of the animals and then prepared a light breakfast. After cleaning up the kitchen he put on his warm coat, packed a lunch and headed down to the barn by the pond to get the dogs and Delightful. They were all very excited and anxious to get out of the barn. Eli then went to the cow barn and put the harness on Old Pet and took him outside and hooked him up to the sled and away they went through the soft snow. Old Pet was at the height of her glory when she was pulling the sled. Eli released the falcon from her tether and allowed the hounds to run alongside the sled. The group traveled out through the meadow east of the cabin as it was pretty flat and easy going for Old Pet. The hounds kept jumping on and off the sled. When Eli got to the east end of the meadow he turned north into the timber and started gathering thick bark off the Fir stumps. In an hour or so he had all the bark he could haul on the sled. Before heading back to the cabin Eli fed all the animals and then sat down and ate his lunch. Life was once again very good on Eli's Goat Mountain.

The weather continued to be mild for the next two weeks. The snow was almost all gone and there were early signs of spring. Eli had lived on Goat Mountain long enough to know that these warmer temperatures would not last. Sure enough on the last day of March it turned cold and very rainy, in fact it rained almost every day for the next two weeks.

TWENTY FIVE

Spring Arrives And With It A Baby Cub

By the middle of April the rain finally stopped and the day time temperatures began to rise. Eli decided that if this weather continued for a few more days he would harness Old Pet and hook him to the small two wheeled cart and go up to the carbonated spring and collect some fresh spring water.

The weather was warm enough so that Eli could open the windows in the cabin in the day time and let the fresh mountain air in. Eli noticed that some of the birds were returning to his Goat Mountain, namely the finches, some of the sparrows and chickadees. Eli decided to check the many bird houses he had placed in trees and on fence posts nearby. Some needed to be repaired. The hounds and Delightful were so glad to be able to spend more time outside.

Eli got a pleasant surprise when he went down to feed the hounds and his falcon. Sampson was out of hibernation and looking like she would be giving birth to her new cub very soon. Sampson acted like nothing was unusual. Eli was very happy about this as Sampson's first cub had been killed by a lightning strike a couple of years earlier. She was of course glad to see Eli, but to her it was as though she had just awakened from a long nap. The sun was shining brightly by the time Eli got back to the cabin and he was very anxious to get going. He fed the animals, made a light breakfast, and prepared a big lunch. He then harnessed Old Pet and hooked him up to the small cart, and brought the hounds and Delightful out from the barn. The trip up the mountain went well. There were some early spring flowers in bloom and many of the birds were returning to Goat Mountain. The group arrived at the carbonated spring about lunch time. Eli filled all of the bottles he had brought with fresh carbonated water and then he sat down and ate his lunch after feeding the animals.

The hounds were having the time of their life just running around in the area around the spring and Delightful was flying high in the sky and enjoying the currents of the warm wind. Suddenly Eli looked up just as Delightful swooped down from the sky and caught a small rodent in her talons. She now had the lunch she had been waiting for since last fall. After spending a couple of hours at the spring Eli decided they should start down the mountain towards the cabin. Old Pet had had a good rest and of course it was all downhill to the cabin. Eli guided Old Pet near the entrance to the cave but he did not stop as he was overcome with emotion. He still could not imagine how different it was going to be on Goat Mountain knowing that at least one of the big hairy creatures would not be around anymore. There was still a question in his mind as to whether or not there might be other big two legged creatures on the west side of the Cascade Mountains.

As Eli guided Old Pet towards the cow barn he saw the barn door wide open. He then realized for the first time that he had been in such a hurry to get going that he forgot to secure the latch on the door. He only hoped the milk cow stayed in the barn or at least in the vicinity around the cabin. He stopped the horse and sled and looked all around but he did not see the milk cow any place outside the barn. He then proceeded on towards the barn. He again brought Old Pet to a stop, got off the sled and proceeded towards the open door. As he stepped inside he knew something was not right. What he saw next horrified him. All that was left of the milk cow was its hide, hoofs, head, and bones scattered around in sections of the barn. Another cougar had struck again. Eli could hardly believe this could happen to him. He was especially saddened because the unborn calf was also destroyed. He was so angry at himself for not securing the door and he rightfully blamed this tragic loss on no one else.

He took the harness off Old Pet, fed him and left the barn. He decided he would clean the mess up tomorrow. He put the hounds and Delightful in the other barn and returned to his cold cabin. He built a fire in the fireplace and before long the cabin was warm. He also built a fire in the wood cook stove. He was so upset that he was not very hungry but he knew he should eat something before going to bed. The last chore he had to do was to place all of the bottles of carbonated spring water in the root cellar. After eating a snack Eli decided to set in his rocking chair and read for a while in hopes that he would be able to get his mind off what had happened. When he finally went to bed he still had a very hard time getting to sleep. It was nearly 11:00 pm when he finally dozed off.

Eli slept in the next morning. After feeding the hounds, Delightful, the chickens and Old Pet Eli prepared himself a light breakfast. After cleaning up the kitchen he went out to the cow barn and spent the better part of the morning cleaning up the mess the mountain lion had created. He knew that every time he went to the barn to feed Old Pet he would be saddened to not find his milk cow there. He also realized that an important part of his food source was now gone and he would be back to using powdered milk, which he did not particularly like. He hoped that he would be able to purchase another milk cow when he went to Colton in the latter part of May.

Eli spent the rest of April indoors a lot as it had rained almost every day on Goat Mountain. The only snow was high up in the Cascades far above Goat Mountain. Eli had not seen any sign of the cougars for a couple of weeks now but he still wondered when their next visit would be. He usually took his 12 gauge shot gun with him when he went outside for any length of time. He also made sure that all doors leading into either barn were well secured.

The weather continued to get a little warmer each day and the days were also getting noticeably longer. Eli decided that if this weather continued for another week he would make a trip down the mountain to Colton. He wanted to see if he could find a milk cow for sale and replenish some of his food supply. He also wanted to visit some of his dear friends and check with his friend Bob Berge to see when he was planning on bringing his crew to Goat Mountain to complete the summer logging activity.

Eli spent the rest of the week getting ready to make the trip down to the valley. He planned to take the hounds and Delightful and he needed to make sure Old Pet had plenty of feed and water in the east pasture. He also made sure the chickens had feed and water. He decided it was nice enough to allow Sampson to remain outside the barn. He wrote letters to each member of his three families so that he could mail them when he got to the Colton Post Office. He was sure there would be mail waiting there for him. He also planned to visit Elaine's cousin, Jennifer Murray.

Eli got up very early to a beautiful clear sky. There was a full moon and the temperature was a balmy forty eight degrees F. Eli fed the animals and readied the hounds and his falcon for the trip down the mountain. He then prepared a hearty breakfast of three poached eggs, country potatoes, and beef jerky. He then went to the barn and started Big Red. He was happy the old truck started right away. All winter long he would go to the barn and start his old trusted truck at least once every two weeks. Eli loved the old truck and would never even consider parting with it, not as long as he was able to live on his beloved Goat Mountain.

Eli left the cabin at about 7:30 am. The roads were pretty soft from the spring thaw so Eli had to drive very slow. The hounds and Delightful were enjoying the ride from their vantage point in their cages on the flat bed of the truck. Big Red performed beautifully and they made it down as far as the old Goat Mountain Community Church by about 11:30. Eli decided it would be a good place to stop and have lunch. As always he fed the animals first and then he ate his lunch. The day was warm and Eli decided to take a short nap before continuing on with the journey.

Eli arrived at Bob and Darlene's place about 3:30 pm. Needles to say it was a happy reunion. The Berge's were so pleased to know that Eli had made it through the long, cold winter in good shape. Eli brought small gifts for Bob and Darlene, things he had made at the cabin when he could not get outside. The Berge's always loved the things he brought them each time he came for a visit. Darlene invited Eli to spend the evening with his family before continuing on to Colton the next day. Eli gladly accepted the invitation. He could hardly wait to enjoy a good home cooked meal prepared by someone other than himself.

Bob and Eli stayed up quite late and Eli was glad to catch up on all the local and national news. Bob told him that timber prices were quite good and they also discussed at least two options for when Bob and his crew would be able to come and do the logging in the summer. Eli said that he would find out when his sons were coming and let Bob know. Eli told Bob about the terrible tragedy of the mountain lion killing his cow. He asked Bob if he knew of anyone wishing to sell a young cow. Bob said that he didn't but that he would ask some of his neighbors.

Darlene prepared a wonderful breakfast of French Toast, home canned fruit and fresh squeezed orange juice. Eli thanked Bob and Darlene for their kindness and hospitality and proceeded on his way to Colton. The first place Eli stopped was the U.S. Post Office. He had letters from all three sons and all ten of his grandchildren. He spent more than an hour reading all of the letters. He was happy to learn that they were all well and the children were all doing well in school.

There was one bit of shocking news. Matt said that his job in Bend was being discontinued and that he was going to fly down to Houston and look for a job there in his field of Landscape Architecture. The company he had been working for had decided to put the work he did out to an outside contractor. Matt had been with the company for at least ten years. They were not excited about having to leave their friends in Bend but they were also excited about the possibility of living near family members in Houston.

Eli's sons had evidently been communicating by phone or mail and all indicated they would like to come to Goat Mountain in July, around the second week, if that would be alright with Grandpa. The children all expressed their excitement about coming to spend time with Grandpa. Eli was so happy about this good bit of news. He looked forward to their visits all year long. He would start planning for their time at Goat Mountain as soon as he got home. Eli went to the Colton market and purchased all of the things he had on his list. He then took the hounds and Delightful to the city park for a while. Eli stopped next at Jennifer Murray's home. Jennifer was very glad to see Eli. She had a nephew and niece visiting her. The children took to the hounds right away and they asked Eli to allow Delightful to show her flying skills, to which Eli quickly agreed. He loved to show off his dogs and his falcon.

Jennifer mentioned to Eli that she had an extra bed room and that he was welcome to spend the night. Eli accepted her invitation. She prepared a wonderful dinner of roast chicken, mashed potatoes and gravy and frozen vegetables from her freezer. She also had freshly baked bread and raspberry jam. For dessert she made a Marion Berry pie. After dinner they spent the evening visiting and getting a little better acquainted. Eli invited her to come to Goat Mountain when his sons and their families arrived for a visit in July.

Jennifer fixed her guest an excellent breakfast. After breakfast Eli thanked her for her hospitality and said good-by. He put Delightful in the cab and put the dogs on the back of the truck. He went back to the Colton Market and purchased a pencil, some letter writing paper, a small box of envelopes and went to the park to write answers to the letters he received. This took him all morning. With the letters in hand he headed to the Post Office and put them in the outgoing mail slot. He made a quick stop at Bob's place to say good-by and tell him when his families were coming in the summer. Bob told Eli that he would plan to bring his logging crew early in June to remove the trees. Bob said that he would continue to search for a replacement cow and that if he found one he would buy it and bring it up to Eli on his next trip to Goat Mountain.

Eli made several more stops to say hello to friends before going to the local Mobile gas station to fill Big Red with gas for the return trip to Goat Mountain. By 2:00 pm he was well on his way home to his cabin in the Cascades. The trip home was uneventful. The spring wild flowers were so beautiful and the grass along the road side was bright green. As soon as Eli parked Big Red he turned the hounds loose and released his falcon from her tether. As he approached the door to his cabin he noticed a note attached to the door with a thumb tack. As he read the note he became very concerned. The note read as follows: Dear Sir, we are officers with the State Game Commission. We have been notified by some hikers that they have spotted some very unusual foot prints while hiking near your property. According to the hikers the foot prints are very large and appear to have been made by a two legged animal walking in an upright position. We would appreciate it very much if you would be on the lookout and get in touch with us if you see any of these reported prints or any unusual large animals. We also want to assure you that we are highly suspect of the hikers story, but we are obligated to check out such unusual reports. The note was signed by Mike Smith and Marty Johnson of the Oregon State Game Commission. It was dated the ninth of May.

This note almost sent Eli into a state of shock. He knew this might happen sometime but he could not believe it had to happen so soon. He tried to stay calm. He knew this could have far reaching ramifications with his life on Goat Mountain. He feared the day when others might now come in search of his hairy two legged animal friends he had come to have so much respect for. These creatures had saved his life more than once. This note was like an exploding bomb shell to Eli. Eli went out to the barn to check on Sampson. He got a wonderful surprise. Alongside of Sampson was the most beautiful new born cub. Sampson was glad to see Eli and to show off her new born cub. The little one was cold black and looked very healthy. Sampson was such a good mother and now she had a beautiful cub to replace the one that had met such a tragic death just a little over one year ago. Next Eli went out to the east pasture to check on Old Pet. Pet came running up to the fence and appeared happy to see Eli.

Eli spent the next week thinking about what might happen next on his Goat Mountain. Needless to say he had some sleepless nights. At times his mind seemed to almost be in a daze. He tried to convince himself that he needed to stay calm and he knew that it was important that he get back to his normal daily schedule. He decided that he would make a trip up to the spring in the morning and go by the cave to check on the big fellow.

Eli woke up to bright sunshine coming through his window. He got dressed and went out to the barn to feed the animals and to check on Sampson and her new born cub. The cub was having its breakfast so Eli left them alone. He let the hounds out so they could get some exercise. He would let Delightful our a little bit later. He put Old Pet out in the pasture by the cabin. After breakfast Eli hooked Old Pet up to the small cart, placed his falcon on her tether and called the hounds. The hounds came running and as soon as they saw Old Pet hooked up to the cart they knew what that meant. They got so excited.

As they approached the cave Eli got the surprise of his life. He saw the one remaining hairy two legged creature standing near the entrance but she was not alone. Beside her was a small 'Big Foot'. It appeared to be not over 3 feet tall. It was very shy and hid behind the big creature. Eli was thrilled! He had no idea that there was even another big hairy creature in the area, even though it did seem very reasonable that there would be. They both looked very healthy and for that Eli was thankful. He hoped they were as glad to see him as he was them. Eli was thrilled to know that there might be a male Big Foot somewhere on the mountain. After giving it more thought Eli concluded that this little fellow was probably the offspring of the male Big Foot that was killed in the terrible battle a few months ago.

Eli and his animals continued on to the spring. The water was ice cold. Eli filled several jugs of fresh water. He then turned Delightful loose from the tether and let the hounds run free. Delightful was only gone for about 5 minutes and she brought back a small rabbit. Again the animal was not hurt and she let it go as soon as she put it down on the ground. Eli loved this bird more than words can express. Eli was busy playing with Big Daniel and Little Anne and preparing lunch when Delightful returned. As usual he fed the animals first and then ate his lunch.

After spending more than an hour at the spring Eli rounded up the hounds and placed his falcon on her tether and headed down the mountain. He took his time going home the long route which brought him to the east end of the meadow by his cabin. As he was leaving the forest he came upon a sight that caused him renewed concern. He found the fresh remains of a small bull Roosevelt Elk. It had evidently been brought down by a mountain lion. The fact that the cougar had killed an elk did not bother Eli as he knew that was a natural part of the food chain but that the kill had happened so close to his cabin meant that he still needed to be very cautious. Eli spent the rest of the afternoon and evening doing chores around the barn and cabin.

TWENTY SIX

Eli's Worst Nightmare Happens

Eli was awakened early in the morning by a knock on his cabin door. He got dressed quickly and opened the door to two total strangers. They introduced themselves as hikers and said they had heard about strange two legged hairy creatures being spotted in the Goat Mountain area and asked if Eli minded if they did some hiking on his property. Eli quickly decided that he must remain very calm and act like he had not ever seen such creatures nor did he believe the story of sightings of strange creatures. He warned the hikers of mountain lions being nearby and said that he would rather they not hike on his property. He kindly asked them to respect his privacy. He told them that he tried to keep his property for the private enjoyment of his sons and their families. They thanked Eli for being so courteous and assured him that they would respect his privacy.

Eli spent the rest of the day making NO TRESPASSING signs to place along his property lines. Fortunately all of his property lines were well marked by surveyors who had surveyed the property several years ago prior to any logging being done by Bob and his crew. Bob had paid for the survey. It took Eli the rest of the week to put the signs up. This is something he had hoped he would never have to do. Eli was having difficulty thinking about anything else but what was happening to his quiet and wonderful life style on Goat Mountain. He knew that life would never be the same for him on his beloved mountain if strangers kept stopping by, searching for strange creatures they had heard rumors of in the area.

Eli decided that he needed to get busy preparing for the coming summer and the visit of his sons and their families. He dreaded breaking the news to them about the turn of events on Goat Mountain.

Spring and the warmer weather brought many changes to Goat Mountain. The cub was growing quickly and, getting used to Eli, the hounds, and the falcon. They all started spending a lot time out in the East Meadow. Delightful was catching small rodents almost every day. The hounds were really loving the warm days, and the freedom to run at will. Eli decided that he needed to make the best of every day and enjoy every moment on his beloved Goat Mountain. He had a feeling this might all come to an end sooner than later.

Eli made several trips up past the cave during the rest of the week. Only once were the big creatures by the entrance. Eli also made an effort to walk a section of his property line each day to make sure the NO TRESPASSING signs were still in place. He never saw any signs of hikers or anyone else during the rest of the week.

Eli got up early the second day of June, fed the animals as usual, and prepared his own breakfast. He was running low on carbonated spring water so he decided this would be a good day to go up the mountain to the spring. He put the harness on Old Pet and hooked her up to the small two wheeled cart. He put his falcon on her tether and allowed the hounds to follow along. By the time they reached the cave it was well after 10:00 am. Eli was concerned because he only saw one of the big fellows. He assumed the little creature was probably sleeping inside the cave.

As Eli and his troop neared the spring they were absolutely horrified to find three young men eating their lunch by the spring. Again Eli knew that he must remain calm. The men introduced themselves and quickly apologized to Eli for not getting permission to be on his land. He asked them if they had seen his NO TRESSPASSING signs. They assured him they had not. Eli believed them. Again they told Eli they had seen an article in the Oregon City Courier about someone spotting a strange two legged creature whose body appeared to be covered with hair, in the Goat Mountain area east of Colton. The author of the article stated that is was his opinion that the story reported by the hikers was all a hoax and that he thought they were just wanting to get some unusual attention. Never the less these young men wanted to take a look for themselves. Eli assured them that he had lived on Goat Mountain for more than fifty years and he had never spotted anything other than the usual animals one would expect to find in this part of the Cascade Range. He kindly reminded them that this was private property and he would appreciate it if they would respect his privacy. They again apologized and told Eli they would leave his property by heading west towards Colton. They also told Eli they would place an article in the local paper stating that they had been to Goat Mountain and found no such creatures and they believed the story about the sighting of strange two legged animals to not be credible. Eli thanked them and watched them as they headed off to the west, finally out of sight.

After the three men left Eli filled his jugs with fresh, ice cold carbonated spring water, ate his lunch and fed his animals. It was time to start down the hill to his cabin. He decided to take the long way home which led to the east end of the big meadow near his cabin. As he approached the meadow he saw a sight that was almost more than he could bear. Blood and animal parts were scattered everywhere. Upon closer examination he could identify the remains of a young male mountain lion. But unfortunately he could also identify the remains of the young two legged Big Foot. Eli broke into tears and was in daze for several minutes. He could hardly believe what had happened. He could only imagine the terrible battle that must have occurred. Now he knew why he had only seen one of the big fellows at the entrance to the cave. Eli sat down by his hounds and Delightful for nearly an hour before heading for home. He decided that he would return tomorrow and bury the remains of the little fellow.

Eli allowed the hounds to remain outside and he also released Delightful from her tether. The hounds were trained to remain near the cabin and his falcon always returned when she heard Eli whistle. Eli went inside and sat down in his rocking chair, placed his head in his hands and wept for several minutes. The events of the past few months and now this tragedy was really taking its toll on Eli. He wondered what would be next. After about an hour Eli finally dozed off into a light sleep. He had only been sleeping for a few minutes when he heard that all too familiar tap on the window. Startled, he looked out the window, but not to his surprise the big creature stood there looking in the window. Eli looked at her and she looked directly at Eli. Eli could see what looked to be a tear running down the side of her face. She looked so sad. Eli got out of his chair and headed for the door. When he opened the door the big creature was already heading down towards the east end of the meadow. Eli knew where she was going but he decided he would not follow.

This was truly one of the saddest days Eli had ever experienced on Goat Mountain. The other sad day of course was when Sampson's cub, Sambo, was killed by a bolt of lightning. This along with curious strangers now coming to his peaceful Goat Mountain, looking for some strange two legged creature that walked in an upright position, had Eli wondering just how much longer he would be able to enjoy the peace and freedom he had been blessed to have for so long. How was he going to discuss all that had happened the past few months with his family when they arrived in a few weeks? Would he be able to share his feelings and his fears with them? What would their reactions be? Only time would tell.

Needless to say, Eli had a very sleepless night, but never the less there was much that needed to be done so he was up and about very early the next morning. After feeding the animals and having breakfast Eli took his shovel and headed down to the east end of the meadow. This was a difficult task that needed to be done. Just before he finished the task of burying the little creature he heard a noise in the nearby forest to the north. When Eli looked he saw his big hairy friend looking down towards him and the nearly completed grave where the remains of her little offspring lay. Eli leaned against his shovel and wiped a tear or two from eyes.

Eli went to the barn and left the door open so the hounds could come out and then he released Delightful from her tether. He also allowed Sampson and her new born cub to come out and enjoy some fresh air. The cub was growing rapidly and was starting to be quite playful with her mother. The cub still would not allow Eli to get too close but Eli knew that would change with time.

School Eli attended through the 8th grade

TWENTY SEVEN

All Three Families Arrive

Eli spent the next two weeks getting everything ready for the arrival of his three sons and their families. There was so much to be done. He spent the first three days just cleaning up limbs that had been broken off from trees in the last heavy snow storm of the winter.

Eli's wood shed was nearly empty so he had to restock it. He hauled many limbs down near the pond so the children would be able to enjoy a large bonfire. There were also some fences that needed to be repaired around the east pasture. This took several more days as he had to go around the entire perimeter of the meadow. The next several days were spent getting the cabin all spruced up and readied for his family. He also spent time putting the tarp over the tent cabin and getting bed frames back inside.

Eli was up early and anxiously waiting to hear the noise of approaching vehicles. He didn't have to wait long. At a little before 10:00 three vehicles came out of the woods and drove straight towards the cabin. Eli could hardly contain himself. He was so excited to see his sons and their wives and his ten grandchildren and Ailene's mom, Elaine. The tears of joy rolled down his cheeks. This had been a long winter and so much had happened.

Eli had prepared a large bowl of pancake batter and the stove was hot and his large cast iron frying pans were ready for cooking pancakes on. He heated some homemade maple syrup that he had made about a month ago. He also had a couple of bottles of wild strawberry jam that he had made last spring. The children were so excited that it was difficult to get them settled down enough to eat. They were anxious to go to the barn and see the new cub and also renew their friendship with Sampson, the hounds and Delightful. Eli still did not know how he was going tell his sons and their families about everything that happened since last summer.

Kim and Ailene offered to do the clean up after breakfast so the others could go down to the barn to visit the animals. The children got the surprise of their lives as Grandpa opened the door and Sampson and the new cub were there to greet everyone. The cub of course was very shy and stayed on the other side of her mother and out of sight of the children as much as possible. Grandpa cautioned the children to not get close to Sampson yet. He would slowly reintroduce everyone to Sampson and her cub. The hounds and Delightful were very excited to see the children. Grandpa took the hounds and the falcon outside and allowed the children to run and play with them. He released the bird from her tether so she could put on a show for the grandchildren.

While the children were playing with the animals Eli decided he would attempt to tell his sons some of the things that had happened since last fall. As he was relating the past events he noticed the deep concern displayed on the faces of his sons. It took most of an hour to tell everything that happened on Goat Mountain since their last visit. Eli told his sons about the female two legged creature giving birth early last fall. He had seen the young one with his mother on more than one occasion.

When Eli got to the part of telling his sons that the young creature was killed by a mountain lion and its father had died from injuries received in what must have been a terrible fight, he became very emotional. All three sons quickly put their arms around their father and expressed their sorrow and concern. They expressed their love and told him that he still had Sampson, the hounds, Delightful, and of course Old Pet and the mother Big Foot.

It was almost noon and time for lunch. Eli and his sons heard the dinner bell ring so they headed for the cabin. The children were still playing with the hounds. Sampson was nearby with her cub and Delightful was soaring high in the sky above. One sharp whistle from Eli and the falcon made a quick decent to the fence rail near the cabin. Eli told the children that he would let them slowly approach Sampson and the cub after lunch.

The children asked their Grandfather if he would take them up to the carbonated spring after lunch. They also asked if they could go by the cave to perhaps get a quick look at the big fellows if they were near the entrance. Eli said that he would love to go up to the spring but that he wanted to take the route at the east end of the meadow so that they could pick some wild strawberries and blackcaps. He was just not ready to break the news to the children about the fate of the young Big Foot and its father. That would have to come in a couple of days.

After lunch the children went with their Grandfather to the barn to get the hounds and Delightful. Siena asked Grandpa if they could take Sampson and the cub but Eli told her that would probably not be a good idea. When they got to the barn to get Old Pet ready for the trip, the children of course wanted to know where the milk cow was. Eli told them that a cougar had gotten into the barn and had killed the cow. They were very sad. They asked their Grandfather if he was going to get another cow. He replied that he wasn't sure. In his own mind he had already decided that he would not. He would just have to get used to using powdered milk.

Eli hooked the small two wheeled cart up to the single tree, loaded several water bottles in the cart and they all headed to the east end of the meadow. The wild strawberries were plentiful as were the wild blackcaps. With everyone collecting the berries it did not take long to fill two one gallon pails. They had not traveled very far when Eli brought the horse to a quick stop. He motioned for everyone to be absolutely quiet and to look up the trail towards the spring. About one fourth of a mile away Eli could see a huge black bear eating what looked to be blackcaps from several plants. All of the adults brought the children to where Grandpa was for a look. The children wanted to see the bear but they also began to express a great deal of fear. Grandpa assured them they had nothing to fear. After viewing the bear for several minutes Eli told the children to watch carefully. He gave an ear drum breaking whistle which caused the bear to stop eating and look in their direction. In an instant the bear was long gone. Eli was careful to avoid the area at the end of the meadow where the young Big Foot was buried.

The group continued on up towards the carbonated spring, picking berries along the way. After collecting several bottles of fresh ice cold water it was time to head back down the mountain. The children begged

Grandpa to go by the cave to which he reluctantly agreed. Eli was careful not to drive Old Pet and the cart too close to the cave entrance. When they approached the cave Eli asked everyone to be especially quiet. Sure enough one of the big hairy creatures was near the entrance. He took one look at the group and slowly moved out a few feet towards the group. Eli was thrilled because in the past he would move quickly back into the safety of the cave. This was truly a first! After staying quiet and motionless for several minutes Eli told the group it was time to move on down the mountain. As they left the area several of the children continued to look backwards towards the cave. The big fellow just stood there. What a thrilling experience this was for everyone. No one was especially frightened any longer of the big hairy, man like creature. Eli was particularly happy as he had not seen the big creature since the night of the death of her little offspring.

By the time the group got back to the cabin it was time to start preparing supper. The berries had to be washed and placed in the cool root cellar until morning. The plan was to make some fresh strawberry jam and also have some of the berries on strawberry short cake made from scratch. The parents all worked together to prepare a fine meal while Grandpa Eli spent time with the children. He was surprised how much each child had grown in the last year. Eli spent the better part of an hour listening to the children tell about things they had been doing during the past year. Again he felt a little remorse in that he did not live close to them so that he could be part of their lives for more than two or three weeks a year. These types of thoughts had been running through Eli's mind more and more lately with each passing year.

After supper the children asked Grandpa if they could have a bonfire down by the pond to which Grandpa Eli agreed. After cleaning up the kitchen area they all headed down to the pond. It did not take long to gather a considerable amount of dried limbs for the fire. Kim brought down a package of marshmallows.

Grandpa asked each member of the family to tell something special that had happened in their lives since last being at Goat Mountain. Some of the happenings were very funny and some were more serious. Everyone had a good laugh when Martin and Mike told about an experience they had on a recent recruiting trips to Wyoming and Utah in the fall. Grandpa was pleased that each child had something special to contribute. The fire finally died down enough so that the children could roast their marshmallows.

Afterwards the children wanted to sing some campfire songs. Mike got out his guitar and played several fun songs while the group had fun singing.

Grandpa told everyone how happy he was that they were all able to come to Goat Mountain this year. Before he ended what he wanted to say the group was terrified by a loud noise that sounded like a woman screaming. The children ran to their parents. Grandpa told everyone that was the scream of a Mountain Lion and that the sound came from far up on the mountain in the direction of the carbonated spring and cave. Matt, Mike and Martin put the fire out while the rest went to the cabin. The children were very happy to get inside. When his sons came inside Grandpa suggested that they make a trip up to the cave and spring in the morning to check on things. He did not want to go into any more detail. The screaming went on for at least another hour. They could all hear the terrible battle that was going on up the mountain. There was very little talking among family members the rest of the evening.

The children were reluctant to want to sleep out in the tent but Grandpa Eli assured them they would be fine and he would be right there with them. The evening was warm and there was a full moon so that made it a little more difficult to get the children settled down in the tent. Finally Elly asked Grandpa to tell them a story, and before he finished with Hansel and Gretel the children were all asleep. Eli had a hard time going to sleep and he shuddered to think what they might find the next day up near the cave.

Eli awoke early as usual but he discovered that Matt, Mike and Martin were already up. They had breakfast started by the time Eli came into the cabin. The aroma of bacon frying was wonderful.

Matt asked his dad to make some homemade biscuits and Martin said he would fry the eggs when everyone was ready to eat. It was only a few minutes until all the children were up and inside the cabin in their pajamas.

After breakfast the children were anxious to go down to the barn and help feed the animals. They were very anxious to spend some time with Sampson in hopes that he would let them get close to the cub.

Sampson was glad to see the children and the cub was not as shy as he was the day before. The hounds were anxious to get outside as was Delightful. Grandpa decided that he would not turn the hounds loose yet as he planned to take them up on Goat Mountain later in the day if his sons still wanted to go and check out what they had heard the night before.

Eli put the harness on Old Pet and hitched her to the small buggy in preparation for the trip up the mountain. He placed several empty jugs in the wagon so they could get a fresh supply of carbonated spring water. They each took a rifle but Eli hoped they would only use them for target practice. He hoped there would be no encounters with the wild animals on the mountain. The children were a little upset when Grandpa told them they would not be able to go on this trip up the mountain.

Eli decided they would take the long route to the carbonated spring. They took two or three empty one gallon cans so they could bring back more fresh strawberries. There was also a cherry tree that had big beautiful Lambert cherries on it this year. Eli had always been careful to prune it each year and get rid of old dead wood. They arrived at the spring by noon. The women had prepared them a nice lunch so they took time to enjoy it by the spring before heading on down toward the cave.

What they saw when they got to the cave was horrifying. There were animal parts all over the place. There were remains of at least one mountain lion and also the big man like creature, that Eli claimed as his friend, was killed in the battle. Eli almost went into shock. It is a good thing his sons were there to comfort him. They did not stay in the area very long as Eli just wanted to leave the area and go back to the cabin. He was subdued on the entire trip down the mountain and for the rest of the day. Fortunately the children's fathers took them down to the barn and explained to them what they found at the cave. The children were saddened and crying as they watched their Grandfather grieve over the loss of his friend. This was a very sad time on Eli's Goat Mountain.

The sun was shining brightly as Eli crept out of bed and was careful not to wake anyone else. He looked at his watch and observed that it was 6:05 am. Eli put on his clothes that he had worn the day before and headed down to the barn to spend some quiet time with Sampson and her cub. They were glad to see Eli. Eli noted how fast the cub was growing and realized before long he would need to release the cub to the wilderness of the Mt. Hood National Forest. Eli took the hounds and Delightful outside where he released the falcon and allowed the hounds to run freely. Eli sat down in an old chair that he often sat in when he wanted to meditate and reflect on his life on Goat Mountain. Once again the thought occurred to him that it might be time to think about leaving Goat Mountain and going to live near his sons and their families in Houston. He could not stand to dwell on that thought very long as it brought tears to his eyes. But with all that had happened in the last couple of years and especially the last year, he knew that he had to face reality.

Before long the sun came up and Eli enjoyed the warmth it provided. He soon heard the cabin door open and all of a sudden out came all ten grandchildren all dressed for the day. Kate noticed a tear that had dried on Grandpa's cheek. She did not ask the question that came to her mind. Elly asked Grandpa if he would take them down to the barn to see Sampson's new baby to which he agreed to do. He cautioned the children to approach Sampson and the cub slowly to see how they were going to react. To his and the children's delight Sampson was glad to see all of them but the cub was still being a little shy. Before long though the cub came around to where the children were and allowed them to get a good look at him. Jacob asked if they might take Sampson and the cub out into the East Meadow in the afternoon. Eli said "we will see how the morning goes".

Pretty soon it was time to call Delightful in and place her on her tether. The hounds were allowed to run free. Before long Kim came out and told the group that breakfast was nearly ready. Kim, Ailene and Elaine had prepared a wonderful breakfast.

There were a lot of little chores that Eli had been waiting for his sons to help him with. Some repairs needed to be made on the cabin roof and also on barn and cow shed. So the entire morning was spent helping grandpa. The children found many ways to entertain themselves, playing with the hounds and Delightful. Grandpa also brought Old Pet out and asked Elaine if she would supervise letting the children ride out in the nearby field to which she was happy to do. There was no saddle for the horse so they just rode bareback. The children loved to ride Old Pet.

Elaine prepared ten numbers on little pieces of paper. Each child drew a number which indicated what order they would ride. Siena drew #1 and Kate drew #10. Old Pet was so gentle with the children and seemed so happy to be ridden and to get the chance to get out of the barn and into the meadows.

Kim and Ailene spent the morning doing some deep cleaning in the cabin and preparing lunch. Time went by quickly and before long Eli and his sons had the repairs completed and sat down on some comfortable chairs that Eli's brother Delbert had made from willows many years ago and given to him for his sixty fifth birthday. They spent some time discussing the events at the cave and wondered how they might tell the children what they had discovered. Mike suggested they tell just exactly what they found and deal with the reactions and the crying that would follow. Martin suggested they wait for a few days. Matt said "no, let's have the discussion right after lunch and get it over with so that we can move on to doing the other things we have planned, like a trip down to Colton and a trip up to the carbonated spring." Grandpa Eli went along with what Mike and Matt said and Martin was fine with that also.

Ailene rang the dinner bell and in a few minutes everyone was back at the cabin and ready for lunch. After lunch Grandpa Eli told the children to stay at the table for a little while because he had something he wanted to tell them. He related the events of the trip to the cave that he and their fathers had made the day before. When he got to the part of telling them that his friend, the big hairy creature, was killed by more than one Mountain Lion, he broke down and cried. The children crowded around grandpa and told him how sorry they were and how much they loved him. The mood at Eli's Goat Mountain was very somber for the rest of the day. Finally along towards evening Eli suggested they build a bonfire down by the pond and roast some hot dogs that Martin had brought from the store in Colton.

Eli awoke to sunshine coming in through the window by his bed. He heard noises coming from outside the cabin. When he looked out the window he was surprised to see all of the children up and playing outside in their pajamas. Their parents were still sleeping, that is all except Matt and Kim. Eli dressed quickly and joined the children outside. They all wanted to go down to the barn and bring the hounds,

Sampson and her cub, and Delightful outside, to which Grandpa Eli agreed.

In about an hour Eli saw Matt and Kim walking towards the cabin with two small pails which were filled with wild blackberries and a few wild strawberries. The children ran to meet them. The hounds followed, but Sampson and the cub stayed behind. This gave Eli a chance to be alone with them for a few minutes. The cub was growing fast and really seemed to enjoy the attention she was now getting from almost everyone.

Matt and Kim took the berries in the cabin and before long the dinner bell rang and that was an invitation to come to breakfast. After breakfast and cleanup Grandpa suggested they take a few moments and plan for next week. The group decided to make the trip to Colton on Monday and then go to the carbonated spring on Tuesday. They planned to spend Wednesday and Thursday picking more berries to make jam with. Eli suggested they leave Friday open.

Everyone got up early Monday morning to prepare for the trip to Colton. It was decided they would take only two cars. The children wanted to take the hounds and Delightful but Grandpa Eli told them that would probably not be a good idea. The children helped Grandpa feed all the animals and do a few other chores. They all loaded into the vehicles and were on their way by 8:00 am. It took all of an hour to make the trip to Colton. Their first stop was Bob Berge's place. Bob and Darlene were very happy to see everyone. Darlene invited them all to supper at around 5:00 pm, prior to their departure for Goat Mountain. They had a short visit and then proceeded on to Colton. They spent about an hour at the Colton Market buying groceries and other supplies. The next stop was Jennifer's home. Elaine rang the door bell. When Jennifer came to the door Elaine introduced herself. They both embraced and a few tears started to flow. It was a happy reunion for everyone. Jennifer invited them all to come in. She offered to prepare lunch but Elaine told her they would like to take her to lunch at the one and only restaurant in Colton. They spent a couple of hours with Jennifer. Eli told Jennifer that Bob Berge would be going to Goat Mountain the first part of next week to do some logging and invited her to come and spend a few days. Jennifer said she would really like that. Eli told her he would arrange things with Bob and stop by and let her know before they returned to the mountain in the early evening.

Eli and his family arrived back at Bob's home about 4:00 pm. Bob and Darlene had prepared a wonderful picnic style dinner which included potato salad, barbequed hamburgers, fresh strawberry short cake and fruit punch. The children played outside while the adults visited inside and around the barbeque. Eli asked Bob if he would be willing to bring Jennifer to Goat Mountain next week? Bob assured him that he would be happy to do that.

The group thanked Darlene for the wonderful dinner and they left to return to Goat Mountain. They made a quick stop at Jennifer's place. Jennifer invited Eli inside while the rest stayed in their cars. After about fifteen minutes Matt thought that perhaps he should go to the door and remind his father that they needed to get going. Kim told him to relax. By this time everyone was wondering what was going on in Jennifer's house. Secretly everyone was hoping that perhaps there might be some chemistry developing between Eli and Jennifer. They were all excited about what might develop next week.

The trip back to Goat Mountain was uneventful. Eli marveled about how much faster the trip could be made in newer automobiles. It had been years since Eli had even ridden in a new car. In spite of this he still preferred his old Dodge 1 ton truck. As soon as they got to the cabin the children wanted to go with Grandpa to the barn so they could see Sampson and the cub. Eli released the hounds and brought Delightful, Sampson and her cub outside for the rest of the daylight hours. Everyone had a great time and got some good exercise after spending a lot of time in an automobile and visiting Eli's friends in their homes.

The children were up before any of the adults and they were excited to go blackberry picking. They all loved the wild berries that grew on Goat Mountain. Grandpa had made handles for all of the one gallon pails he could find. As soon as breakfast was over Grandpa Eli and the children headed for the far end of the east meadow. They took the hounds and Delightful but left Sampson and her cub in the barn. The adults who remained behind said they would do the clean up and prepare the small jars that would be needed to put the jam in.

Grandpa Eli failed to remember the possibility that the children might discover the mound of fresh dirt which covered the burial spot for his small two legged hairy friend that had been recently killed by a mountain lion. Sure enough, they had only been picking berries for about fifteen minutes when Evan hollered to Grandpa and ask him what this mound of dirt was for. Grandpa decided he must tell the truth so he called all of the children around the fresh mound and told them what had happened. As he finished telling of that terrible day tears flowed from his eyes and then several of the children started crying also. By that time Eli wished that he had gone to another area up the mountain to pick the berries. After a few minutes the children settled down and Eli told everyone to get back to picking berries to fill their pails. He had told each child that he would give him/her $1.00 for a full pail of berries. The children had their pails full by around 11:30 so they all headed back to the cabin. Not a word was mentioned to the adults about discovering the small grave or about the crying.

After lunch it was time to start making jam from the berries. This was an adult thing, so the children were sent outside to play for the rest of the afternoon. They had so much fun running with the hounds and watching Delightful perform her flying stunts for them. By this time Sampson was really warming up to the children as was her cub. By the time the dinner bell was heard the children were more than ready to put the animals in the barn and prepare for supper. They were all very hungry. The dinner was topped off with a slice of warm bread and fresh blackberry jam and cold carbonated spring water. In spite of all that had happened recently life was once again good on Goat Mountain.

The children were up early the next morning as they were excited to go picking more wild berries. Ten more pails of blackberries were picked and made into jam. The children's hands were so stained from the blackberries they thought they would have to start school with stained hands.

After cleaning everything up Matt, Mike and Martin suggested they all take a walk in the forest. The children asked if they could take the hounds, Delightful, Sampson and her cub. Grandpa Eli said he thought that would be ok. The wild flowers were beautiful and there were still lots of wild strawberries to eat. They all paused for a few minutes when they passed the spot where Sampson's first cub had been killed. They examined the area that Eli had marked the trees that would be taken this year. Eli's sons had to admit that the areas where trees had been selectively remover appeared to be the healthiest part of the forest. After spending a couple of hours in the forest it was time to return to the cabin and prepare supper. The children and the animals would have preferred to remain in the forest. Sampson and her cub stayed right with the group. Delightful enjoyed the time to soar high overhead and the hounds had a great time checking out every scent. At one point Eli thought the hounds might be on the trail of a raccoon but he quickly called them back to the group. This was not the time to go coon hunting. Jacob, Evan, Benjamin and Archer asked Grandpa if he would take them coon hunting before they left to return to Houston. Eli looked at their Dads to see their reactions to their son's request. All three sons thought it was a good idea. Their mothers were not so quick to give their approval. All three said they would have to think about the idea.

Grandpa Eli was very tired by the time supper was over. He told his sons that he thought it best for him to retire to bed early. As he started towards his bed he got light headed and almost fell to the floor. Martin caught him and helped him to a nearby chair. Fortunately the children were all outside. This caused great concern to the adults in the room. They all told him to just sit quietly for a few minutes. Matt asked his dad if he had had other spells like this before and Eli assured him that he had not. Eli sat in the chair for several minutes and then his sons helped him to his bed. Elaine, who was a retired Nurse, checked his pulse and said that it was above normal but that it should come down after he rested for awhile. After lying down for several minutes the color came back into his face and he assured every one that he was fine. Kim gave him a glass of water and then pulled the curtain around his bed so that he could put his pajamas on and crawl into bed. He was sound asleep within a few minutes. Mike suggested they go outside and discuss the situation. It was decided that they would wait until tomorrow to see how Eli felt before making any decisions as to what actions they might take.

Eli woke up early, got dressed and headed to the barn to feed the animals. Evan was always the first one of the children to get up. He got dressed quickly and heard the hounds outside the tent. He got up and joined his Grandpa who had all of the animals outside. Evan asked if he could take Delightful on her tether to which Grandpa quickly agreed. Evan loved watching the beautiful falcon soar high in the sky.

Before long all of the children were up and playing with the hounds and Sampson and her cub. The rest of the adults were up before long. Eli's sons were very pleased to see their father feeling better and playing with the children. They surmised that he had just over done it yesterday. They decided they would not let him put in such long and tiring days in the future. They wondered what would have happened had they not been there when the incident happened yesterday.

The ringing of the ranch dinner bell meant it was time for breakfast. Eli and the children had worked up a real good appetite. After breakfast everyone helped with the cleanup so it only took a few minutes.

Kate asked Grandpa Eli if they could go down to the East Meadow and spend the rest of the day. Elly and Siena said they would prepare a picnic lunch. Jacob and Evan asked if they could take the hounds and Benjamin asked if he could take Delightful. Grandpa said yes to both. Marina and Brighton asked if Sampson and her cub could trail along. With a little hesitation Grandpa Eli finally said ok. Christine and Archer asked Grandpa if he was going to take Old Pet and the two wheeled cart. Grandpa said that he hadn't planned on it but in the end he agreed to do so. Archer and Christine wanted to ride in the cart. They were the youngest of the ten grandchildren. Kate placed the lunch stuff and carbonated spring water in a small box in one corner of the cart. Eli's sons said they wanted to stay and make some of the small repairs around the cabin and other out buildings. Ailene, Kim and Elaine said they would finish canning the strawberry jam and also make some homemade bread.

When they got to the far end of the meadow Eli looked up towards the spring. What he saw gave him some real concern. A large black bear was eating blackberries. Eli cautioned the children to stay close by. He was very concerned with what Sampson might do when she saw the male bear. The children played with the hounds and the falcon but Eli never took his eyes of the big bear. As it turned out the bear was evidently more interested in eating berries than joining the group, to which Eli was very thankful.

When the sun was directly overhead they all gathered around the cart and had a wonderful picnic lunch. They all thanked Elly and Siena for the lunch. After lunch Grandpa gathered everyone around in a circle and told them some great Old Navy stories. Eli had spent two years in the Navy when he was a young man. The children loved his Old Navy stories although some seemed quite farfetched. After spending a couple more hours in the meadow it was time to head for home. As usual the children didn't want to leave. They especially loved this part of Grandpa's Goat Mountain. On the way home they asked if they could go by the spot where Eli had buried the small Big Foot. It was a sad moment when they reached the spot. Grandpa got all choked up and was in a hurry to move on towards the cabin.

The children were happy to see their parents and Grandma Elaine. Even those who were really not her grandchildren still called her Grandma. The hounds even seemed happy to be back to the cabin. Sampson and her cub headed straight for their place in the barn. Martin said he would put Old Pet in the barn and put the cart where it belonged. Eli gave a whistle and his Falcon came soaring in from high in the sky. It was such a beautiful sight to see her land on her favorite perch.

Eli was very pleased to see all of the little projects his sons had completed while they were gone. He was especially please they had replaced the missing shingles on the roof of the cabin. After a short discussion with their father it was decided they all would spend tomorrow bringing split wood into the woodshed in preparing for next winter. Before long Kim rang the dinner bell. Everyone had really worked up a huge appetite and the dinner that was placed on the table smelled so good. Again the children were too tired for a camp fire and so they all went to bed early. This gave the adults a chance to visit and have an opportunity to discuss many things that had been happening in their lives at home. All three sons were very happy with their jobs and their wives were very involved with their children's schools and being 'stay-at-home moms'. Matt and Kim and their children were getting to like Texas a little better all the time but they still missed their home in Bend and their lifelong friends. They also complained about the hot and humid summer months of June, July and August.

Grandpa Eli, most of the grandchildren, and his sons spent Friday splitting and hauling wood into the woodshed. By the end of the day the shed was full. While they were working with Grandpa Eli Jacob, Evan, Ben and Archer asked their Grandfather if he would take them Coon Hunting tonight. There was a full moon and the temperature was just right. Grandpa said he would check with their fathers at supper time.

If they said ok, and would join in, he said he would love to take them. All three sons thought it sounded exciting. After supper Grandpa Eli got out lanterns for the adults. He prepared some small bottles of water and a small first aid kit. When it got dark they were off for their great adventure.

Eli led the way. They started to the west of the cabin and almost at the bottom of the ranch. This was near the beginning of Mill Creek which flowed off to the Southwest and eventually ended up at Colton and then on to the Molalla River. Eli told the children that they were not going to kill any of the coons. He had trained his hounds to back off once they had them treed. The only time Eli ever killed a coon was if he needed the fur for a new hat or gloves. All of the children had either read or had read to them, that wonderful book, Where The Red Fern Grows. They were pleased when grandpa assured them that the coons would remain free and would probably stay up in the tree the rest of the night, but return to their normal routine tomorrow.

They had only traveled a little way when Old Daniel took off. Little Anne followed right behind. They started yelping and howling and the boys got so excited. They wanted to run after the hounds but Grandpa stopped them. He told them that would be a good way to break a leg or twist and ankle. They followed the yelping sounds of the dogs and finally came to the large mountain maple tree where the coon was holed up. Matt shined his powerful spot light up in the tree and quickly spotted the coon. As soon as the coon saw the light she moved to the other side of the tree. Finally Grandpa Eli called the dogs off and the group continued on their way. They walked about one quarter of a mile and the hounds took off again. This time it was more difficult to follow as the dogs went down into a canyon and back up the other side. Since there was no trail, the going got real difficult. There were blackberry vines, scotch broom, and a lot of Scotch Thistles. The boys were getting real tired but they refused to turn back. After nearly two hours they finally picked up the howling sound of the dogs. By this time it was almost 11:00 pm. Grandpa Eli was exhausted and his sons became quite worried about whether he had enough strength to get back to the cabin. He assured them he could make it after resting for awhile.

Eli called the dogs off and put them on leashes so that they would not go after another coon. After resting for about 30 minutes Grandpa

Eli told them he was ready to head for home. He told them that by going up the mountain side towards the spring they could avoid going through the deep canyon. It only took about 45 minutes to get home. The boys were very tired but excited to tell their siblings about the great coon hunt. All of that would have to wait until tomorrow as the girls were all sound asleep when they got to the cabin. Ailene, Kim and Elaine were all very happy to see that every one made it back safely.

Everyone spent most of the next day doing little chores around the cabin, both inside and out. Ailene reminded Eli that perhaps Bob would come with his logging crew, and of course Jennifer, early next week. They all noticed a twinkle in Eli's eyes when he heard Jennifer's name mentioned.

Eli asked the children if they would like to have a camp fire down by the pond after supper? Their response was of course a resounding yes! They gathered wood and made a huge pile in the usual spot while the adults helped with preparing the evening meal. As soon as the supper dishes and the kitchen were cleaned up it was time to retire to the campfire site near the pond. Michael brought out his old guitar and sheet music with all the neat campfire songs that he had learned during his High School years of being a camp counselor for his father, who taught Junior High Science. Grandpa gave Jacob and Evan permission to bring the hounds down to be with the group. The rest of the children were disappointed that Grandpa would not let them bring Sampson and her cub along also.

Mike gave each child a chance to choose their favorite campfire song. After singing several songs it was finally time to break out the marshmallows, graham crackers, and chocolate bars to make s'mores. It was not long until the younger children began to fall asleep near their mothers, so Ailene and Kim suggested they have one more song and then return to the cabin. Just as they started for the cabin they heard a terrible commotion from the direction of the cow barn. Martin shined his powerful spot light in the direction of the barn and as he did so he saw a huge Mountain Lion pawing at the barn door. He alerted the rest of the group and then let out a loud whistle and the Mountain Lion ran into the nearby woods. Everyone was pretty shook up and the children refused to sleep in the tent so beds were made on the floor of the cabin. Eli and his sons when out to the barn to make sure Old Pet was ok, and she was. They made sure the barn door was secure and then returned to the cabin. Eli thought about tracking the animal down the next day with the hounds, but after careful consideration he decided against it.

Eli was the first one up the next morning and the children soon followed. It was a beautiful morning on Goat Mountain. Grandpa took the children down to the barn to feed the animals. He also did this so that the parents could get a little extra sleep. Just as they were leaving the barn with all of the animals Eli heard the sound of an engine. He guessed that it was Bob and his logging crew. Kate also reminded him that Jennifer would be with them. The children noticed a smile on Eli's face when Kate mentioned Jennifer. The rest of the adults were up and in the process of starting to prepare breakfast when Eli and the children reached the cabin.

In a few minutes Bob and his crew, and yes, Jennifer, arrived. Eli and his sons and their families were so excited to see everyone. Elaine was also happy to see her cousin, Jennifer. Jennifer had never been to Goat Mountain since moving to Colton. Eli invited everyone into the cabin. He asked Jennifer if he could bring her small suitcase inside. Jennifer thanked him.

Elaine, Kim and Ailene asked Eli if it was alright if they invited Bob and his logging crew to have breakfast. Eli said "sure" and with that the ladies got out additional frying pans, more eggs and bacon and every plate they could find in the cupboard. Matt, Mike and Martin set up some tables outside and went to the wood shed to get large, un-split pieces of wood to be used as stools as Eli only had about 6 chairs. The ladies had breakfast ready in about 30 minutes and Kim asked Siena if she would like to ring the dinner bell. This was probably the largest number of people that had ever had a meal at Eli's cabin on Goat Mountain. Eli was so happy to have everyone at his cabin and once again he reflected on how good life was on his beautiful Goat Mountain.

Eli asked the family what they would like to do after breakfast clean up. The children all spoke in unison "would you take us up to the Carbonated Spring and can Jennifer come with us"? The rest of the adults expressed a desire to just stay at cabin and get some more things done on their work list of things that needed to be done. Bob and his crew left right after breakfast. It would take the rest of the day to get their camp set up and get their machinery ready to begin logging the next day.

It took some time to collect all of the animals and to put the harness on old Pet and hook him up to the small wagon. Eli put several empty bottles in the wagon and a couple of small pails for putting berries in. There were still a lot of wild strawberries, blackberries, huckleberries and also some wild blackcaps now. The trip up to the spring was exciting. There were so many beautiful wild flowers and the group saw several young fawns with their mothers. They also saw a couple of red foxes and one badger. They stayed far away from the badger. They passed by the cave but no one said a word about Eli's hairy two legged friends that had once inhabited the cave. Jennifer had not been told anything about these creatures. Eli gave Old Pet some water while the children and Jennifer were filling the water jugs with fresh cold water. Jennifer had her first drink of the carbonated spring water. It was different than any water she had ever tasted. Elly told her that she would probably like it better when it was mixed with Kool-Aid. The children asked Grandpa if they could play around the meadow for a while. Jacob released Delightful from her tether and Ben, Evan, and Archer ran with the hounds. Eli's granddaughters asked if they could pick some spring flowers to take back to the cabin.

With the children gone a short distance away Eli and Jennifer found they were alone for the first time on Goat Mountain. Eli asked Jennifer how she liked the mountain so far? Jennifer could hardly find words to tell Eli how beautiful she thought his cabin, the meadows around the cabin and the mountains were. She was thrilled to be here and thanked Eli more than once for inviting her to his beloved mountain. Jennifer asked Eli how long he had lived here and she could hardly believe it when he told her, more than 25 years this time. She asked if he had been alone all of that time. He told her that his beloved wife had passed away just a few short years after they moved to Goat Mountain. He had been alone ever since. He told her how much he loved having his sons and their families come every year. He also told her how long and lonely the winters were and they were getting a little harder on him with each passing year. Eli told Jennifer that he was born in the very same cabin he now occupied, but that he had moved away when he got married.

He and his wife returned to the mountain when his parents passed away and he had lived here ever since.

Jennifer then shared a little about her past. She had lost her husband in Vietnam. He had been killed by a sniper's bullet just three days before he was to return home. She had raised their two sons and one daughter alone. She never remarried. She had six grandchildren whom she adored. Her two sons lived in Houston, Texas and her daughter lived in Salt Lake City, Utah. Eli asked Jennifer what brought her to the tiny town of Colton, Oregon. Jennifer told him that she and her husband had visited Western Oregon and had driven through Molalla and Colton just prior to him leaving for Vietnam. She was so impressed with the beauty of the area and the closeness to the Cascade Mountains that she thought she might like to live there someday. When she retired from working in the banking industry five years ago she moved to Colton. She also told Eli that her daughter and son-in-law, who lived in Salt Lake City, were moving to Houston. Her son-in-law worked for Huntsman Chemical and the company headquarters was being moved to the Houston area in January. They had five children under the age of ten, and her daughter had asked her to move into their home so that she could help with the children. She also told Eli that she had recently made the decision to make the move. She wanted very much to be closer to her children and their families.

Eli did not want to continue this conversation because he could see where it was leading, so he quickly changed the subject. Eli asked her if she had gotten pretty well acquainted with the people in the Colton community. She knew every one that he named and many more that had moved in, in the last few years. She said that she had recently got to know the Berge's quite well as she had attending their church a couple of times at the suggestion of her daughter who lived in Salt Lake City.

Their quiet time together ended when the children returned to the spring. They were all hungry and so the lunch Elaine had prepared for them was much appreciated. After they finished eating Eli said it was time to head back down the mountain to the cabin as thunder clouds were starting to roll in. The trip home was uneventful and only took about 45 minutes. Everyone helped to take the jugs, full of fresh carbonated water, to the cellar. The girls gave the beautiful wild flowers to their mothers and Jennifer brought the wild berries inside. Eli took

Old Pet over to the barn and removed her harness and put her in her stall after giving her some grain.

The mothers and Elaine prepared a wonderful supper of mashed potatoes, gravy made from the drippings of the elk roast that Bob had brought and a fresh vegetable salad. Elaine made a huckleberry pie from the wild huckleberries the group brought back from the mountain.

After dinner they all went down to the pond for a swim and then a small camp fire. The children could not stay awake very long and Eli and Jennifer were very tired also. Prayers were said and most everyone went to bed early, all except the fathers. They sat around the campfire until it was almost out. This was a special time for Matt, Mike and Martin. They loved to just sit around and talk. This time a lot of their conversation revolved around their beloved father. They wondered if they would ever convince him that it might be time to start thinking about leaving his mountain and living near them in Houston. They also wondered if anything would come of the relationship between him and Jennifer. These were all valid concerns the three sons shared.

As usual Evan was the first one up the next morning. He decided this would be a good time to try making a willow whistle. The last time they were at Goat Mountain his Grandfather had taught him how to make the whistle and he had tried to make one then but was not successful. The willows were a little bit to dry. He went down by the pond a broke off a nice willow limb and brought it back to a stump seat near the cabin. He tried to be as quiet as possible so as not to wake the others. As he was attempting to cut the whistle part away from the rest of the limb he slipped with the knife and cut a gash in his leg. He woke his mother up and she woke Elaine up. Fortunately Elaine was a retired RN and knew exactly what to do. She cleaned the wound and then pulled the skin back together and placed a tight bandage over the wound. She had Evan lay down for several minutes as he had lost a fair amount of blood and looked a little pale. She did not want him to go into shock. Elaine and Kim stayed right by him for several minutes. Before long though he felt better and wanted to continue with the whistle project.

TWENTY EIGHT

The Lost Grandchildren

Eli and his sons spent most of the rest of the day doing odd jobs around the cabin and the barns. The children played with the animals and Grandpa let them take Old Pet out in the East Meadow and ride him in the big pasture. Christine and Siena decided they did not want to join in with the rest of the children. They told Kate they would just watch. After about three hours the children heard the dinner bell ring so they knew it was time to take Old Pet back to the barn and get ready for lunch. When Kate looked around to see where Siena and Christine were, she could not see or hear them. She assumed they had gone back to the cabin so all the rest of the grandchildren headed for the cabin. When they got to the cabin Ailene and Kim asked them where Christine and Siena were. Of course this caused alarm and a great deal of concern when Kate told them she thought they had returned earlier to the cabin. This of course sent every one into an alarm mode. Matt and Mike immediately organized a search with each adult leading a group to begin searching.

They returned to the meadow and tried to follow their tracks but that was to no avail as the ground was too dry. The three sons and their father each led a group in different directions. They began calling and each fired their rifles every fifteen minutes. The rule was to fire twice if the children were found. Everyone forgot about eating, they just wanted to find the children before dark. Martin took his group in the direction of the cave. Matt took his group out into the East Meadow and Mike concentrated on the area west of the cabin. One thing they did not have to be very concerned about was the pond as both girls were excellent swimmers for their age. The great fears they all had were the Mountain Lions that had ascended on the area in the last several years.

Grandpa Eli remembered Siena asking him if he would take her to visit the site where the little cub was killed from a falling tree. He had taken the children to the site several times in the past and he promised her he would before they left to go home to Houston, but in reality he was hoping she would forget about the promise. Every time he visited the site it brought back such painful memories. Just prior to it getting dark Eli decided he would go to the site to see if perhaps Siena and Christine had decided to go there on their own. The site was not very far from his cabin. As Eli approached the site he saw the girls setting down by the marker he had placed their shortly after the cub was killed. The girls were both crying and they were both very happy to see their grandfather. Eli took them into his arms and then he moved several feet from them and fired two shots from his rifle. When the three of them got back to the cabin everyone was waiting for them. Of course the girl's parents were so happy, they were crying. They were so thankful the girls were safe they did not even scold them at the time. Grandpa Eli had them all kneel and he asked Mike to say a prayer of thanks for their safe return.

The meal that was prepared for their lunch was now their supper. Elaine warmed up the beef stew as it was easy to do and only took a few minutes. Everyone was so exhausted, both physically and emotionally, that Grandpa Eli suggested they just spend some quiet time in the cabin and then retire to bed a little early.

Evan was the first one up the next morning. Jacob, Benjamin and Archer soon followed. For some reason all of the girls decide to sleep in. Eli awakened with the noise the boys were making just outside the tent. He got dressed quickly and asked the boys if they wanted to take Sampson, her cub, the hounds and Delightful out into the East Meadow. Their plan was to be well out of sight when the girls finally woke up. The boys were all excited about an opportunity to have all of the animals to themselves, that is all except Old Pet. Eli's grandsons got the surprise of their lives when Elly and Kate came riding Old Pet at a fast gallop after the boys had barley gotten to the east end of the meadow. Grandpa was pleased to know that the girls could bridle the horse on their own now.

Before long the group heard the dinner bell ring so it was time to head back to the cabin for breakfast. Jennifer had prepared the breakfast this morning so Eli had his first chance to try her cooking. She had prepared wonderful omelets filled with small wild sweet onions which Eli had gathered from the hillsides, shredded cheese they had purchased at the Colton store, tiny bits of beef left over from the beef stew and home grown eggs. Everyone complimented Jennifer on the breakfast. Eli not only complimented her but he gave her a hug as he and the children went out to tidy up the tent. Matt noticed a smile on Jennifer's face after Eli closed the door.

After Eli and the children finished making up the beds inside the tent, it was time to go to the barn and feed the chickens and collect the eggs. Eli asked the girls if they would like to collect the eggs and then turn the chickens out into their fenced area. They were excited to be able to do that little chore.

Matt reminded the children that they only had four more days left to spend at Grandpa Eli's mountain ranch. That of course did not bring cheers. The children asked if they could make one last trip up to the carbonated spring to which Eli agreed. Jacob and Evan asked Grandpa Eli if they could stop at the cave. Eli reluctantly agreed. Everyone helped grandpa get Old Pet and the small wagon ready for the trip up the mountain. The girls brought all of the empty jugs for water and put them in the wagon. Jennifer said that she would like to go along. That pleased Eli and the children greatly.

It took about 45 minutes to get to the cave. Everyone was ready for a rest stop, besides it was a very hot day and going into the cave would give everyone a chance to cool off. Of course Eli led the way. Several of the children brought their small flash lights and Eli had his trusty kerosene lantern. As Eli approached the cave he got the surprise of his life. He saw what looked to be fresh tracks of one of the big two legged creatures that he thought were now all gone from the mountain. He did not say a word. He decided that he would not mention this to anyone, not even his sons. After spending a few minutes in the cave it was time to move on to the spring. Again, at the spring Eli saw fresh tracks but he did not say a word. Jennifer retrieved the picnic basket from the wagon and Kate made a fresh jug of carbonated Kool-Aid. They all sat down around the spring and ate their lunch. Again, Eli complemented

Jennifer on the wonderful lunch and the children all told her thank you. Jennifer was really starting to get attached to this family.

By this time Eli was starting to dread the upcoming day of departure. Not only were his sons and their families leaving but that also meant Jennifer would be returning to her home in Colton and preparing for her move to Houston to live with her daughter and her family. Eli realized he needed to stop this line of thought quickly or he would get emotional, and he did not want that to happen at this point.

The children were enjoying playing with the hounds and Jake and Evan were having fun with Delightful. Jennifer suggested she and Eli take a short hike above the spring. There were beautiful spring flowers that were not to be found at lower elevations on the ranch. The wild strawberries were also to be found in abundance. But Jennifer had other motives for wanting to be alone. As they approached a steep part in the trail Eli offered to help her to which she readily agreed by allowing Eli to take hold of her hand. He held her hand until they came to a log across the trail. Jennifer suggested they stop and rest before returning to the children and the spring. Jennifer asked Eli if he had any thoughts about leaving his beloved Goat Mountain. She reminded him of the dangers of living so far from civilization in the winter time at his age. He said he realized all of this, and yes, he had been giving the idea some thought in the last few years, but he just could not imagine himself living any place else and leaving the mountain he loved so much. He could not bear the thought of not having his hounds, his falcon, Old Pet, Sampson and her cub as a big part of his life. She then posed the question: What about your grandchildren? You know they are getting older and you have never been able to attend any of their school functions, their birthday parties, their graduations, the things they participate in at church, etc. The conversation was really getting to Eli and he started to get emotional, and Jennifer noticed a tear or two rolling down his cheek. She decided it was time to end the conversation and head back to the spring.

The trip back down the mountain took longer than usual as the children wanted to stop several times to catch butterflies and watch Delightful as she soared high in the sky. It was nearly 3:00 pm when the group arrived at the cabin. The adults who had stayed behind were all down by the pond enjoying the afternoon shade of the beautiful mountain maple trees that surrounded the west side of the pond.

The children quickly put on their bathing suits and spent the next several hours swimming and playing in the cool mountain spring water that fed the pond. The adults spent the rest of the afternoon visiting. Finally it was time to prepare supper. Eli told the parents that he would stay with the children if they wanted to return to the cabin and prepare the meal. After supper everyone decided to take a short walk out into the east meadow. The children asked if they could take Sampson and her cub, to which Eli gladly agreed. Of course the hounds and Delightful were allowed to join the group. It was a beautiful summer night on Eli's Goat Mountain and life was very good.

July the fourth, Independence day. Eli retrieved his beautiful American flag and placed it in the appropriate place near his front door. This was a ritual he did several times a year. The children were up early and so that meant Eli had to get up also. They all decided to go down to the barn and check on the animals. The first thing Eli noticed was that the barn door was open. He was sure he had closed it the night before. When Eli and the children went inside the hounds and Delightful were there to greet them but Sampson and the cub were not there. Eli was not too concerned as this was certainly not the first time this had happened. The girls fed the hounds and Jake, Evan, Ben and Archer fed the falcon and paid special attention to the beautiful bird. It was not long before the ranch dinner bell rang loud and clear. That meant breakfast was ready. Prior to eating breakfast Eli got out his old family Bible. Under the front cover was a copy of the Constitution and the Bill Of Rights. Eli asked everyone to listen carefully as he read the Bill Of Rights. He then asked everyone to make a comment or two about how thankful they were for the opportunity to live in America. This was a very special time for the entire family and Jennifer. Some even had tears in their eyes as the younger members of the family told how much they especially loved being at their Grandpa's Goat Mountain.

As they were eating breakfast they all heard a vehicle approaching. Eli looked out the window just in time to see Bob and his crew get out of their pickup. Eli asked Bob if they had had breakfast. Bob said they had and thanked Eli anyway. Bob said they were finished with the logging and would be cleaning up the rest of the day and returning to Colton tomorrow. Bob wanted to know if Jennifer would be returning with them. With that Kim and Ailene spoke up and said they would be happy for Jennifer to stay and that they would take her to Colton on Monday. This of course made Eli and Jennifer very happy.

The rest of the day was spent enjoying time at the pond, in the meadows and around the cabin. By evening Eli was getting a little concerned that Sampson had not returned to the barn. He left the barn door open when they returned to the cabin. He was sure Sampson would return by morning.

The next morning Eli was up first and went directly to the barn. Still no sign of Sampson or the cub. Eli decided that he would not get too concerned as Sampson had left for three or four days a couple of years ago.

The rest of the day was spent getting the clothes clean and ready to pack for Monday's departure. This took a lot of time as the only washing machine Eli had was an old ringer type with a small Briggs & Stratton gasoline engine. Fortunately the weather was beautiful and the clothes would dry quickly. Matt, Mike, and Martin spent most of the day helping their father with some last minutes repairs of the cabin and nearby fences. Both barns also needed a few boards replaced and other boards needed to re re-nailed.

The children spent most of the day with the hounds and Delightful. They also spent several hours swimming and playing in the pond as this was the last day they would be able spend so much time just playing and enjoying one another's company. They kept watching for Sampson and her cub to return but that did not happen. If Sampson did not return by tomorrow they knew they would probably never see the cub again.

As night drew near the children asked Grandpa Eli if they could have one last camp fire down by the pond, to which he readily agreed. They all spent some time gathering old logs and limbs for the fire. It was decided they would roast all of the remaining hot dogs and make smore's for supper instead of cooking anything in the cabin. They also enjoyed all of the ice cold carbonated kool-aid they could drink. There were also some fresh vegetables from Eli's garden. The parents told the children they could stay up extra late tonight as they would have to go to bed early tomorrow night as it would be necessary to get up very early Monday morning. They needed to be in Portland at the airport by 11:00 am.

The children had prepared some very cute skits to put on and they also sang several campfire songs. Siena had been taking guitar lessons for the last year but this was the first time she was allowed to play for the campfire. The rest of the children were quite surprised at how well she could play after only having lessons for less than one year.

There was no moon and the night sky was beautiful. Michael Shane pointed out several constellations and the two or three planets that were visible from their location on the mountain. The children were getting very quiet and the parents decided it was probably time to return to the cabin and get ready for bed. Martin offered a very nice family prayer. As they left the pond Eli decided he would stay for a few minutes and make sure the fire was out. He happened to glance across the pond and what he saw caused him to freeze in his tracks. Looking directly at him was what appeared to be one of the two legged hairy creatures he was sure had made the tracks near the opening at the cave and by the carbonated spring. The creature did not appear to be nearly as large as the ones he had befriended for several years, prior to their violent deaths. Eli could hardly believe this was happening. He returned to the cabin but never mentioned a word of what he had just seen.

Since the children were up so late the night before they did not awaken quite so early. Eli and his sons were up early and they were anxious to go down to the barn and see if Sampson had returned. The barn door was still open but no Sampson. Eli was really getting concerned by now but he also realized there was absolutely nothing he could do about the situation. He finally had to face the fact that perhaps Sampson would never return. He began to think that perhaps she had decided to remain with the big male bear they had spotted near the blackberry patch a week or so ago. He started to get very emotional so he had to put those thoughts out of his mind. There were just too many things caving in on him now. His families would all be leaving early in the morning and Jennifer would be returning to her home in Colton.

Eli could feel the loneliness setting in already. He knew he had to shake this feeling off or his families would sense his sorrow and really put pressure on him to consider leaving his beloved Goat Mountain before winter. He was just not ready to think about that possibility at the present time, especially with another Big Foot appearing on the scene.

They were all relieved to hear the ranch dinner bell ring so they returned quickly to the cabin. All of the children were up except Siena and Christine. Eli volunteered to get them up. The ladies had prepared a wonderful breakfast and everyone was very hungry.

They all decided to take one last walk down to the East Meadow. The weather was beautiful and the sun was shining brightly. Kate asked if she could take Old Pet to which Grandpa Eli readily agreed. The children fetched the hounds and Delightful from the barn. There was still no Sampson anywhere around. When they got to the far end of the meadow they all looked up towards the carbonated spring. High on the mountain side they saw a sight that warmed their hearts but caused great concern. In the clearing near some blackberry vines they could see what Eli was sure was Sampson, her cub and the huge black male bear. That was to be the last time Eli ever saw Sampson or the cub. Needless to say this was a hard pill to swallow.

The afternoon was spent sorting the clothes as they were taken from the clothes line in the back yard. This proved to be a monumental job and took several hours. With the packing completed it was time for the ladies to prepare the last supper prior to their departure early the next morning. Elaine made two of her famous apple pies. She also made the salad everyone loved, 'The Green Stuff'. She had gotten this recipe from her mother many years ago. Jennifer made a huge batch of homemade biscuits and they were ever so tasty. No one wanted this day to end, especially Eli and Jennifer.

The sixth of July came and everyone got up early as there was much to do in getting everything loaded into the vehicles. Eli took the children down to the barn so they could say their good-bys to the animals and also Old Pet in the cow barn. The time for departure had finally arrived. At this point Eli could no longer hold back the tears. The children all started crying and all of the other adults, including Jennifer, became quite emotional. Matt, Mike and Martin were the last to give their father a hug.

Eli watched as they pulled away from the cabin and headed down the road towards the woods. All three vehicles stopped just prior to going into the woods. They all got out and waved good- by to Grandpa. Eli did not go back into the cabin for a long time. Instead he went down to the barn and got the hounds and Delightful and went out into the horse pasture. He also turned Old Pet loose in the pasture. He spent the entire morning outside. He was not even hungry by lunch time but he knew he needed to eat something so he finally went inside and made a peanut butter and jam sandwich.

TWENTY NINE

Eli Is Alone Once Again

E li spent the rest of the day outside with his animals. He even walked down to the east end of the meadow to see if he might get a glimpse of Sampson and her cub, with no luck. By this time he began to realize that they were probably gone for good.

As nightfall approached Eli decided that he had better head back to his cabin. About half way back he glanced up towards the cave. In a clearing, not very far up the mountain side, he saw the two legged hairy creature staring down at him. He quickened his pace to his cabin. He hoped this smaller 'Big Foot' would stay far away from the cabin. Eli did not seem to have a desire nor did he have the energy to develop any kind of a relationship with the creature. At this point he just wanted to be left alone.

Perhaps he might feel differently in a few weeks, but certainly not now. He was already so lonely and he just wondered how he was going survive the long winter months away from his family and being so isolated. He also had to admit that he already missed Jennifer. He even began to think about making an earlier than usual trip down the mountain side to Colton.

Then a wonderful thought came into his mind. He should go to the Canby Fair and invite Jennifer to go along. That thought cheered him up and gave him a warm fuzzy feeling. This feeling helped him to have a good night's sleep.

Eli go up early the next morning. After caring for the animals and taking Old Pet out to the east pasture, Eli spent the rest of the day getting things ready for the trip to Colton. He decided he would leave the following Monday. He spent the rest of the week doing little odds and ends around the cabin, things that would need to be done before the fall rains set in. There was still no sign of Sampson and her cub. There were also no sightings of the two legged hairy creature he called Big Foot. For that he was thankful.

Eli awoke just as the sun was shining in through the window on the east side of his cabin. After a light breakfast of oatmeal and fried bread with homemade strawberry jam, Eli quickly cleaned the kitchen area. But deep inside he had a strange feeling that this tranquil life he had enjoyed for so many years might be coming to an end sooner than later. He quickly removed that thought from his mind.

Ely decided he would make a trip up to the carbonated spring and collect several jugs of fresh spring water to take to Bob and Darlene, and of course Jennifer. He harnessed Old Pet and hooker her up to the small two wheeled cart. He made the decision not to take the route that would have led him by the cave, but instead he took the long route which took him to the east end of the meadow and then north to the spring. He thought there would be a better chance of perhaps spotting Sampson and her cub by taking this route and he also wanted to avoid the cave entirely. He spotted several Black Tailed Deer and a Red Fox but there was no sign of Sampson, not even bear tracks.

The Vine Maple leaves were already starting to lose their bright green color and the giant poplar tree at the end of the meadow was starting to lose the green color on its leaves. It had been more than a month since they had received any rain on Goat Mountain and it was getting very dry. Dan and Ann, Eli's coon hunting hounds, were anxious to run and chase the little cotton tail rabbits who lived near the spring. Delightful was freed from her tether so she could search for the small rodents that she loved to dive for every time they came up the mountain side.

Eli filled the jugs with fresh carbonated water and then he sat down on an old log near the spring and ate his lunch. He spent over an hour just reflecting on the events that had occurred while his three families and Jennifer were with him recently. Their visit had been so special and he realized now more than ever just how much he missed his sons and their families. Also, there was hardly a moment when he didn't think about the joy that Jennifer had brought into his life. He could hardly wait for Monday to come. At the same time he also had all these memories of the wonderful life he had had living on his beloved Goat

Mountain. He thought how wonderful it would be if only his sons and their families and Jennifer could be part of his life every day on his mountain but he knew this was a very selfish wish and not realistic.

Eli found a shade tree nearby and before long he drifted off to sleep. He was awakened by a noise that was very familiar to him. He heard something tromping around near the spring. Eli sat up and looked toward the spring. What he saw next caused him great concern. The hairy two legged creature he had seen several days ago was drinking water from the spring. Eli did not move for several minutes. He could hear his hound dogs barking far down the mountain side and Delightful was soaring high in the sky. Pretty soon the smaller 'Big Foot' spotted Eli but just looked at him and then headed towards the cave. Eli knew then that he could not just ignore the creature very much longer. He wondered where its parents were. Perhaps they had abandoned the young one or perhaps they had met the same fate as his other friends.

It was time to head down the mountain so Eli called his hounds in with one loud whistle. Delightful also came and rested on his arm so she could be tethered. Old Pet seemed anxious to leave the spring area. The trip back to the cabin took about an hour as Eli again choose the long route so as to avoid the cave. After unloading the several jugs of carbonated spring water and putting them in the root cellar so they would keep cool, Eli un-harnessed Old Pet and turned her out in the small pasture on the west side of the cabin. He then fed the hounds and Delightful and collected the eggs from the various nests in the barn.

After preparing a light evening meal Eli decided to take the hounds into the forest and examine the area where the loggers had taken the timber. He was always very pleased at how well Bob and his crew were careful to pile all the limbs from the downed trees. They never left a mess. They only took the trees that he had flagged. Eli decided that he would go a little further and check the property line fences and make sure the No Trespassing signs were up as hunting season was not far off. In checking the fences Eli lost track of time and before he realized it darkness was setting in. Eli had not taken his rifle nor had he taken his trusty flashlight. The air temperature was dropping rapidly and clouds had moved into the area. Eli knew that he was more than two miles from his cabin but he had no idea what direction he should take to get home.

Eli decided it would probably be wise to make a shelter and spend the night instead of trying to find his way back to his cabin. He gathered up some limbs and made a pretty good shelter by a rock outcropping near the fence. He also gathered up huge arms full of leaves and grass to cover the ground with. By the time he finished he had made a pretty comfortable place to spend the night. Spending the night away from the cabin did not bother Eli at all. He did wish that he had brought his rifle. As those thoughts ran through his mind he was startled by a sound that he had not heard since his last trip to Montana many years ago. It was the sound of a Timber Wolf. In fact it was not just one but several. Eli kept a tight rein on his hounds. He dared not turn them loose. There was only a sliver of a moon. Eli listened as the cry of the wolves seemed to be getting nearer. His hounds wanted to be freed but Eli knew that would bring disaster. Eli hoped that the wolves were trailing a deer or an elk and not him and his hounds.

The howls of the wolves came closer and closer. Eli knew the only defense he really had was his hounds and prayer. He also realized that his hounds would be no match for a pack of wolves. He poured out his heart to God and asked that his life not end here on a dark night in a skimpy shelter. As he finished his prayer the howls of the wolves seemed to move in another direction and their yelps became more faint. Pretty soon the sounds seemed to be from the direction far to the west, more towards the valley below, in the direction of Colton. Eli was greatly relieved. He quickly offered a prayer of thanks. Never again would he leave the cabin at night without his trusty flash light and his rifle. It wasn't long before he began to relax and in a very few minutes sleep overtook him and his hounds.

The next thing he was aware of was the sun shining into his make do shelter. The dogs were beginning to stir and Eli was now more than ready to get going and make his way back to the cabin. As he neared the cabin he stopped at the barn and fed the hounds, Delightful and the chickens. He also checked on Old Pet. He was glad that he had left the barn door open and pleased to find Old Pet inside the barn munching on some hay.

When he arrived at the door to his cabin he found a note attached to the door. It was signed by the same Game Wardens that had visited him before. The note said they were sorry they missed Eli and that the only reason for their visit was to warn Eli that a small pack of Timber Wolves had been spotted on the west side of the Cascade Range and in the general area of Goat Mountain. They cautioned Eli to be on the lookout and to keep his hounds tied up and to keep a close eye on his horse. They also asked Eli to report any sightings of the wolves to their office on any future trips to Colton. Little did they know that Eli had already heard the howls of the pack, but he had no intention of reporting anything to the Game Commission. He knew this would bring officers to his mountain and this would be a disaster for the small Big Foot that had taken up residence in the cave near the carbonated spring. Eli also realized that there was only a small chance that the creature would survive, with Mountain Lions still being plentiful in the area. All of these things were now weighing heavily on Eli's mind. He was even questioning whether it was wise to leave his mountain for a few days to make the trip to Colton and the Canby Fair, but he had already prepared for the security of his chickens and Old Pet so he was not really worried about what the wolves might do if they returned.

Eli spent the entire day getting ready for the trip to Colton and the Canby Fair. He had made Jennifer a beautiful wood carving of Delightful and he hoped she would like it. He made a new dog kennel for his hounds and a larger cage for Delightful. He also made a large box to put personal items in so they would be secure when he and Jennifer were at the Fair. He planned to ask his friend Bob if he would keep the hounds and Delightful while he and Jennifer were gone to Canby. Eli loaded five jugs of carbonated spring water, two for Bob and Darlene, two for the Martins and one for Jennifer, into the box on the bed of Big Red. He also took three small jars of his home made blackberry jam.

By the end of the day Eli was exhausted and decided to go to bed early as he planned to get up by 5:00 am to get an early start. He had no trouble falling asleep.

Eli was so excited about this trip that he woke up very early the next morning. He knew that Jennifer was the reason for the increased excitement. He just hoped that he was not being over confident about how Jennifer felt about him, after all they had only been together for a few short days. He knew that Jennifer liked Goat Mountain, but he also realized that she might not want to live there full time, as it was so isolated. Besides she had already told him that she planned to move to Houston to be near her family's. He could begin to see that life was getting far more complicated but he was really excited about the recent turn of events. What ever happened he hoped that his beautiful Goat Mountain would always be a part of his life in some way or another.

After a quick breakfast he went to the barn to feed the chickens and to fetch the hounds and Delightful. He put the hounds in the kennel on the bed of the truck and placed his falcon in her new home for the next few days. Next he made sure the truck had plenty of gas to get to Colton and he also checked the oil level in the engine. He also made sure the spare tire was good and the tools necessary for changing a tire were securely stored in the tool box. The last thing Eli did was to give Old Pet plenty of hay and make sure she had an ample supply of water to last for several days.

Eli placed his small box with his personal belongings in it inside the truck so they would stay clean. He looked at his watch and it showed the time as 7:30 am. He was very pleased to be on his way so early. He locked the gate when he left his property.

The trip to Colton was very pleasant. The sun was shining and there was not a cloud in the sky. Eli arrived at Bob and Darlene's house at about 9:30. Bob were very surprised and very happy to see Eli. They unloaded the hounds and their kennel and then they took the falcon from her cage and placed her back in the cage after putting it in a small room in Bob's shop.

Darlene asked Eli if he had had breakfast? He thanked her but said that he had breakfast before he left his cabin. They all went inside and Eli had a chance to tell them the reason for his early visit. Bob and Darlene were very excited to learn of Eli's plans for taking Jennifer to the Canby Fair and they told him that they would be more than happy to take care of the hounds and Delightful. They invited Eli to spend the night, in fact they asked him to invite Jennifer over for supper tonight to which Eli agreed to do so. Eli told them that he and Jennifer would probably travel to Canby on Tuesday so they could be there for the parade on Wednesday morning. The first day of the Fair was also Wednesday and Eli wanted to stay for at least three days of the Fair. Of course he had to run all of this by Jennifer first.

Eli's next stop was at Robert's place. He didn't stay long. He just dropped off two jugs of carbonated spring water a small jar of homemade blackberry jam. Robert's dad asked Eli if it would be alright if he came to his Goat Mountain for a special archery hunt around the middle of September. Of course Eli agreed, he always loved to have Mike and his son come to Goat Mountain to hunt.

Eli's next stop was Jennifer's house. Jennifer was very glad to see him and he was equally happy to see her. He told Jennifer that Bob and Darlene had invited them for dinner around 5:00 pm and wanted to know is she would like to go. Jennifer was very excited to accept the invitation. Jennifer made a quick lunch and then she asked Eli if he thought it would be ok if she make a desert to take to Darlene's place. He told her that he was sure Mrs. Berge would appreciate that very much. He then asked Jennifer if she would like to attend the Clackamas County Fair with him. Jennifer said "yes" before he finished the sentence, she just wanted to know more of the details. She had never been to the Clackamas County Fair since moving to Colton so Eli spent some time telling her things about the Fair. The more he told Jennifer the more excited she got. He told her that the locals usually referred to the fair as the Canby fair. Jennifer asked about how things were up on Goat Mountain. She told Eli again how much she enjoyed her stay at his mountain cabin. Eli was careful not to mention anything about the new sighting of the smaller Big Foot.

THIRTY

The County Fair

Eli and Jennifer had a wonderful evening visiting with the Berge's. As usual Darlene made a wonderful meal and she made a Marion Berry pie for desert. Eli took Jennifer to her home about 9:00 pm and then returned to spend the evening with Bob and Darlene.

Eli spent Tuesday visiting with Mike Smith and his family and their son Robert. Robert was playing on Colton's Little League Baseball team so he asked Eli if he would attend his game in the afternoon. He told Robert that he would and that he would also like to bring a friend. The game was to start at 3:00 pm. Eli went back to Jennifer's house about 2:30 and asked her if she would like to go to the game, to which she said "yes". Robert was the starting pitcher. He pitched four innings and never gave up a run. His team went on to win the game 7 to 2. The Smith's invited Eli and Jennifer to dinner after the game. It was late when Eli took Jennifer home. He told her that he would pick he up about 7:00 am. Jennifer invited him to breakfast to which he readily agreed. He remembered the wonderful breakfast she make at his cabin on her recent visit.

Eli got up early, fed the dogs and Delightful and made final preparations to pick Jennifer up and leave for Canby. He had borrowed two small tents with thick sponge pads and sleeping bags from Bob so they would have a good place to stay for the two night they planned to spend at the County Fair. They planned to eat breakfast at a local restaurant and to eat fair food for the rest of their meals. Eli loved fair food and he soon found out that Jennifer also liked it.

Eli and Jennifer arrived in Canby just as the Parade was starting down the main street. After the parade they went to a camp ground near the Fair Grounds. They choose a camp site and pitched their tends as they knew it would be dark when they returned from the fair. Jennifer placed her tent with the door facing Eli's tent door. The first thing they did after entering the Fairground was to go to Eli's favorite food booth and have some great fair food. Eli and Jennifer spent the entire afternoon visiting every animal barn at the fair. Eli was happy to see some people that he knew from both Colton and Molalla. He was especially pleased to see Robert there with his Herford steer. Eli invited Robert to join he and Jennifer in the evening for dinner at his favorite food booth. He also told him to be sure to bring his parents along.

After dinner Eli and Jennifer went to the Rodeo. Surprisingly this little Rodeo draws some top Cowboys. Jennifer told Eli that this was the first Rodeo she had ever been to. Every event was exciting but of course the bull riding was the big event. Fortunately none of the bull riders were injured and several made successful 8 second rides.

Eli did not sleep that well because of the usual noise that goes with a County Fair. It seemed like people were milling around most of the night. Of course Eli was used to complete quiet and solitude on his Goat Mountain. Jennifer slept much better. They both got up at an agreed upon time of 7:00 am. After a good breakfast at a local restaurant Eli suggested they go out to the Willamette River and ride the old fashioned Ferry Boat. This proved to be a fun experience and another first for Jennifer. When they got back to the Fair Ground they spent the entire afternoon visiting exhibits. Again they went to the barn where Robert kept his beautiful Steer. By this time the judging was completed and Robert won Grand Champion. He was very proud, as were his parents.

As soon as they exited the barn they ran into Bob and Darlene. They agreed to meet a little later for fair food dinner. They also decided to attend the second night of the Rodeo together. Eli was really enjoying his time with Jennifer. They were very relaxed around each other. Their last day at the fair was fun packed. Eli had never ridden the Farris Wheel and Jennifer talked him into riding it for the first time. Eli got pretty nervous when the operator stopped the ride with Eli and Jennifer at the very top. Needless to say, Eli was happy when the ride continued and he was on solid ground again.

The Friday night rodeo was outstanding, except one bull rider got gored and had to be taken to the hospital. The announcer reported that he was in serious condition and asked everyone to remember him in their prayers.

Eli and Jennifer had breakfast at the same cafe they had frequented each morning and then left immediately for Colton. They arrived in Colton about 10:00 am. Jennifer asked Eli if he would stay through Sunday to which he happily agreed. She made a comfortable bed for him in her spare bed room. This gave Eli a chance to introduce Jennifer to more of his old friends in Colton and the surrounding area.

Jennifer made wonderful meals and they had so much fun just being together. Eli was not looking forward to leaving but at the same time he knew that he needed to get back up to his beloved Goat Mountain. After they finished supper Jennifer said that she had something very important to tell Eli. First of all she told Eli that she felt that she was falling in love with him but also he needed to know that she would be moving to Houston in the Spring to be near her children and grandchildren. Eli told her that he had similar feelings towards her. He also told her that he completely understood why she would want to be near her sons and their families in Houston. Eli told Jennifer that he so much enjoyed having his sons and their families spend time with him on Goat Mountain every summer and he expressed how much he missed them the remainder of the year. Jennifer sensed the sadness in his countenance the remainder of the evening.

Darlene called Jennifer around 9:00 pm and asked if she and Eli would like to accompany them to church on Sunday morning. Jennifer then posed the question to Eli. Eli quickly responded that he would love to accompany them to church the next morning and Jennifer was very happy to accept the invitation. Jennifer and Eli talked for a while and then both said good night and went to bed.

Needless to say Eli did not get a good night's sleep. In fact he had a hard time getting to sleep. He could hardly imagine how hard it would be to not have Jennifer living in Colton. He knew that he would never be able to make a trip to Houston and he doubted that Jennifer would have the money to make the long trip back to Oregon. At the same time he could not imagine their relationship ending so abruptly. Jennifer had brought so much joy to him and he so looked forward to future visits to Colton. And now he had to accept the fact that this would be coming to an end come next spring.

The Berge's came by about 8:30 am and Eli and Jennifer accompanied them to Church in Molalla. Eli already knew some of the members but for Jennifer this was her first time visiting the church. As usual the members welcomed them with open arms. Both Eli and Jennifer were very pleased with what they heard and with the friendly and warm reception they received by those they got to meet. On the way home Eli told Bob that he planned to return to his cabin on Goat Mountain early Monday morning.

Jennifer made a wonderful dinner for Eli and they spent the rest of the afternoon talking and enjoying one another's company. There were still a couple of friends Eli wanted to say hello to, so he and Jennifer made some short visits to those folks. As usual they were very happy to see Eli but surprised to learn that he had a lady friend from the area.

Eli was up early the next morning. Jennifer prepared him a light breakfast. They said their good-bys and Eli walked slowly to his truck. When he looked back Jennifer was crying as she waved good-by. This was almost more than Eli could bear. He started his truck and drove slowly away. When he arrived at Bob's place he was so emotional that he drove around the neighborhood several times before going in.

The hounds and his falcon were very happy to see Eli and he was happy to retrieve them. Eli did not mention any thing about Jennifer's plan to move to Texas in the spring time. He did tell Bob that he planned to return to Colton in September to get fresh supplies for the winter. He told Bob and Darlene that he and Jennifer had a wonderful time at the County Fair and he thanked Bob for taking care of the animals. He asked Bob if he planned on coming to Goat Mountain for deer and elk hunting season, to which Bob said without hesitation, "Oh yes, I wouldn't miss that for the world". Eli then loaded the hounds and his falcon into their places in the old Dodge truck, said good-by and drove down to the local gas station to fill the truck with gas. He then drove to the Colton Market and picked up some fresh vegetables and a few other supplies and then started to leave town. He only went a mile or so and then he got to thinking of seeing Jennifer crying. He could not continue towards the turn off to Goat Mountain, instead he turned around and drove directly to Jennifer's house. Jennifer was still outside on the front porch when Eli drove up. Eli parked the truck and as he approached Jennifer she came swiftly to him and they embraced.

He told Jennifer that he noticed her crying and that he could not leave her like that.

She thanked him for coming back and invited him to join her on the porch. They talked for some time and he asked Jennifer if she would like to come to Goat Mountain when he returned in September. He told her that she could return to her home when Bob came for the elk hunting season. Jennifer said she would love to do that.

This time when they parted they were both very happy and there were no tears shed. The drive home to his beloved mountain took about two hours. The hounds and Delightful were very happy to be home. Old Pet came up to fence and ate some apples that Eli brought for her. Eli turned the hounds loose and released his falcon so she could soar in the beautiful blue sky. They all had been pretty much confined to small quarters for over a week. Everything was fine in the cabin and life was good on Eli's mountain once again.

Eli awoke early as the sun was just coming up. He dressed and headed to the barn to feed the hounds and Frightful and then went to the cow barn to turn Old Pet out into the east pasture. He fixed himself a light breakfast and then made a list of things he needed to get done during the remainder of the summer. He spent the rest of the day working on things on his list.

Eli awoke early Wednesday and decided this would be a good day to go to the spring high up on the mountain and get several jugs of carbonated water. After breakfast he went to the barn and got the hounds and his falcon and then went to the cow barn and put the harness on Old Pet. He then hooked her up to the small cart and collected several clean jugs from the cellar. Eli decided he would take the direct route which passed near the opening to the cave. He wanted to see if the small hairy two legged creature might be near the opening of the cave. Not that he intended to pursue any form of a relationship with the creature, but he was curious to see if it was still in the area or if it had moved on to other parts of the Cascades.

As Eli passed the cave entrance he saw no sign of the little creature; however when he got to the spring there were fresh tracks all over the place. Eli filled all the jugs with wonderful ice cold carbonated water. He turned the hounds loose and released Delightful from her tether. He gave Old Pet some grain and water and then sat down to eat his lunch.

As he was finishing his sandwich and getting ready to bite into an apple he heard his hounds barking loudly. Next he heard Anne yelping and he knew she was in trouble. He put down his apple and rushed to the cart to fetch his rifle. He headed quickly in the direction of the sounds his hounds were making. As he got closer the little Big Foot came into view. The hounds would not attack as they were somewhat used to seeing these creatures but this little creature, not being used to the hounds, would charge at them for fifteen or twenty feet and then back off. Eli quickly called his dogs off and started backing up towards the spring.

At least now Eli knew that the little creature was still in the area and was probably living in the cave. This really presented a new problem for Eli. Should he completely ignore the hairy creature or perhaps try to develop a limited relationship with him? He decided he would have to give this some serious thought before making a decision. Eli whistled for his falcon and she quickly came soaring down from high in the sky and landed on his shoulder. He put her on her tether and the company headed down the mountain side. They saw several deer and one small heard of Roosevelt Elk on the way to the cabin. When they got home Eli unloaded the jugs of water and then un-harnessed Old Pet and turned her out into the east pasture.

Eli spent the rest of the day doing little chores that needed to be done from his list. He also decided that he would make Jennifer a pair of gloves and a hat from some of his beautiful fox firs that he had stored in the cellar. He knew this would occupy a lot of his time and he knew that he needed to keep busy. He also decide that he would begin writing letters and have them ready to go if perhaps some hiker should stop by. Eli decided that he would not say too much about his trip to Colton and to the Clackamas County Fair with Jennifer. By the end of the day he had written short notes to each of his ten grandchildren. He would devote part of the next day to writing letters to his sons and daughter-in-laws.

Cemetery where Eli's parents are burried

THIRTY ONE

Delightful Learns A Tough Lesson

After feeding the animals Eli made a simple breakfast of old fashioned Quaker Oat Meal and fried bread. He then spent the rest of the morning outside with Daniel and Anne and his falcon. He allowed the hounds to run free and released Delightful from her tether. He loved to see the hounds run through the nearby fields and to watch his falcon soar high in the deep blue sky. It was fun to watch the bird descend at near lightning speed and pounce on a small rodent. Sometimes she would pick the rodent up in her talons and other times she would wait for the hounds to come and make the kill. There were also times when Delightful would pounce on the animal and then for no reason, let it go free.

Eli was almost ready to whistle for the hounds and his falcon to return to the west end of the meadow, but as he looked out into the pasture he saw a badger only about 100 yards away from where he was standing. Before he could whistle his pets to come to him he saw Delightful make a bee-line dive for the badger. Eli knew this could be very bad. He whistled for Delightful but it was too late. She pounced on the badger and the fight was on. The falcon soon realized that she had made a huge mistake in attacking this ferocious animal. The hounds wanted no part of this battle. Delightful would pounce quickly and then let go and ascend up about 10 feet above the ground. She was very careful not to attack any place near the badger's head. The badger would stand on its hind legs and dare the falcon to attack. This went on for about 5 minutes and finally the bird decided this was a battle she was not going to win. She flew off into the sky and then Eli whistled for her. He hoped that Delightful had learned a valuable lesson from this experience as this same thing had happened once before. Only time would tell.

Eli got back to his cabin about lunch time. He made a quick sandwich from the block of Tillamook Cheese he kept in the cellar. To the cheese he added several pieces of watercress he had collected from the stream leading from his pond. After lunch, and a short nap, Eli spent the rest of the afternoon writing short letters to each son and daughter-in-law. He added these to his collection of letters to the grandchildren.

Eli decided that he would build a small camp fire down by the pond and roast some hot dogs and enjoy the beautiful evening listening to the frogs, crickets and other night creatures. The temperature was 70 degrees with just a slight evening breeze which made the evenings in late August and early September so wonderful on his mountain.

Eli roasted a couple of hot dogs, placed them on some slightly stale buns, added some mustard and then he sat back on his willow chair that his brother Delbert had given him several years ago. He was very comfortable and enjoying the sounds of the night, especially the Great Horned Owl that seemed fairly close by. The fire started to die down and Eli started to get a little bit sleepy. As he got up from his chair he heard the rustling and cracking of limbs across the pond and a little way into the forest. He glued his eyes to the area that the sounds were coming from. Next he saw what appeared to be a dark shadow move between the trees. Pretty soon he got a clear glimpse of the little Sasquatch. The hairy two legged creature never came any closer. He just kept moving back and forth through the trees. Eli watched him for about 30 minutes and then decided it was time to return to the cabin and prepare for bed. He checked the doors to both barns to make sure they were secured. Eli fell asleep as soon as his head hit the pillow.

Eli spent the rest of August building new fences in the east and west pastures. He had been wanting to increase the size of the pastures for some time. He enjoyed this kind of work because he could have all of his animals with him. He would work for an hour or two and then he would spend time with the hounds and hi falcon and then return to the task at hand. The fences were made from split rails Eli made from Western Red Cedar trees that he had asked Bob to cut down the previous year. They were very easy to split and would last in the damp Western Oregon climate for a very long time.

Eli managed to make a trip up to the carbonated spring at least once a week. He would usually go by the entrance to the cave to check on the little hairy two legged creature. More often than not he would not see him at the cave but he would always see what looked to be fresh tracks around the spring. Eli always turned the hounds loose while he was at the spring and he also allowed Delightful to soar in the beautiful blue sky. He loved to watch her ride the wind currents. Without fail she would catch a rabbit or squirrel or chip monk. One thing for sure, Delightful never attacked the ferocious badger again.

THIRTY TWO

The Nugget

On the last day of August Eli decided that he would like to take the hounds and his falcon and go to an old orchard high up on Goat Mountain and camp out for one night, something he had not done for several years. He put the harness on Old Pet and hooked her up to the small two wheeled cart. He put his bed roll and some food for himself, the hounds and Delightful, and of course a jug of carbonated spring water in the cart and headed for the old orchard.

It took him the better part of an hour to get to his camp site. The weather was beautiful, with not a cloud in the sky. The first thing Eli did was to make a fire pit. He brought dry wood and kindling for starting a fire. He made a makeshift table from some old boards that were left from a small shed that someone had constructed near the orchard long before he came to Goat Mountain. The old apple and pear trees still were producing some fruit but it was a challenge to cut around the worm holes. After getting everything set up for his place to sleep and storing the food, he released the hounds and allowed Delightful to be freed from her tether. Before long it was time for lunch. He made a sandwich with some canned venison. After feeding the animals he collected several apples and pears from the fruit trees to top off his meal. It was now time for a well-deserved nap.

The afternoon was spent exploring higher up the mountain side. His property line was only about 300 feet above the orchard but Eli decided to go further up the mountain to an old abandoned mine he had visited many years ago. Legend had it that this was an abandoned gold mine. Abandoned for the lack of every finding enough gold to continue the search. Eli brought his pick along and decided he would scratch through some of the dirt and pieces of granite near the entrance to the mine. He had no intention of going into the mine shaft as he knew the hounds would want to follow. After spending about an hour digging through the pile, Eli turned over a large granite boulder. In doing so he unearthed the largest gold nugget he had ever seen in his life. He got so excited he could hardly contain himself. He spent another hour digging but found nothing. He wondered how he was ever going to find out the value of this nugget. He decided he would try not to even think about it now. He just wanted to enjoy his time camping out and spending time with his animals. Needless to say this proved to be quite a challenge. He couldn't get rid of the excitement he felt within.

Eli had placed some potatoes, carrots and a nice chunk of venison in some tin foil earlier in the day. He then placed these in the hot coals of his camp fire. It was now time to enjoy the fruits of his labor. Before he ate though he fed his hounds, Delightful and Old Pet. After supper he decided he would keep the camp fire going for a while as it was a beautiful evening on his beloved Goat Mountain. Finally the camp fire turned into hot coals and sleep overtook Eli.

Eli awoke to the sound of his hounds wanting to be released and the chirping of his falcon. Even Old Pet was wanting some barley from the sack of grain. Eli looked at his watch and was surprised that he had slept so late. After feeding the animals he prepared breakfast for himself and then put everything away in the grub box in the back of the small two wheeled cart.

Eli decided that he would make one more attempt to see if he might unearth another nugget or two from the pile of granite near the entrance to the mine. After about fifteen minutes of digging he gave up and decided it was time to pack up and head back to his cabin with the one huge nugget safely tucked away in his nap sack.

On the trip down the mountain he passed by the entrance to the cave hoping to see the young Sasquatch. As he neared the cave he tied the hounds to the cart as he did not want any kind of a confrontation. Sure enough the young hairy creature was roaming around outside the cave. Eli past by slowly and continued down the mountain, arriving home a little before noon.

After feeding the animals Eli prepared a small lunch from food he had left over from his camping trip high on Goat Mountain. He unpacked his nap sack which contained the huge gold nugget. He spent the rest of the afternoon doing little things that needed to be done inside his cabin. All the while pondering what he would do with the money he would receive from selling the gold nugget to a buyer of gold. After giving it much thought he decided that he would put the money in a trust fund and distribute it out to each grandchild evenly, to help offset the cost of going to college should they choose to do so.

As usual the months of August and September were very busy months for Eli. He made several trips to his carbonated spring high up on Goat Mountain. This was a wonderful time of the year for picking wild blackberries and making tasty homemade blackberry jam. Eli also picked at least a bushel of pears and placed them in his root cellar to enjoy in the fall time. There were wild onions to collect from the grassy hillsides and other edible tubers. His garden was also coming into full production. The deer fence he had constructed several years ago really helped. He had lots of sweet corn, beets, potatoes, carrots and a variety of squash to harvest and put in the cellar. In addition there was much to be done in preparing for winter. He also spent at least a week harvesting the grass hay from the meadow.

Eli spent most evenings down by the pond as the nights were beginning to cool down a few degrees. On several of these nights he would hear the two legged hairy creature tromping around in the woods across the pond. Once in a while he would even get a glimpse of the creature. Eli noticed that he was getting a lot bigger but for some reason the creature would never come very close to the pond and he would never stay out in the open for more than a few seconds. Eli was fine with that as he had no desire to attempt to develop a more cordial relationship with this hairy creature. He had been saddened enough by what had happened to the others over the past several years.

Eli kept very busy and the months flew by quickly. The Vine Maples high on the mountain side were beginning to turn red and some of the leaves on the large cottonwood trees by the pond were starting to turn yellow. Eli also noticed that some of the birds were beginning to group together and he expected they were preparing to begin their fall migration to the south. The high temperature in the day time was not exceeding 70 degrees. Eli loved this time of the year on his beloved Goat Mountain.

Eli awoke early on the first day of September, as this was the day he started preparing for his final trip of the year to Colton and the valley below. There was much to do as he wanted to leave early Friday morning. He spent the day picking a couple of buckets of the late Himalayan blackberries for making jam. He also set aside a couple of hours for spending time with the hounds and his falcon.

After feeding the hounds, Delightful, the chickens and Old Pet and preparing a small breakfast for himself, the rest of the day was spent making blackberry jam and putting it in the cellar for winter. Eli planned to spend the next few days making final preparations for the trip to Colton on Friday, which included getting his reliable Old Dodge flatbed truck ready to go.

THIRTY THREE

A Happy Greeting

E li woke up a little after 5:00 am, in fact daylight had not arrived yet. After feeding the animals and having a light breakfast it was time to start loading things into the truck. First he loaded the cage for Delightful onto the bed of the truck, up next to the head board behind the cab. Next, he placed the box for the hounds, although they hardly ever stayed in it, next to the falcon's cage. He also prepared a small food box with a few pints of his homemade blackberry and strawberry jam to give to his dear friends Bob and Darlene Berge and Jennifer. He opened the barn door leading into the small pasture and the water tank so that Old Pet could go and come as he pleased. There was still plenty of grass so he didn't need to worry about feed for his horse. The last thing Eli put in his luggage box was the huge gold nugget. He planned to take it into Oregon City to find out its value.

Eli always enjoyed the drive down the mountain side and it was especially beautiful this time of the year. The leaves on the Vine Maple trees were turning red and the leaves on the Cottonwood trees were turning yellow as there had already been a couple hard frost. When he past the old community church he reflected on the times he and his wife had gone together and the wonderful potlucks they had enjoyed at the church when she was alive.

He arrived at Bob and Darlene's place a little before 10:30 am. They were very happy to see Eli and asked if he would stay for lunch, to which he quickly said he would love to. After a wonderful lunch they invited Eli to stay with them for the next few days while he visited Jennifer. He thanked them and told them he would be back a little after dark. Bob agreed to keep care of Delightful and the hounds for which Eli was very thankful. After unloading the hounds and his falcon Eli drove the short distance to Jennifer's house.

They both were very happy to see each other. Jennifer had recently received a letter and several pictures of her daughter's family in Salt Lake City, which she shared with Eli. Her daughter said they would finally be making the move to Houston on the first of October. Eli then unpacked the sack that had a package of gifts for Jennifer. Jennifer was like a little child when it came to opening the two packages. She was overwhelmed with emotion when she saw the beautiful hat and gloves that Eli had made for her. She reached over and gave him a warm kiss on the cheek.

After resting a while Eli asked Jennifer if she would like to go and meet some of Eli's friends that lived nearby. She said she would love to and then she asked who they were. Eli told her they were the Welches', Marlene and Kevin. She told Eli that she knew them well and that she had watched their small children on several occasions.

When they arrived at the Welches' the children were not home from school nor was Kevin home from his job at the mill in Molalla. Marlene was very happy to see both Eli and Jennifer. She had just made several loaves of homemade bread and she insisted on them staying for supper. The children arrived shortly and Kevin followed a few minutes later. Marlene prepared a wonderful meal and then they sat around and visited for a couple of hours. Eli asked each of the children several questions about how school was going and what their favorite subjects were. Needless to say Kevin and Marlene had a few questions for both Jennifer and Eli since this was the first time they had seen these two together. So Eli told them how their meeting came about as a result of Jennifer being related to one of his daughter-in-law's mother, Elaine. Jennifer could see the excitement in their eyes as Eli was talking. The Welches' were pleased with everything they heard and expressed this to both Jennifer and Eli. As they left they expressed their thanks to Marlene for the wonderful dinner.

Eli spent the rest of the evening with Jennifer. They had so much to talk about and they enjoyed being together so much. Before he left he asked Jennifer if she would like to go to Oregon City with him tomorrow. Of course she said yes, as she hardly ever made the trip to that big city. Eli said good-night and gave Jennifer a kiss on the cheek.

Eli got up early the next morning and fed his animals. Darlene fixed a great breakfast and then Bob asked Eli what his plans were for the day. He told him that he and Jennifer were going to Oregon City to do some shopping. Eli did not disclose the real reason for the trip. In fact he had not even told Jennifer about the gold nugget yet. He intended on telling her on the way to Oregon City. He thanked Darlene for the great breakfast and told them he would be home about the same time as last night. Bob told him to be careful in the old truck as there was getting to be a lot more traffic on the highway between Colton and Oregon City. He suggested that he take Beavercreek Road and go through Clarke's Four Corners and Beaver Creek instead of going through Mulino and Carus. The road had more curves but a whole lot less traffic. Eli said that sounded like a good idea.

On the way to Jennifer's house Eli Stopped at a small florist shop and bought a single red rose for Jennifer. When Jennifer answered the door a big smile covered her face when she saw the rose. It appeared that Jennifer was all ready to go. Before they left Eli asked Jennifer for a phone book. He looked up the name and address of the company in Oregon City that might be able to tell him the value of the gold nugget he had found at the old mining site far above his cabin. He wrote the information down on a small piece of paper and stuffed it in his shirt pocket.

Jennifer asked Eli if he wanted her to pack a lunch but he told her that he wanted to take her out to lunch when they got to Oregon City. Eli hoped that a small cafe he had visited on several occasions near the Oregon City Elevator would still be in business. Eli asked Jennifer to bring her camera as he wanted to take a few pictures of the beautiful falls on the Willamette River, which runs right through down town Oregon City.

On the way to Oregon City Eli told Jennifer about finding the huge gold nugget, in fact he had her take it out of the box to show it to her. Jennifer was awestruck with the beauty of the nugget. Eli told her what his plans were for money should he decide to sell the nugget. Jennifer told him that she thought that was a wonderful idea. They were both excited to find out the value.

Upon arriving in Oregon City at about 11:30 Eli drove directly to the address of the local Gold Buyer on 7th Street. When he presented the nugget to store owner the man almost went into shock. He wanted to know where Eli found the nugget and all the details of the discovery. Eli told him that he found it at an old mining site high up in the Cascades but he did not give him any more details. The store owner weighed the nugget and then examined it for several minutes with his magnifying lens. He could find no flaws or cracks in the nugget. He got out his latest publication on mineral values such as gold, silver, and copper. After several minutes he came back to the counter and told Eli his best estimate of the value of the nugget was between two and three thousand dollars. He told Eli the nugget weighed right at twenty four ounces. Eli thanked the man and they left the store immediately. Eli placed the nugget in his small back pack which also held Jennifer's camera.

After leaving the shop they took the elevator down to the lower level of the city and discovered that the little cafe was still open. They had a great light lunch and then made a quick stop at the hobby shop that Eli's father had taken him to a couple of times when he was a small boy to buy a model rocket kit. Next, they walked a couple of blocks over to the overlook of the Willamette Falls and took some pictures. Jennifer had a couple of items of clothing she wanted to buy at J.C. Penny's, so they made a stop there on their way back to the elevator that would take them back to the upper level of town.

Prior to leaving town they stopped and filled the old Dodge up with gasoline. Eli was surprised that the price of gas was 27.9 cents per gallon, about 10 cents less than the station in Colton. They took the same route back on Beavercreek Road. When they got to Clarke's Four Corners Eli turned left on Unger Road as he wanted to drive by the old Clarke's Grange. He had fond memories of the Grange as he had gone there a couple of times with his parents when he was a teenager.

They arrived back at Jennifer's home at about 5:30 pm. Jennifer insisted on Eli staying for dinner. She had it pretty much prepared and so it only took a few minutes to heat up on her small electric range. After dinner Eli asked Jennifer if she would like to walk down to the city park? She said sure, so off they went hand in hand. They sat at a bench alongside the little stream that meandered through the park and talked for over an hour. Jennifer had a chance to tell Eli all about her daughter and son-in-law and her four grandchildren that lived in the Salt Lake.

When she described where they lived it sounded like they lived quite close to where some of his distant cousins lived.

It was nearly dark when they returned back to Jennifer's house. Eli thanked Jennifer for the wonderful day and she walked him out to his old Dodge truck. She invited him for breakfast the next morning to which he quickly agreed to accept the invitation. The next day being Sunday they decided they would attend church together in Molalla after breakfast.

Eli drove home feeling so very happy and pleased with every moment he and Jennifer had spent together. He was also excited to find out the value of the gold nugget. Bob had already fed the hounds and Delightful so Eli was able to visit with him and Darlene for the rest of the evening. Eli told Darlene that Jennifer had invited him to breakfast in the morning and that he would be leaving right after he fed the animals. Eli was pleased that neither Bob or Darlene asked for any details of what he and Jennifer had done while they were in Oregon City. They did talk about the up and coming hunting season and Bob mentioned that he probably would not be coming for deer season but that he planned on coming for the first elk season. Eli asked Bob if it might be possible for Jennifer to get a ride back to Colton with him after the hunt. Bob said that he would be more than happy to see that she got home safely. He and Darlene were so very happy to know that Jennifer would be spending almost two months with Eli at his mountain cabin. In the last few years they were worrying more and more about Eli being alone during the long winter months.

Jennifer prepared a light breakfast of fruit and an omelet. After breakfast Jennifer got ready and they left to go to Molalla for church services. Eli was very happy to see people that he had been introduced to the last time he attended several months ago. They were both so impressed with the talks that were given.

After the services they returned to Jennifer's home in Colton. Jennifer spent most of the afternoon packing as they planned to return to Goat Mountain Monday morning. Jennifer called Bob and Darlene and asked them if they would keep an eye on her home and water the plants and yard while she was gone. They said they would be very happy to do that for her. She also invited them to dinner around 6:00 pm.

After Jennifer finished packing she and Eli spent the rest of the afternoon preparing the dinner. Jennifer had unthawed a chicken and prepared a chocolate cake after Eli went home Saturday evening. Bob and Darlene arrived a few minutes before 6:00 pm. Jennifer spent a few minutes with Bob showing him which plants needed watering and also where she kept the lawn sprinkler and hose.

After dinner they retired to the living room and spent an hour or so just visiting and enjoying one another's company. After Bob and Darlene left Eli stayed about another hour and then returned to his friend's place so that he could feed and tend to his animals before going to bed.

Eli got up early the next morning and went outside and fed his hounds and Delightful. By the time he returned to the house Darlene had breakfast ready. Eli thanked Bob and Darlene for their hospitality and he especially thanked Darlene for the great home cooked meals he enjoyed while staying in their home. He also thanked Bob for taking such good care of his animals. Bob reminded Eli again of the dates he would be coming to Goat Mountain for Elk hunting. It only took a few minutes to load the animals on the back of his flat bed Dodge truck. The hounds seemed especially excited to get going. It's as though they knew they would be returning to their beloved home high up on the mountain side.

The Church Eli attended occasionally as a young boy

THIRTY FOUR

Jennifer Encounters Big Foot

Jennifer was already to go when Eli arrived. Eli had brought along a large wooden box with a lid on top to put Jennifer's belongings in so they would stay clean and dry should they encounter any rain. They stopped at the Colton Market and picked up a few items and then made a last stop at the Service Station to fill Big Red with gas. They were on their way to Goat Mountain by 9:00 am. The trip gave Eli an opportunity to point out several landmarks that were important to Eli when he was a young boy growing up on Goat Mountain. The church that he attended was still being used. The old school building was still standing but no longer being used. Jennifer really enjoyed the drive. They stopped at a beautiful spot where they could get an excellent view of Mt. Hood and had the lunch that Jennifer had prepared. They arrived at the cabin at about 1:30 in the afternoon.

They spent the rest of the afternoon putting supplies away and spending time with the hounds and Delightful. Old Pet was happy to see Eli. Eli set up a small single bed in a corner of his living room and put make shift curtains (sheets) around it so Jennifer would have her privacy.

They fixed a light supper together as they were not very hungry after such a big lunch. Afterwards they walked down to the end of the meadow east of the barn. Eli took the hounds and Jennifer took Delightful on her tether. As they approached the place where the Little Big Foot was buried Eli moved quickly to the other side of the meadow as he did not want Jennifer to notice any change in his countenance. When they got to the very end of the meadow Eli looked up on the hillside in the direction of the cave. What he saw caused him to wonder if he shouldn't tell Jennifer about the two legged hairy creatures because he was sure they would encounter the smaller Big Foot the next time they went up to the carbonated spring to get fresh water. After giving it some thought he decided this was not yet the time. He also saw a herd of, what looked to be, about twenty five Roosevelt Elk. There were at least two huge bulls in the bunch. Jennifer got so excited that she let go of the tether that was keeping Delightful close to her shoulder. The falcon flew a little way but then he returned to Eli in hopes that he would release the tether, to which he did so. They spent the next fifteen minutes just watching Delightful put on her usual air show. Suddenly the falcon dove for the ground and trounced on a small Jack Rabbit. Eli whistled for her to let the little rabbit go. Reluctantly the bird let the rabbit go, frightened but unharmed. Jennifer was having the time of the life. She began to realize more fully why Eli loved living on this mountain so very much. She was already doing and seeing things she had never experienced before in her life.

As the sky darkened Eli suggest it was time to head back to the cabin. He tethered his falcon and called his hounds in and he and Jennifer walked hand in hand back to the cabin. After securing the animals in their barn Eli and Jennifer visited for a little while and then returned to the cabin. They spent the rest of the evening playing a couple of board games and visiting.

The remainder of the week was spent doing little chores around the cabin and just enjoying each other's company. The days were filled with spending time out in the meadows with the hounds and Delightful, preparing small picnic lunches to enjoy outdoors, and taking walks every evening. Jennifer was beginning to feel more at home and enjoying the peaceful setting on Eli's beautiful Goat Mountain.

Eli got up early every morning and fed the animals. This gave Jennifer a chance to sleep in a little and then be dressed by the time Eli finished with his chores. As Eli walked towards the cabin each morning he could smell the wonderful aroma of bacon frying on his Majestic wood stove. When he entered Jennifer greeted him with a kiss on the cheek and a pleasant "Good Morning" greeting. Eli was experiencing joy and happiness that had been missing from his life since his beloved wife had passed away many years ago. But something else was running through his mind that was not so pleasant. He knew in a few short weeks Jennifer would be returning to her home in Colton and he would not see her again, or so he thought, until next spring. He also knew that Jennifer would be moving to Texas at the beginning of summer. He knew that he must not dwell on these thoughts or he would get depressed and Jennifer would want to know what was wrong. He wanted to make these few short weeks with Jennifer a time that he and she would remember and cherish throughout the long winter months.

Each morning after breakfast Eli would let Old Pet out to graze in the east meadow. He was usually back within fifteen or minutes. After cleaning up the breakfast dishes Eli suggested they take the hounds and Delightful out for some morning exercise. The sky was clear and the air felt a little cool. Fall was definitely in the air. The hounds were eager to run and the falcon was anxious to be released from her tether. Eli thought this might be a good time to tell Jennifer about his experiences with these two legged hairy creatures that he had developed somewhat of a relationship with in the last several years. He started the conversation by asking her if she had ever heard any stories about 'Big Foot'? After getting over the shock of being asked the question, she replied that she had heard rumors of there being several sightings recently in the Cascade Mountains but she paid no attention to the rumors. Eli then proceeded to tell Jennifer about his encounters with the creatures over the past several years. She asked him if he had ever taken any pictures to which he replied he had not. Eli could sense some new fear in Jennifer's countenance. He assured her that he had never been threatened by any of the creatures. On the contrary, on at least one occasion, his life had possibly been saved by one of the creatures tapping on his front window, while he was sleeping. When he woke up he noticed his lantern had tipped over, and was still burning. He had forgotten to turn it off prior to falling asleep.

Eli told Jennifer that they needed to take a trip up to the carbonated spring tomorrow to get fresh water. Jennifer was excited about going and asked Eli if they would be going by the cave? Eli told her they could go that way, or go down to the east end of the meadow and then up the hill to the spring. Then they could come back by the cave on the way home. Eli called the hounds in and then whistled to Delightful to return to his arm. They then returned to the cabin and had lunch. After lunch they spent the rest of the afternoon doing little things around the outside of the cabin and preparing for a campfire down by the pond in the early evening.

Jennifer prepared sandwiches and brought several pears from the cellar and put these in a small box along with Kool-Aid made with carbonated water. They walked down to the pond around 6:00 pm and Eli started the camp fire. It was a beautiful fall evening. There was much to talk about as Jennifer wanted to know more about Eli's sons and their families and Eli loved to talk about his grandchildren. Eli also wanted to know more about Jennifer's children and their families. They were enjoying each other so very much and falling more in love. Suddenly Eli saw a movement across the pond, between some large fir trees. At first he thought he would just ignore whatever was moving around but soon the little 'Big Foot' came right out in the open and moved to the very edge of the pond. Jennifer heard the noise and looked in the same direction that Eli was looking. She saw the hairy creature and became very frightened and moved very close to Eli. He put his arm around her and assured her that she had nothing to fear. They sat quietly for several minutes while the creature drank from the pond and then meandered off into the woods. Jennifer never left Eli's side the rest of the evening. They enjoyed the sandwiches and fruit and sat by the campfire for a couple of hours. Finally Eli suggested they return to the cabin. Before leaving they put the campfire out.

The next morning Jennifer prepared another great breakfast on the wood cook stove. While she cleaned up the kitchen area Eli put the harness on Old Pet and hooked her up to the small cart. He then loaded in several empty water jugs and brought the hounds and frightful from the barn. They both prepared a lunch and loaded everything in the small cart and headed for the carbonated spring. Eli avoided going by the cave on the way up the mountain to the spring. When they arrived at the spring they both saw many fresh foot prints made by the hairy creature but he was no where around. Eli turned the hounds loose and released Delightful from her tether. Eli did not allow the hounds to go towards the cave. The falcon put on her usual air show and Jennifer really enjoyed every minute of it.

After lunch Eli and Jennifer walked hand in hand to a pear tree that was about 100 yards from the spring. They picked a small bucket full of beautiful Bartlett Pears that were just turning yellow. The hounds were enjoying every minute trying to catch a small jack rabbit and Delightful saw the action from high above. Suddenly the falcon dove down and picked up the small rabbit and lifted it about 20 feet off the ground before Eli whistled the command for her to release the catch. The little rabbit quickly scampered into the protection of a wild blackberry patch.

The afternoon was quickly passing and Eli suggested they prepare to head down the mountain. It only took a few minutes to fill the water jugs with fresh cold carbonated spring water. Eli called in the hounds and whistled for Delightful to return so he could attach her to her tether. Eli guided Old Pet so they would pass directly in front of the cave. Sure enough, the Little Big Foot was out at the entrance of the cave. Jennifer still appeared to be somewhat frightened and sat very close to Eli. He assured her that she had nothing to worry about. They continued on down the mountain and arrived at the cabin in the late afternoon. They placed all but one of the jugs of water in the cellar. Eli took the harness off Old Pet and turned her loose in the pasture east of the barn, while Jennifer took the hounds and the falcon to the barn and fed them and the chickens.

They both worked together in preparing a light supper. Afterwards they were very tired so they sat on the couch and just talked about families and friends. The days were getting shorter and the temperature really dropped when the sun went down. Eli built a small fire in the fire place and they sat and talked till almost 10:00 pm. The conversation finally led to Jennifer again telling Eli that she planned to move to the Houston area in late spring or early summer of next year. She was still not ready to ask Eli if he would consider leaving his beloved Goat Mountain and moving to Houston. Perhaps she was afraid of his answer if he said no. At the same time Eli was thinking how hard it was going to be just being away from Jennifer the entire winter. He realized she would be leaving in a few days when his fiend Bob called for her at the end of his Elk hunt. He refused to even think about the time when Jennifer would leave her home in Colton and move to Houston, and the fact that he may never see her again. It was with these thoughts running through his mind that he said goodnight to Jennifer and retired for the night. Needless to say both had a difficult time going to sleep.

The next three weeks went by quickly. Eli and Jennifer prepared meals together, spent time with the animals, took two more trips up to the carbonated spring, and enjoyed at least three more campfires down by the pond. They only saw the little Big Foot one more time and that was on the last trip to the carbonated spring.

The day finally arrived that they both dreaded. Eli's friend Bob arrived a little before noon. He informed Eli that he had had a very successful hunt. He invited both to come out and see the huge bull elk that he had bagged. Bob had left it hanging high from the huge limb of a maple tree near his camp site for three days. He suggested to Eli that they skin the animal and leave the hide for Eli to make whatever items he wanted to make from the hide. He also told Eli that he wanted to leave him a portion of the meat. Eli was pleased to accept the offer. He would smoke and cure the meat and fill several two quart bottles for canning the meat. All three worked on this project for the rest of the afternoon.

While Eli and Bob cleaned everything they had used in the processing of the meat, Jennifer prepared a wonderful supper. After eating they all decided to take the animals out to the pasture east of the barn, as they had been kept inside all day. Bob enjoyed watching the hounds chasing small rodents and observing Delightful soaring high in the sky. It seems as though the falcon did a little extra when she knew strangers were around. This time she remained high in the sky and decided to leave the small rodents to the hounds.

Just as the group was getting ready to leave to return to the cabin something happened that Eli had not planned for. As Bob was looking up at a small clearing on the mountain side he saw a sight that startled him. He asked Eli if he could borrow his binoculars. He then gave the binoculars back to Eli and told him to take a look at what he was seeing. With this Eli knew he had to finally tell the whole story of his experiences with these two legged hairy creatures to his friend. When they got back to the cabin Eli spent the rest of the evening sharing his many experiences with these creatures over the last several years, with his good friend. Bob assured Eli that he would never reveal any of this to anyone, except his wife Darlene. Eli thanked him for that promise.

A cool weather front had moved into the area during the night and when they all awakened there was a light covering of snow on the ground. Jennifer and Eli prepared a nice breakfast of fresh elk meat, scrambled eggs and fried bread while Bob loaded the meat into his

Polaris Ranger Crew for the return trip to his home in Colton. After breakfast Eli helped Jennifer put her things into the Ranger. Bob would drive the Ranger to the site where he had left his 4 X 4 Ford Pickup.

It was now time to say good-by. Eli shook hands with his friend Bob and then held Jennifer tightly. They kissed each other and said good-by. Jennifer began to cry but Eli realized he had to hold back his tears as he knew this would just make parting even harder for the woman he had come to love so very much. The last four weeks had been like Heaven on Earth for Eli. He could only hope these wonderful memories would sustain him through the long winter months ahead. He knew it would be May or early June of next year before he would see Jennifer again. Before they left he assured Jennifer that he would come to Colton as soon as possible in late spring and spend time with her before she moved to Houston. He found joy and sorrow in telling her this. He could not even imagine how difficult it was going to be to say a final good-by at that parting. He also knew that he had decided many years ago that he fully intended to spend the remainder of his life on his beautiful and peaceful mountain property that his parents also loved so dearly. With these thoughts in mind he waved good-by one last time as Bob and Jennifer stopped the Ranger for just a moment before disappearing into the forest.

THIRTY FIVE

The Christmas Surprise

Eli spent the rest of the morning spending time with his hounds, his falcon and Old Pet. He fed the chickens and made some repairs on the chicken wire fence that protected the chickens from skunks, weasels, and the sly old fox. After lunch he decided to take the animals out into the east pasture for the afternoon. The storm had passed and the light dusting of snow was gone. The temperature had reached a balmy 58 degrees. The Vine Maple leaves on the mountainside were now a bright red and the leaves on the large maple and alder trees were yellow. Eli had plenty of wood in the shed, hay in the barn loft, and good feed for the hounds, Delightful, and the chickens. He was well prepared for the winter months with material things, but he wondered if he was prepared for the loneliness that lay ahead? Only time would tell!

Eli kept as busy as possible during the rest of November and well into December. Snow started falling around the middle of November and continued to fall off and on for the first three weeks of December. Eli was glad that he had checked out several good books to read from the library in Colton. The librarian knew that he would return the books on his trip to Colton in late spring or early summer. Eli missed Jennifer so very much. He marked each day off from his calendar but realized that it was still several months before he would be seeing Jennifer again, or so he thought. He was also glad that he had given her several letters to mail to his sons, daughter-in-laws and grandchildren.

As the snow piled up it became more difficult to take the hounds and Delightful out very far from the cabin. He had to break the ice on the pond so the animals could get water to drink. He also kept several jugs of fresh water he collected from the small creek that flowed from underneath the ice on the pond, in his root cellar. Nothing ever froze in his cellar as it was mostly below ground level and the walls were at least a foot thick and filled with sawdust. Eli always kept a path open to both barns, his wood shed, and the root cellar. Evenings were the most difficult and lonely times for Eli. His thoughts always turned to the wonderful times he had had with his families during their visit in the summer and the special weeks that he had spent with Jennifer. As he said his prayers each night he always expressed his thanks for his sons and their families and for bringing Jennifer into his life. Eli was being blessed in so many ways, especially good health. One thing about being isolated from the rest of the world during the long winter months was that he was not exposed to all the germs that city folks were exposed to, for which Eli was very thankful.

December 24 (Christmas Eve-Sunday)

Eli awoke to bright rays of sunshine coming through his kitchen window. When he looked at his trusty Elgin pocket watch, given to him by his father, he was surprised to see that it was nearly 8:30 am. He started a fire in the wood stove in the kitchen and also in the fireplace. Within a few minutes it was toasty warm in the cabin. As usual he went to both barns and fed all the animals, including the chickens, before fixing breakfast for himself. He took his measuring tape so that he could measure and record the snow depth. The snow measured almost five feet deep right in front of his cabin. Eli brought in a small Douglas Fir tree, that he had put in his woodshed several weeks ago, and placed it on a stand in front of the main cabin window. He placed the few homemade decorations he had collected over the years on the tree, with a beautiful white Angel on the very tip of the tree. Jennifer had brought him a Christmas Present, and had made him promise not to open it until Christmas morning, so he placed it under the tree.

The temperature outside was twenty eight degrees Fahrenheit. Eli decided this would be a good day to stay inside, sit by the fire and read. A couple of weeks ago he decided he would read the Four Gospels, Matthew, Mark, Luke and John, before Christmas. He only needed to complete John and this would be the perfect time to do that.

After a light lunch Eli sat down in his rocking chair near the fire and started reading. He had only read a few minutes when he heard the sound of an engine. He could not imagine who would be out in weather like this and with the snow so deep on his Goat Mountain. The sound got closer each minute. Eli got up from his chair and went to the window. In a few minutes the Snow Mobile pulled right up next to the front door. Eli could not believe his own eyes. Bob, Darlene and Jennifer got off the machine. Eli hurried to the door and welcomed them with open arms. He could not hold back the tears as he embraced Jennifer. Bob and Darlene were beaming with joy. Jennifer was crying tears of joy. Eli held her for several minutes. Bob had attached a small sled to the back of his machine. Before he took off his warm snow mobile outfit he returned to the sled and brought in several bags of groceries and several presents. He told Eli that he and Darlene's children had decided they would not be able to come to their home for Christmas this year so he and Darlene asked Jennifer if she had any plans for the holidays. When she replied that she didn't, Bob asked her if she would like to go to Eli's cabin for the Christmas holidays. She started crying when he asked her. She told Bob that would be the best Christmas present she could ever have.

Eli was still in an almost state of shock. He was overwhelmed with happiness and joy. He could not believe this was happening. While his visitors were taking off their snow clothes Eli put the groceries away. He put the small turkey, that was still partially frozen, in the sink so that it could continue to thaw. There was so much to talk about. The four of them spent the rest of the afternoon just talking about the things that had happened in their lives in the last two months. Bob and Darlene had made a trip to Canada to visit their daughter for Thanksgiving. Jennifer also got a surprise when her family arrived unexpectedly from Houston the day before Thanksgiving. Jennifer wanted to know if Eli had seen the young Big Foot recently. Eli told her that he saw him on both trips he had made to the carbonated spring in November and early December. He said that he did not expect to see the creature again until spring time. In the past, the hairy two legged creatures spent the winters in and around the cave. They lived off the small rodents that dared to come out near the spring. There always seemed to be water running out from under the ice at the spring and the animals would come for water. In the past Eli had even found the remains of young deer near the spring. He assumed they had been killed for food by his two legged man like friends or a mountain lion.

Eli asked Jennifer if she would like to accompany him to feed the animals and of course Jennifer was more than happy to do that. Darlene said that she would prepare supper while they were gone. Eli always kept a clear path to both barns, regardless of the depth of the snow. The hounds and Delightful were very happy to see Jennifer. Eli suggested to Jennifer that they take the dogs and the falcon outside tomorrow, weather permitting. They also fed the chickens and checked to make sure they still had plenty of water. There were only a few eggs to collect as the hens appeared to be going into their molting season. Next they went over to the horse barn. Old Pet was also glad to see Jennifer. While Eli got down some hay from the loft Jennifer took the currycomb and combed Old Pet's neck and sides. The old horse loved this attention. Jennifer suggested to Eli that they take Old Pet out tomorrow and just walk her back and forth in the path to the other barn. Eli thought this was a great idea. Finally they heard the dinner bell ringing so they hurried back to the cabin.

Darlene had a wonderful dinner prepared, mostly from the groceries they had brought. She also made some homemade buttermilk biscuits, which Eli loved so much. After dinner Jennifer and Darlene cleaned up the kitchen and finished putting everything away. While doing this they talked about the menu for the Christmas dinner they planned for tomorrow. Jennifer said she would make and apple pie.

Afterwards Jennifer, Darlene and Bob put the presents they had brought under the small Christmas tree. Jennifer was please to see the present she had given Eli earlier, under the tree. While they were doing this Eli got out two of his camp cots and brought out the two thick foam pads from under his bed. He placed two of the camp cots in the corner of the kitchen area. He got a long piece of clothes line rope and tied it to a nail on each side of the wall. He then took a blanket and put it over the rope so Jennifer and Darlene could have some privacy. Bob said he would sleep on the small couch.

With sleeping arrangements made Eli asked the group if they would like to play a card game called Hearts. They all said they were very familiar with the game and would love to play. Eli lit every oil lamp that he had and placed them around the cabin. Eli and Jennifer played as partners and Bob and Darlene played together. They decided they would trade partners with each game.

They all had a wonderful Christmas Eve. Eli suggested to the group that they finish the day reading from the Book of Luke in the New Testament. Everyone had the opportunity to read several verses. At the end of the reading Eli asked Jennifer if she would offer a prayer. After the prayer Eli filled the fire place and closed the damper. By doing so he knew the cabin would stay warm all night. Bob prepared the wood range in the kitchen so all that would be required in the morning would be to light the paper with a match.

December 25th (Christmas Day-Monday)

Everyone slept in until about 7:30 am. Eli and Bob were the first to get up. Eli asked Bob if he would like to go with him to feed the animals. The hounds and Delightful were glad to see Bob. Before leaving the barn Eli collected the few eggs and then they went to the horse barn to feed Old Pet. When they got back to the cabin Darlene and Jennifer had prepared a light breakfast of Quaker Oat Meal, fried toast and fruit.

There was not a cloud in the sky nor was there any wind. Eli reminded Jennifer that they had decided yesterday to take the animals outside for a couple of hours. They both put on their warm coats and headed out to get the hounds and Delightful and Old Pet. Fortunately the snow had by now a pretty hard crust so the hounds were able to run and play on top of the snow. Jennifer release Delightful from her tether and she immediately flew high in the sky. Old Pet was so happy to be outside even though they just walked him between his barn, the cabin and the other barn. Eli and Jennifer were happy to be alone for a couple of hours. Jennifer told Eli that she was already dreading the time when they would have to say good-by in a few short days. Eli agreed, but he said "let's just enjoy this wonderful Christmas day and the great blessing it is to be sharing it together," to which Jennifer agreed whole heartedly.

When they returned to the cabin they were pleased to see that Darlene had already started preparing the turkey and Bob was helping with whatever Darlene wanted him to do. Jennifer immediately started making the apple and pumpkin pies. Eli peeled the potatoes and prepared the table for dinner. They were enjoying each other's company and working at the same time. Eli had to pinch his self and see if this was really happening or was he just having a beautiful dream. He could hardly wait to write letters to his three sons, telling them about this unbelievable surprise. He would send the letters with Jennifer so she could put them in the mail when she returned to Colton.

While the turkey was cooking the group decided to take a break and open the gifts from under the small Christmas tree. The gifts were simple but beautiful. After opening the presents they sang several Christmas Carols. This truly turned out to be one of the most wonderful Christmas' Eli had ever experienced.

The next three days went by all too quickly and the time had come for Eli's guest to prepare to return to their homes in Colton. Bob announced that they would have to leave early the following morning. The day prior to their departure was spent visiting, spending time with the animals and hauling a good supply of wood from the woodshed to the front porch. After supper the group decided to play hearts and dominos. Finally everyone was getting pretty tired and sleepy so they decided to retire to their beds as they knew 6:00 am would come early. Just as everyone was settling down and almost asleep they heard a terribly loud screaming sound come from the direction of the horse barn. Eli and Bob jumped up quickly. Put some clothes on an grabbed two rifles and two lanterns and headed for the horse barn. Eli and Bob immediately recognized the screaming sounds as those of a mountain lion. Eli and Bob knew they had to enter the barn from a small door on the back side of the barn. They realized that it would not be wise to confront the animal by coming in the door that the cougar had evidently come through. As they entered the barn Eli fired off one shot from his rifle and the animal screamed and immediately escaped through the open door. Old Pet was terrified, but when Eli examined her he discovered no marks so evidently the lion had not attacked. Perhaps the cat realized that the horse was a lot bigger than he was and could probably land some pretty wicked blows with those huge hind legs. Eli and Bob stayed with Old Pet for some time. Eventually the horse settled down and Eli felt that it was ok to leave and return to the cabin. Eli made sure the door was closed and secured. When they got outside the barn Eli fired off a couple more rounds from his rifle. He was pretty sure the mountain lion was long gone by now. Bob asked Eli why he didn't just shoot the cat as they entered the barn. Eli explained to him his thoughts about killing the wild animals that he shared his beloved Goat Mountain with. He told Bob that the only time he had killed a mountain lion was when his own life was threatened. Bob said he understood.

When they entered the cabin the ladies were terrified. Eli told them what had happened. Eli saw that Jennifer had tears running down her cheeks. He immediately went to her and held her in his arms and assured her that everything was alright now and that the mountain lion was long gone. He told the women that Old Pet was fine and that the lion had not attacked him. They all were very thankful for that. They all had so much adrenaline running through their systems that it took more than an hour for them to again return to their beds. The remainder of the night was peaceful and quiet.

As usual Eli was the first one to wake up the next morning. As he was putting on his clothes he heard Jennifer probably doing the same thing. When she came out from behind the hanging blanket they both greeted each other good morning. Eli asked Jennifer if she would like to go with him to feed the animals to which she happily agreed to do so. It was still dark so Eli took a lantern. Jennifer was still a little frightened from what had happened last night so she stayed very close to Eli. After the hounds, Delightful and the chickens were fed they went to the horse barn. Jennifer was so happy to see Old Pet. She asked Eli if it would be alright for her to brush the horse down with the currycomb. Eli told her that would be wonderful. After she finished she asked Eli if they could just set for a few minutes and talk. They sat down in a small stack of straw that Eli had used for bedding when he had a milk cow. Jennifer told Eli how concerned she was for his safety, with him being alone for the next several months. Eli assured her that he would be fine. He reminded her that he had been living alone for the last twenty five or more years. He also told her how much he appreciated her coming to spend this special time of the year with him. He also told her how much he had come to love her and that he would miss her terribly. He again promised her that he would come to Colton as early in the spring as possible to spend time with her before she moved to Houston. When he finished that last statement she started to cry. Eli held her in his arms for several minutes. Finally it was time to return to the cabin.

As they approached the cabin they could smell bacon frying. Darlene had breakfast nearly ready and Bob had everything ready to load into the sled behind the snowmobile. No one said very much during breakfast. Bob and Darlene could see that Jennifer had been crying.

After breakfast Jennifer put her things into her suitcase and brought it to the sled. The dreaded time had finally arrived when they had to say their good-bys. Eli and Bob shook hands and Eli gave Darlene a big hug and thanked her for all the wonderful meals she had prepared. He then held Jennifer in his arms. It was so hard to let her go. She had tears streaming down her cheeks and Eli had difficulty in holding back his tears. He finally helped her onto the snowmobile and off they went. He stood waving until they got out of sight. All of this time Jennifer was waving back at him.

THIRTY SIX

A Happy New Year's Day Indeed

Eli decided he would go down to the barn and spend the rest of the morning with the hounds and his falcon. As he walked towards the barn several thoughts kept running through his mind. If this departure is so difficult how will I ever say good-by to Jennifer when she moves to Houston? Why did I ever let myself fall so deeply in love with her? Why couldn't we have just been casual friends? In the end the overriding thought was, she has added something to my life that has been missing for many years.

Even though it was quite cold, the sun was shining and there was no wind. The hounds and Delightful were anxious to get out side. The chickens had no desire to leave the warmth of their nests. Eli released the hounds and he also released his falcon from her tether. The hounds were able to run on top of the deep snow as the crust was very hard, in fact there were places where Eli could even walk on the snow. He even took Old Pet outside and walked her on the paths between the cabin and both barns. They stayed outside until it was time to go in for lunch. Eli fed the animals and then returned to his cabin. The cabin was warm inside but there was definitely something missing. He made a light lunch and then sat down and picked up one of the books that Jennifer had given for Christmas. The title of the book was 'Where The Red Fern Grows.' As soon as he learned the book was about a boy and his two hound dogs he immediately put everything away and spent the rest of the day reading. Several of Eli's grandchildren had told him about the book when he took them coon hunting, but he had not read it. The only thing he got up for was to put wood in the fire. When it started to get dark he lit two lamps and continued reading. He finally stopped when he realized that he had not done his evening chores nor had he prepared anything to eat for himself.

In his prayer that night he thanked God for the wonderful gift of bringing Jennifer into his life and he also thanked Him for the wonderful Christmas in which his dear friends, Bob and Darlene, had brought Jennifer to spend this special time with him.

The next morning Eli didn't get up very early as there was really no reason to do so. The weather had really turned very cold. Eli dressed warmly and after building a fire in the fire place and the kitchen stove he headed to the barns to feed all of the animals. He glanced at his outdoor thermometer and noticed that it was just 10 degrees F. None of the animals seemed to want to go outside. There were no eggs to gather so Eli did not stay out very long.

When Eli got back to his cabin it was nice and warm inside. He prepared a light breakfast of oatmeal and bread that he toasted on top of his wood cook stove. He spent most of the day doing little projects inside. He had decided sometime ago that he would make a leather vest for Jennifer and make a leather billfold for each grandson and a small leather purse for each granddaughter.

He knew this would keep him busy for a couple of months.

By late afternoon he needed to go outside and get some fresh air so he went to the barns to feed the animals. The hounds were getting pretty restless as was Delightful so he decided to take them outside for a few minutes. Even though it was very cold the hounds were happy to run and play on top of the snow and his falcon was happy to be able to soar high in the sky. This lasted for about one half hour and they were all ready to return to their barn. After supper Eli spent the rest of the evening reading from 'Where The Red Fern Grows'.

December 31, Sunday, New Years Eve Day. The weather was still very cold. After building fires and doing the morning chores Eli started working on the billfolds. After lunch he heard the sounds of roaring engines approaching his cabin. He rushed to the window and could not believe what he was seeing. All three of his sons got off their snowmobiles and headed toward the cabin. Eli flung the door open and rushed to his sons. He was speechless. They all went inside quickly. Eli could not contain the tears nor could his sons. They were very happy to find their father in good spirits and good health. The boys were hungry. They had stopped at the Colton market and brought three boxes of groceries, including some fresh produce and several gallons of milk. Eli was very pleased that they brought several dozen eggs as he was not getting any from his chickens. Martin volunteered to fix some breakfast while Matt and Mike brought things in from the small sled that Matt had pulled behind his machine.

Each son brought letters for Grandpa from each of their children. After breakfast they all wanted to go to the barns and check on the hounds, Delightful and Old Pet. Eli told them about the attempt made by a mountain lion to get at Old Pet, while his friends Bob, Darlene and Jennifer were visiting him. This just added to their concerns about the safety of their father continuing to live alone on Goat Mountain. There were so many "what ifs"?

Eli changed the subject quickly and even wished he had not told them about the mountain lion incident.

The wood supply on the porch was getting a little low so Mike suggested they spend part of the afternoon bringing wood from the woodshed to his front porch. As usual, Martin came up with a lame excuse that he should stay inside and tidy up the cabin and keep the fires going. Eli responded that he thought that was a good idea since Martin had prepared a great breakfast. Matt and Mike just shook their heads and rolled their eyes. This was just the way it was when they were younger and still at home. They all laughed it off and went to work bringing in the wood. Matt asked his dad if he had seen the young Big Foot lately? Eli told him that he had seen him on several occasions prior to the heavy snow falls. He told his sons that the hairy creature probably stayed near the cave and the spring as it was quite difficult for him to get around in deep snow.

The wood project only took about an hour. With that done it was time to return to the warmth of the cabin. When they got inside they were a little surprised to discover that Martin had the Monopoly game all set up on the kitchen table. They knew their father loved to play monopoly and they had never beaten him in a game yet. This was a very relaxing time and his sons had a lot of questions for their father. All of their questions were leading up to one big question. Finally Martin could not wait any longer. He asked his dad how things were between he and Jennifer. Eli responded with "I thought you would never ask". Eli then spent the next hour telling them about the trip to the County Fair with Jennifer and the time they had together when he brought her to Goat Mountain when he made his annual fall trip to Colton for supplies. He told his sons that his friend Bob Berge took her back to Colton after finishing his elk hunt. Next he told them about the surprise visit during the Christmas holiday. All of this is just what his sons wanted to hear. They hoped this would help the plans they had for their father, fall into place. All three knew the real reason for this visit at this particular time of the year.

The Monopoly Game went as expected. Eli ended up with the orange and purple properties and the railroads. Martin had the red properties. Mike had the light blue properties and Boardwalk and Park Place. Matt had the yellow and green properties. The problem for his sons was that Eli was able to get hotels on all of his properties while they were only able to get two houses each on their properties. Furthermore, they all kept hitting at least one of Eli's properties on every go-around. It was finally time to prepare some supper so the boys conceded the game to their father.

Matt and Mike said they would prepare the meal while Eli and Martin went out to feed the animals. In addition to two lanterns Eli also took his 10 gauge shot gun. Just as they headed toward the barn Eli spotted a mountain lion approaching the horse barn. He guessed it was the same animal he had scared away while his friend Bob was with him. He immediately fired a round from his shotgun to scare the animal off. He decided then and there that the next time he went out he would take his rifle. When Matt and Mike heard the shotgun go off they opened the door to see what was going on. Martin told them everything was ok so they went back inside and continued with the meal preparation. This incident gave the boys one more reason to want to proceed with the plans they had for their father.

Matt and Mike prepared a very nice evening meal while Martin played his Dad a couple of games of Checkers. The results were the same as the Monopoly game. Neither of Eli's sons had ever beaten him in either game. When they were younger and still at home, their mother would tell him to let them win once in a while, but they would hear nothing of the sort.

After supper they all sat around the fireplace and reminisced about the wonderful life they had been blessed with. The boys also told Eli how much they still missed their mother. Eli expressed the same sentiments. Neither son had yet developed the courage to approach their father on the reason for their un-scheduled visit. In the back of Eli's mind he had pretty much figured it out, although he said nothing. He had already made up his mind as to what his answer was going to be if they brought up the subject.

January 1 (Monday, New Years Day)

Matt got up early and started the fire in the wood stove and the cook stove in the kitchen area. He had a roaring fire when his brothers and father got up. He checked the outdoor thermometer and it registered 10 below zero. The sky was clear so he knew it was going to be a very cold but sunny day.

Mike said he would fix breakfast and Martin and Matt agreed to go with their father to feed the animals. The hounds had burrowed into a pile of straw and Delightful was near-by. The chickens were all in their warm nests. Next they all went to the cow barn to feed Old Pet. The horse had her winter coat on so she was fine. Eli gave her a little extra grain and plenty of good grass hay.

By the time Eli and his sons returned to the cabin Mike had breakfast almost ready. All that was left to do was toast some bread on the hot surface of the cook stove. Martin offered the blessing on the food and within a few minutes the food was consumed by four hungry men. After cleaning up the kitchen and putting everything away they all decided to put on the snow shoes and take the animals outside for awhile. The top six or eight inches of the snow was frozen very hard so they were able to walk on top of the snow. It was a beautiful sight to see the falcon soar high in the sky. She always put on quite a show. Martin brought a pair of binoculars and his camera. When they got to the east end of the meadow Martin looked up on Goat Mountain towards the spring. What he saw startled him somewhat. He handed the binoculars to his father and told him to take a look. Eli immediately recognized what Martin had spotted. He told Martin that what he had spotted was The Little Big Foot that he had been telling them about. The only thing was that the hairy two legged creature was not very little anymore. He appeared to be heading towards the carbonated spring. The snow was frozen so deep that he appeared to be walking on the surface as were they. They all watched him until he got out of sight behind some trees. They spent a couple of hours in the meadow and then returned the hounds and Delightful to their barn. They were all glad to be back in the warm cabin.

After lunch they decided to put a puzzle together. It was a beautiful Nativity Scene that Eli got out each Christmas. Eli decided this would be a good time to tell his sons about the great time he had on his trip to Colton in late June. He also told them in more detail about some of the things he and Jennifer did at the Clackamas County Fair in Canby. Next he told them about bringing Jennifer to Goat Mountain when he went to Colton for supplies in September. She stayed until his friend Bob came for the hunting season. Again, this was exactly what his sons wanted to hear because they knew that Jennifer was going to be moving to the Houston area early next summer. Their hope was that Eli would soon follow.

Matt prepared a Ham and put it in a Dutch Oven and then placed it in the wood stove oven right after lunch. Mike made an apple pie from apples Eli had collected and kept in his root cellar. Martin made a salad with the recipe called the German potato salad. The unique thing about this potato salad was that it was served warm. It was an old family recipe that was handed down from his grandmother on his mom's side of the family. It has been a family favorite for many years. They did all of this prior to working on the puzzle.

The ham was ready by 5:30 and the puzzle was complete, so it was now time to eat. Eli gave a beautiful prayer. He was so thankful to have his sons with him. This was truly a wonderful New Years Day, one that he would never forget. After all he had spent many New Years Days alone over the last several years. The dinner was superb. The apple pie was the best ever. Mike had it down to a perfection. The only thing that could have made it better would have been a scoop of ice cream on top.

THIRTY SEVEN

The Plan

After cleaning up the kitchen area Mike got out his guitar and played some Christmas Hymns, even though Christmas was almost seven days ago, while the others sang. This was a very special time and Eli was loving every minute. At the same time he was already dreading tomorrow as he knew his sons had to leave to return to Houston and their families. They ended the evening by singing Silent Night Holy Night. After the singing ended Matt, the oldest son, told his Dad that there was something all three of his sons wanted to talk with him about. Mike was evidently pre-selected to be the one to present the plan, which was in fact the main reason for their unannounced visit, to their father. Mike asked his dad if he would consider leaving Goat Mountain and moving to The Woodlands, Texas so that he could spend more time with his three sons and their families? Martin chimed in and told his dad that the grandchildren missed him so very much. Matt promised his dad that they would bring him back to his beloved mountain at least once a year, in the summer time. They reminded him that Jennifer would be moving to the Houston area early next summer. Mike also told his dad that they all were very concerned about his health. Matt's home was on a little over an acre and he had a small guest house on the back of the property. He told his dad that he would be more than welcome to live in the guest house, rent free, for as long as he wanted.

Eli knew this conversation was coming and he was prepared. He told his sons that he could not give them an answer at this time. This was something he would have to think about for several months. He thanked them for their deep concern for him and he thanked Matt for the generous offer. It was getting pretty late and they were all ready to call it a day. Mike suggested they offer a family prayer and Eli asked Martin if he would say the prayer. This had been a wonderful Day. Eli told his sons that he loved them very much and they expressed the same love for their dad.

The next morning Eli got up before anyone else, started a fire in the fireplace and wood cook stove, and then went back to bed, waiting for the cabin to warm up a little bit. The cabin was warm within a half hour. Everyone awakened about the same time. Eli got dressed quickly and asked Martin if he would like to go with him to feed the animals. Matt and Mike said they would prepare breakfast. Martin and his dad returned in about 20 minutes and breakfast was ready. After cleaning up it was time for his sons to finish packing and get everything loaded in the sled. This took about 30 minutes. It was time to head down the mountain to Colton. Eli hugged each one of his sons and thanked them for coming. He was so sad to see them leave as he knew it would be six long months before he would see them again. As usual his sons stopped their machines just prior to entering the forest. They waved good-by to their father.

Eli went back into the cabin and sat by the fire place for a couple of hours. He couldn't help but reflect on the last conversation of the prior evening. His thoughts turned to Jennifer and her moving to Houston early next summer. At the same time he thought about the great life he had here on his beloved Goat Mountain. He thought about the peace and quiet he enjoyed every day. He loved his hounds and Delightful and his old work horse, Pet. He thought about the many trips he had made over the years to the carbonated spring. He reflected on the many encounters he had had with the hairy two legged creatures. He knew that he would have none of this if he moved to Houston. What would happen to his animals, the cabin, the barns and the remaining Big Foot? What would happen to his beloved Goat Mountain, the meadows, the old pear and apple trees, and most especially the carbonated spring? He repaired the spring box every year to make sure the animals could not get into the spring. This insured the water to be clean and pure for drinking. There were just so many things that he had to think about over the next six months or so. With all of this he also had to thing about his newfound relationship with Jennifer. She had brought so much joy back into his life. Would he ever see her again?

At lunch time Eli didn't seem to be very hungry. He decided to go down to the barn and spend some time with his hounds and his falcon. They were all very glad to see him. The sun was shining and there was no cold wind so Eli decided to take the animals outside for a while, even though it was very cold. The hounds loved running on top of the frozen snow and Delightful loved flying high in the sky, looking for any small rodents that might be out and about. Eli even took Old Pet out of the barn and let him walk around on the trails to the cabin and the other barn. This was always good therapy for Eli when any of his family or friends left after a visit. Finally as the sun started to go down Eli called Delightful in and took her and the hounds to their barn and fed them. Next he took hold of Old Pet's halter and put her in the barn. He gave her plenty of good grass hay and a small amount of grain.

As he turned towards the cabin he heard a noise coming from the direction of the pond. He followed the path he had made to the spring just above the pond. He had only gone about twenty yards when he froze in his tracks. Through the trees on the other side of the pond he saw a mountain lion attacking a cow elk. Eli made fast tracks to his cabin and got his rifle. He had no intention of shooting the cougar but he wanted the wild animal to know that he was not welcome any place near his cabin or the barns. Eli fired a couple of rounds and the cougar took off. Eli knew the mountain lion would be back to reclaim the rest of his kill. He went to both barns and made sure the doors were well secured and then returned to the warmth of his cabin. He knew this was part of nature. The mountain lion is at the top of the food chain and will prey on all weaker animals.

Eli spent the rest of the afternoon and evening tidying up the cabin and preparing a light supper. He also spent considerable time reflecting on his son's visit, especially the part where they invited him to come and live with them in Houston. He had no intentions of making any decision concerning such a move in the near future. He loved his Goat Mountain so much, his animals, and the peace and quiet. He knew that he had several months to think about their proposal.

Eli kept pretty busy for the rest of January. The weather warmed up the last two weeks of the month so Eli was able to spend a lot of time outside with his animals. It took him almost a week to make a path through the snow down to the east end of the meadow. He never saw the mountain lion again but he did see the skeletal remains of the cow elk it had killed earlier.

THIRTY EIGHT

A Record Snowfall

The two legged hairy creature he called Little Big Foot evidently stayed near the cave and carbonated spring. Eli also spent a lot of time reading and carving wood things. His sons had brought him a very nice set of carving tools on their visit, with books of instructions. He had lots of vine maple and cedar from which to carve items. This proved to be a great pastime and very challenging.

On the first day of February the snow started falling again and it snowed almost every day for three weeks. It was a challenge just to keep the paths to the barns, the spring by the pond, the root cellar and the wood shed open. This occupied a couple of hours of Eli's time each day. He was careful to not over exert himself and he only worked when there was a break in the snowfall. He actually enjoyed the work and the exercise. He let the hounds and Delightful out when he was working. They were always happy to get outside of the barn and to run and play in the snow. Delightful kept looking for small rodents but was never successful with the deep snow. The hounds could no longer run on top of the snow so they were always running up and down the paths to the horse barn and the spring. They loved playing in the snow and eating the fresh snow.

On the twenty first day of February, Eli awakened to a beautiful clear sky. The sun was shining through his front window. It had finally stopped snowing. When Eli went down to the barn to feed the animals he decided to bring back a large kettle full of fresh, clean, white snow. He loved making homemade ice cream. He took a little bit of canned milk, three eggs and some sugar and mixed these up in the bowl full of snow. It was delicious. He even gave a little bit to the hounds and

Delightful. They loved the snow ice cream. Eli spent the rest of the day doing odd chores inside the cabin, reading and making lunch and supper. He started putting a puzzle together that his sons had given him on their recent trip to the mountain. After a light supper Eli fed the hounds, Delightful, and the chickens. He then went to the horse barn and fed Old Pet. Just as he was returning to the cabin it started snowing again. He continued working on the puzzle until it was time to go to bed.

For the next week it snowed almost every day. As usual Eli spent a couple hours each day keeping the necessary paths open. On the last day of the month Eli measured the snow in front of his cabin. It measured 84 inches. This was the most snow he had seen on Goat Mountain in years.

It snowed a little bit almost every day during the first week of March. Eli was getting very anxious to see the sun and so were the animals. He still had plenty of wood and plenty of food and the animals were well fed but they were all getting quite restless. Finally the snow stopped and the temperature started to rise a little bit each day. The weather made a big change during the last week of the month. The snow started to slowly melt and there was sunshine every day. Eli was able to spend a lot of time outdoors with his animals and they loved it. By the end of the month there was less than three feet of snow on the level. The snow was gone from the paths Eli had made and they were all happy to be able to walk on wet grass and fallen leaves.

THIRTY NINE

April Sunshine Brings May Flowers And Birds

The warm weather continued throughout most of the month of April and the snow continued to melt rather quickly. Eli expected there would probably be some flooding down in the valley. Eli started seeing some bare ground out in the east meadow. Water was pouring into his pond from the melting snow and the creek leading from the pond was running very high. More birds were returning to the mountain. The robins were starting to build nests in their usual trees. The Dark Eyed Junkos were everywhere. There were Western-Scrub-Jays, Stellar-Jays and Loggerhead Shrikes. Spring was in the air and Eli and his animals loved it. They spent several hours each day outside. Eli hoped they would be able to make a trip to the carbonated spring in a couple of weeks. Another big change was that his chickens started laying again. Eli had not had eggs for breakfast for the last couple of months. A great blessing was that he had enjoyed very good health. He had not had one sick day all winter. Eli thanked the Good Lord each day for all of his blessings. Also, he was getting very anxious to see Jennifer again but that was still a couple of months away. With the heavy snow pack he knew the road leading down from his mountain would not be passable until late May or early June.

Eli finished the carving of two beautiful cedar flower pots for Jennifer. He also made her a small jewelry box from cedar. He also made little bird carvings for each of his ten grandchildren. He carved a beautiful small cedar bowl for each daughter-in-law and Elaine. He made each son a pair of leather moccasins. He also made hats from Raccoon hide for Bob and Arlene. All of this kept him very busy for the entire month of April. He had completed the billfolds for his sons and grandsons and small purses for his granddaughters earlier.

By the end of the first week in May most of the snow was gone from the open hill sides on his mountain. With a few more days of sunshine Eli figured he would be able to take Old Pet and the hounds and Delightful up to the carbonated spring. He was very anxious to check on Little Big Foot and to get some fresh water from the spring.

The day finally arrived for the trip to the carbonated spring.

Eli got up early, made breakfast and then fed the animals. By noon they were well on their way up the mountain side. They had to be a little careful as there were still some very wet places but after an hour they were near the entrance to the cave. Eli saw no sign of Little Big Foot near the cave; however when he got to the carbonated spring there were foot prints all over the place. He was very happy about this. He now knew that the hairy creature had survived the long winter. Eli filled several jugs with fresh carbonated water. He gave Old Pet some oats, fed the hounds, and called Delightful down from the blue sky. It was now time to head back down the mountain. The sun was shining brightly as they passed the entrance to the cave. Sure enough Little Big Foot was sunning himself against the rock wall at the entrance to the cave. Eli kept the hounds on their leashes as he slowly passed the cave. Little Big Foot watched the group as they passed by but never left his place in the sun. He seemed completely unconcerned. Eli was sure that he did not feel threatened at all. This made him very pleased. The group continued on down the mountain and arrived back at the cabin just as the sun was going down.

Eli put the hounds and Delightful in their barn, fed them and the chickens. He then collected the fresh eggs and took them inside his cabin. Next he put Old Pet in his barn and fed him some more oats and meadow hay. As he walked back to his cabin he thanked God for the wonderful day and the beauty of his beloved Goat Mountain. There was no place on earth like it in the spring time. The trees were starting to bud out. Little ground flowers were starting to bloom. The pussy willows were starting to bud out with their beautiful white color. The delicate wild strawberry plants were starting to bloom. Even a few of the Rhododendrons were starting to bloom with their beautiful deep pink colors.

FORTY

Eli Gets An Unexpected Visitor

The next morning Eli awoke to a beautiful spring day. The sun was shining brightly through his front window. Eli was a little surprised that he had slept so late. He quickly dressed and went to both barns and fed the animals. While fixing breakfast Eli heard the noise of an engine. He could not imagine who would be coming this early in the spring time. As the four wheel drive pick-up came closer he quickly realized that it belonged to his good friend Bob Berge. Immediately Eli left his breakfast detail and went out to greet his friend. Did he ever get a surprise! Jennifer jumped out of the pick-up and ran to him. Eli was beside himself. Words could not express his joy at seeing Jennifer. They both had tears in their eyes, tears of joy! Bob stayed in the pick-up for a minute or two to let them enjoy the moment alone. In a few minutes they all went inside the cabin. Eli brought out some more eggs and peeled a couple more potatoes to make hash browns. He had brought in the last slab of bacon from his root cellar the night before. Bob and Jennifer brought in their suit cases and several boxes of food supplies for Eli. Bob told Eli that Darlene was not able to come as she was expecting her mother to arrive from Canada.

After eating a good breakfast and cleaning up the kitchen area they all sat down near the fire place and visited. Jennifer wanted to know what Eli had been doing to keep himself busy during the long winter months. That gave Eli a perfect opportunity to bring out some of his carvings. He gave Jennifer the two cedar flower pots and the small jewelry box. Jennifer was speechless. She told Eli how beautiful these handmade carvings were and that she would treasure them forever. He also gave Bob the hats he had made for him and Darlene. Bob thanked him and also expressed how grateful he was for their friendship.

Jennifer was anxious to go to the barns and see the hounds and Delightful. She was pleased when Eli told her that they all had survived the long winter in good shape. Eli also mentioned that he had not been sick even one day for which he was very thankful. Bob asked if they could take the hounds, Delightful and Old Pet and go down to the east meadow. Jennifer suggested they pack a small lunch and spend a good part of the day outside as it was so beautiful. Eli suggested they take a small bucket and pick some wild strawberries.

The meadow was just starting to turn green and come alive. The birds were everywhere. Robins, Jays, Juncos, Red Tailed Hawks, Meadowlarks, the Oregon State Bird and even some Western Blue Birds. In another month there would even be more birds returning for the summer. The early spring flowers were beautiful. They all enjoyed watching Delightful soar high in the sky and then dive for a small rodent. The hounds were loving every minute. They appeared to be very happy to see Jennifer again. Jennifer asked if they might make a trip up to the carbonated spring tomorrow. Bob thought that would be a good idea but Eli was not too quick to agree, but finally said ok. He did tell Jennifer and Bob that on his trip to the spring a week or so ago he did see the Little Big Foot at the entrance of the cave. He also assured them that the hairy creature seemed completely unconcerned when they passed by the cave. He also told them that he was very pleased to discover that the creature had survived the long winter in what appeared to be very good condition. Eli could tell that Jennifer probably wished that she had not even suggested the trip to the spring. She was still very leary of these man like creatures.

As the sun was starting to get lower in the Western Sky Eli suggested they head back to the cabin. They had had such a good time in the meadow watching the hounds run free and also watching the falcon soar high in the sky. Old Pet came when Eli whistled for her.

When they arrived at the cabin it was time to prepare supper. Jennifer offered to prepare supper while Eli and Bob fed the animals, gathered the eggs and secured the animals for the night. Eli built a fire in the wood cook stove and fire place prior to going out to the barns. When Eli and Bob returned to the cabin Jennifer almost had supper ready. The meal was wonderful and both Eli and Bob thanked Jennifer. It was a real treat to have a meal fixed by someone other than himself. The green salad that Jennifer fixed from fresh vegetables they had brought from Colton was so good.

After dinner they sat at a small card table by the fire place and played Hearts until it was time to go to bed. It only took Eli a few minutes to put up the curtain and comfortable cot for Jennifer. Bob slept on the small couch with his sleeping bag. Eli asked if he could offer a prayer before they all retired for the night. He filled the fire place with wood, closed the glass doors and partially closed the damper.

Eli woke up as the first rays of sun came through the front window of the cabin. He dressed quickly, got the fire going in the fire place and then started a fire in the wood cook stove. By this the time he finished with the fires Jennifer was up and dressed. He invited her to go with him to feed the animals. They were as quiet as possible, trying not to wake Bob. Jennifer loved feeding the hounds and Delightful. While she did this Eli fed the chickens. As they approached the horse barn they noticed the door wide open. Eli panicked and ran inside to see if Old Pet was ok. Old Pet was in her stall munching on some hay left for her the day before. Eli remembered that he had forgot to secure the door to the barn and evidently the wind had blown it open. He breathed a sigh of relief and promised himself that he would not make that mistake again. The outcome could have been vastly different had a mountain lion been in the area.

Jennifer still had not had the courage to tell Eli the reason for her unexpected visit. When they got back to the cabin Bob was up and starting to prepare breakfast. Jennifer offered to help for which Bob was thankful. Eli added wood to both the fire place and the wood cook stove. It was only a few minutes until they were setting down to a wonderful breakfast of hot oatmeal, scrambled eggs and fried bread. Eli love Jennifer's fried bread. After breakfast Eli said it was time to get ready to go up on the mountain.

While Jennifer prepared a box lunch, Eli and Bob put Old Pet's harness on and hooked her up to the small cart. They put several clean glass water jugs in the cart. By the time they got underway the temperature was 67 degrees, a beautiful day in deed for a trip to the spring. Eli allowed the hounds to follow along by the cart and Jennifer kept Delightful tethered to a handle on the side of the cart as they moved up the mountain side. As they approached the spring Eli gave Old Pet a command to stop so that he could tie the hounds up to the back of the cart. It was too late. Big Daniel took off for the cave as soon as he saw the hairy creature near the entrance. Eli, Jennifer and Bob all tried to call him back, but to no avail. Jennifer held on to Anne or she probably would have joined Daniel. As Daniel got closer to Little Big Foot the hairy creature gave one loud scream. With that Big Daniel turned tail and headed back to Eli as fast as his four legs would carry him. The creature then went back into the cave. Everyone was pretty upset as they proceeded on to the carbonated spring. Again, there were fresh tracks all around the spring. Eli noticed that there were also two distinctly different size of tracks; however he did not bring this to the attention of his guests. They were still very nervous as neither of them had ever heard the scream of these hairy two legged creatures before. After filling all of the jugs with ice cold carbonated spring water it was time to have lunch. Jennifer and Bob never took their eyes off from the direction of the cave. Eli tried to assure them that everything would be ok but he could tell they were still nervous and seemed to want to head back down the mountain side. In fact Jennifer suggested they take another route back to the cabin.

The trip down to the far end of the east meadow was uneventful. From there it only took about fifteen minutes to get back to Eli's cabin. Eli and Bob unharnessed Old Pet and put the hounds and Delightful back in their barn. Jennifer took the remains of the picnic lunch to the cabin and stored the jugs of fresh carbonated spring water in the root cellar. Bob said that he would like to take a short nap. This gave Eli and Jennifer a chance to be alone. Jennifer asked if they could go down by the pond to which Eli quickly agreed. Jennifer thought this would give her a perfect opportunity to tell Eli her reason for her unexpected visit to Goat Mountain. She started the conversation by talking about her daughter and son-in-law, who were now living in Houston, and her sons and their families who also lived there. Eli in turn told her about the surprise visit he had from his three sons for New Years. He also told Jennifer that his sons had strongly urged him to consider leaving Goat Mountain and moving to Houston in the summer time. He had given it a lot of thought but could still not make that huge decision. Jennifer knew how much Eli loved his home here on Goat Mountain. This gave Jennifer a perfect opportunity to tell Eli that she had made a decision to make the move to be near her family in Houston the first week of June. She also told him that she had sold her home in Colton and that the deal was set to close on the 31st of May.

This all came as a huge shock to Eli. He knew that Jennifer planned to move sometime during the summer but he thought it would be later in late summer. He had hoped they would be able to spend a lot time together come summer. He had planned to make several trips to Colton as soon as the road down the mountain dried out. This new development would change all of his plans, but would it help him in making his decision as to whether or not he should leave his beloved home and way of life on Goat Mountain? Only time would tell. Right now all he could think about was losing Jennifer. He had fallen in love with her and he was so looking forward to spending time with her in the summer time. It was all he could do to hold back the tears. Those tears seemed to flow more readily as he aged. Jennifer sensed his sadness and came into his arms. He held her tightly for several minutes. They sat in silence for several minutes. The silence was broken by the noise chickens make when they lay their eggs. Eli suggested they go to the barn and collect the eggs and feed the hounds and Delightful. They walked hand-in-hand to the barn. As they walked inside the barn Jennifer told Eli that she needed to return to Colton in the morning. This again made Eli feel very sad. He told Jennifer that he would go down to Colton the last week in May and help her with final preparations for her move.

When they got back to the cabin Bob had started preparing supper. Jennifer helped while Eli brought wood inside for the cook stove and fireplace. There was very little talking during supper and Bob assumed the reason being, that Jennifer had told Eli about her plans to move to Houston the first week of June. He sensed the deep sadness in Eli's demeanor. He wondered to himself how all of this would turn out. He knew that both Jennifer and Eli had very deep feelings for one another. After supper Jennifer washed the dishes and cleaned up the mess Bob made in preparing the meal. They all sat around the kitchen table and played Hearts. The mood was rather somber. After about an hour of playing hearts Jennifer suggested they all retire to bed, as she and Bob wanted to get an early start on their return trip to their homes in Colton the following morning.

Jennifer was up and getting things packed in her suitcase when Eli woke up. He quickly fixed a fire in the wood cook stove and insisted Jennifer and Bob have breakfast before leaving. Eli prepared the breakfast while Jennifer and Bob packed things in Bob's pickup. There was not a lot of talking during breakfast. Jennifer could sense Eli's sadness. She loved Eli and hoped that he would make the decision to also move to Houston to be near her and his sons and their families. But she also knew how much he loved his home on Goat Mountain.

It was so hard for Jennifer to say good-by. She could see the tears welling up in Eli's eyes. Bob and Eli shook hands and then Eli held Jennifer for several moments. It was finally time for them to head back to their homes in Colton. Eli watched them as they drove away. As usual Bob stopped the pickup at the edge of the forest and they both got out and waved good-by one last time.

Eli went back inside the cabin and sat in his rocking chair for several minutes. In the back of his mind was the ever nagging decision he knew he must make in the next few months. Whether to do what his sons and Jennifer wanted him to do, that being leave his home on Goat Mountain and move to Houston, or to stay in his peaceful home in the Cascade Mountains of Western Oregon. This would never be an easy decision for him to make.

Eli spent the rest of May making repairs on the two barns, the wood shed and the cabin. As usual the deep snow had taken its toll on the buildings. Every spring it was necessary for Eli to spend a couple of weeks making repairs. The fence around the horse pasture needed to be repaired and that work took a couple of days. Eli wanted to get most of this completed before he made the trip to Colton in late May or early June. The weather was warm and the animals loved being outside every day.

FORTY ONE

Eli's Dream

Eli was surprised he was able to get so much done in such a short time, especially since he was usually thinking about the upcoming decision he knew he had to make very soon. The beautiful spring weather, the spring flowers, and the warm spring breezes made the decision even more difficult.

Eli finished the repairs on the building on the 30th of May. He decided that he would make a trip to the carbonated spring on Memorial day as he wanted to leave for Colton on the 1st of June. Eli got up early, prepared a quick light breakfast and fed the animals. He harnessed Old Pet and hooked her up to the small two wheeled cart. He put several clean jugs in the cart as he wanted to take fresh carbonated water to Bob and Darlene and Jennifer. He packed a big lunch and food for the animals. Eli stopped in front of the cave but so no sign of the two legged hairy creature. This caused some immediate concern. As they approached the carbonated spring his concerns vanished as the creature was drinking from the spring. Eli brought Old Pet to a quick halt. He kept a hold of the hounds and Delightful. When Big Foot saw him he slowly meandered off into the forest above the spring. He looked very healthy, for that Eli was thankful. Big Foot did not seem frightened of Eli and the hounds at all. That also made Eli very happy.

After lunch Eli released the hounds and allowed Delightful to be free from her tether. He even allowed Old Pet to graze in the nearby mountain meadow. Eli thought this would be an excellent time for him to kneel and ask God for help in making the difficult decision that he had to make very soon. He had come to realize that he could not make this decision on his own. He had the faith that he would get an answer but he didn't know what it would be or when the answer might come.

After he finished lunch he decided this would also be a good time to take a nap as he had gotten up very early that morning. As he slept he had a dream. In his dream he saw Jennifer crying as she got in her U-Haul truck, which was loaded with all of her belongings, and pull away from her house. He got in his old flat bed truck with the intention of catching up with her and telling her that he had made his decision, but he could not get the old truck started. He walked over to his friend Bob's place to get help in starting his truck. Bob and Darlene were not home. He walked back to his truck and sat for what seemed like hours. He finally admitted to himself that Jennifer was gone and that he may never see her again. That thought startled him and he awoke from his dream in a panic. It was a moment or two before he realized it was just a dream. Everything seemed so real. Wow, was he every happy that it was only a dream. He wondered then if this was an answer to his prayer. But what was the answer? Should he stay on his beloved Goat Mountain or should he in-fact move to Houston.

Eli called his hounds in and placed Delightful on her tether. He filled all the water jugs and hooked Old Pet up to the cart. As they passed the cave Big Foot was standing at the entrance. Eli slowed Old Pet to a very slow walk but the creature seemed completely unconcerned. The rest of the trip down the mountain was uneventful. Eli put all but three of the jugs in the root cellar. He un-harnessed Old Pet and put the hounds and Delightful in their barn. He collected the fresh eggs and returned to his cabin. He spent the rest of the day getting ready to leave for Colton the next morning. There was much to do as he had made some things to take to Bob and Darlene and Jennifer. He also spent an hour or more writing letters to all three sons as he wanted to mail them when he got to the post office in Colton.

Eli was up before sunrise. After a quick breakfast he fed the animals and turned Old Pet out in the east pasture. He hoped that nothing would bother her while he was gone. He had not seen or heard the mountain lion in several months. He loaded the water jugs and other items in the truck. He put the hounds in their pen on the back of the truck and put his falcon inside the cab. They were on their way by 8:00

am. The trip to Colton went very well. The road was dry and thankfully there were no downed trees to contend with.

Eli stopped at Bob and Darlene's house first and left the hounds and Delightful with Bob. He arrived at Jennifer's house about 10:00 am. When Jennifer heard his truck coming down the road she ran to meet him. They were so happy to be together again. The joy Eli felt quickly turned to sadness as he saw the U-Haul truck parked in her driveway. Eli also knew that he must face reality. The fact remained, Jennifer was moving to Houston to be near her families and would be leaving in about a week. There was much to be done in the next few days and Eli was glad that he was there to help. Jennifer had arranged for some of her neighbors to help with loading the heavier things into the U-Haul. She had everything well organized and neatly packed in boxes. She had a huge moving sale a week ago in which she sold most of her furniture, except her bed, rocking chair and a few lamps. She did not sell her refrigerator or kitchen range.

Eli suggested they go to the local cafe for lunch. Jennifer called Bob and Darlene and invited them to join her and Eli to which they happily agreed. They had a great lunch and talked about Bob and Jennifer's last trip to Goat Mountain. Eli told them about his recent trip to the carbonated spring but he did not mention anything about his dream. He had decided that he probably would not even tell Jennifer about the dream. After lunch Bob and Darlene went to Jennifer's house to help with the packing and loading of the U-Haul. The neighbor men arrived about 3:00 pm and loaded the heavy items in the front of the truck. They were careful to wrap everything with the blankets provided by U-Haul. This took several hours. Jennifer had purchase snacks and soda pop for the helpers. She was so appreciative of their kindness and help. She had so many good neighbors and it would be difficult to leave the many friends she had made in the Colton and Molalla area. Eli, Bob and Darlene were a great help in marking and organizing the many boxes of clothes, dishes, etc. Jennifer decided it would probably be best to wait until morning to load the boxes.

Darlene invited Eli and Jennifer over to her house for supper to which they gladly accepted the invitation. Darlene had prepared a wonderful stew in her slow cooker. After supper they sat around and talked until about 9:00 pm. Eli drove Jennifer home and they sat and talked until about 10:30. Jennifer could not bring herself to ask Eli if he had made his decision yet. Perhaps she was more frightened of what his answer might be. Deep inside her mind she had convinced herself that his answer would probably be to stay at his beloved Goat Mountain. She knew how much he loved his peaceful life on the mountain, with all of his pets and wild animals. Eli had deer and elk that would come right up to his back yard and eat grass. He had squirrels and chipmunks that would eat out of his hands. He had birds that nested in bird houses that he had made, every spring. Much of his food came from the wild berries and roots that he collected on the hillside and fields around the cabin. And there was the cold carbonated spring water that was his for the taking. All he had to do was bring it down from the mountain. And after all, how could he leave the hairy creature, not knowing what it's fate might be, when he was not there to protect it from folks from the big cities like Portland and Salem. All of these thoughts kept running through Jennifer's mind. Eli kissed her good night and drove slowly to Bob's house. Before leaving Eli told Jennifer that he would take her to breakfast in the morning around 8:00 am.

Before going to bed he thanked Darlene and Bob for being so kind to him. He told Darlene that he was going to take Jennifer to breakfast at the local cafe the next morning. Bob said that they would be able to help Jennifer if she needed them the next day.

Eli got up early, took a shower and fed his animals. When he arrived at Jennifer's house she was ready to go to breakfast. They had a wonderful breakfast but did very little talking. Jennifer kept hoping that Eli would volunteer his answer. They stopped at the post office so Eli could mail his letters to his sons. Jennifer wondered if he had given his answer to his sons in their letters. If so, why wouldn't he tell her? The truth of the matter was that Eli, in fact, had not made a decision yet. He was still waiting for an answer to his prayer he had offered up on the mountain by the carbonated spring. He kept thinking of the dream and still wondered if the answer was in the dream. But nothing was clear to him as he mulled the dream over and over in his mind a million times.

They started loading the bigger boxes into the truck as soon as they got back to Jennifer's house. Eli asked Jennifer when the new owners were going to take possession. She told him that the closing would be on Thursday and they would start moving in on Friday. This startled

Eli a little bit. For some reason he had thought that Jennifer would not be leaving for a week or so. He was beginning to wonder if he would have his answer before she left. He knew that he had to be patient and that God answered prayers on his time, not necessarily on man's time.

Bob and Darlene arrived a little after 11:00. Darlene helped Jennifer pack the remaining dishes while Eli and Bob continued loading boxes. The U-Haul truck was almost two thirds full by lunch time. They stopped working and went to the local cafe for lunch. After lunch Jennifer suggested they take a two hour break and drive in to Molalla so she could say good-by to some of her friends from the church. Bob and Darlene said they had some shopping to do so they asked if they might ride along. The two hours turned into three and then four hours. Eli had a great time talking with Jennifer's church friends and Bob and Darlene enjoyed the time they had to shop and visit with some of their friends. They met back up around 5:30 pm. Bob said that he would like to treat Eli and Jennifer to a nice dinner at the new Black Bear restaurant that had just opened in town a couple of months ago.

They arrived back at Jennifer's house about 7:00 pm. The men continued loading boxes until almost dark. By the end of the day they only had a few items and boxes left to load. The men said they could probably be finished loading everything by 10:00 am the next day, Thursday. Darlene told Jennifer she would come in the morning and help her clean and prepare the home for the new owners.

Darlene asked Eli to bring Jennifer to their house for breakfast instead of going to the local cafe. She prepared a wonderful breakfast of bacon, eggs, hash-browns and whole wheat toast and had it ready when Eli and Jennifer arrived. After breakfast they all went to Jennifer's and the men finished loading the U-Haul while Jennifer and Darlene cleaned. Everything was done by early afternoon. The new owners had already arranged to have the power put in their name on Friday. They stopped by late in the afternoon to see how everything was going. Jennifer was so happy that her home had sold to a young couple that had two small children. He was going to teach at Clarke's School at Clarke's Four Corners, a distance of about 6 miles from Colton. His wife was a stay-at-home mom. Bob and Darlene had a chance to be among the first to welcome the Adams family to the community. When they asked Eli where he lived he pointed to a lookout tower high on the side of the Cascade Mountains. He told them his cabin was just below the tower on Goat Mountain, about twenty five miles away. Nothing else was said about Goat Mountain or why Eli lived there. Eli assured them that they had moved into a great community where neighbors looked out for one another and in fact knew each other.

After the Adams left it was time for supper. They all went to the local cafe for the evening meal. The owner of the cafe knew that Jennifer was moving the next day and he had arranged a surprise dinner for her and some of her close friends. When she arrived with Eli, Bob and Darlene was she ever surprised. They had a wonderful special meal prepared by the owner and his wife. The owner had put up the 'closed' sign so they had the entire restaurant to themselves for the rest of the evening. Jennifer was overwhelmed by the entire evening's event. She had a hard time holding back the tears several time during the evening.

Darlene had insisted that Jennifer spend the night at their house. After all there was nothing left in her house. Her bed was in the U-Haul, as was everything but some traveling clothes and personal items. They sat up and talked until about 10:00 pm. Bob and Darlene went to bed first. Eli and Jennifer sat on the couch together, but neither said very much. Eli just held Jennifer in his arms. Jennifer kept waiting for the answer but it never came.

Darlene was up early. She had breakfast almost ready when Jennifer got up. Eli was already up and out feeding the animals. Bob was helping Darlene. Darlene had prepared omelet's, a fresh fruit dish and whole wheat toast. She noticed that Jennifer was eating very slowly. Eli hardly said a word during breakfast. After breakfast Eli told Jennifer that he would take the U-Haul to the gas station and fill the tank, check the tires and make sure everything was ready for the long trip to Texas. Jennifer had promised him that she would only drive during daylight hours and no more than 8 or 10 hours a day. She had blocked out a week to make the trip.

Darlene and Bob arrived at Jennifer's house just as she closed and locked the door for the last time. As Eli walked her out to the U-Haul truck she kept hoping he would give her his answer as to whether or not he would consider leaving Goat Mountain and move to Texas. Still nothing! She said her good-bys to Bob and Darlene and then went to Eli. He held her in his arms for several minutes. Finally she could not hold back the tears. Tears were also running down Eli's cheeks. Jennifer began crying almost uncontrollably. She wanted his answer but she dare not ask. It was finally time to get in the U-Haul and head south towards Texas. Eli kissed her one last time and then let he go. In a few minutes she was out of sight but certainly not out of mind, nor would she ever be. As the truck disappeared from his view he thought of the dream on the mountain side near the carbonated spring a couple of weeks ago. He still didn't know if his answer was in his dream. Why was this so difficult?

Bob and Darlene insisted that he stay with them for a couple of days. They showered him with attention. Bob even offered to take him fishing in the Molalla River. Eli reluctantly accepted his offer. He really wanted to just go home to his beloved Goat Mountain and be alone with his animals. Bob caught several rainbow trout but Eli only caught succors. Darlene had a nice dinner ready when the men got home. She and Bob were also waiting for an answer from Eli as to what his plans were. They had mixed feelings about the possibility of him moving to Texas. How could an old man move from the peace and tranquility of Goat Mountain to a city with a population of nearly three million people?

Bob asked Eli if he would like to ride over to Estacada and back with him and Darlene. Eli had not been to Estacada in several years. It had really grown since the last time he was there. He had almost forgotten about the huge Clackamas River that ran through the town. The only three towns that he had gone to in the last 20 years were, of course, Colton, Molalla and Oregon City. He had recently gone to Oregon City to have his gold nugget looked at. Darlene asked Bob to make a stop at the Thriftway Super Market so she could pick up a few items. They arrived back in Colton about 9:00 pm. After a small snack they all retired to bed as this had been a very long day.

Darlene had breakfast ready when Eli got up. Bob was in the living room reading the morning paper. Eli apologized for sleeping in so late, but Darlene reminded him that it was just 7:00 am. Eli and Bob went out and fed the hounds and Delightful. The animals seemed to be wanting to get back up to their home on Goat Mountain. They were restless and really not too interested in eating very much.

After breakfast Bob suggested he and Eli go and visit some of his friends and do a little grocery shopping in Molalla to which Eli agreed.

Darlene had some things to do with her Garden Club in Colton so she was happy that the men folk would be gone for most of the day. After visiting some mutual friends Bob and Eli stopped at the local Thriftway Super Market. Eli had made a grocery list on the way to Molalla so he was pleased that he was able to get everything on the list at one store. With their shopping and visiting complete it was time to return to Bob's home in Colton.

Darlene had a wonderful supper ready when they got home. After the meal and clean up they sat out on the back porch and visited until almost dark. Eli thanked Darlene and Bob for their kindness. He was really glad that he had stayed a couple of extra days with them. He also told them how much he missed Jennifer and how uncertain he was about any future plans for the two of them.

The next morning Bob invited Eli to attend Church with them in Molalla to which he readily agreed. The church service was wonderful and Eli was happy to see some of the folks he had met the last time he attended. He was surprised that so many of the members remembered him and seemed so happy to see him. He felt so welcome. Of course some of them asked him about Jennifer. It seems as though only a very few of them knew about her move to Texas. They only stayed for one meeting as Eli needed to get back to Bob's house. He needed to get the hounds and Delightful loaded on the truck and get headed back to his home on Goat Mountain. He wanted to get home in the early afternoon as there was much to do after being gone for several days.

Darlene made lunch while Eli and Bob got the hounds and the falcon loaded onto the truck. Eli also put the supplies he had purchased into the large enclosed wooden box on the back of the truck. After lunch Eli took a few minutes and wrote a short letter to Jennifer, hoping that it would arrive at her son Matt's home before she arrived. He told her how much he missed her already. He also wrote short notes to each son. He asked Darlene to please mail them on Monday.

FORTY TWO

Eli Prepares For The Visit Of His Families

Eli stopped at the local service station and filled Big Red up with gas. He was on his way back to his mountain by 3:30 pm, and arrived home around 5:00 pm. The hounds and Delightful were so glad to be home. Eli released the hounds and allowed his falcon to fly freely while he unpacked everything. He went to the east pasture and whistled for Old Pet. As soon as she heard his whistle she came running. Needless to say they were all very glad to be home on their beloved mountain. Everything was just how Eli had left it. The chickens were out of food and there were several dozen of eggs to be collected. Eli allowed them to leave their secure home in the barn and run freely around the cabin and horse barn for a couple of hours.

After unpacking and putting everything away Eli put all the animals back in their respective barns and fed them. He then prepared a light supper and sat down to reflect on all that had happened in the last couple of weeks. He kept thinking of the dream he had had and still wondered if the answer to his prayer was in the dream.

The next several days were spent getting things ready for the coming visit of his three sons and their families. They were scheduled to arrive on the third of July. He knew that he must make a decision as to his plans by the time they arrived.

On the twenty first of June, Eli decided this would be a good day to go to the carbonated spring. After feeding the animals and preparing a light breakfast Eli harnessed Old Pet and hooked her up to the two wheeled cart for the trip up to the spring. He allowed the hounds to run alongside and placed Delightful on her tether and attached it to the cart. He loaded several water jugs and made a lunch to eat at the spring.

As they approached the cave Eli Placed the hounds on their leaches. As they were passing by the entrance Eli saw two of the hairy two legged creatures. One was much larger than the other one. They appeared to be completely unconcerned with him or the animals with him. This pleased Eli greatly. This caused him to wonder how he could every abandon these creatures and the other animals that he had come to care about on his beloved Goat Mountain. He knew that if he left it would only be a matter of time until the public would be all over this mountain. They would discover the carbonated spring and the two legged creatures. He could not bear to think about what the end result would be.

After lunch Eli filled all the water jugs and called the hounds and his falcon in. He then decided to take a short nap before heading down the mountain. A strange thing happened. He had the exact same dream as before. He awoke in a panic just as before. He could not get this dream out of his mind during the entire trip down the mountain. They took the route back that took them to the east end of the meadow, which was east of the horse barn, so they did not pass the cave. He still could not see how there was anything in the dream that might be an answer to his prayers.

When he got back to his cabin he busied himself in putting the carbonated spring water in the cellar and unloading the little cart. He spent the rest of the afternoon setting in his favorite old wooden rocking chair under the huge Mountain Maple tree near the pond, reading a book that Jennifer had given him before she left. The title of the book was 'The Cay.' Even with that, it was hard for him to get his mind off the dream. The hounds and Delightful were enjoying their extra time outside. With the nice summer weather it was difficult to keep the animals inside their barns. Old Pet had lost most of her winter coat and was really enjoying the green grass in the east pasture. The chickens also enjoyed being able to run freely during the few hours that Eli allowed them to be outside. The only trouble was that Eli was not getting many eggs as they were laying wherever they happened to be at the time.

Eli's reading came to an abrupt end when he heard a chicken making a terrible racket. The noise was coming from the small fenced yard behind his cabin. Eli rushed to the rescue but it was too late. Just as he got near the cabin he saw a red fox running towards the woods with the chicken in its mouth. With that he rounded up the rest of the chickens and put them in their barn. They were all pretty shook up and seemed happy to be back inside.

He put the hounds and Delightful in the barn and then whistled for Old Pet so that he could put her in her barn for the night. Eli really enjoyed spending almost all of the day outside. He dearly loved this time of the year and once again, life was very good on his beloved Goat Mountain. Eli kept very busy during the last week of June. He spent a lot of time making presents for each of his grandchildren. He carved a different animal for each one.

Eli woke up very early on the second of July. He needed to put the finishing touches on each wood carving. He also spent some time outdoors with the animals and made a quick trip up to the carbonated spring as he wanted to have fresh spring water for the family when they arrived the next day.

Again he decided to take a quick nap before heading back to his cabin. For the third time he had the same exact dream. He awoke in a panic just as before but this time he finally realized that the answer to his prayer was clearly in the dream. He now knew exactly what he must do. He was now prepared to give his sons the answer to their proposal and would be able to send a letter to Jennifer with his answer. He decided though that he would wait until the next to the last day of their visit.

On the return trip down the mountain he passed close to the front entrance to the cave. As they neared the entrance Eli not only saw the two hairy creatures he had seen the last time, but there was now a third member of their family. This one appeared to be a female. Again, they acted completely unconcerned as Eli and his animals passed by. Eli was pleased to see the family now complete. The hounds and Delightful had now become accustomed to these creatures so there was very little reaction from either one.

The rest of the day was spent doing a few little odds and ends in preparing for his families arrival tomorrow. This indeed had been a good day for Eli. He felt very good about the decision he had finally made regarding his decision as to whether he should remain at his beloved home on Goat Mountain or move to a completely strange and far away part of the country. A part of the country with drastically different weather and no mountains and severe heat and humidity in the summer months.

July the third found Eli up well before the sun came up. He fed the animals, gathered the eggs and put Old Pet out to pasture. As he was returning to the cabin he heard vehicles coming through the woods. His families were coming in three vehicles. They all stopped about 300 feet from the cabin and all the children got out and ran toward Grandpa. As usual, the reunion was full of laughter and tears. Immediately Eli commented on how much each of the children had grown. He managed to give each child a hug and each one gave him a kiss on the cheek. Matt told him that he had a special gift and letter from Jennifer for him. They all insisted he open the gift right away. When he opened the gift he had a hard time holding back the tears. Jennifer had enlarged and framed a picture that his friend Bob had taken of the two of them just prior to her moving to Texas. Eli put her letter in his pocket and they all went inside the cabin.

The children wanted to see the animals right away. Kim and Ailene said they would fix breakfast while Grandpa Eli took everyone down to the barn to spend time with the hounds and Delightful. Just as Eli was going out the door Kim asked him if he had seen any of the hairy two legged creatures since last summer. Eli acted as though he never heard her question and proceeded on with his sons and the children to the barn. Of course the hounds and Delightful were very excited to see the children. Eli opened the barn door and let the hounds run free but he kept Delightful on her tether. They all walked over to the pasture where Old Pet was eating grass. As soon as she saw everyone she came running.

When they got back to the cabin breakfast was ready. Eli excused himself for a few minutes while he read the letter from Jennifer. It was a wonderful letter in which she told Eli how much she missed him. Eli was pleased that she did not ask if he had made a decision about leaving Goat Mountain. Jennifer also asked about all the animals. Eli was surprised but pleased that she did not ask about Big Foot.

After breakfast and clean-up the children asked Grandpa if they could take the hounds and Delightful out into the east meadow. He said "yes," and that he would go with them. His sons and daughter-in-laws said they would put supplies they had brought from Colton away. Grandpa Eli had a wonderful time with all ten of his grandchildren. They enjoyed watching the hounds running and chasing everything that popped it's head up. It was also thrilling to see Delightful dive in an attempt to catch a small rodent. The weather was beautiful and several of the older children commented on how nice it was to be out of the extreme heat and humidity of Houston. Evan had wandered off to the north side of the meadow and in doing so he kept looking in the direction of the carbonated spring. All of a sudden he saw what looked to be three black bears far up on the hillside. He hollered to Grandpa to come quickly. Fortunately Eli had remembered to bring along his binoculars. Eli got so excited that he almost dropped them as he raced towards Evan. Sure enough there were three black bears, one appeared to be quite young. Eli wondered if one of the three was Sampson. The other children came quickly and Eli let each one look through the binoculars. Jacob asked if they could go up to the carbonated spring tomorrow, to which Eli quickly agreed.

Grandpa whistled for Delightful and put her on her tether and they all headed back to the cabin. It was time for lunch. The children were excited to tell their parents about seeing the black bears. After lunch the children put on their swimming suits and everyone spent the afternoon at the pond. The adults relaxed and talked while the children swam. Eli was surprised that no one asked him whether he had made his decision about leaving his beloved Goat Mountain, for which he was thankful. Again he decided that it would be best not to tell them of his decision until the day before they were to leave. Matt had told him during lunch that they would only be staying through July 10. All three sons had to be back to work on Monday the 12th.

July 4th (Independence Day) (Sunday)

Eli got up early and put the flag up on the flag pole in his front yard. There was a little wind and the flag looked so beautiful flowing in the breeze. This was going to be a wonderful 4th of July with all of his family with him on his beloved Goat Mountain. Matt, Mike and Martin all brought an abundance of fireworks to light off out in the east meadow in the late evening.

The children all got up as soon as they heard Grandpa rustling around. Most of them slept in the large tent as usual. They all went with Grandpa to feed the animals and Old Pet. When they got back to the cabin the adults were all up and they were all helping with preparing breakfast, that is all except Martin and Mike. They had taken their new Nikon Monarch binoculars and headed out into the east meadow to look for birds. It seems as though both of them had gotten quite interested in birding in the last couple of years in Texas.

When breakfast was nearly ready Siena asked if she could ring the dinner bell. When Mike and Martin got back to the cabin they had quite a story to tell. They called their Dad aside and told him that they had seen two of the hairy two legged creatures high up on the hillside towards the carbonated spring. They were able to see them quite clearly with their binoculars. Eli suggest they go ahead and tell everyone what they had seen. Eli asked the children if they still wanted to go to the carbonated sprint after breakfast. They all said "YES," without any hesitation.

After breakfast and clean up Eli put the harness on Old Pet and hitched her to the two wheeled cart for the trip up the mountain. Five of the youngest grandchildren piled into the cart while Eli, his three sons and the other grandchildren walked along side with the hounds. Archer held Delightful by her tether as he rode in the cart. Eli decided to take the short route to the spring, which passed close by the entrance to the cave. None of the hairy creatures were by the entrance so the group continued on to the spring. After filling all of their water jugs, Eli told the children they could play nearby. This gave him a chance to visit with his sons. He told them how much he missed Jennifer but he did not say a word about the decision he had made concerning their wanting him to leave Goat Mountain, and move to Houston.

It was soon time to call the children and animals in and head back down the mountain. They took the long route back to the cabin. They still did not see any sign of the hairy creatures nor the black bears which Evan had seen a couple of days ago. As they were nearing the cabin Jacob asked his grandpa if he would take him coon hunting. Eli told him that he would think about it but that he wanted to discuss it with his father first. Benjamin, Archer and Evan all said that they would also like to go. After a short discussion with their fathers it was decided they would go tomorrow night.

When they got back to the cabin Ailene and Kim had lunch ready. They had prepared sandwiches, watermelon, strawberry flavored carbonated water, and chips. After lunch it was nap time for the men folk. The children went outside and played with the hounds and

Delightful. Kate took charge of the falcon. Kim gave the younger children rides on Old Pet.

When Eli woke up he woke his three sons and they all went down to the east meadow and gathered old limbs and logs for the campfire, in preparation for the fireworks which would begin as soon as it got dark enough. They chose an area out in the middle of the meadow so as to have a safe place for lighting off the fireworks. The grass was still very green from all the spring and early summer rains on Goat Mountain. They made sticks for everyone to roast their hot dogs on. By the time they were finished with the preparations they saw the mothers and the children heading their way. They brought all the supplies which would be needed for the evening activities. The children started to get really excited. To start the evening off Matt, Mike and Martin each took turns discussing with the children the significance of this special day of the year. Eli was very impressed with how much the children knew about this holiday. Elly spoke up and reminded her Grandpa that they spent a lot of time in their Texas schools studying the history of Texas and the United States.

After everyone got their fill of hot dogs, chocolate smore's and chips it was time for the fireworks to begin. All three sons helped with lighting off the fireworks. They brought the fireworks from Texas where almost everything was legal to purchase. Most of these fireworks were not allowed to be sold in Oregon. The display went on for almost thirty minutes. It was so beautiful and exciting. There were hundreds of AWS AND OOOS. Every one clapped and cheered at the conclusion. It was almost 10:30 pm when they finished. The adults put out the fire while the mothers gathered up the small children and the supplies. Everyone was very tired and ready for bed by the time they got back to the cabin. In fact Shane had to carry Christine most of the way, as she had fallen asleep in her mother's arms by the campfire. They all knelt by the couch and chairs as Eli led them in a beautiful family prayer. They all agreed that this was the best Fourth of July they had ever had. Mike agreed to sleep with the children in the tent. The rest slept in the cabin. They were all asleep in a few short minutes.

Most of the following morning was spent out in the forest cutting the large rounds of wood into small pieces and stacking them so that they could be hauled into Eli's wood shed before his sons returned to

Houston. When noon arrived they were all very happy to hear the dinner bell ring. That meant it was time for lunch. The mothers had prepared a wonderful meal of sandwiches, carbonated strawberry lemon aid, chocolate cake and chips. After lunch Eli hitched Old Pet up to the two wheeled cart and his three sons and the grandchildren spent the afternoon hauling wood into the shed. This was hard work but many hands made the task a little easier.

FORTY THREE

Grandpa Collapses

After supper it was time to prepare for the big coon hunt that Eli had promised his grandsons the day before. A lot of preparation was necessary for such an event. Matt, Mike and Martin would carry back packs with water, first aid kits and snacks. Matt would carry Eli's small 22 rifle. The older boys were asked to carry gunny sacks. Eli said that he would keep hold of the hounds, which always proved to be a difficult task indeed. Each person had a flashlight attached to his baseball hat. Neither mother was very supportive of this whole event and they had no trouble voicing their concerns.

Finally it was dark enough to begin the hunt. It only took about fifteen minutes to reach the far end of the east meadow. The hunters continued on about one quarter of a mile to reach a small creek that ran through Eli's property. There were some large mountain maple trees that grew along the creek bed. This was usually a good place to find coons. Martin shined his light down on some damp dirt next to the stream and saw fresh coon tracks. With that Eli released the hounds and they immediately started following the scent of the coons. They had only traveled a short distance when the hunters heard the familiar sound a hound makes when it has treed a coon. In a few minutes the hunters were standing at the base of a huge maple tree. Mike shined his powerful spot light high up in the tree and there sat a huge ringtail. Eli decided to let this one go so he took the dogs by their collars and led them away from the tree. He had trained the hounds to do this several years ago, as it was his policy only to kill a coon if he needed it's hide for making clothes, such as hats and gloves.

In about fifteen minutes Eli decided to release the hounds again. He was having a difficult time holding them back. They were only gone a few minutes when the hunters heard that all too familiar bawl for the second time tonight. This time they were not standing by a large tree, instead they were at the bottom of what appeared to be a snag of an old fir tree. It was no more than thirty feet tall.

Near the top was a large cavity on one side of the tree. Eli was sure the coon or coons were holed up inside the hole. This time the hounds would not leave the treed coon. In the past they would only leave if they in fact actually saw the coon. Finally Eli took one hound by its collar and Mike took hold of the other coon. They literally had to drag them away from the tree.

Jacob, Evan, Ben and Archer were having the time of their life. For Ben and Archer this was their first coon hunt. The terrain started getting a little rough and the creek took a turn to the south. Eli could hear a waterfalls so he knew he was not far from the end of his property. He decided to turn the hounds loose one more time before returning to his cabin as it was almost 11:00 pm. and he was getting pretty tired. The hounds took off at a dead run and before long they had treed another coon. The hunters had to proceed more carefully as the trail along the creek bed became quite steep as it approached the falls. Suddenly Eli became very dizzy and slumped to the ground. His sons and grandsons came quickly to his side. He appeared to be unconscious. Matt checked his pulse and discovered that he had a very rapid pulse. They moved him away from the creek to a more comfortable place. Mike dampened his handkerchief and placed it on his father's forehead. Eli came to quickly and asked what happened. Martin told him that he had passed out and that he needed to stay quiet and rest for a while. It was decided that Mike and the grandchildren would stay with Eli while Matt and Martin went to retrieve the hounds. They only traveled a short distance and found the hounds at the bottom of a huge maple tree. When Martin shined his light up in the tree he saw not one coon but three on one limb. Again they had to drag the hounds away from the tree. When they got back to where their father, and the rest of hunters were Eli was feeling much better. Mike asked his dad about how long it would take to get back to the cabin? Eli told him that they were actually just a short distance from the cabin but the trip back would be pretty much an uphill climb. Matt and Mike walked right with their father, one on each side. They took their time getting back to the cabin, arriving just a little before midnight. The group decided that they would not awaken the mothers. Matt helped his father get into bed while Mike and Martin helped the grandsons get to bed. Matt sat by his father's side until he was sure that he was sound asleep. He checked his breathing and pulse and they seemed to be back to normal. All three sons went outside to talk about how they might proceed with telling their wives in the morning of the incident and also to discuss how best to proceed in convincing their father that he really needed to move to Houston. Their concerns about his health were very much on their minds as they retired to their beds for the night. Sleep did not come easy for either son.

FORTY FOUR

The Decision

Eli's three sons were already up and dressed when he woke up the next morning. Eli quickly put his clothes on and suggested they all go out and feed the animals. He told his sons that he wanted to talk to them in private. Thankfully the grandchildren nor the mothers were up yet. After feeding the animals Eli and his sons sat down on a couple of old benches in the hay mow of the horse barn. His sons listened as Eli told them of his earlier decision not to move to Houston but he also said that he was rethinking that decision after what happened last night. His sons listened intently. Eli said that he had had a dream in the night and in this dream he had traveled to Houston and Jennifer had met him and he had proposed marriage to her, to which she gladly accepted. That was all there was to the dream, no other details of the move or what might happen to his beloved Goat Mountain.

Needless to say his sons were ecstatic. They told their father how happy they were that he was, in fact, considering the move and they assured him that this was no doubt a wise decision. They also told him they would help him with whatever he decided to do with his property, even if that meant keeping it for a while and returning each summer for vacation. Eli told his sons that his good friends, Bob and Darlene Berge, had said that they would be more than happy to spend the summers at Goat Mountain and thereby maintain the cabin and property should he decide to move to Houston. This sounded like a good plan to all three sons.

When they got back to the cabin all the children were up. Evan spoke up as soon as she saw Grandpa. He asked him how he was feeling? Kim picked up on his question quickly and asked Evan why his asked?

With that the three sons said they all needed to set down and talk about what happened last night near the end of the coon hunt. The mothers and granddaughters listened intently as the fathers related the events of the previous night. Kate, Elly, Marina, Siena, Brighton and Christine all rushed over to Grandpa and put their arms around him and gave him a hug. Eli told the group that he was feeling fine and that he had an important announcement to make to the entire group. He then proceeded to tell them the same thing that he had told his sons a few minutes earlier. They were all very happy that he was considering the move.

By lunch time he told everyone that he had made the final decision to make the move to Houston. The adults spent the rest of the afternoon beginning to work out the details of the move. It was decided that Mike and Martin would stay behind and rent a U Haul truck to move what little bit of furniture Eli planned to take. He had decided that he would leave most of his furniture so that Bob and Darlene would not have to move furniture back and forth, should they make the final agreement to stay at the cabin during the summer months. The next big decision was what would he do with the hounds, Delightful and Old Pet. He hoped that Bob would also take his animals. That would make things so much more simple. There was nothing he could do about leaving the hairy two legged man like creatures. He was just glad that he had had very few personal encounters with the ones that occupied the cave now.

Matt suggested that he and his father make a trip to Colton the first thing in the morning and talk over his plans with Bob and Darlene and get their final decision as to whether they would like to move to Goat Mountain in the summer time.

The children spent the entire afternoon swimming in the pond and playing with the hounds and Delightful. They all finished the evening with a bonfire and a hot dog roast down by the pond. The evening was warm and the stars were shining brightly. There was just a sliver of a moon. As they were putting out the fire Eli looked across the pond and into a clearing in the nearby trees. Looking back at him were the two of the three hairy creatures he had seen several days ago up on the mountain side. Eli said nothing but quickly turned his flashlight off and acted like he had seen nothing.

Before going to bed Jacob and Evan came to their Grandpa's side and put their arms around him. Evan told his grandpa that he knew how hard the decision to leave Goat Mountain was. They both told him how much they also loved his mountain and they hoped they would all be able to come every summer for a vacation. They also told him how much they were looking forward to him living near them so he could attend all their school and athletic events. Elly piped in and said how much she was looking forward to him attending her high jump and other track events. With that every other grandchild told their grandfather how excited they were at the prospect of having him and Jennifer living nearby, as Jennifer's home was also in The Woodlands.

Matt and his father got up early the next morning, ate a little breakfast and headed for Colton. Matt took his rental SUV so the trip down the mountain did not take very long.

Bob was very surprised to see them. Darlene asked how things were going with all the family at the cabin? Bob asked why the others did not come along? Eli told them that they had come to tell them of his decision to move to Houston. He also gave them a summary of what had happened on the coon hunting trip. He told them that his initial decision was not to move to Houston at this time but the events of the coon hunt had caused him to reconsider his earlier decision. He also told them of the dream he had. Before he could ask them whether or not they would still consider spending the summers at Goat Mountain, Bob interrupted him by telling him that his offer to move to the mountain was still on the table. Eli and Matt told them how happy they were to have he and Darlene spending the summers at Goat Mountain. Eli said that he hoped his entire family would be able to come back and spend a couple of weeks at the mountain each summer. Bob said that would be wonderful and would give he and Darlene a chance to spend a couple of weeks in their own home each summer.

Darlene fixed a wonderful lunch for Matt and his father before they headed back to the mountain. Matt asked if he could use their phone to call the U Haul company about renting a small truck to move his father's belongings. Eli also asked if he could use their phone to call Jennifer and tell her of his decision. Jennifer was beside herself with the good news of Eli's decision. She told him that she could hardly wait to see him. She was crying tears of joy when she hung up the phone. Eli also had tears flowing down his cheeks. He now knew for sure that he had made the right decision and that his prayers had been answered.

Bob told Eli that he would love to have the hounds, Old Pet, Delightful and the chickens. This also made Eli very happy. It seems like Heavenly Father was making everything fall into place. Eli was feeling better and better about his decision as the hours went passing by. He and Matt thanked Bob and Darlene for the wonderful lunch and told them they would be down to pick up the U Haul truck in a couple of days. Before leaving town they picked up several boxes from the grocery store to pack things in.

The trip back to the ranch only took about an hour. Everyone was waiting to hear of Bob and Darlene's decision. Matt told everyone that things had worked out just as Eli had hoped they would. He told the group that he had rented a U Haul truck and that they would pick it up on Friday.

The next two days were spent packing and deciding what and what not to take. Again the children spent the time at the pond or playing with the hounds and Delightful. They tried very hard to stay out of the way of the adults. Things went better than expected with the packing. Eli saw everything that went into the boxes.

Matt and Mike left early Friday morning for Colton to pick up the U Haul. Eli said that he would like to stay and spend time with the children and the animals. His decision was sinking more deeply into his mind and he was starting to think about how sad it would really be when the day came that they would pull away from his beloved ranch and head down the mountain. He also knew it would be very difficult to say good-by to the animals he love so dearly. They had spent so many wonderful years together, most of the time with no one else around. He realized he had to keep busy and not dwell on those thoughts too much. He had to keep thinking about how wonderful it was going to be to spend, what he hoped would be, the rest of his life with Jennifer and his sons and their families.

Matt and Mike returned shortly after 12:00 pm with the truck. After lunch the adults started loading things into the truck. The children all played with the hounds and Delightful. Eli told Martin, and the mothers that had stayed behind, that Bob and Darlene would be moving into the cabin shortly after they all left to return to Texas next week. By evening they had almost everything loaded, except what they needed for the rest of their stay in the cabin. Eli retrieved the gold nugget from the secure place where he had placed it several weeks ago. He only showed the nugget to his three sons. They were overwhelmed with curiosity when they saw it. They bombarded their father with questions. He decided that he would relate the whole story of the find to them. They asked him what he intended to do with the nugget. He told them if he sold it he would use the money to help pay for the grandchildren's education, should they decide to go to college. Of course no one knew the actual value of the huge nugget at this time. The nugget was larger than a baseball and was very heavy.

It was decided that Matt, Mike and their father would drive the U Haul to Texas while the rest of the group would fly home on Sunday. It would be necessary for both Matt and Mike to call their boss at work and request additional days off when they got to Colton Monday morning.

After supper the children asked if they could have another bonfire down by the pond, to which Eli readily agreed. They roasted marshmallows and sang several camp fire songs. Siena asked Grandpa if they could all go up to the Carbonated Spring one last time tomorrow. Eli said he had already planned on spending tomorrow morning at the spring with the children and the animals.

Eli woke early, before anyone else was up. He went out and fed the animals. He put the harness on Old Pet and hooked her up to the two wheeled cart for the last time. When he returned to the cabin everyone was up and dressed. The three mothers had breakfast ready, which consisted of pancakes, scrambled eggs and the last of the bacon. Eli told the mothers that they would not need a lunch as he and the children planned to be back to the cabin by noon.

Eli took all ten grandchildren, seven of the youngest rode in the cart. Eli and the oldest three walked. They took the short route, which passed right by the cave, to the spring. As they passed by the cave all three of the hairy two legged man like creatures were standing at the entrance. The children got close to Grandpa, and Jacob and Evan held the hounds by their collars. Marina held the tether of Delightful tightly. They did not stop at the cave but proceeded on to the spring. The creatures did not seem to be bothered by their visitors. This made Eli very happy. Once they got to the spring they filled the few water jugs and placed them in the cart. Marina released Delightful from her tether but they did not release the hounds. Eli fed Old Pet some grain and gave her some water in the grain bucket. The children did some exploring nearby while Eli sat on a nearby stump and reflected on the wonderful years he had been blessed to enjoy living on his wonderful Goat Mountain. Again he realized that it was going to be very hard for him to make the departure from his cabin and the ranch. The one consolation was that he fully intended to return for a couple of weeks each summer with his family and what he hoped would be his wife, Jennifer.

The time passed quickly and before he knew it, it was time to call the children in and head back down the mountain. Eli decided to take the long way back to the cabin. This route took them to the far end of the east meadow. As they approached the meadow Evan spotted three black bears eating black berries along the edge of the meadow. Eli stopped Old Pet immediately and gave out a loud whistle. As soon as the bears saw the group they left the meadow and headed into the woods further east. The group stopped by the black berry vines and ate all the berries they wanted. Eli filled a small pail with berries for those that stayed at the cabin. Before leaving the meadow Eli went over to the spot where he had buried the two legged creature he knew as Little Big Foot, the one that had been killed by the mountain lion. He stood by the spot in silence for several minutes reflecting on the sadness he felt when he discovered its dead body more than a year ago.

Eli's sons and daughter-in-laws spent the morning packing for the return trip to Houston as they had to be at the airport by 4:00 pm on Sunday. The mothers had a wonderful lunch prepared when the group got back to the cabin. Eli suggested they eat outside under the shade of the huge maple tree near the horse barn.

After lunch Eli excused himself and stated that he would like to go into the woods alone to visit a couple of sacred places where some sad events had occurred. He assured the group that he would only be gone a short while, not over an hour. With some hesitation his sons said that would be fine. He went directly to the spot where he had buried Sampson's cub. He had driven a steel rod into the ground so the spot was easy to find, even though a lot of weeds had grown up around it. Again, he spent several minutes thinking about the joy this little bear cub had brought into his life and how sad it was when his friend, Bob Berge, brought the news of its death to him that morning. It was painful but necessary for him to re-live these sad happenings before he left his mountain. Next he went to the site where he had buried the remains of his faithful old milk cow, that had been killed by the mountain lion. When he returned to the cabin his sons could see that tears had fallen down his cheeks. Ailene and Kim each gave him a big hug. It was not necessary to ask questions about where he had gone, everyone knew exactly where he went. Nothing more was said about the last hour.

The rest of the afternoon was spent getting the cabin ready for Bob and Darlene's move-in next week. There was plenty of wood in the woodshed, in case a cold spell came along before they moved back down to the valley to their home in the fall. Bob would bring his four wheel drive pick up to the ranch and they could use Eli's old red truck to go to the spring. Bob had told Eli that he would store the old truck inside the horse barn so it would be there for the family to use when they came in the summer time. Eli told Bob that he had given Big Red to his son Mike upon his death and that it would be up to him as to what he wanted to do with it at that time.

After supper the entire group took a walk down to the east end of the meadow. Eli asked if each one would tell about some of his or her favorite experience in coming to Goat Mountain. Of course some of the experiences were very funny and a few were very sad. Everyone said that the trips to the carbonated spring were among their favorite experiences. Siena and Elly both told how much they enjoyed riding Old Pet. The grandsons said their favorite experiences were playing with the hounds and Delightful and the coon hunts, except for the last hunt when grandpa had fainted. They laughed and talked all the way to the end of the meadow and back to the cabin. By the time they got back it was time for the children to go to bed. Matt said that it would be necessary to be on the road by no later than 9:00 am in the morning. They would need to take the hounds, Delightful and the chickens to Bob's place. Old Pet could stay in the barn and pasture. They would fill the stock tank with water, which should last until Bob and Darlene arrived next week. Eli called all the children around him and asked if the entire family could kneel one last time for family prayer. They were all excited to do this. Eli asked his oldest son Matt to offer the prayer.

July the eleventh, Sunday, the day of departure from Eli's beloved Goat Mountain had finally arrived. Eli and his sons collected the few chickens and put them in small boxes. They put the hounds in back of Martin's rental pick-up. Eli gave Delightful to Kate to hold by its tether for the trip down the mountain. Eli and Shane went to the horse barn and filled Old Pet's water tank with fresh cold spring water. By the time they got back to the cabin the mothers had breakfast ready. After clean up it was time to load into the three rental vehicles and the U-Haul for the trip down the mountain. Eli locked the cabin door as he was the last one to leave the cabin.

Eli told his sons that he would like to walk alone to the edge of the forest to the spot where they always stopped to wave good-by. Everyone else loaded into the rental vehicles and the fathers drove slowly to the spot where Eli would join them. Eli walked ever so slowly, turning around many times to have one last look. Old Pet came to the edge of the pasture and just looked in Eli's direction. A large buck Mule Deer ran out of the forest and into the horse pasture. Eli glanced down towards the pond and was surprised to see the three hairy two legged creatures getting a drink at the far end of the pond. He had never seen them this close to the cabin so early in the morning. Chipmunks scampered across the road in front of him as he slowly continued towards the waiting vehicles. Eli looked through his binoculars one last time high up on the mountain side towards the carbonated spring and to his delight he saw two large and one small black bear foraging in the what appeared to be blackberry vines. He wondered if one could be Sampson?

As he neared the vehicles he could no longer hold back the tears. When the children saw him with tears running down his cheeks they all started crying. Even all the other adults could not hold back a few tears. For everyone this was truly a time of sadness but also a time for joy. Grandpa was going home with them. Eli had no way of knowing that this would be the last time he ever saw his beloved Goat Mountain.

The End

EPILOGUE

E li and Jennifer were married shortly after he moved to the Houston area. They purchased a home in the small town of Navasota, Texas. They were only a short distance from Jennifer's families and from Eli's three sons and their families.

One of the first things Eli did after getting settled in his and Jennifer's new home was to set up a Living Trust. He placed the property on Goat Mountain in the trust as well as the large gold nugget. He directed that any money received from selling the nugget be set aside in 10 equal shares for the ten grandchildren's college education. His three sons were the beneficiaries of the trust. He did not place he and Jennifer's home in the trust. That of course would go to Jennifer should he die first.

Eli's son Mike, inherited the old Dodge truck. He had it restored and enjoys driving it around The Woodlands on Saturdays.

Eli and Jennifer enjoyed five wonderful years together prior to Eli's death from complications from pneumonia. Unfortunately Eli was never able to return to his beloved Goat Mountain as he developed a respiratory problem that required him to be on oxygen at night, and there was no electricity at his cabin on Goat Mountain nor would he be able to tolerate the elevation.

His friends, Bob and Darlene, moved to Goat Mountain each summer. When they learned of Eli's death, they traveled to Houston to attend his funeral. Shortly thereafter they were able to purchase the entire property from Eli's estate, for the appraised value of the land and the timber. The author has no way of knowing what ever happened to the hairy two legged man like creatures that used the cave as their home. It is only assumed that they still roam the High Cascades. Bob and Darlene still have Big Dan and Little Anne and Delightful.

Eventually the gold nugget was sold for several thousands of dollars, and the money was used to help pay for the grandchildren's college education. The money from the sale of the property on Goat Mountain was divided evenly between Eli's three sons, after inheritance taxes were paid.

Eli standing by his old Doge flat bed truck

Edwards Brothers Malloy
Ann Arbor MI. USA
June 1, 2016